# The ESCAPE

Clare Harvey is a former army wife. Her mother-in-law's experiences during WWII inspired her novel, *The Gunner Girl*, which won both The Exeter Novel Prize and The Joan Hessayon Award for debut fiction. Clare lives in Nottingham with her family. Find out more about Clare on her website: http://clareharvey.net or catch up with her on Twitter: @ClareHarveyauth or Facebook: ClareHarvey13.

*Also by Clare Harvey:*

The Night Raid
The English Agent
The Gunner Girl

Praise for Clare Harvey:

'Will delight all those who love a good wartime story'
**Dilly Court**

'Brilliant. I was swept away by this unforgettably powerful tale of love and courage in the face of war. This beautifully written, pacy and impressively researched story binds together a group of flawed individuals in an intricate and fascinating drama, full of heart-stopping moments. Clare Harvey writes with a directness and an honesty that pins you to the page' **Kate Furnivall**

'The sense of period, the descriptive prose and the superb writing make *The English Agent* a real page-turner. Clare is certainly a gifted storyteller' **Ellie Dean**

# *The* ESCAPE
## Clare Harvey

**SIMON &
SCHUSTER**

London · New York · Sydney · Toronto · New Delhi

A CBS COMPANY

First published in Great Britain by Simon & Schuster UK Ltd, 2019
A CBS COMPANY

13 5 7 9 10 8 6 4 2

Simon & Schuster UK Ltd
1st Floor
222 Gray's Inn Road
London WC1X 8HB

Simon & Schuster Australia, Sydney
Simon & Schuster India, New Delhi

www.simonandschuster.co.uk
www.simonandschuster.com.au
www.simonandschuster.co.in

A CIP catalogue record for this book
is available from the British Library

Paperback ISBN: 978-1-4711-6189-6
eBook ISBN: 978-1-4711-6188-9
Audio ISBN: 978-1-4711-7628-9

Typeset in the UK by M Rules
Printed and bound by CPI Group (UK) Ltd, Croydon, CR0 4YY

For Chris, forever

*Double exposure (noun): the repeated exposure of a photographic plate to light, often producing ghost images.*

# Chapter 1

**January 1945, Nazi Germany**

*Detta*

At the sound, her fingers stilled. She had been about to type the letter 's'. The type hammer stopped halfway to the paper. Her ring finger quivered above the key. She looked up. The windowpane shivered as the droning swarm passed overhead: wave after wave of bombers in battle formation, like migrating birds in autumn, heading west. Heading west?

Detta's eyes flicked away from the window. Frau Schmidt was partway across the room, carrying a cup of coffee. Irmgard was licking an envelope, pink tongue protruding from her thin lips. Both were frozen mid-action, heads tilted as they looked out of the window at the ranks of bombers. Detta followed their fixed gazes out of the window, to where the planes still flew. From here it was impossible to see what markings the aircraft had. She didn't need to. They were flying in from the east, heading west. There would be red stars on their bodywork. Starlings. What was a flock

1

of starlings called? A murmuration – a murderous murmuration, she thought distractedly, watching the bombers pass overhead.

And then they were gone. The skies were back to the usual white-grey, and the sound was just a distant vibration. Detta turned to look at Frau Schmidt; the older woman merely squinted through her spectacles, and continued walking towards the boss's office with the coffee mug. But the coffee had spilled in her shaking grasp: brown tears on the pale grey lino as she shuffled away. Irmgard finished licking the manila envelope and let it fall like a trembling autumn leaf onto the stack in front of her.

Outside, where the planes had passed, were the silent, snow-laden skies. Inside, feet pattered along the endless Reichsbahn corridors, typewriters chattered, filing cabinet drawers swooshed open and clunked closed. As if nothing had happened at all. But there was a taste in the air, thin and salty: fear.

Frau Schmidt was already walking back towards her desk. Irmgard scratched her head and picked up another envelope to lick. The spilled coffee lay unnoticed on the floor. Detta wondered if she should get a cloth and wipe it up before someone slipped. But her hands were still stuck above the keyboard and it felt impossible to move. Carry on, that's what she should do. Ignore what had just happened and carry on. Perhaps they could all conspire in the pretence that they hadn't just seen and heard the Russian bombers, heading west, right into the heart of the Reich.

Detta felt a pull in her chest and her throat constricted. Breathe, she told herself. Just breathe. The hand on the big clock by the door jerked forward. What would Mother be doing now, she wondered? Preparing lunch? If there were guests then it would be lentil soup with smoked sausage and rye bread. But there hadn't been any guests at the inn since before Christmas, and what was the likelihood they'd have any today, this nondescript January day? No, there would be no guests at the inn. No guests, but visitors? She thought of the image of a Russian T–34 tank she'd seen on a newsreel last year, beetling across the steppes. Not that kind of visitor, not yet, surely?

'After I've finished these I'm going for lunch.' Irmgard's reedy voice broke in on Detta's reverie. 'Want to join me?' Her eyes had a glassy look. She had never invited Detta to join her for lunch before.

'How kind of you to ask.' Detta let out a breath as she spoke. She flexed her fingers over the keyboard, pushed the carriage release, lifted the lever, and turned the platen knob. She pulled out the sheet of paper and placed it in a yellow file marked 'Herr Meier', hoping that Irmgard wouldn't notice that there was just a line and a half of text, an unfinished sentence, on the pale cream page. The letter 's' still hovered indecisively above the Simplex's keyboard. 'I just need to pop this down to Herr Meier and I'll be with you.'

'Can't you put it in the internal post?' Irmgard said, between desultory licks.

Detta pushed the 's' back into its position in the ranks of

metal type hammers, and picked up the yellow file. 'Sorry. It's urgent.' She managed a smile. 'I won't be long.'

Irmgard's desk faced away from the door, and Frau Schmidt was peering at something in the purchase ledger. Neither noticed Detta plucking her handbag and coat from the stand on her way out.

She paused in the corridor. Breathe, she reminded herself. If anyone asks, you are dropping off the file for Herr Meier, that's all. She didn't dare put her coat on yet – too obvious. To her left, the corridor stretched away towards the main stairs. Herr Meier's office was on the floor below, overlooking the atrium, where the receptionist sat with the signing in and out sheets. Detta checked her watch. It wasn't yet midday: too early to sign out, even for an early lunch break. If she went down the main stairwell she'd be stuck. To her right were the stationery cupboard, the meeting room and the kitchenette. And at the end of the corridor a fire door.

Detta turned right. She forced her shaking legs to walk, even though everything was telling her to run. Don't make it obvious. Slow down. Her feet tapped along: one-two-three. Slow, slow, almost there. She could see the smooth handle of the fire door; imagine the rush of cold air as she opened it. A couple more steps would be all it took.

A door suddenly opened to her right. 'Fräulein?' She turned with studied casualness. To look bored, that was it. Look bored even if it feels as if your heart is about to explode. It was Herr Hauptmann: balding, myopic blue eyes and a smell of mothballs about him.

'Yes, Herr Hauptmann?'

'The meeting's running on – could you ask Frau Schmidt to sort out having a tray of sandwiches sent up from the canteen?'

Detta nodded. 'Yes, Herr Hauptmann.'

'Good, good. See to it, then.' The door slammed shut. She could hear muffled voices from inside. Should she go back, tell Frau Schmidt about the sandwiches? But then Irmgard would see her, and she'd be forced to stay, have lunch. There'd be no escape. The tug in her chest came again. She touched the silver locket at her throat, thinking of Mother, and of home.

Three careful steps and she was at the fire door. With delicate slowness she pushed down the bar and opened it just wide enough to slide out. The first breath was like needles as the icy air assaulted her. She pushed the door to. For a moment she glanced down at the zigzag mesh of steps, tethering the brickwork like a piece of bad hemming. She knew better than to touch the railings in this weather, but there was no time to fumble in coat pockets for gloves. No time at all. She began to trot down the icy metal steps, trying not to think about what would happen if she fell. Down, down, down. Her chest was heaving by the time she reached ground level.

A path led from the back of the Reichsbahn building to the road. Across the road was the wide façade of the station. She could hear a train whistle, see the distant puff of smoke. Wasn't there a Breslau train just before midday? She dropped

Herr Meier's yellow file on the frosted ground, and broke into a run.

## Tom

He thought he'd imagined it at first, but no, there it was, definite low buzz, coming from beyond the trees. Hope twisted deep in his guts.

When was the last time he'd felt hope? Back in the Beaufighter when they made their final approach to the German ship, as they let off the torpedoes into the inky sea, and the ship's ack-ack burst forth. Job done, they'd thrust back up, through the exploding air, towards the safety of the cloud cover. Thinking his luck had held, he'd reached, swift and surreptitious, to touch the place on his flying jacket, beneath which his uniform badge lay like a charm: *Per Ardua Ad Adstra* – through adversity to the stars. That had been hope, what he felt in the instant before it happened. Then there had been the sickening judder of something hitting the port wing, and suddenly it was like being inside a crumpling piece of tin foil, all reflected light and sharp, sudden sound.

He hadn't felt hope since.

Now Tom blew on his fingers and stamped his feet, waiting, to be certain. The woods were pitch-dark and still. Snow pooled in the spaces between the tree trunks. He'd come out of the hut for his usual pre-lunch constitutional: three times round the perimeter and a pause to check what birds there were. Ever since he arrived at this Stalag Luft he'd been training his visual memory so that he could paint them in flight – nothing much about at this time of year except the odd starling. Perhaps if he ever got out of here, got back to real life, he could follow his dream, and go to art college. Until now it had seemed a fantasy.

Until just now.

The sound was getting louder, but still he couldn't see anything. He looked up at the watchtower on his right. The sentry up there had heard it, too. He seemed to sniff the air, bristling like a dog. Tom reached out with his right hand. He touched a barbed-wire spike on the perimeter fence, sharp as a thorn – a physical sensation to remind himself that he couldn't be dreaming.

Now would be a good time to escape, Tom thought, with the soldier intent on the noise in the sky. At the next watchtower the sentry also had his head tilted back, listening. Carpe deum and all that – seize the moment and make a dash for freedom, whilst all the goons had their heads in the clouds. Should he? But what would be the point? If those aircraft really were what he thought, then it could only be a matter of weeks before they were liberated. He imagined Red Army T-34s rolling westwards across snowy planes. Weeks? Days, even.

The noise was louder, now, a rhythmic drone. And there they were, rising from the treeline, not directly overhead, but passing across his line of vision and to the right: south of the prison camp, on a westerly course. There was a buzzing hum as the angry silhouettes spilled across the wan skies. Tom thought of witches on broomsticks. *Hexen*, that was the German word for witches, wasn't it? Some poor German city was going to be hexed all right, once those Pe-2s reached their target.

Tom saw the sentry's helmet slip back to show a slice of grey hair, and even from this distance could see the man's mouth gape open at the spectacle. The sound of muffled cheers came from inside the huts, increasing in volume until they eventually drowned out the noise of the passing bombers.

The Russian planes disappeared, outpacing the shrunken winter sun. Where had they taken off from, and what was their range? What was the target – Oppeln, Breslau, or somewhere further west? All those cities that had been out of range of the Brits and the Yanks were within striking distance for the Russians now.

'Uncle Joe's coming!' Tom called out to the sentry, adding '*Onkel Joe kommt sofort!*' just to make it abundantly clear. The soldier span round and cocked his weapon. Tom grinned, lifted his hands in sarcastic surrender and began to saunter back to the hut. He knew the man wouldn't shoot – only last week Tom had given him a bar of chocolate from a Red Cross parcel for his granddaughter's birthday, and the man had given him half a tube of lapis blue paint in return. They had an understanding, of sorts. 'For you the war is over,' Tom muttered, as he walked back across the frosted dirt. He glanced back at the patch of sky where the bombers had passed, thinking of the old soldier and his precious granddaughter.

'For you the war is over.'

## Detta

She'd made it in time. There was the Breslau train, steam-wreathed and chuntering. The guard was just walking along and slamming all the doors, but there was one still open near the rear of the train. She ran across the platform towards it. It should be pretty empty inside, she thought, not like the 5.30 – usually she had to stand all the way home. In an hour she'd be with Mother, and this overwhelming panic would be gone.

Detta reached the open door at the same time as a fur-coated woman with a large pram, coming from the opposite direction. She stepped aside to let the woman on first. The woman didn't even bother nodding her thanks, so intent was she on getting the enormous baby carriage on board. It appeared to be stuffed full of shopping bags, but a small white-mittened hand waved out from under the hood – there was a child under there, somewhere under those bundles. The woman jerked and shoved the pram through the open door. Detta was about to offer help when the guard came running, breathless and beetroot-faced. He put a hand out towards the woman. What in God's name was she doing, he wanted to know. She couldn't take that thing on the train. There was no room. There was no time. The woman, scrawny profile like a scythe, ignored him, and continued to push the pram up the carriage steps.

It was only then that Detta noticed how full the train was. Had all these other people felt the same intuitive tug of panic she had, when she saw the Russian bombers flying overhead? Had everyone else had the same idea, downed tools and fled, without waiting for proper procedure, authorisation, or permission? It certainly looked that way. People were packed like bottled plums, all stood up, no room to even squat down on the corridor floor. And they weren't the usual lolling-headed commuters or gossiping housewives, either. She glimpsed a Wehrmacht soldier with a bandaged head, an old man with no teeth, whole families, bunched up and glum.

From inside the pram the child started howling. The guard was trying to tug the pram away from the doorway, but the woman continued to heave it upwards, at a forty-five-degree angle, even though it was obvious there was no room. The passengers started shouting abuse at her, but the woman carried on in silent determination. Detta saw the white-mittened hand wave, and the edge of a white fur bonnet from under the pram hood. Not a baby, but a young child – old enough to sit up, at least. The guard continued to yell at the woman. The woman ignored him. The train hissed steam. The pram tilted upwards, but hands from inside the carriage tried to push it back. The passengers swore. The guard tugged at the pram handle. The woman pushed in the opposite direction. A disembodied hand from inside the train began to pull the door to. The child screamed louder.

It happened quite suddenly, like a popping cork on a bottle of Sekt: the pram overbalanced, the child sprawled out onto the platform, right next to the white-painted edge, and the train door began to swing closed, pulled by hands from inside. As the pram toppled, Detta stepped aside, and managed at the same time to get a foot on the train step. The pram contents slewed across the platform, and the woman crouched over her fallen child. The guard was shouting '*Gott Verdammt!*' but Detta had a foot inside the train. The door thudded painfully against her shoulder; she was half-way inside.

*Oh get in, then, but close it after you. Leave that silly cow and her brat. We need to go* – a hoarse voice behind her, a hand tugging her sleeve.

Detta could see the woman clutching the squalling child close, safe from the platform's edge. As she did so, the guard kicked the fallen pram away, and blew his whistle: a shrill cry. A hiss of steam and the train shunted forwards a notch. Detta was being pulled inside, but the door hadn't yet slammed shut.

*Quick, girl, the train's leaving. Get in.*

She caught a glimpse of the woman's sharp face as she hugged her screaming child, features forged in desperation. Already the platform had begun a slow slide backwards as the train began to move. Detta pushed the door open with her free hand, and held it out for the woman.

*What the hell are you playing at? Shut that bloody door!*

But the woman grabbed her outstretched hand, and Detta

managed to pull both mother and child onto the train. They fell backwards into the angry mound of passengers. The guard was still shouting '*Gott Verdammt!*' as he slammed the door behind them. His puce face was left behind the smutty glass as the train began to ratchet away. Behind him on the platform lay the spilled contents of the pram. Detta glimpsed a silver candelabra and a black leather boot – gone as the train sped up and they left the station behind. She put a hand out to steady herself as the disgruntled voices continued.

*We shouldn't even have stopped in Oppeln. There's no room for anyone else to get on. What a shower of shite.*

Someone tutted. The child's cries reduced to sobs. Detta turned. A little girl – a graze on her forehead where she'd tumbled from the pram. The woman rocked her and comforted her as best she could in the crush. 'Thank you,' she said to Detta.

'*Nicht zu danken,*' Detta replied: nothing to thank me for. I only did what any decent person would have done, she thought. And yet nobody else had helped, not even the guard, whose job it should have been to assist passengers. What has happened to us all? Has this war robbed us of our decency?

She was crushed as close as a lover to all these selfish people, could smell the damp fur and wool of their winter clothes, the hint of body odour and bad breath and the stale smoky air. There was an indecency in the intimacy of it. 'Where are you going?' she said to the sharp-faced woman as the child's sobs subsided. 'Visiting relatives?' The woman gave a mirthless laugh, and looked away.

From across the corridor other voices chipped in, and Detta listened:

*I'm headed for Berlin; my sister's there.*

*You'll be lucky if she's still there, with all the raids.*

*Well, where else can I go?*

*You'd be better off in the countryside — more food, fewer bombs.*

*But I don't know anyone in the countryside. Besides, I'd rather be with my sister. It's important to be with family in times like these.*

*Sod the family. I'm going to keep heading west until I meet the Tommies or the Ammies.*

*How can you say such a thing?*

*Only a fool would wait here for the Ruskis.*

*You're talking about joining the enemy — that's treachery.*

*But, dear lady, perhaps treachery means freedom?*

*How can you say such things? It's a betrayal of the Reich!*

*All I'm saying is that betrayal could mean escape . . .*

'What about you. Where are you going?' The woman had turned back to speak to Detta. Her daughter was sucking a thumb now, resting a sleepy head on her mother's shoulder.

'I'm just going home,' Detta said, reaching up to fiddle with the chain at her neck. 'I felt a little — a little strange at work, so I thought I should head off early. I usually take the 5.30.'

'Lucky you did. There won't be a 5.30 today.'

'I beg your pardon?'

13

'This is the last train across the Oder, dearie. There won't be any more trains.'

'What are you saying?'

The woman looked at her as if she were stupid. 'Well, they're hardly going to want the Red Army catching the 5.30 to Breslau, are they?'

## Tom

'I'm telling you, that wasn't thunder,' Tom said.

'Well, what was it then? Sounded like thunder to me.' Gordon was intent on his task of turning an old corned beef tin into a cup, rubbing the metal warm-soft and turning the sharp edges inwards so that it wouldn't cut the drinker's lip. He'd got quite expert in putting old cans to other uses these past few months (since D-Day, the escape committee had given up asking for digging utensils). The other members of the hut were rehearsing an am-dram production. Except for Albert Ward, who was in sickbay with suspected pleurisy.

'Artillery.'

'No. Couldn't be. The Reds couldn't be this close. Clancy in hut fourteen said the last BBC report put them over one hundred miles away from Silesia.'

'When was the last time Clancy's lot managed to tune in?' He put the tip of his finger out to touch the painting he had pinned to the wall by his bunk: dry, at last – he could send it home with today's Red Cross post.

'Well there's been nothing the last couple of days – goons

not keeping to their usual scheds, so it's been impossible to get a safe spot of time.' Gordon looked up from the half-finished cup. 'D'you really think they could cover that much ground so quickly?'

'I'm telling you, it's Uncle Joe,' said Tom, as another faint rumble reached them. 'Right, that's it. I'm going out to take a look.' He'd been in the process of writing home. He hadn't mentioned seeing the planes yesterday in his letter, didn't want to get anyone's hopes up too soon. But if the Red Army were almost upon them – well, that really would be something to write home about. Tom dropped down from his top bunk, shoved his feet into his boots and began to lace them up. It was freezing out there, twelve degrees, apparently, but if something was going off, he wanted to know about it.

'I'll join you, pal,' Gordon said, getting up and reaching to the lower bunk for his coat, which doubled up as an eider-down these days.

Tom pushed the hut door open and stepped out, blink-ing, into the sudden whiteness. It looked as if they weren't the only chaps with the same idea. Men were streaming out of their huts as if it were morning roll call. The sun was already hidden beneath the pines. Occasional glimmers of low golden sunshine pierced the gaps in the trees, but the night was beginning to draw in. It was past four already – it would be dark soon.

The men stood a distance from the perimeter fence, wait-ing and listening, but there were no more rumbling echoes, and Tom began to wonder if they really had heard what he'd thought. Perhaps it was just distant thunder, or a blast from a far away quarry.

But as they stood, shifting from foot to foot, and rubbing their arms in a vain attempt to stave off the biting chill, they began to hear another sound, and see something moving in the trees. A memory ran through his mind: reading *Macbeth* at school, that bit where the witches warned of a moving forest. Birnham Wood, wasn't it? The trees beyond the perimeter fence were like Birnham Wood: thick suddenly with encroaching forms, a column of men were trudging through the pines. The only sound was the swish of their strange striped clothes, and the crunch of footfalls on crusted snow. At the front was a soldier in a green-grey greatcoat, carrying a weapon with a fixed bayonet. He did not even glance up at the camp guards in the watchtowers. The stumbling queue of men didn't come right up to the camp, but turned away, following a track through the trees that wound round behind, away from the road. Some wore caps, some had brown blankets slung overhead like shawls. Even at the distance of some thirty yards or more, through the barbed wire and the branches, Tom could see they were thin as skeletons. Many had no shoes. A stench drifted like putrid fog. The men inside the wire stood in silence as they passed by. As the last one disappeared, Tom heard a retching sound. He turned. It was Gordon – yellow bile streaming from sagging lips.

Tom put out a hand to touch his hunched shoulders.

Gordon picked up a handful of snow, wiped his face and straightened up. They both turned away from the trees and began to walk back to their hut. The other men were all silently drifting inside, too. Once inside, they sat down together on Gordon's bunk. Gordon slumped forward, face in his hands. Neither spoke, but their proximity was comfort enough.

Nobody who'd known them from 29 Squadron back in West Malling would have expected to see them like this. Tom had kicked up a ruckus when Gordon was selected to pilot *Dirty Gertie*, their Beaufighter. Tom was an RAF regular, had qualified back in '38, had seen it through the Battle of Britain. Gordon was a conscript, still wet-behind-the-ears (at least, that's what Tom told their CO). But the answer came back that Flight Sergeant Harper was a promising pilot who needed the experience, so Tom's choice was navigator on night fighter sorties, or being posted to a training regiment in the Midlands. Tom had put up and shut up for the sake of his career, but there remained an undercurrent of resentment: he'd rather have been at the fighter's controls than twenty foot back in a Perspex bubble.

But afterwards they'd become known as the Siamese Twins, he and Gordon: Tom was Gordon's memory, and Gordon was Tom's left leg, each the other's crutch, for months into their incarceration, until they both began to mend. How many times had he told Gordon about their last sortie together, going over the details again and again?

Reminding him how they'd set off on that frosty February night, flying with the other two Beaufighters, coddled between layers of cloud above the Channel, then cutting their engines and diving down to the target, sending up that final, guilty prayer in the rush of descent. But although the shrapnel wound in Tom's leg healed, and he could walk again, Gordon still remembered nothing of that night, or the immediate aftermath. Each time Tom retold it, Gordon immediately forgot, the memory erased like a sandcastle with high tide.

Now Tom patted Gordon's back. 'I know, old man,' he said, swallowing down his own grief at what they just witnessed. A moment later two of their fellow inmates returned, still in the costumes they'd been wearing at the dress rehearsal.

'Bastards,' said Edward, his greasepaint smeared, revealing pale stubble beneath.

'But why are they moving them?' Oliver began to loosen his paisley cravat. 'Why not just leave them to the Russians?'

'Evidence.' Edward sagged down on the opposite bunk.

'Evidence?' Oliver slung the cravat over a nail in the wall.

'Of what's been going on in the concentration camps. Don't want the Allies to know what utter evil shits they've been.' Edward put his head in his hands.

'But we're prisoners of war, Geneva Convention and all that, they wouldn't evacuate us, would they?' Oliver said, still standing, rumpling his blonde hair and frowning. The thudding rumble sound came again, louder this time. Tom thought: that's not thunder, that's heavy artillery. The Red Army is closing in.

Oliver carried on talking, raising his voice above the barrage: 'They wouldn't evacuate us. They'll all just do a bunk and leave us here to be liberated by the Russians, won't they?'

But nobody answered.

# Chapter 2

## November 1989, West Berlin

*Miranda*

I lift the camera to my face. Through the lens I see the crowds of East Berliners push towards the barrier, looking like an audience at a gig, waiting for the main act to come on stage. They have been massing for hours in the cold glare of the security lights. But the red-and-white striped bar, the wire-mesh fencing and the miles of concrete wall stay put.

I am exactly where I want to be. It is for this that I extended my overdraft, skipped my dissertation tutorial, and left a note for my housemates saying I'm not sure when I'll be back. This – being in the right place at the right time – will more than make up for it when it comes to the shots I'll get for my portfolio and degree show.

If it happens.

Border guards look on, fingering their guns. But they neither speak to their fellow citizens, nor cock their weapons in warning. The half-moon rises higher in the clear sky, the crowd growing by the moment, as word gets out about Schabowski's press conference, but still there is an impasse. The night is stretched: tense and full.

It was Quill who got the tip-off. Some press contacts of his said there were rumblings in East Berlin. Then last weekend there was the huge Alexanderplatz demonstration, hundreds of thousands of frustrated 'Ossis' shouting for Gorbachev's help: revolution was in the air. But the newspaper Quill works for – the *Sunday Correspondent* – didn't have a Berlin stringer, let alone a photographer. Quill volunteered to cover the Berlin situation, and his editor agreed. I've come along as a freelance press photographer. The editor knows we're an item, Quill and I, and he's fine with that. What he doesn't know is I'm still a student, that this is my first professional job.

I lower my camera. The moment is yet to come. The throng of bodies on my side of the crossing shift and swell. It is freezing, even in the crush of humanity, and I shiver. I turn to look at the West Berliners. Some have started lifting lit cigarette lighters and waving them, causing a sparkling sheen on the shadowy mass, like a starling's wing. The tension is palpable, air thick with anticipation.

'Let them in!' someone shouts from the back of the crowd.

'Freedom!' another voice calls out. The chant suddenly ripples through the crowds from West to East, crossing the barricades, a murmur that rises to a shout: 'Freedom! Freedom! Freedom!'

There is a scuffle by the barrier on the Eastern side. I lift my camera and zoom in. 'Just let us through,' a bearded man says to a border guard, and as he speaks he reaches out. 'We'll come back again. We just want to visit, that's all. That's what Schabowski promised!' The guard lifts an arm to block the man, but as he does so, the man makes a lunge forward. I click the shutter. Is this it? The 'Tiananmen moment', when peaceful protest erupts into violence? I keep the viewfinder to my eye and hold my breath.

'No violence!' A woman pulls the bearded man back, and the soldier lowers his arm. 'Freedom, not violence!' she yells, and the crowd echoes her voice.

'Freedom, not violence! Freedom, not violence!' Chanting fills the air on both sides of the border crossing. And still we wait.

Freedom, not violence: Quill likes to talk about the power of peaceful protest, of autonomy, of giving people their voice. I have seen him, pint in one hand, cigarette in the other, pontificating on the importance of self-determination to Dieter and Petra, our contacts and temporary hosts out here. He never picks up on the irony, the schism between the political and the personal. He can be talking about human rights and autonomy, then, if he notices me catching another man's gaze, will, lightly but deliberately, touch my inner wrist with his lit cigarette tip. Afterwards he always apologizes, explaining it's because he cares so much for me that he can't bear the thought of other men even looking at me.

Love and fear produce the same panic-surge of adrenaline: when I'm with Quill I'm not certain which it is I feel, anymore.

The crowd moves, and I am pushed up against the mesh fence. I see an older border guard emerge from the security buildings, say something to his younger colleague, who strokes a gloved hand up and down the barrel of his weapon, as if calming a dog. What are they saying? I'm too far away to hear. What is the order? To open fire, to release water cannons? Bodies are shoving me against the fence and I struggle to keep my camera up to my face. The older border guard goes back inside.

Then, through the wire, I see the red-and-white barrier begin to lift, and the East Berlin crowd surge forwards. A huge cheer goes up and the Ossis rush forward, faces like children on Christmas morning. The crowd on my side pulses, clapping, laughing, crying, as the first of the East Berliners are suddenly, without warning, allowed through to the West.

I snap the faces as they cross. Each pauses just beneath the lifted barrier, even with the crush pushing them forward. They stop in nervous joy, and seem to check for permission, before taking a breath and stepping over into the West. And I capture their individual moments of release. History spills with a click onto celluloid. But even as I shoot their baffled ecstasy, I think: this isn't it; this pelt to freedom is only half the story.

My film runs out, and I move further away from the barrier, along to the point where the wire mesh of the crossing gives way to the concrete wall, to find space to change the canister. It is a fiddly operation, and I am shoved and shunted by the exuberant crowd. I fumble, cursing my freezing-numb fingers for not working quickly enough, for what if I miss it: the moment – the moment when the picture is the story. I wind the new film on, shove the empty canister in my pocket, and click the camera back in place. I shift the viewfinder into position. I can see the back of the customs office, below the watchtower.

And there, through my lens, is a female border guard: blonde hair and pointed nose, mouth curving downwards. She stands next to an older, portly, male colleague – the one I saw giving the order to lift the barrier. He's taken off his cap, and his grey-haired head is in his hands. As I watch, the woman reaches out to pat the man on his arm. He lowers his hands from his face. I zoom in and catch his anguished expression, and lip-read the words he shouts out at the passing crowds of ecstatic Easterners. 'This is treachery. This freedom is a betrayal!'

I see the mercury glint of a single tear on his cheek as he lets himself be pulled into his colleague's embrace, with the sea of freedom seekers and the candy-striped barrier raised in the background. I click the shutter. That is the moment: the truth of it.

Then the border guards go inside, and I take more photos of the reunited Berliners: the joyful, tearful reunions and gasping optimism of it all. I find myself smiling, then laughing, as a heady mix of emotion wells up inside.

I join the crowd pushing through the late-night streets where the lights blink through pulled curtains and music spills through open doors. Cars chug past as if it's rush hour, speeding west, spewing fumes and honking. All around is the sound of weeping, music, laughter as the bottleneck of the Berlin Wall checkpoints are unstoppered.

I duck into a bar to use the bathroom. As I wash my hands, I catch my reflection in the liver-spotted glass above the sink: platinum-blonde cropped hair, red lips, black polo neck, denim jacket, camera swinging like a pendulum. I look every inch the ambitious photography student, taking her chances at the Berlin Wall. There's not even a glimpse of the little girl who used to cry herself to sleep to the sound of her parents' rows. I suppose they were trying to protect me by not arguing in front of me, waiting until I'd gone to bed. But sound travels in old houses: under ill-fitting floorboards and through rusting pipework. My childhood lullabies were the hissing volley of insults and occasional smash of glass. I frown at my reflection, slick on more lipstick, and banish the memories.

I go out into the packed bar, order a Coke, and perch on a high stool by the counter at the window to drink it. On a building site across the street yellow cranes stand idle like giant question marks. Through the smudged glass I see two lads stumbling from a side street. One shoulders the other, half-carrying him. Their four-legged stagger continues past my line of vision. Someone has been celebrating a bit too hard, I think, watching legs splaying at awkward angles, heads lolling. As I look, one of them falls, a slow-motion underwater tumble, landing with limbs slewed out over the kerb, one hand dangling into the gutter between two parked cars. The other pirouettes, wide-eyed, calling back over his shoulder for help, but nobody comes. He crouches next to his friend. The fallen boy's pink-pale arms hang limply out from a khaki vest. I see a trickle of vomit slide from his gaping mouth.

Crowds jostle the pavement, but nobody else seems to have noticed. They need help. I put down my Coke and jerk from my seat, but as I do so I see a man run across the road, dodging traffic and pedestrians, his long coat and blue scarf flapping out behind him. He must see me looking through the window, and makes an urgent gesture as he runs, staring at me, holding one arm to his face, little finger and thumb poking out: telephone – telephone for an ambulance.

I turn and yell at the woman behind the bar, point out of the window at the enfolding scene, and she calls back to say she'll phone right now. The man in the long coat kneels at the kerbside. As I watch, he pushes the fallen youth's dirty hair from his face, lifts the chin and pushes a finger inside the lips to clear the airways, then tilts his body sideways, into the recovery position. He stands to take off his coat, covers the lad's shivering torso. I check with the woman behind the counter, she says the ambulance is on its way. I knock on the window. The man looks up, and I give him the thumbs up, mouth *Krankenwagen kommt*: the ambulance is coming. I notice his eyes: twin blue sparks glimpsed through the dirty plate glass. He nods, then turns his attention back to the casualty. The curious and helpful have started to crowd round, and medical help is coming. I'm not needed.

I am guiltily relieved that the man with the blue scarf beat me to it. Incidents like this remind me of my father, that winter evening, when I came home from school to find him. I remember the feel of the telephone dial: three nines. I remember his slack-jawed drooling mouth, and the eyes rolled up, unseeing. I remember the guilty relief as the woman on the end of the telephone line told me not to touch him, just to wait for the paramedics. I remember phoning Mum at work to tell her he'd been taken away, and her saying not to worry, he'd be fine. It would all be fine.

An ambulance appears, a red pulse in the gloom. The casualty is taken away and the Good Samaritan evaporates into the night. I can't help but wonder what Quill would have done, if he'd been here. Would he have sat with the youths, undertaken emergency first aid, seen them safe on the ambulance, or would he have carried on walking on the opposite side of the street, muttering about 'useless Berlin junkies not knowing when they've had enough'? I think I know the answer. I leave the dregs of my Coke and go. I rejoin the crowded pavements and start walking again.

Just before dawn I reach the Brandenburg Gate, see the water canons spewing upwards on the Eastern side, still trying, vainly, to stop the drunken clamberers. An American news anchor is broadcasting from a dais; TV cameras snout over the Wall behind him. Quill and I are not the only ones who had a hunch about Berlin, it seems. A well-wisher thrusts an open beer bottle into my right hand, assuming I'm from the East. I trail my left hand along the Wall, tracing the texture of graffiti like Braille as I go, swigging from the bottle. For a while I manage to be part of the picture, just another face in the extraordinary night.

At Checkpoint Charlie the crush is like a mosh pit. A US soldier leans against the uplifted barrier: white teeth and cigarette, surrounded by girls – as if he's a rock star, not a border guard. I am drawn to Cafe Adler, thinking vaguely of sitting down, but inside the cafe is even more crowded than the street.

I am about to leave when I see the flash of blue. It is Petra's coat. She has her arms round someone; her toffee-apple bob falls back over the fake fur. Figures jostle past and I lose sight of her. There's a shout from the bar: 'No more beer! We're out of beer!'

'Then let us drink wine!' A returning bellow from a latter-day Marie Antoinette – a huge man in a sheepskin coat to my right. The cafe erupts into laughter. I realize who the wine-demander is.

'Dieter!'

He turns and engulfs me in a bear hug. 'What a night, what a night!' We laugh, and when he puts me down I catch sight of Petra again. Quill stands next to her, swigging from a magnum of champagne. He has his back to me, but Petra turns, sees me, touches Quill on the arm. His head swivels, his white teeth show. He rubs a finger across his nose, and thrusts the bottle at Petra.

'Miranda!' He pushes his way towards me through the throng. 'You're here.' His arms are around me. His lips are on mine: the taste of champagne on his breath as he kisses me. He pauses. 'You okay, baby?' He looks into my eyes. 'I was worried about you, going off on your own like that.'

'Yeah.' When I blink, I can blank him out, just for a split second. 'I'm fine.'

'Did you get good shots?'

'I think so. I've run out of film, now, anyway, so . . .'

'Well done. Good girl. We'll get them couriered off ASAP. I've already faxed my copy.' He gestures round at the packed cafe, the open checkpoint outside. 'This – this is history in the making, isn't it? This is everything we wanted!' He takes a step back into the crowd to hold me at arm's length. His handsome fists dig into my upper arms, and I imagine the rose-coloured fingerprints on my flesh. 'And it's just the beginning,' he says, mouth breaking into an even wider grin. 'For Germany, and for us, Miranda!' He pulls me towards him, crushing me close. But the camera is between us, like a fist in my solar plexus, and the line of his jaw is hard against my skull.

Over his shoulder I glimpse Petra gazing at me with a mixture of envy and sympathy. I shut my eyes, and wait to be released, thinking of the crowds chanting for freedom, as

Quill holds me tight to his torso. Slowly he lets go. I open my eyes, letting his face swim back into focus: the lock of black hair, smudge of five o'clock shadow, dancing green eyes – the face I fell in love with, and now I've begun to fear.

'I'm sorry, Quill, but I can't stay in Berlin any longer,' I say, emboldened by the events I've witnessed this extraordinary night. 'I want to go home.'

# Chapter 3

**January 1945, Nazi Germany**

*Tom*

His fingers scrabbled at his chest, but there was nothing here. No ripcord. He cried out, but his voice was lost in the suffocating rush of air and he was falling, into the blackness, twisting and falling. God. Oh, God.

Awake. Shivering and sweat-drenched, eyes staring unseeing into the darkened room, chest bellow-pumping, breath loud and fast in the quiet air – the familiar nightmare. Tom pushed his hands over his forehead and into his hair, wiping away the cold sweat.

He stared out into the darkness of the sleeping hut, mind scrabbling just as his fingers had been just now, trying to find something to clutch, remembering the aftermath. He remembered the remains of the plane plummeting ahead of him, orange flames extinguished by the inky sea. He remembered the wind pulling him shorewards, landing in a hollow in the dunes, pulling the chute in, expecting at any moment to hear the roar of military jeeps, or tramp of jackboots, but there being nothing but the distant crash of waves and swish of wind through the marram grass. Then, noticing the dampness on the flight suit – at night-time, blood isn't red, it's the same dark grey as the North Sea. Crawling up the dune, seeing the distant blur of a supine figure at the shoreline, still attached to the billowing chute. He remembered calling out, voice snatched and hurled away inland, and nobody answering.

No. Don't think about it. Why dwell on it? How could you possibly have got back to Blighty from that: an amnesiac and a shot-up cripple, even had the locals had links to the Dutch Resistance, even had there been safe houses. It was hopeless from the moment *Gertie* took a hit. Think about something else. Anything else. Even Hitler. No, not him. Stalin? Yes. The Russians, think about the Russians.

Tom exhaled. His own breath felt warm in the chill air. Uncle Joe is coming. Soon he'd be free. Within weeks he could be back home at the rectory. He thought of the smell of roasting meat, the silky feel of an eiderdown, dark-green monkey-puzzle tree branches glimpsed through a sash window, and the distant sound of church bells. He forced his breathing to slow, fumbling fingers re-buttoning the pyjamas where he'd torn them open in an attempt to pull the invisible ripcord. He'd lost a button. Never mind. Hunt for it in the morning. There'd be all day to find the bugger and sew it on, nothing else to do except sit and wait. Ever since they'd heard the Russian artillery the other day, all camp activity had stopped: amateur dramatics, language classes, art, even the footballers seemed less eager to start a game. All they did was listen to the thunder of the guns, trying to calculate how close the front was, how soon they'd be liberated.

He listened. The rumblings of the Russian guns were silent for now – even soldiers had to sleep at some point, he supposed. He imagined high-cheeked blackbeards in their T-34s, curled up like hibernating bears. Did any of them have nightmares, he wondered? Won't we all have nightmares by the time this sorry mess of a war is over?

Instead of distant ordnance, he could hear the faint sound of rhythmic breathing from the other men in the hut. His own bunk wobbled a little as Gordon grunted and turned in his sleep. The hut was windowless as a crypt, so he could only guess whether there was a frost-shrouded moon above the trees and a diamond-studded sky outside, or whether the clouds were a silent pillow fight, dousing the camp with fresh downy whiteness.

Nightmare banished, sweat dry, Tom suddenly felt the cold, and lay back down, dragging the blanket over his head and pulling himself into a foetal knot, to hug in as much warmth as possible. He could relax now. It was rare to get the dream twice in a night. If he could just get warm again, he might be able to sleep through until morning roll call. And tomorrow he'd find the blasted button and sew it on. It would give him something to do, at least.

It was only because he was still awake that he heard:

footfalls running across the parade ground, guards being called down from watchtowers. What was that all about?

Two sets of footsteps passed right by the side of the hut. Tom strained his ears to catch the muffled German. 'Shit,' said a voice. 'But we haven't prepared for this.'

'Shut up,' came the response. 'It's the Fuhrer's orders.' The footsteps and voices moved away.

Tom sat up again, wide awake. Something was about to happen, but what?

### Detta

'Tell your mother I owe her – if there's anything I can do . . .' Frau Moll's brow puckered as Detta handed over the basket of eggs. A uniformed man banged out of the Schloss door and ran down the front steps to the army truck that was idling on the gravel driveway below them. He hurled himself into the passenger seat and the truck skidded away. They paused to watch it veer and slip down the track, and onto the main road, where it slewed left towards Oppeln. Trudging in the opposite direction of the racing truck was the now-familiar sight of clots of refugees heading towards Breslau. Detta could just glimpse her mother at the doorway of the Deutches Haus Inn, opposite the church, ready with mugs of ersatz coffee for the passing travellers: she wouldn't ask for payment, and none of them would stop for food or a bed for the night. It had been like this for days, ever since the trains stopped running and they heard the first bombardments.

The army truck was out of sight, now, but Frau Moll still

gazed at the patch of main road where it had last been. 'They eat and eat,' she said. 'But how can I refuse them a decent meal, when it might be their –' she didn't finish the sentence, interrupted by another one of those angry artillery booms that had become a percussive accompaniment to their lives these last few days.

'Mother says she'll keep sending as many eggs as we have, it's not a problem. The hens are still laying, despite–' Detta cleared her throat, unable to say the words: *despite the noise of artillery fire from the approaching front* – because saying it out loud somehow made it more real. Instead, she let her voice trail off, touching the place where her scarf wound into her fur coat, beneath which the locket lay. 'And in any case, we have no guests at the Deutches Haus at the moment, unlike you.'

'Well, I'd hardly call them guests,' Frau Moll turned away from the road and lowered her voice. 'It's not as if I had a choice, is it? But still, one has to make the best of things in these times.' She attempted a bright smile, but succeeded only in showing a glimpse of her pearly little teeth, leaving lines of anxiety netting her eyes. She drew breath. 'Feels like there's more snow coming, don't you think? Would you like to come out of the cold for a while? The children would love to see you.'

'I should get back,' Detta said, but she hesitated, feeling sorry for the older woman. Frau Moll's high-ranking husband was a prisoner of war in England. The army had recently requisitioned the Moll Schloss, now the front was moving west, and she'd been living with her three children in just two rooms, whilst the rest of her palatial home was used as a field HQ and officer's mess.

'They loved it when you came and taught them those French nursery rhymes,' Frau Moll said. 'They get so bored without school, and it's too cold to let them play outside for long. Maybe you could come and give them a little French tuition – I would pay you, of course.'

'I have to take something to Father Richter, and I promised I'd go back and help Mother,' Detta gestured in the direction of the refugees. Another boom of distant shellfire came, and Frau Moll winced. 'Tomorrow,' Detta said. 'I'll come over tomorrow morning and I'll bring my big book of Perrault Fairy Stories for the girls.'

'They'll love that. And it's always useful to know another language, you never know when you'll need it; one can never start too young. Thank you, dear.' Frau Moll held the basket of eggs in her right hand, but with her left she reached out and touched Detta's cheek with her fingertips. 'Thank you,' she repeated, before turning away.

Detta heard the Schloss door thud shut as she walked down the granite steps to the driveway. She was fond of Frau Moll, and of the flaxen-haired Moll girls, with their chubby knees and china-doll eyes. But why would Frau Moll want them to learn French at a time like this? It was irrational. But then, wasn't everything irrational at the moment? Detta thought of the gunfire, the soldiers, the vehicles that sped through the village at all hours. There had been blood on the road by the baker's shop yesterday morning. They said a Wehrmacht soldier was shot by the SS for trying to desert. Dead if you fight and dead if you don't – none of it makes any sense, Detta thought. Her boots slipped through the thin crust of ice and into the deep snow underneath as she took the shortcut through the trees.

The path took her past the French forced workers' barracks. Usually by this time in the morning they'd all be at work, mending the tracks or oiling the points or whatever it was they did (she wasn't sure – all she'd ever had to do was drop off occasional notices from the Reichsbahn head office that she'd translated into French, just lists of rules or information about meal entitlements or changes to working hours). But today, just like yesterday, and the day before that, they hadn't even left their barracks, although some of them had Polish girlfriends who'd been working the land nearby, and they'd been seen coming and going, even after curfew. There had been no sign of Herr Frankel's car, though – in fact, now she thought about it, his car hadn't been there since she came home early on the last train from Oppeln. He was quite well-connected in the Nazi party – perhaps someone had tipped him off about the situation.

The barracks windows were shuttered from the cold, but the building itself was a flimsy construction, shoved up in a rush a few years ago, when the French forced workers were moved into the village to work on the eastbound railway line. As Detta passed the plasterboard walls she could hear

37

the curlicued vowels of the French workers from inside. She recognized them: Henri and Jean-Pierre, two of the men she often met when she brought round translated orders from the Reichsbahn. When they'd complained about having no contact with home, she'd managed to persuade Herr Meier to let them have paper and pens, and to cover the cost of posting their letters.

*Ah, they're all bitches!*

*Not at all, I'm taking mine with me, when the Reds get here.*

*I thought you had a girl back home in Rouen?*

*The war changes things, though, doesn't it? Remember I had that anonymous letter saying that some Nazi boy had been sniffing round her . . .*

*And you believe it?*

*I don't know. But I know I'm very fond of Ana, and I think we could make a go of things, if she comes with me. God, I can't wait to get out of here.*

*Not long now, JP.*

*How long do you think? A week?*

*Maybe less – haven't you been listening? They're definitely closing in.*

*Perhaps you're right. I'll tell her to start packing her things.*

A week or less, Detta thought, carrying on past the barracks and joining the icy rutted track that wound down beside the church, parallel to the main road. Would the Red Army really be here so soon? And what would happen then? Some of the refugees had muttered about what had happened in Prussia. No woman is safe, they said. Detta didn't want to think about what that meant.

She looked up at the blue arch of sky. Mistletoe pom-poms burred the naked trees. The cold made the bones in her face ache, but at least there was still some sunshine glinting off the snow. There was another sudden rumble, as if the pale sun itself was belching ordnance. Detta hurried on. It was too cold to linger and remember the summertime walks she used to have with Rolf under these trees, more than a year ago now, before he too got sucked into the grey-green Wehrmacht machine, and never came back. At least she hadn't been in love with him, she thought. At least it had finished before it had properly started. They'd been spared that. She thought of Frau Moll struggling in the Schloss, and Oberst Moll locked up in a British prison camp. Yes, war was easier without love, she supposed.

She squinted into the glare. But there were black clouds in the distance, piling up above the Oppeln road. Frau Moll was right: it would snow later.

It had snowed that night they first heard the Russian guns, she remembered. Initially nobody had been quite sure what they heard. The lights had flickered, and the radio went dead. It must be an electric storm, Mother told the customers in the lounge bar. The lights came back on again, and people began to smile and chat, reassured. But then the radio stayed obstinately silent, nothing but a dull hiss where there should have been music. The thudding rumbles got louder until it was impossible to pretend that what they were hearing was just a storm. The snow settled into drifts outside and all the customers evaporated into the night. The next morning the soldiers arrived at the Moll Schloss and dawn light showed the first dark clump of refugees limping along the main road.

Detta carried on walking. The barrack block was behind her now, and the church on her left. It was like something from a children's picture book: the orange and white paint-work made it stand startlingly out against the bright blue sky, with its onion-shaped spire poking heavenward. She passed in front of the church, heading for the manse. Father Richter would be at home, and Mother had sent him a gift, a small bottle of homemade plum brandy, that bulged in her coat pocket ('In times such as these, holy spirit might not be enough – Father Richter might need some of the real stuff,' Mother said with a grim smile as she'd handed the bottle to Detta).

She had just got to the old beech tree by the roadside, with the hole in the trunk, when a sudden rush behind unbalanced her, making her rock on her heels. A column of tanks thundered along the main road: fast as ambulances, white-painted, gun turrets jabbing forwards, like a giant manic rosary – on and on and on, stringing along the road to Oppeln, the same way the truck had gone just now. At last they passed, and the road was empty again, save for an old man at the far end of the village, leading a cow on a rope. She could still feel the vibration of the tanks when another booming roar burst through the air. The truck and the tanks were rushing to the front line, but how far away was it? How long until her home village became a battlefield?

Detta lifted a gloved finger and touched her cheek in the same place where Frau Moll had caressed it just a few minutes earlier. She gulped in a breath of the icy air and turned away from the road and into the path that led to the manse. At least Father Richter was still here. At least he hadn't run off like Herr Frankel and the other party members. Father Richter wouldn't abandon them; he'd stay with them, no matter what.

No matter what?

She pulled her hand from her cheek.

What exactly do you think is going to happen, Detta?

She took the smooth brandy bottle from her pocket as her feet crunched up the path. She wouldn't think about it. She would not think about what was coming their way. She reached the front step and knocked on the door, waiting for the priest to answer.

# Chapter 4

**November 1989, Exeter**

*Odette*

'Darling?' I wake with a start and reach instinctively towards the right-hand side of the double bed. But it is cold, empty.

The wave of panic-grief is swift, washing over me and crashing in an instant. In the beginning it would last all day, this disorientation of drowning loss. But that was more than twenty years ago. Now it is an occasional blow, catching me off guard.

For a moment I stare up at the ceiling rose and the silver chain that holds the glass lampshade, trying to ignore the scent of pipe smoke that always lingers after these incidents. He has been gone longer than we were ever together, but there is still this torn-up feeling inside.

I push myself out of bed with a soft grunt, trying to ignore the twinge at the base of my spine. I would, of course, prefer to roll over and have a quiet weep into my pillow for the man I lost. But what is the point? Life goes on. It is Friday, and this morning I must go and check up on the typing school. I take the girls cakes as a treat, and talk over any administrative issues that Sue, my capable manager, might need me to deal with. Afterwards, I have my shampoo and set, a gossip with the hairdresser, and I change my library books. I come home for afternoon coffee, and spend the rest of the day reading. Occasionally I may dine with a male friend in the evening, or he may take me to a concert. I've not been a nun since my husband passed. But they never go very far, these little affairs. The problem is that no man can ever come close to being what he was to me.

I reach for the curtains, feeling suddenly light-headed as I draw them open, and have to lean heavily against the cool glass pane. When my vision clears I see a seagull whirl up above the rooftops, swirling invisible spirals against the windy grey skies. It is just low blood pressure, I'm sure, nothing to worry about. I take a breath, straighten up, and begin to get dressed.

I head to the bathroom, passing my favourite watercolour of his in the hallway: the blue-black night, the curls of barbed wire, the moon behind the watchtower – he even made incarceration seem romantic, somehow.

I splash cold water on my face, and catch my bisected reflection in the mirrored medicine cabinet. Not bad for an oldie, I think, and smile at myself. Nothing wrong with a little vanity, even at my age – especially at my age. I take my face cream from the shelf and smooth it on. Then the ritual begins: foundation, rouge (they call it blusher these days, don't they?), powder, grey eye shadow, black mascara, and my favourite red lipstick, poking up like a cheery steamship funnel: preparing a face to meet the faces.

I remember a time when my beauty routine consisted of nothing more than a slick of Vaseline on my lips and running a broken comb through my dirty hair. I reach towards the empty space at my clavicle, as I recall the girl I once was. I tut at my reflection, then brush out my sleep-flattened silver curls and pat them into place. Stop thinking about that. It was a lifetime ago. Leave the past where it belongs, dear. I pick up the hairspray canister, shut my eyes, and spritz, the gin-and-tonic taste of it on my tongue and up my nose.

In the kitchen I spoon ground coffee into the Italian pot and tamp it down with the back of a spoon. I turn on the hob and go through to the living room to open the curtains, whilst I wait for it to percolate. The light is flashing on the answerphone. Someone must have called when I was in the bathroom just now. I play the message: 'Hello Mum, it's Helen. Have you seen the news? Have you heard from Miranda? I've got to get to work now, but call me later, won't you? Bye.'

I run my ring finger over one eyebrow, pushing down a stray hair. My daughter and granddaughter are not on speaking terms. I'm tired of being dragged in as an intermediary. Can't Helen call Miranda herself? And what news is she talking about? The coffee pot gurgles and hisses from the kitchen. Coffee first, family squabbles later, is that not so, darling? I glance across at the photograph of my husband on the mantlepiece. He smiles at me, pipe clamped between his teeth, paintbrush in one hand, chubby-kneed toddler Helen on his hip, easel and Devon coastline in the background. He smiles, but says nothing.

I am ready for distraction, so I turn on *Good Morning Britain* and sit down with my cup of brown-gold, inhaling the fragrant steam. There is footage of crowds of people coming through a barrier, at night, people laughing, weeping, clutching each other. The film cuts to a graffitied wall, and a news reporter on a floodlit dais. Then we are back in the beige studio, and a man with a sandy moustache says something about the incredible scenes from the Berlin Wall. He turns to his co-presenter, who gives a nod, and enthuses about the surprise opening of the border last night providing a happy ending for so many families who've been kept apart for decades by the division of East and West Germany. On the screen behind them the footage plays out: tearful embraces, a sea of bodies surging along the West Berlin streets. Indeed, says the man, looking seriously into the camera, but what world leaders will have to ask themselves this morning is: 'What happens after the fairy-tale ending?'

I take a sip of my coffee: hot and pungent. *What happens after the fairy-tale ending?* What nonsense they talk, these TV people. I get up and switch off the television.

Why should events in Germany be any concern of mine?

# Chapter 5

**January 1945, Nazi Germany**

*Tom*

*Nein. Lass ihn. Er stirbt nicht*: No. Leave him. He's not dying. Tom pushed the rifle barrel from his friend's neck. 'Come on, pal, let's get you up,' he continued in English, heaving at the fabric of Gordon's coat, but Gordon was slumped on a snowdrift at the wayside, eyes closed, and wouldn't move.

Tom sensed the muzzle nudging back, blurted more German: 'No, I'm telling you, he just needs to get on the casualty wagon; he's not dying. Leave him alone!' He looked along the rifle barrel to the guard's face. The older man gazed blankly back. They'd shot a POW yesterday, when he'd got to the stage when he could neither walk or even sit upright, and left his body in the ditch by the road.

'Keep walking, you,' the guard replied in English, gesturing with his weapon. Tom knew that if Gordon hadn't carried him, that night back in the winter of '42, he'd have been done for. His mind slipped back to that night on the Frisian Coast, just after it happened:

Heaving and shunting across the frozen sand to the studded line of wooden groynes that stamped a double line between dunes and sea, where the tethered body lay. A snail trail of blood behind him as he crawled, dragging his injured leg. Tears of relief at seeing a chest moving gently up and down under the flying jacket, cheeks warm beneath the smashed goggles. Then the crushing loneliness as the other man wouldn't wake up, lay unresponsive as a corpse.

Trying to shift Gordon further away from the encroaching tide, but his own injured leg heavy as lead, anchoring him to the sand, and everything feeling thick, underwater-slow, and so very cold. Exhaustion hitting like an axe blow, and the foam-topped waves moving inexorably towards them, up the beach, with the incoming tide.

The icy sea lapping Gordon's boots. *Come on, old man*, but Gordon not moving. A larger wave splashing, soaking them both. *That's it, we're done for – the skipper's out for the count, and I'm too weak to move any further.*

But the cold seawater must have roused Gordon: seeing his eyes open wide, head lifting up from beside the wooden stake he'd bashed it on in the chaos of landing. Gordon was conscious, they were both alive, and there was still a chance.

Confusion, Gordon blurting nonsense, staggering upright, pulling off the smashed goggles and not knowing what they were, who he was, even his own name. *You're my skipper. We took a hit. The plane's gone down. We're behind enemy lines. You are Flight Sergeant Gordon Harper, and I'm Warrant Officer Tom Jenkins. I'm your navigator and I'm injured, I'm so sorry. I'm so sorry, old chap.*

A clumsy fireman's lift, and the sea becoming sky as Gordon carried him inland, upside down, in the direction of the distant lights. The feel of his forehead thudding against the leather of Gordon's flight jacket, and seeing the discarded parachute pulsing in the wind, thinking it looked like a giant jellyfish on the shoreline.

He must have passed out after that, because the next thing he remembered was choking awake in a dark, smoky room, and the simultaneous sweet-sharp scent and sting of surgical spirit being poured into the open wound on his leg.

Gordon had saved his life. And he'd be damned if he let his skipper end his days being slotted in a ditch by one of the goons. Now, looking through the swirling snow at the German guard, Tom shook his head. 'Not without my friend. He's not dying, he's just exhausted. He needs rest. He needs to be on the casualty wagon.' The straggling column of prisoners of war limped along in his peripheral vision. The snow hissed down from the sky, muffling the sound of trudging boots on the track. The casualty wagon was nowhere to be seen.

'Leave us,' Tom said. 'I'll help him. I'll be responsible for keeping him walking.' The guard shrugged, and Tom heard him click the safety catch back on his weapon as he turned away to where the line of dark trees ranged and the column wore on into the blizzard. 'Come on, chum.' He tried again to lug Gordon up. No good. Tom recalled how it was icy seawater that finally revived Gordon that night. He grabbed a handful of fresh snow and shoved it in his pal's face. Gordon's eyes sprung open. 'Fuck off,' he slurred like an angry drunk.

'That's more like it. But I'm not fucking off anywhere without you, old man.'

Somehow, he managed to get Gordon to his feet, slung one of his arms round, and shouldered the load. It was hard going with the full weight of a grown man to support, face pulled tight against the driving snow. But what else could he do?

The forced march tramped onwards. It was still day, and yet it felt like night. The guards at the front of the column had torches that waved a silver web under the darkening skies. At one point they were called to a halt in a copse. Tom and Gordon stopped under a tree whose branches seethed angrily overhead. Through numb fingers he managed to light them a cigarette, trying not to think about frostbite. He passed it to Gordon, letting his friend taste the warming smoke first. Nearby another dysentery-ravaged man jack-knifed, too cold and weak to even move aside and drop his trousers. He wasn't the only one. Gordon had been like that for two days now. They were a reeking squad. When they set off again Tom heard the guards shouting down the line. No more stopping until they'd all crossed the Oder.

The thud-crash of artillery snapped at their heels, getting

gradually fainter with each forward pace. The Russians may have reached their old Stalag Luft by now, Tom thought. They would be plundering discarded Red Cross parcels, looting and raping their way through the nearby village. What the Red Army foot soldiers did was no secret. And who could blame them? It was no worse than the Wehrmacht had inflicted on the Russian people, just a couple of years earlier.

The sky had started to clear, but it was dark by the time they reached the river. Sunset had happened unseen behind the blizzard clouds. Stiff, rusty reeds poked up through the ice at the edge. It was wide as a lake. On the opposite side scrubby bushes littered the banks and a startled bird cried out. The rising moon was a sharp crescent in the foamy sky, like a razor blade against a sudded cheek.

Gordon grunted as Tom staggered a little, tripping over the uneven ice at the river's edge. They began to inch across. Labouring across drifted snowy fields had been easier than this uncontrolled slither. Again and again they fell. In the end Tom had to drag Gordon bodily across the ice, like a fleshy sledge. Would they be able to rest at the other side, Tom wondered? There didn't seem to be any cover – perhaps they'd have to keep on walking.

The first night of the march they'd slept in an abandoned brick factory, and every man had been given half a slice of black bread and a mug of thin soup to drink. There was no bedding, but at least they had some food inside them, and space to lie down. The second night they'd slept in a barn. Some of the men had tried hiding in the rafters, but the camp commandant had ordered a head count, and when it was found that men were missing had ordered the guards to shoot up into the roof space. Tom recalled the blooded thud as a body fell to the floor. The commandant said that for every man who tried to escape, five would be shot. There were no more escape attempts after that, although men had still been shot – men who were too weak to walk, men like Gordon.

As they neared the western side of the Oder, Tom saw the remains of a blown-up bridge further along the bank. The guards were already setting up camp: rubberized ground-sheets spreading like inkblots into the snow. 'Is this it?' Tom looked round at his exhausted comrades. 'What are they expecting us to do? Build a bloody igloo for the night?'

In the end they huddled close, taking it in turns to be on the outside, in the killing wind. Tom rubbed Gordon's kidneys through his greatcoat. They dozed standing, like cattle.

At daybreak the sky cracked with blue. Gordon's breathing was careful-slow, but he was still alive. They were both alive. The men began to move from their night-time formation. Tom saw the old guard from camp, the one who'd swapped oil paint for Red Cross chocolate with him. 'How much further?' Tom said, thinking that now they'd crossed the Oder they must surely be close to their destination. He could probably manage one more day of lugging Gordon, if he knew there would be rest and food at the end of it, and not another sleepless night of lethal cold.

'I don't know. Word is we might go on to Fallingbostel,' the guard said.

'Where?' Tom said, thinking he must have misheard.

'Fallingbostel,' the guard repeated.

Tom's mind whirled, struggling to remember his navigation maps. 'But that's more than four hundred miles northwest of here. How can we walk all that way?'

'Keep your voice down. Anyway, I don't know for sure.'

Just then a rolling barrage came from beyond the far side of the river, the Russian artillery yawning into action for the day.

'Right, move out!' the guard said.

The curdled pool of men groaned and shuffled back into line, turning their backs on the sunrise, and heading slowly westwards once more, through the snowdrifts, away from the light. Gordon hung like a lodestone from his shoulder. He couldn't take another four hundred miles of this, none of them could.

## Detta

Detta scraped away the thin coating of frost from the inside of her window and then licked her fingertips, as if she were still a little girl, stealing icing sugar from the top of a cake. She looked down through the hole she'd cleared in the glass. There was no military traffic: the road was empty, for a change. She looked through the bare branches of the line of beech trees to the manse opposite. Had Father Richter drunk the plum brandy she'd dropped off yesterday? She imagined him sipping slowly, hunched by the last of the heat from the kitchen range, poring over his big copy of the Bible by the light of a single candle. He wasn't usually much of a drinker, but who knew – nobody seemed to be their normal selves these days. Past the church and up through the trees she could just glimpse the curved portico of the Moll Schloss. She had promised Frau Moll she'd return, hadn't she? But yesterday's blue skies had gone, replaced with lumpen grey clouds, and snow fluttered over the church spire and the denuded birch trees.

One of those booming gun sounds came. Was it her imagination, or did her windowpane quiver, this time? With each new morning the frontline slid closer.

Her bed was made (years of helping Mother with the guest house at weekends and school holidays had given her a housekeeper's discipline: hospital corners, and sheets pulled so tight you could bounce a pfennig on them), with her satin eiderdown plump and smooth. On top was a small leather suitcase, not much more than a weekend bag, really. Inside the case was a change of warm clothes, spare underwear, flannel, toothbrush, comb, soap and toothpaste and a small sewing kit with scissors. The case was only half full, because Mother had said to leave plenty of space for food. Her mother didn't want to leave ('Your father and I have been building this business since before you were born. It's not just our home, it's your legacy,' she'd said, pulling the empty case down from the top of the wardrobe and handing it to Detta), but the message came last night that if the front line got close then there might be forced evacuation of the whole village ('Evacuation to where, that's what I want to know,' Mother said, pushing her lips together in that way she had), and they had to be prepared.

What would happen if they left? Who'd look after the chickens and the pig? What would happen to their things? Detta looked at the beautiful china doll that her father had bought for her third birthday, not long before he died. The doll was in a wicker pram, in the corner of the room by the wardrobe, and there was a basketwork trunk of shop-bought doll's clothes, sent by Aunty Hedwig from Hanover every year on her birthday, until she was ten – half her life-time ago, now.

She walked over to the pram and ran her hand along the wickerwork. Nineteen was far too old to still have a doll in your bedroom. Or a book of fairy tales, she thought, looking at the line of books on the mantlepiece, with the Perrault collection at the far end. She thought of the Moll girls. A gift might distract them. They could read one of the fairy stories in French and then learn the main words: sleep; forest; prince; kiss; wake; love; marriage. She took the book from the shelf and put it into the pram with the doll, then put the basketwork hamper of clothes on top. Another thudding bang came, then, and she jumped, knocking the pram. The doll tipped out onto the rag rug. Detta shivered, remembering the upturned baby carriage on the station platform. Was that only a week ago? Where was that little girl now, she wondered, as she gathered up the things and lugged them downstairs.

'Detta, where are you off to?' Mother's voice drifted from the kitchen.

'I'm going up to the Schloss. Frau Moll wants me to teach some French to the girls, and I'm taking them my doll to play with.'

Her mother appeared from the kitchen doorway, in her grey woollen dress, with layers of burgundy and navy cardigans over the top – the thinner she got, the more she felt the cold, it seemed. 'Can you drop this off with Father Richter on the way?' She held out an old shoe box, tied with string. It was surprisingly heavy. 'The silver,' Mother said, without being asked. 'Your christening things, the candlesticks, the teaspoons and cake forks from our wedding set, the bonbonnière, and the rose bowl. We can't take them with us, but I'm not having some Ruski getting his hands on it. Tell Father Richter I've dipped them all in wax, in preparation, so he can just bury the box as it is.'

'Bury it?'

'There's an empty grave. He's burying all the church plate tonight. There's space for our odds and ends, too, he says, keep them safe until this is all over.' Detta touched the locket at her neckline. 'No, you're best off keeping that. Keep your watch on, too. I'm wearing all the jewellery your father gave me – we may well need to hock it. Reich marks won't be worth the paper they're printed on, if it's anything like last time.'

Detta nodded, and put the heavy box in the doll's pram with the other things. Her mother, unusually demonstrative, gave her a swift hug, bones poking through the layers of woollen padding. She smelled of cinder ash and chopped onions, coffee and Chanel – the odd mix of hard grind and glamour that defined her. She spoke into Detta's hair as they embraced: 'I know you promised Frau Moll, but don't be gone too long, will you?'

Detta stooped to wheel the doll's pram into the hallway, took her blue scarf and fur coat from the stand in the entrance hall and pushed the pram over the front step. The snow was falling more heavily now, and she pulled the scarf cowl-like over her brow, and lifted the doll's pram into her arms, struggling to keep the contents from spilling out onto the icy road. For once there was no traffic, no one about at all, and she crossed over without having to pause for military vehicles or refugees.

Father Richter must have seen her approach, because as she passed the old beech tree with the hole in the trunk, the manse door began to open. He invited her in, his grey-streaked beard catching snowflakes as he poked a head out from inside. Detta passed on her mother's thanks for him burying the silver. He asked if she'd like a cup of herb tea, but she said she needed to go to the Schloss, explaining about Frau Moll and the promise of French lessons for the girls. 'Russian would be more useful than French,' Father Richter said, as he took the heavy box from her. But his head was turned away, and his voice so low that he seemed to be speaking to himself more than to her, so Detta didn't reply.

They said their goodbyes and she heard the soft thud of the heavy oak door behind her and turned back into the snow. She decided to take the shortcut to the Moll Schloss, thinking that it would be quicker than the estate road, even though it would be heavy going with the fresh snow, which was coming down harder, now.

The snow was calf deep with a thin frozen crust on top, but powdery soft underneath, so she had to lift her feet with each crunching step. She clutched the pram, which slithered in her gloved grasp but at least it wasn't so heavy now she'd offloaded the silver.

The manse and the church offered a little shelter from the blizzard, but further up the path blinding flurries of snow swirled into her eyes. The boom of the artillery fire sounded even louder in the open air, and her mind flicked back to the packed suitcase on her bed. How much longer had they got?

The snow was turning to hail, blasting into her face and stinging like needles on her cheeks. She pushed her chin down and laboured on. She'd made a commitment to Frau Moll, and she was going to keep it.

On the curve of the track, past the French barracks, where it narrowed into a path, she was suddenly confronted with a straggling column of men being led by a Wehrmacht soldier with a rifle slung over his shoulder. From a distance they looked like a more orderly version of the refugees that had been traipsing along the main road this past week. But as they passed she could see that they were all men, prisoners of some kind, trousers the same charcoal blue as the underbelly of snow clouds.

Detta stood still, even though the biting wind blasted into her face, watching as the men passed. They looked thin and ashen, with several days of stubble on their faces. Most wore scarves of some sort draped over their caps, and blankets draped round their shoulders, so it was impossible to tell which uniforms they wore, or what nationality they were. They shuffled past in silence. As the last few men in the line drew level, she noticed one of them was supporting another man, who slumped like a sandbag from his right shoulder. The supporting man would have been tall, if he hadn't been burdened down by the weight of his comrade. He wore a long grey coat. As he passed, he raised his head and looked straight into Detta's eyes. She gazed back, not blinking, looking at his stubbled face with the chinks of blue eyes under frosted brows. Then he turned away and limped forward.

The column passed; Detta began to walk along the Schloss path once more, but she turned to look back through the hail at the trudging men. As she did, she noticed that the man in the long grey coat had also paused, and turned back to look at her. From this distance his eyes were like tiny blue sparks seen through the snow-veil between them.

There was an uncomfortable sensation inside her, like numb-cold fingers thrust in front of an open fire. She turned away from his gaze and forced her legs to move, back along the path, towards the Schloss, and by the time Frau Moll answered her knock, the strange feeling had passed.

### Tom

The roadside trees seemed to topple towards him as Tom staggered beneath Gordon's weight. '*Schnell!*' The disembodied voice of a guard from somewhere through the snow told him to hurry up. But he couldn't move any faster, didn't want to hurry, even had he been able. If he could, he would have turned round, back towards that village they'd just passed through, back to the impossible girl with her dark-eyed stare.

The guard prodded him in the ribs with the barrel of his rifle, causing him to lurch forward. His boots slid and caught on the rutted ice of the farm track.

If he hadn't paused to look at her, he wouldn't have fallen so far behind the rest of the column. The guns boomed again. A half-starved black cat sped out from a ditch.

The young woman had seemed oddly familiar. It was like bumping into one of his sister's now grown-up schoolfriends at a crowded Tube station – familiar and unfamiliar at the same time. But that young woman couldn't possibly be anyone he knew. She was German. She was beautiful.

The column jerked away into the blank distance ahead of them. Men dropped out occasionally to relieve themselves in the ditch. The roadside snow was spattered brown-red with their diarrhoea. It was inevitable that he'd succumb eventually, too, and then who'd look after Gordon?

He thought again of that woman. She had been wearing a dark brown fur coat with a sky-blue scarf pulled up over her head. Her cheeks were chill-flushed pink and her eyes melting-dark. He hadn't been able to see the colour of her hair, as it was covered by the scarf. But he thought he knew what it would be like to have her bend over him, and have a long dark mane cascade over, like the whispering bough of a willow. She had been carrying something, large and ungainly, and he'd had a stupid, chivalrous urge to let Gordon go, run over and say, 'Here, let me help you with that,' and carry her load through the snow to wherever it was she was headed.

He frowned. Forget her. You're never going to see her again. In a few days the Red Army would overrun the village. He knew what would happen to her then, if she hadn't had the good sense to flee. Something caught in his throat at the thought of what the Russians would do to her. She was only a German, but nobody deserved that. He shook his head. He'd never see her again. He needed to focus on keeping himself and Gordon alive. 'Alright, pal?' He turned to his friend, who nodded, lacking the energy to speak. Were they really to be force marched all the way to Fallingbostel?

There were some tumble-down farm buildings up ahead and the men were ordered inside one of them. The stench kettled as they were herded inside: shit and piss and silage combined. At least it was warmer than outside. Some lit cigarettes, and the smoke drifted up in the fetid air.

Tom managed to get Gordon the edge of an old hay bale to sit on. Gordon's cheeks were hollowed, the skin beneath his stubble waxy-pale. The floor was filthy, so most men squatted on their heels. Small rectangles of black bread were handed out amongst them.

The guards made a fire in the barn next door and put a pot full of snow on to heat up. They brought through cups of tepid water made salty with the addition of an over-diluted stock cube. Word went round that they'd picked up a bag of potatoes from the village. There was talk of them being boiled, or roasted in the fire's embers. 'Is this us for today, d'you think?' Gordon's eyes were hopeful orbs in the gloomy fug.

A man squatting on the floor beside Tom must have overheard the comment. 'Why don't you find out?' he said. 'You speak a bit of German, don't you?' Tom nodded. 'Go on then, see if you can't find out what the goons have planned, old boy.' The man had a ginger moustache, and one of those saw-edged public schoolboy voices that assumed compliance, and Tom found he was pushing himself to his feet before he'd thought to question it. He nudged his way through the crouched forms and out into the farmyard. The wind had got up, whipping up stray bits of straw and grit. Tom squinted his eyes and walked the few paces to the next barn, where the guards were preparing food. He stood by the doorway, was about to knock, when he felt someone shove past him. The commandant barged through the barn doorway, not seeming to notice that Tom was there.

'I'm going to walk on to the next village and find a working telephone.' The commandant chopped his words like an axe on logs. 'Follow on when the men have eaten. I should have clear orders by then.'

Tom looked through a gap in the rotten wood to see the guards huddled round the fire, the commandant facing them with his hands on his hips. 'But, sir, aren't you hungry, don't you want to wait and get something to eat?' Tom recognized the voice of the paint-tube guard, the one who'd let slip to him about Fallingbostel. The commandant made an impatient gesture, and strode back out of the barn, almost banging the door in Tom's face as he went. Tom watched as he strode on up the road, westwards, to where the skies were clearer, the sun a hint of silver behind the retreating clouds.

Tom went back to the barn and over to the man with the ginger moustache. 'The goons don't seem to have a clue. The commandant has just flounced off up the road in search of a telephone. I think they were just told to get over the Oder, and now they don't know what to do next.'

Tom thought about the commandant striding off into the whiteness. It was he who'd been doing the head counts. It was on his orders that the barn rafters had been strafed on their second night, and he who'd decreed five men should be shot for every attempted escapee. But he'd be hundreds of yards away already, and he wasn't coming back to collect them when they moved out.

Tom turned to Gordon to say something more.

But Gordon had disappeared.

# Chapter 6

## November 1989, West Berlin

*Miranda*

'Are you awake, baby?' I hear his voice in my ear, feel his breath on my cheek. I open my eyes. My tongue seems to be stuck to the roof of my mouth. It makes a clicking sound as I pull it down. He kisses the top of my head, and stacks the pillows up behind my shoulders. He's already shaved and dressed, I notice. 'Stay where you are. I'm bringing you breakfast in bed.' He disappears into the little kitchen.

As I become fully awake I remember last night: the Wall, the photos, my decision. I need to pack up my rucksack. I mustn't forget my passport, hidden with Quill's at the bottom of the fruit bowl (the improbable hiding place that Petra said would be the last place any thief would think of looking). I can either hitch to Holland and get the ferry or splurge the last of my overdraft on a flight. I'll decide once I'm on my way.

There is a clattering, the faint scent of something burning, and he comes back with a tray and places it on top of the quilt: a slice of buttered toast, and a glass of orange juice. When he's being like this, when there's just the two of us together, I almost think we can work it out. But playing the solicitous lover is not enough to keep me in Berlin with him any longer.

'I meant what I said last night,' I begin.

'Shut up and let me look after you,' he says, patting my leg beneath the quilt. I take a gulp of the juice: delicious, freshly squeezed. I glance at the fruit bowl on the window sill. There are no oranges left – he's squeezed them all for me. The fruit bowl is empty.

Completely empty.

'So, what have you done with our passports?' I try to sound casual.

'You can't leave me, Miranda.'

'Where's my passport?' His face is sullen, blank, like a boy caught with his hand in the pick 'n' mix. 'It was in the fruit bowl. What have you done with it?'

'Burnt it, didn't I? If you must know. Happy now?'

I'm not sure if I've heard him correctly. 'You did what?'

'I burnt it, alright? You can't go, Miranda. I need you here, with me.' He leans in to stroke my hair away from my forehead, reminding me of the first night we kissed, of how special I am, how important it is that I stay with him. He tells me to eat up the toast, the breakfast he made because he loves me and wants to look after me.

He has that look in his eyes. The strand of black hair that

falls over his eyebrow twitches like a cat's tail. I know better than to argue, so I swallow the toast, dry as cardboard in my constricted throat, as he watches me finish every last crumb. Afterwards he tells me I should shower and get dressed. Dieter and Petra are planning a party and they need to turn our bed back into a sofa and clear the room. I do as I'm told.

When I come out of the shower, Petra has already put our bed away and cleared the living room floor. She says Quill has gone out with Dieter to get beers and sort a sound system. In the kitchen there is the acrid scent of something burnt, ashes in the plughole. I look in the bin, but there's nothing there. He actually did it then, destroyed my passport, so desperate to keep me close. Below the soft wool of my jumper the scabbed cigarette burns itch. I should have left Berlin sooner. I never should have come.

On the pretext of tidying up I stuff my few belongings into my rucksack. I tell Petra I'm just off to get a few more shots of the Wall for the newspaper, and leave the basement flat.

The yellow phone booth is at the end of the street, on the corner. I walk past a neon-lit massage parlour, a Lebanese takeaway called Falafel Station and the orange *Imbiss* kiosk: lunchtime customers are propped against the counter, eating sausage and chips. A stray Alsatian dog begs, hoping for leftovers. Pigeons flap, and the traffic roars past the junction.

I telephone the British Consulate in West Berlin to see if they can help. No, says the unhelpful woman at the other end of the line. There's nothing they can do for me today, unless I can get to the Embassy in Bonn before 5 p.m. But as Bonn is 600 kilometres away, and it is already midday, I know it's impossible. I will have to wait until after the weekend. Frustrated, I hang up.

I slip down to the underground station. On the U-bahn I sway along with my fellow passengers, staring at the blank tunnel walls. Without my passport, I'm stuck. Perhaps if I wait until Quill is in a better mood he'll see sense, agree to drive me the 1000-mile round trip to the West German capital. After all, without ID I can't even get into East Berlin at the moment, and Quill's editor might need to send us there for a story. I decide to do what I said, take some more photographs, and give myself a chance to make a plan. I get off the U-bahn at Kochstrasse station.

From the station exit I see the crush of TV crews and journalists at Checkpoint Charlie. But I'm looking for a different angle. I turn right. Further along, at the end of Jakobstrasse, five small boys are playing football, using a section of the Wall as a goal. A burned-out red 2CV is abandoned on a piece of waste ground, by a gigantic billboard of full-colour cowboys against a backdrop of cattle and mountains. 'Go West!' is splurged in red type – West is a brand of cigarettes, but it feels like an advert for the emerging diaspora from the GDR. I lift the Leica, but change my mind, reaching instead for the Rolleiflex in my rucksack, an old 1939 camera (state-of-the-art in its day). My grandmother gave it to me when I started my photography degree course; it used to belong to my grandfather, which I suppose makes it a family heirloom, of sorts.

The Escape

You have to hold the Rolleiflex like a prayer, just below the centre of your chest, and the double-mirror lens works like a kind of reverse periscope. The effect, in the shots, is to lift the horizon, making subjects appear somehow more heroic.

It seems right to use a Second World War-era camera here in the forgotten underbelly of Berlin: everywhere I look I see walls pock-marked with bullet holes, rubble-strewn abscesses in once-grand terraces. I think about how it would have been in 1945. Echoes of that time are everywhere, just beneath the surface: ghosts in the pitted stonework, like a double-exposed film. When the boys' ball comes my way I kick it back, and they grin their thanks.

I walk on. There is a space of waste ground between the raggle-taggle street ends and the Wall, wide enough for army jeeps to barrel round on patrol, although there are no sign of them now. Weeds, dog mess, and used needles scatter the pitted concrete.

I pause and look up over the Wall. Stabs of midday sunlight through grey clouds create a halo above East Berlin. Then something twitches in my peripheral vision. Up ahead I see a group of youths, huddled, tussling with something. There is movement: grunting, thuds. Perhaps some rival gang member is getting a good kicking? I should walk away. But I don't. I lift the Rolleiflex to my chest, like a shield, and close in. My shoes crunch on broken glass. As I approach I hear the young men are chanting something – what?

'*Mauer muss weg!*' comes the shout – *The Wall must go!*

67

The forest of denim and leather gives way easily as I arrive at the scene, as if they expect me. A young man with his sleeves rolled up is wielding a sledge hammer at a piece of graffiti-scrawled wall. The grunts and thuds I heard from a distance are the sounds he makes as he attacks the concrete. His sinewy arms bulge, and another piece of the Wall comes loose. There's already a jagged smile appearing in the Wall, a glimpse of the other side.

Eventually the young man gives up, to cheers, backslaps and more chants: *Mauer muss weg: the Wall must go!* He passes the sledge hammer on to his curly haired friend, who shrugs off his jacket and rolls his shoulders in readiness. I carry on photographing them.

I run out of film. None of them notice as I slip away. I begin to retrace my steps, back towards Kreuzberg. I'm going to the apartment, to the party, to Quill. I tell myself not to worry, that the weekend here is an opportunity to take more photos. Quill is right. History is happening, and it is a privilege to witness it.

As I can't get a new passport until Monday, I'm trapped here, so why not celebrate freedom, along with everyone else in Berlin today?

# Chapter 7

**January 1945, Nazi Germany**

*Tom*

With the hot potato in his hands he could begin to feel his fingers again. Good, they weren't frostbitten. When Tom had been eavesdropping on the guards, Gordon had fallen asleep, and slipped, unnoticed, in to a recess behind the hay bale in the barn wall. When Tom returned, he was momentarily panic stricken, thinking the bugger had gone and done a Scott of the Antarctic on him, but he'd found him quickly enough, wedged in the corner, snoring into the mouldy straw.

Tom chewed on the glorious boiled potato. It was hard and starchy, the skin green-grey and slippery. But it was hot, and it was food. From his squatting position next to the ginger moustache man, Tom looked up at the barn. There was a hole in the roof through which occasional snow flurries fell like fairy dust. But the rest of it was solid enough, roof tiles supported by huge oak-hewn wooden rafters. The eaves were brown-black shadows behind the beams. There were birds up there, a couple of pigeons fluttered – someone had made a vain attempt to lure them down with a piece of potato skin, thinking of roast pigeon, but the birds weren't stupid. Tom looked up. The struts were huge, wide as a man, and that dirty grey colour of aged wood, almost the same colour as his greatcoat.

The guards were still in the next barn, smoking and gossiping, taking their time, emboldened by the absence of their boss. Sometime soon they'd drain their mugs, pack the handcart, and someone would bellow '*Raus!*' at the POWs. Then they'd all be off again into the endless, angry chill, so cold it numbed their thoughts as well as their limbs. On the march it was as if everyone forgot their dreams of escape into the liberating arms of the Reds, and focussed merely on the next step, the next breath. He'd have to carry on shouldering Gordon's weight until – until what? Would the time come when he'd have to let them put a bullet in his pal's neck and leave him by the wayside? Perhaps he'd ask the goons to do him a favour and finish him off at the same time. Perhaps that was how his war was destined to end. He chewed the remaining scrap of potato and swallowed it down.

Tom thought again of the commandant, loping lupine up the track, miles away by now. He thought of the woman in that last village, the pulse of recognition as their eyes met. And he thought of the photograph that Gordon kept of his wife, Dorothy, tucked in the breast pocket of his uniform, underneath the RAF badge, above his heart. He touched the spot on his own greatcoat then, on the left. He couldn't feel the insignia through the thick cloth, but he knew it was there. 'Sod this for a game of soldiers,' he muttered, as he pushed himself upright. He nudged past Ginger Moustache and leant over Gordon. If anyone were looking, which they weren't, it would merely seem as if he were waking up his chum ready for the march. 'Stop snoring and lie still for me, will you?' he said, shaking Gordon's shoulder, and Gordon opened his eyes and moved his chin a quarter of an inch downwards in acknowledgement.

Just as he expected, there were footsteps and scuffling outside, the barn door was flung open, and the call came: '*Raus! Raus!*' The groaning throng began to lumber to their feet. He could see the guard's pale face, his shouting mouth, but the man didn't bother coming in to rouse them, just yelled into the gloom.

There was such a scuffling crush as everyone got up, that nobody took much notice of Tom grabbing the disintegrating hay bale and shoving it over Gordon. He kicked some muck and twigs over the top, too. It was dark over this side, and you could barely tell. He caught Ginger Moustache watching as he scrabbled to scatter the last few bits of straw, but the man looked pointedly away as soon as their eyes met.

The prisoners had begun to shuffle out into the barnyard. Tom realized he'd need to be quick. All he had to do was get up that strut and into the rafters, quick as climbing the apple tree in the garden back home. His fingers scuffed the disintegrating brickwork as he reached up.

'*Schnell!*'

Damn. The guard was back, waving his rifle. Too risky. Tom filed out into the aching cold with the others. The driving snow stung his cheeks. They began to walk, along the track, following where the commandant had gone: fresh snowfall had already covered his footprints. Tom fell in beside Ginger Moustache, who raised an eyebrow, but said nothing.

It was easier to walk without Gordon to support, and he managed to work his way up the column. Eventually he came across Oliver, his old hut-mate. He was limping a little, with blisters, but hadn't yet succumbed to dysentery. They paused to clap clumsy arms on each other's shoulders, then carried on trudging ahead. There were no guards in the centre of the column, but even so, Tom moved in close enough to whisper. 'Say cheerio to the others for me.'

'Beg pardon?' Oliver's voice was almost inaudible, muffled behind the scarf he had wrapped over his face.

'I'm off. Don't let on but send Edward and the others my best, won't you?'

'Are you mad? You'll get yourself slotted!'

'If any of the goons notice, just say I've got the shits.'

There was an old oak tree up on the left, with a broad trunk, and beyond it the track curved away to the right. As they drew level, Tom headed towards it, making a show of fumbling with his fly. There was a ditch at the side of the road, too, and the tops of scrubby bushes poked through the snow drifts.

Tom crouched down, watching the column plodding past. He resisted the urge to lie down, below the line of sight, because if anyone saw him lying in the ditch he'd be shot — for attempting to escape, or being too ill to walk — either way he played it.

The column was almost past now. The snow was still sheeting down, and everything was grey-white and blurred. If any guards saw, surely they'd think he was just another diarrhoea-sodden POW crapping in the bushes. But this was the most risky bit. There was a guard at the tail end of the line. If he were spotted now, the guard would wait for him, nudge him with the barrel of his weapon back to join the others.

Then he spotted Ginger Moustache, who'd dropped right back, lumbering alongside the sickies and the tail-end goon. He was walking on the guard's right-hand side. Tom crouched behind the oak tree, to the guard's left. Just as they approached, he heard Ginger Moustache strike up a conversation: 'I say, old boy, is it true we're headed to Breslau?'

'*Wie bitte?*' The guard turned to respond. He was close enough for Tom to hear the soft crunch of his solid army boots on the snowy track beside him. He held his breath. Counting the seconds along with the footfalls: one, two, three . . .

'Breslau, someone said, but that means heading north, doesn't it? And I suppose you want to keep on going west, given the circumstances, don't you?'

'Breslau?'

'Yes, are we going – *farhren wir nach* – *Breslau?*'

There was a pause then, and for a moment Tom thought the guard had stopped.

'Breslau? I don't know. We are waiting for orders.'

The sound of the boots came from beyond the tree trunk now. Tom counted . . . sixteen, seventeen, eighteen . . . his chest bursting with pent-up breath. He closed his eyes, willing time to pass.

'What would you do, if you were in command?' Ginger Moustache's voice was further away.

'Command?'

'Yes, if you were the commandant, what would you do? Take us to Breslau, or head west? What would your command decision be?'

Tom could barely hear the footfalls now.

'We are waiting for the orders.' The guard's voice wavered with impatience, but it was harder to hear, turning the corner.

. . . Twenty-nine, thirty . . .

The voices eased into the distance and Tom exhaled with careful slowness. The muffled boom of a gun came from the east. He waited a little longer, to be certain.

Finally, painfully, he unwound from his crouching position. Pins and needles burnt his legs where they'd been bent for so long. He stamped his feet to get rid of the sensation. The road was empty in either direction now.

Tom checked once more before setting off. Could anyone see? No, they were gone, hundreds of men simply swallowed up in the wintry landscape. He walked along the ditch, just in case – if he did hear or see anything he could drop to the ground and be hidden from the road. He made slow progress, squinting into the snow, and stumbling over hidden branches in the drifts.

The sound of the artillery came again, and he smiled. He was walking towards the booming of the guns, at last: towards the farm buildings, towards Gordon, towards the Russian front.

Eastwards – towards home?

# Chapter 8

## November 1989, West Berlin

*Miranda*

The apartment door is open, so I walk in, dangling the bottle of red wine I've picked up from the corner shop on the way, and dropping my rucksack in the hallway. Music blasts from the stereo. There is an old tin bath full of ice cubes and beer bottles on the hallway floor. In the kitchen a woman in a green cocktail dress winds an arm round the neck of a black bloke in tight jeans, and plants her face on his. I go through to the living room, crowded as a nightclub, the sofa-bed shoved out of the way against the wall, the speakers thumping. The air is thick with the tang of marijuana smoke. Everyone has made an effort: heels and dresses, shirts and aftershave. Dieter has even installed a miniature light set on top of the sound system: coloured lights flash along with the beat.

My gaze trawls the room. Here and there guests are huddled around tiny mirrors upon which white powder is chopped and scraped into wispy white lines by razor blades, taking it in turns with rolled-up twenty Deutschmark notes: one nostril, then the other. I try not to look shocked at the blatancy of the cutting and snorting, and take refuge behind my Leica lens, snapping shots of the partygoers, some of whom grin and wave, like celebrities on the red carpet.

'Miranda, where have you been?' It's not Quill but Petra who grabs me. Her Berlin bob is swept back and glistening, a black silk shift dress shimmers, her glossy lips part. 'Dieter, look who's finally here!' she calls out. Then I see Dieter, fat joint in one stubby hand, bottle of beer in the other.

'Where's Quill?' I have to raise my voice to be heard.

'He just went out to the phone booth to make a work call.'

'I'll go and find him,' I say. I need to check in with the picture desk anyway, make sure my shots have arrived. I pull away from Petra's grasp, pass the grinding bodies in the kitchen, grab my rucksack, and go back outside into the grey afternoon. The clouds have thickened and the graphite sky pushes down on the angular rooftops. I turn up the collar of my jacket against the cold.

My stupid heart lurches when I see him, turned away from me, black hair flopping forward, broad shoulders filling the phone box. I reach the booth and stand close to the glass, directly behind him. But he doesn't notice me. I wait. Petra told me it was a work call, and that concerns me, too, with everything that's been going on, so I do not think of it as eavesdropping. Not at first.

'Is that you, mate? Finally. Took your sweet time about it ... the line's shocking, isn't it? Is it just as bad your end?

Okay, okay,' he raises his voice, shouting to be heard. 'So, mate, you've heard the news, obviously. It's a bit sooner than anticipated, but, you know, time and tide . . .' I lean in against the glass. At first I'm just hearing, not actively listening. 'So you need to sail to Salcombe as usual, but this time Jules will be there to meet you. The pair of you are going to go together to Coors' place on the coast of the Netherlands – I'll fax the details . . .'

Why? Why is he telling people to sail to the Netherlands? What has this got to do with our piece for the *Sunday Correspondent*?

'Jules will cut the stuff en route, and Coors will deal with it from there on in. He's a good chap: solid, yeah. His fiancée is an air hostess with Interflug and we've got the customs at Schoenberg and Stasi chaps sewn up, too . . . What? I do wish you'd do your bloody prep, mate. Schoenberg is the airport in East Berlin and the Stasi are the state police. For fuckssake.'

He shifts the receiver to the other ear, then, and I think he's going to turn and see me, but he doesn't. And I know I should walk away, or at least let him know I'm there, but I don't do that either. I carry on listening.

'We've got to move now, to get control of the supply routes, take advantage of the chaos and steal a march on the others . . . What's that? You'll have to speak up, mate.'

He straightens up, and I am sure he'll catch sight of me now. But the traffic zooms past, reflections play on the glass panels, and still he doesn't notice me there, just beside him.

'My what? My front? My cover? What are you talking

about? Oh, you mean the gorgeous Miranda. No, she's not going anywhere, I've made sure of that, so yes, to all intents and purposes I'm just an innocent journalist with his photographer girlfriend, covering the Berlin situation for the foreseeable future. It's perfect. Even better because as far as she's concerned, it's the truth. And you know what, her shots are so good that I can file any old shit and they'll publish it as a picture-led piece. Which gives me more time to focus on the operational side of things this end. Yeah, I know, right . . .' He starts to laugh.

I knock on the glass. He looks up, sees me, smiles his toothpaste smile through the pane. 'Talk of the devil – here's my precious pet now. Gotta go mate. Ciao.' He hangs up, pushes open the booth door.

'Miranda!' He steps forward to embrace me, but I pull away.

'I heard,' I say.

'What?'

'The whole conversation you just had, with whoever it was.'

'Baby, listen–' He holds his hands out, palms upwards, head to one side. 'It's not what you think . . .' I shake my head and take a step backwards. 'Oh come on, it's just cocaine. It's just a lifestyle choice,' he says. 'It's not like that shit that did it for your dad.'

'You know nothing about my dad.' I hear my voice waver, feel the heat rising in my chest.

'Miranda, look. It's business, that's all. Now the Eastern

Bloc is bound to open up, there's a huge potential gap in the market. If we get in first, we can make a killing.'

'A killing?'

He nods, smiling into my eyes, not hearing my tone, thinking he's brought me round.

'No, Quill. I won't be your 'front' or your 'cover' or your 'pet' or however else you think of me.' I make a move to go, but he grabs my wrist, twists my arm up behind my back. The wine bottle falls and smashes on the pavement. He pushes me inside the booth, then lets go of my hand, spins me round, and shoves me up against the phone.

'I need you,' he says, pushing his face in close. His expression is a mixture of anger and bewilderment.

'It's over,' I say. 'We're over.' I can't meet his gaze, and look away, hearing the growl of cars and a distant shriek of police sirens.

I don't know how I expect him to respond, but not like this. It comes, sudden as a hammer blow. A buzzing in my head, a moment of blackness. I hear myself cry out as if it is someone else – disembodied, apart. And then I open my eyes and I am back here in the phone box with him. I feel it then: a bursting pain in my right brow.

'You headbutted me?' Even as I stutter out the words, it seems impossible. 'Why?'

'Knock some sense into you.' He turns and pushes open the booth door. 'I'll see you back at Dieter's.' And he lets the door shut behind him, trapping me inside. I watch him go, through the grimy glass, shrinking into the Berlin afternoon.

He is so certain I'll follow that he doesn't even turn back to check.

I steady myself with my fingertips against the phone booth, head reeling, mouth dry, feeling the thud-rush of my racing heart. I close my eyes for a moment and catch my breath. There is a knock on the glass. I start, thinking it might be Quill, returned, to apologize, to hold me, tell me sweet lies about how much he loves me and how everything will be okay. But the grubby pane holds the face of an old Turkish man with caved-in cheeks and two-day old stubble, gesturing at me to hurry up. I push open the booth door, pass the old man, and pick my way over the shattered remains of the wine bottle. I walk away, in the opposite direction of the apartment.

A fine drizzle starts to fall, enfolding me in a chill mist, as I traipse along the pavements. The whole of West Berlin is partying today. Every building I pass seems to have music blaring. The undercurrent of a bass beat changes with each block, syncopating with the throbbing pain in my forehead.

Eventually I reach Jakobstrasse, past the burnt-out car and the billboard, cowboy colours now turning monochrome in the lowering light. I follow the strip of waste ground, winding between the homes and the barricades. It begins to sleet. Icy rivulets run down inside my jumper. I reach up to wipe drips from my forehead and my fingers graze the swelling bruise on my temple.

Then I see it up ahead: the crack in the Wall that was just

a smile earlier on has turned into a jagged 'Oh' of dismay. The young men have all gone. I am the only person here. No border guard or patrol dog in sight. I put out a hand. The Wall is still smooth where the graffiti paint sticks, but rough around the edges of the hole. The metal reinforcements show like ridged spines in the smashed space. One is bashed sideways, giving just enough room to let a person through.

The leaden clouds have made twilight of the daytime, but through the Wall security lights veil the sleet – a waterfall shimmer, light at the end of the tunnel.

I take off my backpack and feed it through the space between the metal reinforcements, dropping it onto the sand on the other side. Then I lift one leg across. I push, struggle, the metal struts pinch, the broken concrete snags my clothes, but I shunt and pull free.

As I make it through to the other side, I pause, just as I'd watched the Ossis do as they passed through the barrier last night. I hesitate, and take a breath, looking across at the chunky outlines of East Berlin, a grey huddle beyond the searchlights and raked sand of the death strip.

Then I step forward, into the East, escaping.

# Chapter 9

**January 1945, Nazi Germany**

*Detta*

Odd that it should have been the growl of a truck that woke her, not the roiling thunder of the front line, which had continued throughout the night. The booming thuds and jarring vibrations had had a strangely calming effect on Detta's strung-out nerves, and she slept a full, uninterrupted seven hours, for a change. It was the sound of the engine that made her shoot up, eyes wide in the dark, run across the cold floorboards to unshutter the window and scrabble at the frosted pane to see.

The vehicle careered up the main road, coming from the Oppeln direction. Everything was monochrome in the moonlight, and it was hard to make out what colour it was. Detta strained her eyes as the truck zoomed close. What was that marking, dark grey on the side of the cab? She sucked in a breath. Was it a star? The truck passed beneath the guest-house. No, it was a cross – in daylight it would have been red – on the cab door and on the flapping canvas covering the truck bed. The truck skidded on the ice as it turned past the barracks and veered up the estate track.

Not the Red Army, then. Just an ambulance. They must have started using the Schloss as a field hospital, now the front was getting closer.

She was about to close the shutters, feeling the cold now her panic had abated, but just as she began to push the slats to, she noticed a movement in the churchyard, between the manse and the church. There was the dark shadow of a figure moving amongst the gravestones. Her breath clouded the windowpane and she had to wipe it continually as she watched. Who or what was it? Or they? For a moment she thought she saw two shadowy forms staggering between the tombs in the darkness.

She blinked, reminding herself of Father Richter's promise to bury the family silver in an empty grave. That would be it. It must have been his cassock billowing out that made her mistake him for two lurching figures. The space on the window was clouded over again with her condensing breath. She closed the shutters and went back to bed.

She'd been up so long that the bed had cooled, sheets shroud-cold as she crept back under the covers, hoping to snatch a little more sleep before daylight. You stupid girl, she told herself, worrying about churchyard ghouls, like a little child. There's more to fear from the living than the dead, she thought, listening to the symphony of guns outside, and waiting for her body to warm up.

The Escape

But neither heat nor sleep enveloped her, and eventually she decided to get up, pulling on her woollen dress and thick stockings. She tried a hopeful flick of the light switch in the hallway, but of course there was nothing, so she lit the candle in the saucer on the Ottoman chest and made her way downstairs. The third stair down creaked, as it always did, and just before she reached the bottom she heard the faint, strangled cry of the Muller's old rooster, across the way.

Detta pushed open the kitchen door. Mother was already up, curlers in her greying hair, a green serge overcoat belted over her dressing gown and nightclothes. She knelt in front of the kitchen range, poking kindling onto yesterday's embers. 'It was just a field ambulance,' she said, without turning.

'I know. I saw.' Detta put her own candle down next to the other two on the table and they glittered like Orion's belt. She didn't mention the figures amongst the gravestones. After all, it had to be just Father Richter, surely? But she could have sworn there were two. No, her eyes must have been playing tricks. And in any case, it was dark out there, and her windowpane was smeared with condensation. 'Coffee?' She reached for the tin of ground acorn and chicory in the cupboard by the sink.

Her mother half turned from the hearth, sharp features limned rose gold by the embers' light. 'Use the real stuff.'

'Brown-gold?'

'I've had enough of that other muck. In any case, we may as well use it up,' she added, poking another stick on the fire.

Detta took the coffee grinder and the precious cannister of

beans from the back of the cupboard. Coffee beans were so scarce. They'd only had real coffee on special occasions since the start of the war. Would today turn out to be a special day, Detta wondered, turning the brass handle to grind the beans.

A louder crump-thud than usual came from outside, making the floorboards shiver. The three flames leapt in their saucers. Detta finished grinding the coffee, filled their old Italian coffee pot from the tap, tamped the ground beans into the funnel-shaped filter and screwed the lid on. In the silence that followed the guns, the rooster crowed again. Mother stood up, closing the range door, as Detta reached over to put the coffee pot on the hob. Some years ago Detta had outgrown her mother, who seemed to be shrinking daily as the war toiled on. 'They're not getting their hands on our silver or our coffee, or anything else if I can help it,' Mother said, rolling her head to either side, and reminding Detta of a strongman she'd seen at the fair as a child, the way he'd eased his shoulders when limbering up to lift the huge weights. Mother went to open the shutters and Detta blew out the candles. The bitter-rich scent of brewing coffee wafted across from the range.

The guesthouse kitchen was south-facing: the warmest place to be in winter, harvesting scraps of sunshine through the double windows all day long. The inside of the glass was frost encrusted, although the splashes of winter sun and the warmth from the fire would mean that the ice would eventually clear from these windows, unlike those in the rest of the building. It was impossible to see through the crystalline blur into the kitchen garden: the rosemary bush, bay tree, hen house and pig sty. All you could see were two rectangles of charcoal blue haze, as the night sky slowly lifted. It was almost the same colour as that prisoner's coat had been on the path yesterday. Detta frowned. Why dwell on that? He was either kilometres away, or dead, by now. She turned away from the window, rubbing her arms to warm them, waiting for the coffee to come to the boil. Mother began to lay out the things for breakfast: plates from the dresser, black bread from the crock, honey from the cupboard. There were still a few sticky crystals clinging to the insides of the jar.

Detta recalled how once, as a girl, one boring Sunday afternoon, she'd stolen down to the cellar with the pfennig she'd 'forgotten' to put in the church collection box. Feeling guilty about the sinful penny, she'd crept down the dark back stairs and into that hidden world of wagon-wheel cheeses, sausage wreaths, barrels of brandy, and a culinary library of preserving bottles and cans. She'd found the lid loose on one of the honey jars. First she'd dipped in a finger, licked the sweetness. Then she'd taken the coin from her pocket, and dropped it into the jar. She stayed for ages watching as it sunk with excruciating slowness in viscous amber limbo. She still didn't know why she'd done it. There would have been easier ways to hide her guilt: popping it in the till, or in her mother's coat pocket – even her six-year-old self would have known that.

She felt like that pfennig now: the tortuous torpor of the fall – so slow, so inevitable.

'I packed my case,' Detta said, watching her mother bustling about, but Mother didn't answer. The staff had already been paid off. Many in the village – the ones who had relatives further west – had already left. But still, only a few days ago the town clerk had been round to check that every household still had their obligatory swastika flag and photograph of the Fuhrer on display. There was still the possibility that 'traitors to the Reich' could be bundled into the back of a black van and taken away, never to return. 'Couldn't we go to Aunty Hedwig's?' Detta said.

'There's no food in Hanover and they've been bombed to buggery. Going there would be suicide. It will be a miracle if Hedwig makes it through.' Mother put her hands to her face as she spoke, and then pulled them away as she finished the sentence, with a sharp inhalation of breath.

'But what about ... what about when the front moves west?' Detta said.

'The Reds will move through like locusts, and for a while it will be terrible. But later on this will still be a main road, you know, and tired Russian travellers will also need a bed to sleep in, food and drink. We'll have to change the name, of course. How does Russiche Haus sound?'

'But Mother, you heard what the Prussian refugees said about what the Red Army have been doing.'

'People say lots of things. Your father worked himself to death – literally – building this place up from scratch. When we arrived, there was nothing. You won't remember that, of course. This place gave you your education, young lady. We could never have afforded to send you to Ursulinen Kloster if your father was still a waiter and I was a shop girl, and without your languages you would never have got that good job at the Reichsbahn, don't forget.'

'But I got the French from you, Mother, and that's what got me the Reichsbahn job.'

'Pff.' Her mother made a swiping gesture with her hands, as if her French ancestry were of no consequence whatsoever.

'But if – when . . .' Detta still couldn't say it out loud: *When we are overrun by the Red Army, what will we do then?* Her face must have betrayed her thoughts, because her mother continued.

'Don't be naive, Detta. Remember your mother is from Alsace. I know a thing or two about swapping sides when the time comes. We'll have to lay low for a while, naturally, but then, you know, people are people and business is business, and it will all settle down, you'll see.'

Her mother had been through a war before, and thought she knew how to survive it. But it's different this time, Detta thought, remembering the look on those refugees' faces when they'd recounted what the Russians had done. She shook her head, but didn't have the energy to argue. 'I'll go and collect the eggs, shall I?' she said instead, but then the pot hissed to the boil, and her mother said to warm herself with a drink first, and poured the steaming coffee into china cups. Detta lit two cigarettes. They both sat down at the table, took a sip of coffee, and then a drag of the cigarette, savouring the mix of roasted flavours, not speaking. The breakfast things lay untouched between them.

Detta had almost finished her coffee when the phone went. Mother sighed. 'It's a miracle the lines are still working,' she said, beginning to push herself up from her seat.

'I'll get it,' Detta said, draining the last precious sip of coffee and taking her half-smoked cigarette with her as she slipped out into the dark corridor.

The nagging phone crouched toad-like, next to the hotel register and the black-framed photo of Herr Hitler shaking hands with the old chancellor. Detta reached for the receiver with her left hand, keeping her cigarette in her right. Behind the reception desk was the large gilt-edged mirror. Detta caught a brief glimpse of herself in the dull glass: unbrushed hair and owlish eyes. God, what a fright. But better to look as plain as possible with what's coming, she thought grimly, picking up the receiver.

'Deutches Haus Inn, how can I help?'

'Oh, good, it's you. I didn't want to trouble your mother.'

'Father Richter? What is it?'

'Can you come over to the manse?'

'Now?'

'As soon as you can.'

'What is it, Father?'

'It's . . . I need your help with something. It's quite urgent. Can you come?'

'Of course,' Detta said, frowning at her reflection and flicking ash into the marble ashtray on the counter. 'I'll come as soon as I can.'

'And Detta . . .'

'Yes.'

'Don't mention it to your mother, not just yet, will you?'

'She'll want to know why I'm going out, Father. I'll need to tell her that I'm coming over to yours.'

'Yes of course. But don't tell her why.'

'But I don't know why.'

'No, of course not. Good. Well then, I'll see you shortly?'

'Yes. I just need to brush my hair, and I'll be with you.' She hung up.

That moment, then, when the telephone made a chiming thump into its cradle, and the Muller's silly rooster made his third reedy crow of the morning, that was the moment it all changed. It was as if someone had picked up that big jar of sickly honey from the cellar shelf, with the coin still sliding through the goo, lifted it high and dropped it – *smash* – onto the flagstone floor.

# Chapter 10

## November, 1989, East Berlin

*Miranda*

'Emergency travel documents take two working days to process,' she says, looking at me as if I am stupid. She has large, gold-rimmed glasses that make her eyes look like a fish's. She has a slight squint, too, so when she speaks it's as if there are two of me, and she's addressing us both.

I am at the British Embassy. Quill was right, he did knock some sense into me. I remembered that there are two British Embassies in Germany: one in the West German capital of Bonn, and also one in the East German capital in East Berlin, within walking distance of the Wall.

'And where did you last see your passport?' the administrator says, jotting a note on a pad. Behind her, above the counter, are two metal-rimmed clocks, like an echo of her glasses, showing London and East Berlin time. The hands jerk forward as I look. My head aches, and I have started to feel nauseous.

'In a fruit bowl, in a friend's apartment,' I say, knowing how ridiculous I sound.

'It's not possible it's just been mislaid? Moved by your friend, perhaps?'

'No, it's definitely gone.' I recall Quill's sullen face and the burnt remains in the kitchen sink.

'Right, well, that's logged for you, Miss Wade, and here's your confirmation.' She hands me a slip of typed paper, which she has dated and signed. 'So I'll see you again on Wednesday afternoon.'

'Wednesday?'

'Two working days, Miss Wade. Today is Friday, and as it's already . . .' she makes a show of turning to look at the clocks on the wall, 'past three, it's too late to begin to process your application today. Two working days means Monday and Tuesday, so if you come back on Wednesday it should be ready for you. But I'd wait until after lunch. We might be quite busy with other things, what with everything that's been happening recently.' She waves a hand at the crowded lobby.

'I see,' I reply. 'Wednesday afternoon then. Thank you.'

She gives an unsmiling nod of acknowledgement and I turn away. I can't get back home until next week. I am stuck in East Germany for five whole days, alone.

I walk across the marble floor towards the exit, side-stepping men in suits, thinking of what I heard Quill discussing on the phone, remembering the look on his face, and the impact of his head slamming against mine. I can't go back, can I?

There is a public telephone near the Embassy doorway. I pause, wedge myself beside the window and I let my throbbing temple rest against the cool glass. I pick up the receiver, and dial, asking the operator to reverse the charges.

## November 1989, Exeter

*Odette*

'You were right about him, Gran.' Her voice is small and tinny down the long-distance line.

'Miranda?'

'He turned out to be ... to be not very trustworthy, just like you said.' Her voice wobbles, and my heart gives. My granddaughter, my only grandchild. What has happened to upset her like this? I want to go to her, hold her, comfort her, just as I did when she was a toddler with a scraped knee, or a teen who'd flunked a school test.

My cigarette lies smouldering in the cut-glass ashtray, abandoned when I picked up the phone. Next to it is my coffee mug, imprinted with my lipstick from the first couple of sips. 'Why don't you take a break from college and come to visit me this weekend?' I say. 'I'll pay your train fare and I'll take you to tea at Tinley's – how does that sound?'

'I'd love to, but I can't. I'm in Berlin.'

'What?' My insides contract. So that was what the message from Helen was about this morning.

'We went over on the ferry on Sunday. Quill said he had a hunch about the situation, and he's got friends out here, so—'

'So you just ran away to Germany without telling anyone?'

'We left a note at Mum's when I picked up my passport. I thought she might have mentioned it. Anyway, Quill was right – you've seen the news?' I nod, forgetting she can't see me. 'Gran, are you still there?'

'Yes, yes I saw on the news, about the Wall.'

'I got some really good shots last night. Quill thinks the *Sunday Correspondent* will definitely use at least one of them to accompany his piece.' Her voice is dull and reedy, like a child who has been forced to recite a poem.

'That's good, isn't it?' I say, thinking that her course tutor might forgive a mid-term absence in her final year if she gets one of her photos in a newspaper.

'Yes, and it will look great in my portfolio.' Her voice has dropped almost to a whisper. I strain to hear. 'He says he wants Quill and I to do more stuff together. Quill . . .' I hear a muffled sob at the other end of the line.

'What is it?' I say. 'Has he done something?' She doesn't answer, but I hear her uneven breath. 'Miranda?'

I have only met him once, this boyfriend of hers, but once was enough. When you've been widowed at forty, you understand something of men with charming smiles, predatory eyes, and open-topped sports cars. All I wanted was for Miranda to take care of herself, realize not all men were to be trusted. 'Don't give away the goods too soon,' was all I actually said. But by that stage she was already under his spell.

'Has he hurt you?' I say, expecting a tawdry tale of night-club infidelity.

'Yes. He ...' I hear the effort it takes to choke out the words. 'He headbutted me.'

'Oh, darling.' I pause, collecting myself. I had expected petty philandering, not assault. I want to scream interrogations, but I'm wary of overreacting. I do not want to send Miranda spinning back into this man's arms simply because I cannot keep my cool. 'Is it bad – have you seen a doctor?'

'No. It's just a bruise. I probably shouldn't have wound him up. It's just that I found out something about him and—'

'It's not your fault,' I interrupt. 'Whatever was said, whatever the situation was – and you don't need to tell me anything about it if you don't want to – you need to know that his violence is not your fault. Is that clear?' I hear her sniff. The line between us crackles. 'Miranda, you are not to blame. Are we clear?'

'*Sonnen klar,*' she says. *Clear as sunlight.* She has reverted to German, as if she's a little girl again.

'You're not with him now?'

'No, he's back at the apartment with the others, celebrating; they are having a party.'

My mind works quickly. 'Okay, go to the airport and call me when you get there. We'll see when the next flight to Heathrow is and book you on it. I'm sure they'll be able to take my credit card details over the phone. I'll drive to Heathrow and pick you up.'

'I can't, Gran. Quill's destroyed my passport.'

'What do you mean?'

'He burnt it. We've not been getting on, since we got here, but when I said I wanted to go home, he insisted I stay. We had a row, and . . . I don't really want to go into all of it now, but anyway, he burnt my passport. I've been to the British Embassy, but they've said they can't get me emergency travel documents until the middle of next week, so I'm stuck. I'm sorry. It's kind of you to offer to get me home, but there's nothing you can do. I can't face going back, not yet, at least. Maybe later on when the party's over, later on tonight. I'm sorry, I just wanted someone to talk to.' She sighs.

'But you can't!' I cannot bear the thought of her returning to that man.

'I don't know where else to go. I'm stuck here till Wednesday at the earliest.'

My brain panic-whirs. There must be something I can do to keep her safe from him. 'Where are you now?'

'At the Embassy in East Berlin.'

East Berlin, not West. I have a sudden surge of hope. 'I know someone in East Berlin,' I say. 'She'll look after you.' I know the address off by heart, from all those years of secretly-posted Christmas cards. 'Don't worry, I'll call her once you're off the phone. She might still be at work, so give it an hour or two, so she'll be home when you get there. Now, write this down . . .'

Afterwards I hang up the phone and stand still in the middle of the room, arms out, embracing the dead air, giving my mind a chance to process it all. Debussy has come to an end on the LP, and the speakers hiss an empty groove. I lift the needle and switch it off.

For most of my adult life – the last forty years or more – I have managed to forget. But today, memories have come jostling to the fore, no matter how many times I turn off radios or televisions or stride quickly past news-stands. Even the hairdressers were talking about Germany today.

I look round the flat: my dead husband's watercolours dot the walls, and his pipe sits in a drawer in the antique davenport. This is where I belong. This is home. This is my life now. For forty-four years I have not even looked at a map of my homeland. I lift my hands to my face and cover my eyes. My husband was adamant, after what we'd been through, and I agreed: Germany was to be left in the past. The day I married him, I became British, end of story.

End of story.

I drop my hands and go back to the table, picking up my glass. I take a sip of bitter coffee, and light a fresh cigarette. I pull aside my net curtain and look out through the sash window across the cathedral green. There is a couple walking along next to the row of shops, under the portico. They are holding hands, and walk up the steps of the Clarence Hotel. The door opens, and for a moment the pair are a tiny conjoined silhouette, before being swallowed up inside. I remember being that couple. I remember that night so well. That's why I chose to move here, when he passed. So I could sit at the window and replay the memory every day. I let the curtain drop and turn inside.

I go over to the mantlepiece, taking a deep drag from my cigarette. My husband looks out of the silver-framed photograph, teeth gripping his pipe stem. I tap my cigarette ash into the crystal ashtray, and pick up the phone. I dial zero and ask to be put through to international directory enquiries. I give the operator the same name and address I gave Miranda. There are strange crackles on the line, but eventually I hear the telephone ringing at the other end. I take a nervous drag and count the rings: one, two, three … I am about to give up when a voice finally answers.

'*Hallo? Wer ist das, bitte?*'

I start at the sound of her, after all these years, speaking German, and I almost drop the receiver. 'Gwen? Is that you?'

# Chapter 11

## January 1945, Nazi Germany

*Detta*

'Don't say yes unless you're certain.' The priest's face was all lines and shadows in the candlelight. He took Detta's hand; his fingers were dry as twigs. The air smelled of wax polish and the dried roses in the vase next to the candelabra. Frau Hecketier had kept the manse spotless until she left, just last week, spirited away by grandchildren in Dresden. Father Richter was without a housekeeper, and Detta assumed this was what he was asking, although he'd seemed so anxious and cryptic about it.

'I'm happy to help out, if that's what you need,' Detta said. She no longer had her Reichsbahn job, after all, there weren't any guests in the inn, and the odd hour reading French fairy tales to the Moll girls barely counted as a prior commitment.

Father Richter cleared his throat, and squeezed her hand. 'You see, Detta, what I'm asking from you is more than just

help with housework. I didn't want to say over the phone . . .'
He cleared his throat again, opened his mouth as if to speak,
but stayed silent. Detta lifted her mouth in an uncertain
smile. Father Richter had always been so kind, almost a
replacement for her real father, in some ways. But had the
stress – all these war years of having to hide his true feelings
about the Nazi party, preach against his convictions – had it
finally got to him?

'Thank you again for hiding our silver,' she said, to fill the
awkward silence.

'Not at all,' he said. 'I . . .' he began, but there was a sound
from upstairs, then a creaking floorboard above their heads.
Detta's eyes flicked up to where the unlit light bulb swung
slightly in its flowered shade. She shivered, remembering the
shadows she'd seen in the churchyard last night. The priest
dropped her hand. 'Shall we go through to the kitchen to
talk?' he said, and without waiting for an answer, turned to
walk down the dark corridor.

His kitchen felt warm: the range must have been on for
some time, and there was a salty smell in the air, as
if someone had been cooking soup. There were dirty
dishes in the sink, too: bowls and spoons. But the shutters were still closed, even though it would be fully light
outside by now.

'Shall I make a start on these while we talk?' Detta said,
moving over to the sink. She didn't mind helping. It would
give her something to do. It was just strange that the priest
should be making such a song and dance about asking.

'No, please sit. I'll do us some herb tea.' He went over to the range to move the kettle onto the hob.

'I'll just open the shutters then, shall I?' Why was he wasting candle wax when it was already daylight?

'Why not?' He made a casual gesture with his hand. Detta's necklace swung like a pendulum as she reached to pull open the shutters. There was no frost on the windows – she was right, the kitchen fire must have been going for quite a while already to melt it. Outside, the sky was fuscia beyond the Schloss, birch trees jerking their mistletoe baubles, and scratchy grey clouds scudding across a livid sunrise. It had stopped snowing, but all you could see of the priest's rose garden were stubbled tops of thorns, poking up through the pink-tinged drifts. The gate through to the churchyard was unlatched, swinging dizzily in the wind.

She sat at the table and blew out the candle. Father Richter placed a cup of mint tea in front of her and sat down opposite. He took a sip of his own before speaking. 'I've known you since you were a little girl, and I know you to be competent, loyal and trustworthy,' he said, looking at her from under his bushy brows. He put his mug down, then pushed his hands together into a prayer position and tapped the joined hands against his lips. 'You have a little medical knowledge?'

'Well, I was the first-aider for our office, but that hardly means—'

'And you speak English,' he said, cutting her off. 'But what I'm asking is very dangerous. We could both be shot.'

He rested his chin on his prayer hands, and looked into her eyes. And that was when she began to comprehend his cryptic words.

'I saw some prisoners being force marched through the village yesterday,' she said. 'Were they British?'

The priest nodded.

'And did one of them escape?' She thought madly, stupidly, of the prisoner in the long coat, with the blue eyes. But it couldn't have been him, could it?

'Two. Airmen.'

'And they're here?'

He nodded again.

Detta's mind worked. Two *terrorfliegers*, here in the village? The SS would surely be on their way.

'One of them is in quite a bad state. They need medicine, food and rest. And it's impossible for me to change my routine. It's too obvious: the whole village knows my whereabouts at any time of day, but you ...'

Detta knew what he was asking. She was out and about all the time, to the Schloss, to the bakery for bread, to the Muller farm for milk, always running some errand or another, especially since she was no longer going to work every day. Father Richter wanted her to help him with the British escapees. Could she?

'Is the church still unlocked, Father?' It was her turn to interrupt. He nodded. 'If you don't mind, I'd like to get a second opinion,' she said, gesturing with her head in the direction of the church.

'Of course.'

She left her un-drunk tea and Father Richter let her out of the side door. As she turned right towards the church, she looked up at the upstairs window – the floor with the creaking floorboard would be in that room – but the shutters were closed and she couldn't see anything up there. She heard the door close behind her and she pushed out into the windy morning.

Inside the church air was still as a mill pond, cold as a tomb. She clasped her hands and closed her eyes. *Dear Father, I need your help . . .*

What to do? A good, patriotic citizen would rush to tell the authorities that the local priest was harbouring escaped enemy prisoners. Of course, she'd never betray Father Richter. But Mother had always taught her not to take sides, to keep her head below the parapet. *The way to survive is to work hard, smile, and keep your opinions to yourself,* she used to say. *Politics is bad for business.* (When, at the start of the war, Father Richter had once implied in a sermon that some of the Nazi party policies were unchristian, Mother had simply stopped attending church for a while, claiming to be too busy with the guesthouse to attend – avoiding all the furore and the questioning from party officials.) *Dear Lord, give me guidance, I pray . . .*

The wooden pew was hard beneath her buttocks, and a blue circle pulsed behind her closed lids. She could smell the faint smoky-sweet waft of incense left from the last Mass.

She flexed her fingers against each other. God would want her to do the right thing. But what was the right thing? To risk her life as a traitor to the state? And for what? The war was almost over. The Russians, the British and the Americans would all snap up the Reich and Germany would cease to exist.

But Father Richter had asked her. He had put his faith in her. Could she do it, this treachery? *Dear God . . .*

She heard the sound of the church door being pushed open behind her. It would be Father Richter, coming to ask her decision. Detta opened her eyes and turned her head, still not knowing how to answer him. But what she saw wasn't the black splash of the priest's cassock against the white-washed walls. What she saw were two men dressed in grey uniforms – 'grey dogs' – the SS. They strode down the aisle like an impatient groom and best man, boots echoing on the marble floor.

'Check the sacristy, Weber,' the taller one said to the squat one, who nodded and headed off to the side of the altar. Detta dropped her head again, as if intent on her prayers. But she kept her eyes open. Her interlocked fingers were clammy with sweat. 'I'm very sorry to interrupt your prayers, Fräulein,' the tall one said, not sounding sorry at all. Detta lifted her head to look at him: pale, elongated features like dripping candlewax.

Detta unclasped her hands. 'It's fine, officer. I was just leaving anyway.' She stood up.

'Before you go, have you noticed anything unusual here?'

'No. What are you looking for?'

'Two British *terrorfliegers* escaped yesterday. We've just had word.' He inclined his head to one side, looking down at her, blocking the exit from the pew. There were scuffling sounds from the sacristy.

'You think they might be here?'

'They often try the churches first. Those British seem to think the priests are a soft touch. Problem is, they often are. You'd think that someone whose job it is to explain the difference between right and wrong to our children would know better than to harbour an enemy of the state, wouldn't you?'

'You would, officer.'

There was an awkward pause. The taller SS officer still blocked her exit. The squat one came tramping back across the nave. 'Nothing doing. Where else, boss?' He joined the tall one at the exit to the pew. His bull neck bulged red above his too-tight collar.

The tall man cast his eyes round. 'Have a good look, under the altar and so forth, but this girl says she's seen and heard nothing, isn't that right, Fräulein?' Detta nodded. He shook his head, turned away, leaving a little space at the pew's end, but not enough for her to get through without having to brush past him. Was she free to leave? The shorter man was using his pistol barrel to lift up the tapestries that hung from the altar and peer behind them. 'I think we need to talk to the priest, Weber, don't you?' the tall man called over to his colleague.

'Yes boss.'

'Would you know where I can find your priest, Fräulein?'

'Father Richter?'

'Oh, that's his name is it? Father Richter – where would he usually be at this time in the morning?'

Detta swallowed. It felt as if her upper teeth had been magnetized and the lower row replaced by an iron strip. There was tremendous effort in opening her mouth and forming the words, but somehow she did it.

She was certain, now, what God wanted her to do: 'Father Richter will be at home in the manse. I can take you there, I'm going that way myself. If you'd like to follow me, gentlemen?'

## Tom

He'd been dozing in the chair when the knock came. There was no time to do anything except open his eyes and wipe the trail of saliva from the side of his mouth, where it had slid from his lips as he slept. Gordon sat up in bed, but Tom motioned for him to lie back down. There was a plan, in case the manse was searched. The priest had loosened the floorboards under the bed, and they were supposed to slide underneath. Tom glanced through the shutters, craning his neck to look down on whoever was below.

As he looked, hope and despair assaulted him at once. He could see the sky-blue scarf of the girl from the path, but just behind her, on her right and left shoulders, were the grey-green tops of field police caps. Damn. He held out a thumbs-down to Gordon, who immediately slid out from under the covers and began wedging himself into the floor space. Tom ran across the room to the bed, but there was only room for them to get in one at a time. Tom pushed at Gordon's struggling limbs. 'Fucking splinter,' Gordon hissed, as he wrestled himself into the too-small gap. Tom lay down, ready to follow him.

'I'm coming now!' The priest's voice came from the corridor below. How loud it was, Tom thought, how easily sound travels in this house. Gordon was still struggling to get under the boards, making faint grunting sounds with the effort, and the wood scraped and creaked as he went. The priest could probably hear him from the hallway and so would anyone coming in through the front door.

The triple knock came again. 'Just need to unlock ...' the priest said loudly from below. Gordon was in. Thank God, now it was his turn. But then there was the sound of the door opening and voices. He froze. If he moved now, they'd hear downstairs. He lay still, planning what to do. He'd keep still and quiet, pray they'd not come up as far as this room – but if they did, then what? As gently as he could, he began to pull the covers from the bed, trying not to shift his body weight at all as he did so. He heard the voices from the hallway.

'Good morning, Father Richter.' It was her voice, the woman with the blue scarf, the woman on the path, the beautiful, lethal girl. 'I just met these two officers in church.

They're looking for some escaped *terrorfliegers*, but they didn't find them in your church. Shall I start with upstairs or downstairs today, Father?' she carried on without seeming to draw breath. 'I can leave the study until later, if you're planning your sermon. Or shall we have a cup of tea before I get started?'

The priest cleared his throat before speaking. Tom could hear it – so he stopped trying to pull the covers over himself, worried that even a small movement would give away a telltale sound. 'A cup of tea sounds like a good idea, Detta,' Father Richter said. (So, her name was Detta, and she was the priest's housekeeper. But she'd brought the SS to the house, so she was a Nazi.) 'I'm afraid I only have peppermint, you know how it is, but it's warm, at least, and I have some honey to sweeten it with. Gentlemen?' There was a pause in which Tom imagined the two officers exchanging glances. Then he heard a male voice saying no, thank you, but did he have any knowledge of the escaped prisoners?

A set of footsteps moved away then, but they didn't sound like military boots, the footfalls were softer. Tom imagined the girl walking off along the corridor.

'*Terrorfliegers?*' the priest asked. 'No, I haven't seen any-thing like that. How many?'

'Only two. And we think they may be in the vicinity.'

'Well, they're not here. We're all German in this village – nobody would hide those who murder our people. Look for yourselves.'

The soft footfalls returned along the length of the corridor below, with another noise, a kind of dull clunk-thunk – the housekeeper must be carrying a mop and bucket. 'I'll just start with the bedding and the floors upstairs then, shall I, Father, as we're not having tea?' her voice came again.

'As you wish, Detta,' Father Richter said. The clunk-thunk sounds moved up the stairwell.

At any moment those two officers would tramp up the stairs behind her and barge into the upstairs rooms. Would they all be shot immediately? Or would they make a show of it, drag them into the main street and do it in front of the whole village?

'If you see or hear anything unusual, or you catch some local gossip about it, or someone lets something slip in confession, you must report it immediately. Immediately, is that understood?'

'Yes, officer,' Father Richter said.

'You too, Fräulein.'

'Of course, officer, immediately,' the girl's voice came from the top of the stairwell, just a few paces away from the door.

'We'll be making house-to-house enquiries, so if you do remember seeing anything suspicious, then you can tell us straight away. We'll be in the village a while. Good morning, Father, Fräulein.'

'Good morning.'

The door slammed. There was the sound of boots tramping on the street outside, moving away, across the road. Tom let out half a breath. It wasn't over. The housekeeper was coming with her mop and bucket. She'd discover them, then run out onto the street to tell the police. It felt like the way a cat toys with a mouse – releasing it just to claw it back to certain death. The footsteps and the clunking sound of the mop bucket stopped outside the door. The door handle moved. She was about to find them. It was too late.

Tom jumped up, lifting his hands above his head in surrender. I tried, was all he could think, remembering his muckers on the march, trudging mindlessly forward into the remains of the Reich. At least I damn well tried.

Then, oddly, there was a soft knock, and the door slowly opened. She didn't have on the blue scarf or the fur coat. She had one finger on her pursed lips. Her eyes flicked round the room.

'Oh,' she whispered. 'I thought there were two of you in here.'

## Detta

The man had his hands above his head. He was wearing a blue-grey uniform, and she noticed the pilot's wings above his left breast pocket. She looked at his face. It was him. It was the man she'd seen on the path.

He looked straight into her eyes as he lowered his arms. He looked pale and drawn, exhaustion bowing his body, but his eyes held the same spark of blue she remembered. He recognized her too, she could tell. She hesitated, a knot forming deep in her gut.

There were footsteps coming up the stairwell behind her.

Father Richter came in, went across to the window, and looked out through the shutter slats. 'It's fine. They're in the Mullers'.' He turned back. 'Tom, this is Fräulein Detta. She's going to help us. Detta, this is Tom.'

Detta reached out, ready to shake hands, but the airman ignored her and swivelled to face the priest. 'She brought the SS here,' he said in near-perfect German.

'But I thought it would be even more suspicious if I tried to keep them away,' Detta replied. 'They were asking for the priest; they would have come here anyway. At least I was able to—'

'Escort them onto the premises yourself?' the airman interrupted.

Heat rose in her chest. How dare he question her motives? She had put herself in danger trying to help. 'I could have directed them upstairs if I'd wanted to. God knows you were making enough noise with your shuffling about up here. Why else do you think I tried to get them into the kitchen for tea? Why else do you think I went and got the mop and bucket out?'

He still hadn't turned back to look at her. 'You may as well have put a signpost up: *Terrorfliegers, this way.*'

'I was only trying to cover up the sound of the creaking floorboards. And if they had decided to search upstairs, they would hardly have started off in the room I was cleaning. I was trying to buy you some time.'

'Of course you were.' He raised an eyebrow as he turned back to face her.

'Now then. Please.' Father Richter took a pace in between them, holding both palms downwards as if physically suppressing their quarrel. 'Detta, you will have to excuse Tom. He is understandably nervy. Tom, you can trust Detta.'

'Can I, though?' His eyes were hard as he looked at her. 'How do I know she won't betray us?'

There was a beat, then, as nobody answered him. Detta realized her own right hand was still stuck out, awkwardly, for the abortive introduction, and let it drop to her side. She took a breath. The air tasted of grime and desperation. She switched to speaking English, the good, formal English that the nuns at Ursulinen Kloster in Breslau had drilled into her for all those years: 'We are not all Nazis, you know.'

She watched his expression change. His eyes softened at the sound of his native tongue. Then he frowned. 'The fact that you speak English doesn't alter my concerns.'

'When the SS were here I would only have had to nod in this direction, and you would have a bullet in your head by now.'

'And so would Father Richter. How do I know you weren't just protecting him? How do I know you won't just find another way to turn us in without implicating the priest?'

'You really think I'd do that?' She was aware of her chin jutting out as she spoke. 'Really?' She stared into his ice-blue eyes, watching how his pupils swelled as he returned her gaze. Then he blinked, dipped his head, and turned away.

113

Father Richter, unable to understand the volley of English, looked from one to the other, tugging his beard. From outside came the muffled sound of a military vehicle slowing as it approached the estate junction, beyond the barracks.

'He thinks I'm not to be trusted,' Detta reverted to German as she spoke to the priest.

Father Richter took a step towards the airman and placed a hand on his shoulder. 'We need Detta. She's the only one who can bring extra food and medicine here without arousing suspicion. As God is my witness, she is on our side.'

'You can get hold of medical supplies?' The airman turned away from Father Richter to look at Detta again.

She nodded, thinking of the ambulance she'd seen going to the Schloss last night. 'I think so, yes.'

'Good.' He rattled off a list of items he needed urgently. 'If you can get those, as soon as possible.'

'I'll try.' Their eyes locked again, and this time he didn't turn away.

'Thank you.' He cleared his throat. 'I appreciate the position you're being put in by helping us, and I'm very grateful.' He held out a hand towards her. 'Tom Jenkins. *Sehr erfreut.*'

She hesitated, then held out her own right hand. 'Detta. How d'you do.'

Their fingers touched in a brief, formal handshake. At his touch it felt as if there was a pull at the knot in her stomach. He fixed her with his gaze. 'You won't betray us.'

She shook her head, even though it was more of a statement than a question. 'I want to help you in any way I can.'

'Wish someone would bloody help me.' A muffled English voice came from under the bed, and a filthy hand grappled the floorboards.

'Please excuse Lazarus over there, manners were never his strong suit.' Tom smiled then. 'Be over in a sec, Gordon, just need to check the SS aren't still on the prowl before we get you out.'

# Chapter 12

## November 1989, East Berlin

*Miranda*

I am about to close my Filofax, stash it in my rucksack and head out of the Embassy into the sleet when I think of someone else I need to call. I check my contacts pages and lift the receiver again.

'Ah hello there, Miranda, can you pass me over to Quill for a moment please?' I phoned the *Sunday Correspondent*'s picture desk, but it is Richard, the editor, who answers.

'Sorry, what was that? This line's terrible, I'm afraid.' A trench-coated man pushes through the exit and the glass Embassy doors let in a gust of damp autumn air.

'Quill – I need a word with him. Is he there?'

'Sorry, no. He's not with me right now. He's back at the apartment, there's a party.'

'Yes, I imagine there would be a fair amount of celebration going on.' I hear Richard's nasal chuckle. 'Well, get him to give me a call when you see him, won't you? Got some queries about his copy.'

'Okay,' I say. 'And did you get my shots?' I hold the receiver so close to my ear that it hurts.

'Yes, they're great,' Richard says, and I exhale. 'Really well done with these. You've got some talent for catching the moment, that's for sure. The photos are exactly what we need. It's just the words that need some, er, clarification.'

'So I'll get a picture credit?' I say.

'Of course. Let me make a note of your full name for the subs.'

'It's Wade,' I say. 'Miranda Wade.'

'Good, good. Right, well I think what I'll need you guys to focus on now is getting some really strong human interest stories for next week,' Richard says. 'You know, families being reunited after years of separation by the Wall, et cetera.'

'Yes,' I say. 'I think I get the idea. And you're happy with what you've got for this Sunday?'

'More than happy. Keep sending over whatever you can. Obviously we'll need portraits to go with any human interest stories that Quill digs up, and it would be good to include some decent photos of East Berlin, too, so we can compare and contrast lifestyles between East and West Berliners. And anything else you've got.'

'Could you use some shots of youths dismantling the Wall? I took some photos earlier of a group of young men attacking the Wall with a sledgehammer and I thought—'

'Perfect. Brilliant. Send them over as soon as you can.'

'Only I took them with the Rolleiflex.'

'I have no idea what that means, but our picture-desk guys can cope with most things – just get them over asap. Look it's crazy here today, I can't talk, but send over anything you've got, as soon as you can.'

'Will do. Thanks, Richard.' The line goes dead, and I hang up.

The main streets are still choked with cars heading towards the Wall border crossing points, and the air is thick with the metallic tang of exhaust fumes and the chug of two-stroke engines. Sleet runs like sideways tears on windscreens. I find a courier office just off Pariser Platz and get the Rolleiflex film sent off to Richard in London. When I come out the weather has begun to lift.

Pedestrians hunch their shoulders against the icy air and hurry past, all except one: a middle-aged man in a check jacket and homburg, who mutters something about changing money. I nod, and we duck into a side street. I exchange some of my Western marks for East, at a rate of four to one. The Eastern notes are as flimsy as Monopoly money, stuffed hastily into my jeans pockets. The man dissolves into the chilly afternoon.

Gran said her friend might be at work, so it's too soon to head over there yet. I think about what Richard said, and decide to take some shots of East Berlin. I walk along the grey car-choked streets, then cross the bridge to Museum

Island. The baroque dome of the restored cathedral is a dull reflection in the mirrored bronze windows of the Palace of the Republic. At Neptune Fountain a young GDR soldier walks hand in hand with a blonde girl in a pale pink beret and matching coat, oblivious to all but each other. The love-drunk pair make me think of a photograph of Gran and Granddad just after they were married, on VE day: him in his RAF uniform, and her holding his hand, smiling in the spring sunshine in front of the carved grey stones of the cathedral. They were happy together for twenty years, until the worst of marriage wreckers came along: cancer. I never met him, but I know he was the love of her life. I take the East German couple's photo, hoping to capture the adoration in the soldier's eyes as he looks at his girlfriend. Did Quill ever look at me like that, I wonder?

The vertiginous Telecoms tower is a stiletto heel rammed through a Christmas bauble. At its base teenage boys mess around on skateboards. I snap them when they're not looking, imagining what readers of the *Sunday Correspondent* will think: they don't look cowed by communism, they look like teenagers the world over.

At Alexanderplatz station the early commuter rush spills onto the train: mostly men, in long coats, carrying briefcases, avoiding eye contact, heading off early on a Friday afternoon to homes in the suburbs. Last night's momentous events at the Wall seemed to have passed most people by. There is nothing of the giddy optimism I photographed at the border crossing last night. Here in the East everyone seems to be carrying on as normal, despite streets jammed with the westbound traffic. I board the train with the businessmen, but it's too crowded to sit down. I feel my heart thudding, faster than it should, just off the beat of the train on the tracks: an adrenaline disco going on inside me.

After five stops the coloured lights of the fairground at Treptow Park flicker past like fireworks. For a moment I'm reminded of going on the ghost train at the Ottery St Mary fair with my dad, rattling along the tracks, screaming happily at the unconvincing ghouls. I try to work out when that must have been: I can't have been more than seven, if Dad was still around.

I give way to the memories: the bedtime stories Dad conjured from thin air, the touch of his fingertips brushing my hair from my face as I turned away to sleep. Sometimes he'd be happy, full of energy, and after school we'd rush to take the bus to the beach, dance on rainy sands, and storm the amusement arcades. Other times his eyes drooped, and he'd say he was too tired for anything, and I'd make us both sugar sandwiches and watch old cowboy films on TV with him. I didn't mind, sitting together in the half-dark. But Mum did, when she came home from work to find curtains drawn, dirty washing-up, and overflowing ashtrays.

Still thinking of my father, I get off the train at Planterwald, the next stop along the line. A tarmac path runs beside the river Spree. On the opposite bank there are factories and a belching power station. I take a photo of the cityscape, then walk on, past empty benches and litter bins.

I ask a solitary dog walker – a woman in a quilted grey coat like a raincloud – the way to the park. Her terrier licks my hand as I ruffle his ears, and the woman points to a path through the woods to my left. I thank her and head off. Soon I see the top of the big wheel through the trees. As I walk on the big wheel disappears, the trees are too tall and close, but I start to hear music. Blown by the breeze an amplified pop song falls unevenly between the tree roots: Kylie Minogue singing 'I Should Be So Lucky'. The ground is slippery with wet earth and fallen leaves. I notice fungus growing like coral in a gap in a tree trunk.

Funny how some childhood memories stick, but don't make sense until years later. I remember one argument that didn't wait until after my bedtime. Dad's friends had been over all afternoon: air thick with blue smoke and John Martyn albums on the stereo. They'd painted a mural on the living-room wall of a woman with rainbow-coloured hair and a dress made of snakes. I remember Mum throwing open windows, chucking things in the bin, shouting that she could cope with weed, but she drew the line at mushrooms. I must have been about five or six. I thought they were having a row about gardening.

It was after that row that Gran came for me, explaining – in that non-specific grown-up way that didn't clarify anything – that Dad was 'unwell' and Mum was 'busy', and I'd be staying at hers for a while. 'A while' meant every weekend, school holidays, and sometimes, when things were at their worst, during term time too.

The fairground is buried in the middle of the forest, like a dream. Coloured lights are strung between trees. Despite the weather, and what's going on at the Wall, there are a handful of customers staggering windblown and giggling between rides. Music crackles through the tannoy and the air smells of fried food. I take photographs: three shiny cars proceeding in collision-free circles on the dodgems; girls and boys clutching steering wheels of miniature fire engines and jeeps, eyes saucer-wide as they travel slow circles beneath the clanking carousel.

After Dad was sectioned, it was Gran who used to take me to Ottery St Mary fair. But I was older then, and bundled into the back of her car with my schoolfriends, Karen and Julie. Gran didn't come on the ghost train, she waited in the car park with a flask of coffee and Radio Three, whilst us three teenagers screamed and careered around. She didn't mind waiting, she said, it was nice to see me having fun with my friends. I suppose she must have seen how much I missed Dad, and did what she could to compensate.

Suddenly ravenous, I go to the open-air cafe for a bratwurst served up on a grey cardboard plate. I also have a lemonade – in East Germany even the lemonade is different, it's not fizzy and clear, but lime-coloured and still, and actually tastes of lemons. A black leather punk with a Billy Idol sneer shouts something at a scruffy man with a bottle of vodka poking out of the pocket of his green parka. They begin to exchange insults, and neither notice as I take the picture of their brawl.

As I snap their snarling mouths and scowling brows, I recall that row with my mother, the last time I saw her:

*Don't preach to me, Miranda. He's not welcome here, ever again.*
*You have no idea what it was like living with that man. He is*
*ill. He was a total nightmare to be with.*

    *At least he cared.*

    *What's that supposed to mean?*

    *At least he tried to make it to my school plays and prize-givings. Yes, he was late, stumbling over chairs, a bit of an embarrassment, but at least he made the effort.*

    *One of us had to take some responsibility and bring some money in. I'm sorry I wasn't always there, but my job was – is – demanding, and someone has to pay the bills.*

    *You worked late because you wanted to. You went to all those 'important' conferences because it was a way of avoiding your junkie nutcase husband and your disappointment of a daughter.*

    *How can you say that? How can you even think that?*

    *Because it's true, Mum.*

And so it went. Dad's been incarcerated for more than ten years now in a mental institution. But he never did anything wrong, not really. He was only ever a danger to himself. Now he's on the right medication he should be allowed home, not locked up like a criminal. That's what I tried to tell Mum last summer. We haven't spoken since. I can't say I miss her in my life. I was always closer to Gran anyway. She practically brought me up.

I drain the last of my lemonade and head to the roller coaster. In the bull-nosed red car I clutch the cold steel of the safety bar, made shiny by thousands of expectant hands. I'm ratcheted up the ice-cream cone mountain, until I'm high above the treetops. In the distance, glimpsed through city blocks, the tip of the Telecoms Tower pierces the sunset. I grab a quick shot of the bloodshot Berlin skyline, the swooping roller coaster struts and the silhouetted profiles of my fellow riders.

Here we are, this cargo of paying pleasurers, boys feigning cool, girls giggling, sons smiling expectantly at fathers. We're poised on the brink, the point of no return.

It would have been just after that row with Mum that I met Quill for the first time. He was covering a gallery preview for a piece in the colour supplement, but his photographer hadn't turned up. I happened to be there with my Leica, and he co-opted me. It was serendipity, he said. It was fate. Within a week I'd pretty much moved into his riverside apartment. I'd never been out with someone so much older, wealthier, so much more experienced. With Quill it was all flashing lights and thrill-seeking, a multi-coloured surge of panic-love.

Here we go: the sheer terror of descent. We scream, white-knuckle fists hanging on for dear life, the blur of colour through the tunnel, the two-second fall that fills your eyes with tears, reason abandoned in the whoosh, the crash that never comes.

Except sometimes it does.

The ride stammers still, and I touch the spot above my eyebrow as I wait for my car to be unlocked by the greasy-haired attendant. Sometimes in the roller coaster of a relationship the crash does come. And what do you do then?

It's time to get off the ride.

# Chapter 13

**January 1945, Nazi Germany**

*Detta*

Her footfalls made barely a sound on the thickly carpeted stairwell. Detta felt like a thief, stealing soundlessly upstairs. But the front door was unlocked, and a medical orderly had waved her past the rows of groaning men on stretchers that cluttered the hallway.

It was true, then, the field hospital had been moved here, which could only mean that the one in Oppeln was already in danger of being overrun – were the Russians as close as that? The air held the pungent-sweet mix of iodine and surgical spirits.

Until now the music room had been reserved for the Moll family's exclusive use, even as the Brigadier's team swelled, and the Schloss was filled with grey uniforms, green telephones and cartons of manila files. But now the baby grand piano was shunted in the corner by the coat stand, boxes of medical supplies toppling on the varnished wooden lid. The music room was a hospital ward, and Frau Moll was banished to her bedroom like a naughty child. But which was her room? The medical orderly hadn't known.

A blonde-haired woman on horseback stared down from her gilt-framed oil painting at the top of the stairwell, looking bored of the blood-stained bandages and the scurrying medics in the hallway down below.

Detta paused, unsure, gloved hand on the marble balustrade. There was a gallery leading off ahead of her: a line of closed doors to the left, and windows looking out onto the wooded parkland on the right. At the far end was a large window with a window seat. A couple were sitting there, silhouetted against the light like a cameo brooch in reverse. Perhaps she could ask them which one of the doors was Frau Moll's room.

The couple's foreheads touched. The pale winter light shining between their chins and chests made a heart shape. Sweet, Detta thought, that army nurses and doctors could snatch moments of love, even in such circumstances as these. At the thought of the couple's intimacy an image of the airman's face flashed into her mind's eye. When he looked at her she had that feeling, like walking in from a blizzard to the heart of a kitchen: too much, too soon – a dizzying rush. His eyes asked questions that she didn't know how to answer. She blinked. Focus on why you're here, Detta.

'Excuse me,' she called out, pulling her hand from the bannister and beginning to walk along the gallery. The couple pulled apart as she spoke. 'I'm looking for Frau Moll.'

'Detta?' The woman started, jumping away from the man. It was only as she drew close that Detta finally recognized her.

'Frau Moll?'

'I wasn't expecting you so early.'

'No, but I couldn't sleep last night, so I've been up for hours already.'

'Well, who can sleep, with this –' an artillery boom came on cue '– racket going on day and night. And as you can see we've had some disruptions here, too.' From the doorway behind them came the muffled sound of Tchaikovsky on the gramophone and some high-pitched giggles.

Detta looked at the man. He was young – younger than Frau Moll, but not by much, she realized. She had always thought of Frau Moll as a bit of a matron (she had three children, after all), but the colonel's wife had married young, her high-ranking husband a full twenty-five years her senior. Thinking about it, she might not even be thirty. 'This is Johann – Corporal Johann Mann.' The corporal must have been in his mid-twenties, with deep brown eyes behind thick lashes.

'Good to meet you.' As they shook hands Frau Moll explained that Johann was the Brigadier's driver, and had been tasked with helping the family move some of their things upstairs when the rest of the house was converted for hospital use.

'And also sometimes there are things to discuss regarding household management and the brigadier sends Corporal

Mann because he's so busy himself with strategic matters,' Frau Moll's words came tumbling out.

'Of course.' Detta nodded. Johann excused himself and said goodbye to them both. Detta noticed that his accent was similar to her own mother's, that tinge of Alsace-Lorraine in his voice. She saw how Frau Moll watched him walk off down the corridor, only pulling her eyes away when he was out of sight downstairs.

'Won't you come in?' Frau Moll said then, opening the door behind her. Inside, the three Moll girls were dressed in tutus the same colour as the drifting snowscape outside. Swan Lake played on the gramophone. The air was warm from the fire in the hearth, and smelled of wood smoke and lavender. It was exactly as you'd expect the master bedroom of a Schloss to be: four-poster bed, Chinese silk counterpane, dressing table with a triptych of mirrors and rows of crystal scent and make-up bottles. A string of pink pearls hung from one of the mirrors and pattered against the glass with every booming vibration. Detta noticed her old doll in the wicker pram in the corner by the cheval mirror. 'Girls, look who's here!' And Detta was caught up in hugs and kisses and demands to watch their ballet. Tchaikovsky's violins sawed on in the background, jumping occasionally when there was a distant thud of artillery or a nearby thump of an overenthusiastic *pas de chat*.

'This is my music,' Detta told them after the display, explaining how her mother had been hoping to train as a ballerina in Paris, until the last war had ruined her dreams.

'This was my mother's favourite ballet, and that's how I got my name.'

'Detta?' The eldest girl, Lisl, looked at her as if she were stupid. 'There's no Detta in Swan Lake, silly.'

'Not Detta. Odette – my real name is Odette.'

'Oh. And are you going to tell us some French stories again today, Fräulein Odette?' The three girls held hands, gazing up expectantly at her, looking like an oversized daisy chain: blonde curls surrounded by white tutus like petals. 'Not today, I'm afraid. I just came to ask your mother for something.' Detta turned her head to include Frau Moll, stood with one hand on the windowsill, looking out over the white landscape. Her lips were pressed together, as if she'd just blotted her lipstick – or she was withholding a secret. As Detta watched, Frau Moll turned away from the light. 'Remember yesterday when you said if there was anything you could do?' Detta said. Frau Moll nodded. 'Well, there is. I need some medicines.'

'Are you ill, Fräulein Detta?' Helga, the middle child, bit her plump lip.

'No, they're not for me, don't worry.'

'Your mother?' Frau Moll said. But Detta didn't answer. She wasn't going to lie.

'I need charcoal tablets, camphor ointment, sulphur powder, methylated spirits, and bandages,' Detta said. 'It's quite urgent.'

Frau Moll opened her mouth as if she were about to say something, but then closed it again. She rubbed her hands together as if they were cold, even though it was quite warm in the room, with a fire blazing in the hearth. 'I'll see what I can do,' she said, and left, closing the door behind her. Tchaikovsky came to a scratchy halt, and the guns boomed away beyond the treeline.

Whilst she waited for Frau Moll to return, Detta chatted a little with the girls in French. They'd remembered the story from the day before, and they said their mother had been testing them. 'She's making us call her *Maman* instead of *Mutti*,' Gisela said, blinking her blue eyes.

'Corporal Johann speaks French, too,' Helga said. 'But he doesn't tell us fairy stories, like you do.'

'He's been teaching French to Mutti – to Maman,' Lisl corrected herself.

'Has he? That's nice,' Detta said, thinking of Frau Moll and the corporal sitting in the window seat together, and of the corporal's Alsace accent. Frau Moll's husband was captured by the British three years ago, and he'd been away at war a year already before that. The youngest child, Gisela, was only a babe in arms when he left. Why was Frau Moll so keen to learn French, at a time like this? Was she betraying her husband?

Detta suddenly recalled the words of the man on the train from Oppeln: could betrayal mean escape?

She was roused from her thoughts by the door opening. Frau Moll was back. She brought the basket that Detta had left behind with the eggs yesterday. It was full of medicines. 'I put in aspirin, too,' Frau Moll said. 'But you can't leave with it like this, wait . . .' She opened the wardrobe and pulled out an orange silk embroidered shawl and put it over the top of the packages, before handing the basket to Detta. 'There.'

Detta thanked her and promised the Moll girls she'd come back as soon as she had time. Frau Moll said she'd see her out, 'just in case', gesturing to the stolen first aid supplies hidden under the shawl. The two women walked back downstairs together. Another ambulance arrived as they reached the front door, and they had to stand to one side in the vestibule. Detta tried not to look, but there was the dirty-sweet scent of blood and burnt flesh as the stretchers were rushed past.

'Thank you again,' Detta said.

Frau Moll cleared her throat. 'The SS were here, first thing. There were reports of escaped *terrorfliegers* in the village.'

'Yes, I heard that, too. I was in church when they searched it,' Detta said. Don't make me lie, she thought. Please don't make me lie. She, too, cleared her throat. 'The girls tell me you've been taking French lessons from Corporal Mann,' she said, pulling her scarf over her head and shifting the basket to her left arm.

'Fräulein Detta,' Frau Moll said, and she reached out then, touched Detta on the cheek as she'd done the day before, but this time she kept her fingertips there a moment longer, and scanned Detta's face. Detta looked back into the anxious grey eyes and said nothing. Frau Moll sighed. 'In times such as these, only God can judge us,' she said, at last, and let her hand drop to her side.

There had been a lull in the cacophony of guns, but it started up again then. Detta and Frau Moll mouthed their goodbyes through the thunder.

Detta began to make her way down the steps, thinking of the airman, and feeling again that discomforting tug inside her as she imagined him waiting for her in the manse.

### *Tom*

'Close but no cigar, Fritz,' Tom muttered to himself as he pulled the skin on his cheek taut. The razor blade was steady in his hands. He felt – how did he feel? Not safe, not that. Safe was a flabby word, comforting as a steamed pudding. He was unlikely to feel safe until he was in a Lyons Corner House on a drizzly June afternoon. What he felt now was more like it had been when the crew had managed to offload, dodge the flak and were on a smooth home run: alive – more alive than he'd felt in years, he thought, scraping off the stubble and the grime with the edge of the blade. Alive and a bit cocksure. His half-sudded reflection smiled back at him in the glass: careful now, sunshine.

He thought back to how it had happened: staggering back in the biting darkness, eastwards along the road they'd come. By the time they'd reached the village there were flickers of dawn on the horizon. You didn't have to be a vicar's son to have faith in a church, but it helped. They'd been almost at the door when that truck careered up the main road, and they'd had to duck for cover behind a gravestone and a mound of fresh earth, so newly dug that there wasn't even any snow topping it. Lucky the priest had seen them as they hadn't made it as far as the church. If they'd hidden there, the SS would have discovered them for certain, the girl said.

The girl: Detta. Tom squinted at his reflection and shaved off another line of stubble. There was that swimming feeling when he looked at her, like déjà vu. Did she feel it too, he wondered? Tom's body ached for rest, but his mind was racing as if he'd swallowed one of those wakey-wakey pills they used to take before sorties.

A huge thud, then, as one of the big guns went off in the distance. Tom's hand slipped and he nicked his cheek. He dropped the razor in the sink, and grabbed for something to blot the blood.

That was when he heard the knock at the door – the SS, back to resume their search? He sprinted across the room to his hiding place.

# Chapter 14

## November 1989, East Berlin

*Miranda*

*Grunau*. The name is inscribed in angular 1930s black capitals on white metal oblongs nailed to the station walls. I need to get to 109 Street, where a woman called Frau Karger lives. Gran says she'll be happy to put me up until my passport's ready. The S-bahn guard wears a navy blue peaked cap with a blood-red band. She points me in the direction of the tram stop across the road. The street is wide, clean and almost empty of cars. Overhead lines twitch with electricity as a tram the colour of vanilla ice cream clatters to a halt.

There is no conductor on board, just a red-lipsticked driver, chewing gum, and I can't see a ticket machine anywhere. The men – it is all men – in front of me slide their tickets into a grey metal puncher and beat a hole with the flat of their hand. There is an assumption of honesty here. Feeling like a criminal I slink into a seat at the front, but nobody seems to notice or care that I have dodged my fare.

The tram runs parallel to the road and then veers off sideways through a forest of bare silver birch, pale and limb-like as we pass.

I get off at the first stop and walk along the tree-lined road. Down one side I glimpse an expanse of water, pewter in the late afternoon light. Youngsters in grey tracksuits jog down the centre of the street, pausing periodically to do push-ups or star jumps. A man with a moustache stands by one of the boathouses, giving blasts on his whistle and gesticulating. I stop one of the joggers to ask directions. Running on the spot, she points out the way. I thank her and cross the road.

On my left is a detached house with an overgrown garden and a white Lada on the drive: number two. This must be it. I feel suddenly nervous and apologetic, turning up at this stranger's house. My feet crunch on the gravel drive. There is a bell hanging on a chain beside the wooden front door. I pull it, and it jangles, but nobody comes. I knock three times and wait. There's no response. Maybe she is out, still at work? I am about to turn away, when a light comes on, and I hear footsteps on a tiled floor. The door begins to open. I take a breath. '*Guten Abend, Frau Karger,*' I say, as the doorway reveals sheepskin slippers, beige slacks, a blue polo-neck jumper, and a face framed with pale grey-gold curls. I hold out a hand and introduce myself in the polite way my grandmother taught me when I was a little girl: '*Sehr erfreut.*'

'Oh, it's you. I expected you sooner, dear.' She answers in English, a voice like the queen. She smiles as she sees my outstretched hand. 'I think we can dispense with that kind of formality, being family.' Her arms are around me, a softly powdered cheek against mine. She is the same height as me, and smells of fried onions and lavender water. 'So lovely to finally get to meet my great-niece,' she says, holding me at arm's-length and regarding me with round, blue eyes.

'Great niece?' I say, stupidly.

'Are they still too ashamed to talk about me, back home?' she says, letting her hands drop. 'Oh well, come in out of the cold. I'll make tea, shall I?'

## November 1989, Exeter

### Odette

'So, are there any more skeletons in the closet?' Helen slices carrots and peppers into tiny ribbons as she speaks. I have just driven round to tell her about Miranda, and how I've sent her to Gwen's to escape from her abusive boyfriend. But Helen is infuriatingly flippant. 'No millionaire cousins in Australia, or hidden stashes of family silver?'

'I thought you'd be a bit more concerned about your daughter,' I say, watching as she pushes the red and orange strips into a neat rectangle on the chopping board.

'I don't think she wants my concern. You know she hasn't spoken to me for months, not since we had that row about her father.'

(That row: they are both right, and I can't take sides.)

'I only found out she'd gone to Berlin because her

137

boyfriend – the one who's apparently so awful – thought to leave a note when they came round to pick up her passport,' Helen says, putting down her knife.

'Miranda told me he headbutted her,' I say.

'Then she's well out of it, with good old "Red Gwen".' Helen is opening the fridge, and peering inside. 'Anyway, Miranda's a grown woman now. She needs to learn to take care of herself. When I was her age . . .' Helen's voice is muffled by the fridge door.

'When you were her age you had a husband, a baby, and you were one term into your masters degree,' I complete her sentence. She straightens up, slams the fridge closed, and slaps a plastic bag on the work surface. We lock eyes for a moment. She has blue eyes, like her father, and Gwen. Neither of us speaks, but I know we are both remembering those days, twenty-one years ago: a squalling, colicky baby, Jono changing nappies by day and stacking shelves by night, and Helen struggling with the demands of academia and motherhood. I helped as much as I could. To everyone else it seemed that I was being a wonderful support, a dutiful grandmother. But doesn't altruism always have a seed of selfishness? It is only now I can admit the guilty truth to myself: baby Miranda helped fill the gaping hole that widowhood had opened up, and circumstances meant that in many ways she soon became more of a daughter than a grandchild. I often wonder how much of this Helen has already guessed: that her unplanned student pregnancy and marital strife gave me a new sense of purpose when I most needed it.

I blink, now, breaking our gaze. 'So, what's his name?' I say, changing the subject, nodding at the food preparation. Mackerel parcels are Helen's second-date staple. I open the cupboard door behind me and pass her the baking paper.

'Keith,' she says, accepting the dodge, complicit in leaving the past behind. 'New history tutor, just moved down from Surrey. Recently separated. Will parsley do instead of dill?' she mutters to herself, pulling sprigs from the potted plant on the windowsill. 'I suppose it will have to.'

I wonder if Keith will last any longer than Marcus, Trevor or John, as Helen chops the leaves and pulls two sheets from the roll of baking paper. The radio is on in the other room. It seeps through the open kitchen doorway, a late afternoon drama: someone sighing and talking bitterly about betrayal. My mind returns to Miranda. I check my watch. Hopefully she's arrived at Gwen's by now.

'Aren't you worried at all?' I say.

Helen slaps the fish onto the paper. 'Not really. The separation was fairly amicable, apparently, no kids, and his *decree nisi* is due to come through next month. Anyway, it's early days.'

'I mean, about your daughter.'

'Well, you've told me you've sent her off to this secret communist aunt of mine. I'm not sure what else we can reasonably be expected to do from this end.' She stuffs the vegetables and herbs into the wetly gaping mackerel bellies.

'Miranda says she can't get replacement travel documents until Wednesday. That's four days. What if Quill comes to

Clare Harvey

find her in the meantime? Or, worse still, what if she goes back to him and doesn't come home at all?'

'How is he going to find her?' Helen wraps up the stuffed fish in their paper shrouds.

'He's a journalist. He'll have contacts. And she's in the East, now. She's probably already being tailed by the Stasi.'

'But even if he's got contacts in the Stasi, and he tracks her down, why on earth would she go back to him, after what he's done? My daughter may be many things, but she's not stupid.'

'But what if she thinks she's in love?' I say, watching Helen rinse her fingers in the sink and dry them on a tea towel. 'Love makes people do stupid, dangerous, life-changing things.' Helen gives me a sharp look. She thinks what I've just said is a comment on her own drug-fuelled partying student days with Jono, before Miranda's unexpected appearance. She turns away, taking off her red-checked apron and hanging it on the hook on the back door. But my words weren't meant as a reproach. I was thinking of the stupid and dangerous things *I* did for love myself, once upon a time.

'You need to find a distraction, then,' Helen says, turning back to face me with her hands on her hips. 'When Miranda was little, and about to do something naughty, you always used to say not to tell her off, just to find a distraction for her.'

'But she's not a child anymore —'

'Doesn't the principle still apply? Send her off to take photos of something – more skeletons in closets or hidden family silver, I don't know. Give her something else to think about, if you're worried about her going back to Mr Wrong.' I shake my head. Helen doesn't seem to be taking this seriously at all. Rain sputters at the kitchen window. Helen's house is wedged into the side of the hill, windows half submerged against the pavement. Outside, beyond the reflections in the pane, I see legs and a bulging carrier bag jolt past, at an angle. 'Look, Mum, you're welcome to stay and meet Keith if you want . . .'

I take the hint. 'No, I should get going. I only popped round to tell you about Miranda.'

'And I'm glad you did.' It is unexpected, the hug. A swift kiss on the cheek is all I usually get from my daughter. Helen smells of L'air du Temps and gutted fish. 'Thank you for pointing Miranda in the right direction. But try not to worry about her. She's a tough cookie, really.'

'Like her mum,' I say. Stiff tendrils of Helen's spiky hair-sprayed hair graze my cheek like twigs as we embrace.

'And her grandmother.' She gives me a final squeeze and pulls away. 'Now, shoo. I need to hop in the shower before Keith gets here.'

In the car going home my windscreen wipers smudge drizzle across the glass, and my headlights waver in the gloom. Helen told me not to worry about Miranda, but how can I not? Unlike me, Helen hasn't met Quill, doesn't know what kind of man she's dealing with.

As I signal to turn off the clock-tower roundabout there's a sudden tingling in my arm, and it's hard to even push up the indicator. For a split second it is as if all the streetlights have been turned down on a dimmer switch, and the road stretches, thin as a razor blade, away to infinity. But then the moment passes. A funny turn, that's all, low blood pressure or something, to be expected at my age, I suppose. When I get home I must make sure I have something to eat, I think, as I slow down to wait at the traffic lights by the museum.

A distraction, Helen said, send Miranda off to find skeletons in closets and family silver. I take my hand off the steering wheel for a moment and touch the hollow where my neck meets my chest.

Skeletons and family silver: Helen's flippant comments ring truer than she realizes.

## November 1989, East Berlin

*Miranda*

'I was a traitor, coming to live here with Karl-Heinz,' my great-aunt Gwen says, laying out photographs in front of her like tarot reading on the kitchen table. 'At least, that's how my family viewed it. For me it was an escape.'

Her house smells similar to my grandmother's flat in Exeter: coffee, cigarette smoke, dried flowers. Great-aunt Gwen tells me why she's been erased from my family history. 'You won't know this, but post-war Britain was a grim place. It was as if the whole country was convalescing. There was an enormous pressure to settle down, to do small, safe things with our lives, do you see?' She glances over at me and I nod, even though I'm not sure I do see.

'I'd just been demobbed, but my former boss – a colonel on the brink of retirement – had proposed. Mother and Father were desperate to get me settled. But I could see exactly how my future would play out if I said yes: going to bridge parties, walking tubby Labradors, flower arranging for the local church, and, in time, becoming a glorified nurse for my elderly husband. Don't get me wrong, I was flattered, and very fond of the old boy, so I asked him to give me the weekend to think about it.' Gwen takes a sip of tea before continuing.

'I took myself off to a Wagner concert. Actually I hated Wagner, still do, but a girlfriend of mine had a ticket she couldn't use, and I needed the distraction. On the way to the bus stop I got chatting to a Marxist musicologist who happened to be taking the same bus to the same concert. That was Karl-Heinz.' She puts her elbows on the table and her hands together, as if about to pray.

'I fell in love with the man, the ideology was just part of the package. He wanted to help build a new Germany, in the East. So we married, and I went with him. That was more than forty years ago, now.'

'And you never came back?'

'During the Stalinist era I wasn't allowed, but I wouldn't have been welcome, if I could have. Ditching a decent life as a colonel's wife in favour of marrying a penniless German-Jew refugee, and becoming a communist to boot? They thought

I was mad. They were thoroughly ashamed. Do you know, the only person who even sent me Christmas cards was your grandmother.' She sighs and taps the photograph on the top left of a dark-eyed man holding a violin under his jutting jaw. 'That's Karl-Heinz, taken just before we met,' she says.

'Handsome,' I say, although I think there is something cruel about the set of his mouth. 'I can see why you fell for him. And is he . . .?' I hesitate, not quite sure how to continue. There is no hint of a male presence in this house.

'He passed away earlier this year,' she says, her chin jutting with odd defiance as she speaks. 'His heart.' I begin to say that I'm sorry for her loss, but she interrupts me. 'How can you be sorry? You never met him. You barely know me. I miss him, but he was not an easy man to be with. In many ways his passing was a release.' She pauses, and I realize that she's not looking into my eyes, but at the spot on my right temple where the bruise has begun to swell. 'You know how some men are,' she says.

I nod. I do know how some men are: men whose love falls as quick as a declaration of war, and who annexe you into their own lives within days.

'More tea?' Gwen's chair scrapes on the tiled floor as she gets up.

'Please,' I say. As she goes over to refill the teapot, I look down at the other photographs laid out on the wooden table top. One in particular catches my eye: a man in RAF uniform, leaning against the fuselage, smiling a languid smile into the lens, as if war will be of no more consequence than a

Sunday afternoon cricket match on the village green. 'Is that Granddad?' I say, pointing. Gwen turns with the teapot. 'Yes, that's Tom. Rather dashing, don't you think? No wonder all my old school chums had pashes on him.' She comes back with the tea and refills our cups, then sits back down beside me. 'And here are your grandparents with your mother.' She gestures at a christening photo: Granddad still in uniform, Gran in a slim suit with thick shoulder pads and a hat, and a baby trailing frothy lace. 'Your grandmother sometimes put photographs in with her Christmas letter,' Gwen says, 'so I kept up with the family news. Look, here you are.' I sip the tea: warm and sweet. The photograph she's pointing at is an awful posed studio shot: Mum, Dad and I all smiling effort-fully for the professional photographer, against a backdrop of fluffy clouds (my front teeth are missing, and I hold both parents' hands as if trying to tug them together). Next to it is an earlier photo of my mother in her graduation robe, hair hanging down from her mortar board in wispy, hippy-ish waves. I am in that photo, too, I realize, but unseen: the large pregnancy bump hidden beneath the billowing gown. I would have been born a week later, slap-bang in the middle of the summer of love.

'Thank you for showing me these,' I say, thinking how odd it is that this woman I've never met has been keeping track of our family history all these years. 'But what's this one?' Almost beneath Gwen's right elbow is a sepia postcard that has been torn in two and taped back together. The edges of the tape curl up yellow.

'Oh, I only came across this one a few weeks ago, when I was clearing out Karl-Heinz's office. It was in a book of poetry your grandmother lent me. The book had mildew and some spilled red wine had stuck pages together – it was ruined – but as I was throwing it away, this fell out. It must be your grandmother's, and I thought you could take it back to her when you go.' She pushes it across the table to me.

On the front of the torn-mended postcard is a village scene, dominated by a half-timbered house. In front of the house is a space where cars are parked, and there's a sliver of road showing. Right in the foreground is a single bough from what looks like a beech tree. At the bottom, in thick angular script, it says: **Deutches Haus Gasthaus, Lossen**. I turn the card over. On the reverse an address is scribbled in faded pencil. Gwen leans in. 'That's your grandfather's handwriting, and that address is our childhood home: The Rectory. You might remember it.'

I do vaguely remember visiting my great-grandparents in South Devon, as a very young child. I turn the postcard back to the picture side. 'But this isn't a photograph of the South Hams.'

'No, I think it must be a picture of your grandmother's old house in East Germany, where she grew up,' Gwen says. 'That's why I thought she'd like to have it back.'

'But I thought she came from Colmar in Alsace?' I knew Grandma spoke German, of course, she taught me, but she always claimed to be from a German-speaking part of France.

'That's just what she told people. It was easier that way.

Everyone was so unrelentingly vile about the Germans. It was her own mother who came from Alsace, apparently. Anyway, you can give it to her when you next see her, and tell her I'm sorry about the book.'

I pick up the card. My gaze travels the points of a triangle: the creased brown postcard of an East German village, Gwen's careworn face, and, outside, through the kitchen window, the very last ribbon of Prussian blue escaping from the Berlin sky.

I feel as if I've slipped through the looking glass.

# Chapter 15

**January 1945, Nazi Germany**

*Tom*

Her eyes glinted and her cheeks were flushed from the cold. 'I'm sorry.' She pulled the blue scarf away from her face as she spoke. 'I shouldn't have knocked; I should have come in the back way. I didn't think.' Her English was accented and imperfect. She lent over and pulled the heavy bookcase completely free so that Tom could stand up from his hiding place in the alcove. A couple of leather-bound volumes fell to the floor as he uncurled from the hidden hole, limbs burning with pins and needles. Her head was lowered as she reached for the fallen books, hair falling forward in a waterfall. She put them on the shelf.

'It's okay. We're all a bit jumpy,' he said, pushing the bookcase back into position.

'That's a bloody understatement,' Gordon chipped in, as Father Richter helped him out from the space under the floorboards. Tom smiled. It was good to hear him speak, starting to recover.

She straightened up. 'You're right to be scared. They could come back at any time.' She brushed her hair from her eyes and looked at him. 'We might not always be as lucky as we were this morning. We'll have to think about moving you on as soon as your friend is able.'

Move them, but where to? Surely no one but a priest would consider having an enemy on the run in their home. Tom was about to respond when the priest cut in, saying he had to go and perform a christening. 'I have to stick to my routine. It will be noticed, otherwise. I'll be back as soon as I can.' He was gone, then, leaving them alone with Detta.

They stood quite close, him and her, not having moved away from the bookcase. How long had it been since he was this close to a woman? He was aware, suddenly, of his unbuttoned shirt, the air cool against his chest. 'Well, then,' he said, stupidly, fumbling to do up his buttons. She looked pointedly away. He glanced across to Gordon, who was watching them both. There was the clunk from downstairs: the priest closing the front door behind him, and the metallic scrape of his key in the lock. 'So, um, don't let us keep you. If you have cleaning to do, and so forth,' he said.

'Cleaning?' she repeated the word in English, and looked at him as if he were mad. But she was the housekeeper, wasn't she? She lapsed into German then. 'I've brought you some medication. I think treating your friend is a higher priority than housework, don't you?' He nodded, and she gestured to the basket she'd put down by the bedstead. 'If you want to get those opened, I'll go and get us some warm water and a sponge and we can get started.'

'Yes of course.' He went over to the bed, where Gordon lay on top of the covers. In the doorway, she stopped, and it was like an echo of when they'd first seen each other on the path, in the snowstorm. The air contracted between them. His lungs felt tight. She held his gaze, but didn't speak. She feels it, he thought. She feels it, too. But then she turned away and went downstairs.

'Let's see what we've got for you, old man.' Tom lifted the orange cloth from the basket and sat on the edge of the bed to look through its contents. 'Charcoal tablets for your shits; sulphur powder for the lesions; meths for the blisters . . .' He turned the familiar packages over in his hands – they were German army medical supplies, he'd worked with these before, but where the hell had she got them from? '. . . Camphor ointment for your swollen joints, and bandages. And aspirin, too. The girl's a bloody miracle worker.'

'Is she?' Gordon's voice had an edge to it.

'What?'

'She's a good-looking woman.'

'Yes, I suppose she is.' Tom tried to sound casual.

'You think after all we've been through I don't know you, Tom Jenkins?'

'Don't catch your drift, old man.'

'We're so close to freedom. Don't scupper it.'

'I don't know what you mean.'

'Like hell you don't,' Gordon said. Tom heard the sounds of vehicles passing on the main road in front of the manse, and the bell began to toll in the church. 'You're fanny-struck,' Gordon said, pushing himself up so that his face was closer to Tom's. 'But remember that she's German and in a few days' time the Reds will be here, and—'

'I know. I know. Leave it, will you?'

'I'm just saying, it's futile as well as dangerous.'

There were footsteps on the stairs. 'Stow it. She's coming back.'

And there she was, with an enamel bowl of water and a clean towel. Tom bathed Gordon's legs and feet, and dried them off. Detta sprinkled sulphur powder and dabbed meths on the blisters. Gordon winced. 'Fuck,' he said.

'Well, that's one word that doesn't need translation,' she said in German, making Tom smile. 'But it's not some-thing the nuns would have put on our vocabulary lists if it were,' she added, pouring more meths onto the patch of lint she held.

'I didn't know they taught English in German schools,' he said.

'They did in mine. You know, there are quite a few words that sound the same in English and German, but they mean something different. Sister Maria used to call them "false friends". Like *angst*, for example. It translates as "fear" in English, but for you the word angst means something dif-ferent, I think.'

'Existential dread,' Tom said, squeezing camphor ointment

onto his forefinger and beginning to rub it into Gordon's swollen knee joints. He caught Gordon rolling his eyes, and thought about what his skipper had just said, about it being futile and dangerous to get to know this German girl. Was she a 'false friend' or did his feelings translate perfectly? He'd probably never find out. After all, she was already talking of moving them on.

He picked up the bandage and began to wrap Gordon's foot where she'd finished treating the blisters.

'Where did you learn to do dressings like that?' she said, watching him.

'I was a medical orderly in the Luftwaffe hospital in Hohemark for a while. They like to put us prisoners to good use, when they can.'

'I didn't know that.' She was still watching him. He cut the bandage.

'Would you mind just ...' She knew what he was asking, and put her forefinger on the spot where the tail end of the bandage was, keeping it tight whilst he knotted it. Their fingers brushed against each other.

'How long have you been a prisoner?'

'Since 1942 – two years, eleven months and one day. How long have you been a housekeeper?'

'I'm not. I'm a bilingual secretary. I do German to French translation for the Reichsbahn, because they have lots of French workers at the moment. Or at least, they did.'

'Oh, I thought ...'

'I'm just helping Father Richter out. He's an old family

152

friend. I can't go to work at the moment. They stopped the trains last week. I was on the last train to cross the Oder.' He noticed her worrying the silver locket on the chain at her neck. 'Everyone said I was lucky to get out when I did. But, you know, I think of my colleagues in Oppeln – I don't know what's happened to them. And it's not like they were good friends or anything, but … I feel guilty, somehow. Sorry, I don't know why I'm telling you this.' She got up. The water sloshed in the enamel bowl as she picked it up. 'I'll make you two some lunch and then I'll have to go home or my mother will worry. She'll send out a search party for me, which,' she raised an eyebrow, 'is the last thing we need right now.'

Tom watched the way her black dress clung to her hips as she walked from the room.

'Jesus Christ,' said Gordon. 'What was that all about?'

'Shut up and take one of these,' said Tom, tossing him the bottle of aspirin.

### Detta

'Who is it?' Her mother's voice was muffled behind the heavy oak door.

'It's me, Mother, who else would it be? And why is this door locked?'

There was a clunk-scrape as the door was unbolted inside. Her mother opened it just wide enough to let Detta in, then slammed and bolted it after her. 'Where have you been all day? It's almost dark.'

'I told you I had to go to help Father Richter at the manse, and I went up to the Schloss, too, to see Frau Moll and the girls. Anyway, it's not late – why have you locked up already? I know we're not exactly overrun with customers these days, but even so.' Detta took off her scarf and coat and hung them on the stand.

'We've got visitors,' Mother said, pulling her cardigan tight across her chest and folding her arms.

'Visitors?'

Mother inclined her head in the direction of the games room that opened off the reception area. Detta took the few steps it took to cross the hallway and looked in. The fire was lit. Green–black shadows wavered in the corners of the room, and the shutters were already closed. The room smelled, as it always did, of smoke and wood polish, but now there was something else, an undercurrent of something more pungent. Detta paused, and her mother joined her in the doorway. 'They came this afternoon,' she said. There, on the billiard table, were the twin mounds of two grown men, stretched out underneath a travel blanket. One snored, shifted in his sleep so that the blanket fell away, revealing the grey sleeve of his uniform. Their caps lay discarded on the floor.

'Wehrmacht?' Detta said. Her mother nodded.

The one who'd moved had blonde hair, his curls kissed orange in the firelight. From this distance he looked like Rolf, Detta thought, and her throat constricted. But, she reminded herself, Rolf was dead: killed in Italy. His mother had had a telegram, and Father Richter had given a memorial service – they couldn't have a proper funeral without the body. Detta had cried like a gushing tap, and then seen Rolf's mother and felt guilty for her tears. What right had she to grieve for Rolf? They had only been seeing each other such a short time; she hadn't really known him well at all. Her despair was tinged by self-pity, thoughts of an imagined future with Rolf that she'd never have, and she'd hated herself for that.

'They came asking for food and drink. I let them in out of the cold, but when I came back from the kitchen I found them like this.' Her mother spoke in a low voice. Detta noticed, then, the untouched dishes of lentil soup on the table by the hearth. 'They are younger than you, Detta, just canon-fodder, poor things.'

'You can't let them stay. If you're discovered harbouring deserters . . .' Detta thought of the blood on the snow in front of the bakery last week, and of the voice of the SS officer this morning.

'I know that.' Her mother sighed and ran a hand over her brow.

'This isn't like you, Mother. You never get involved.'

'But look at them. They are just boys.' And Detta knew that her mother was thinking about Rolf, too, and about all the other village youths, who'd been barely big enough to come into the public bar for a beer before the war lassoed them away.

Detta's mind whirled. Army deserters at home, escaped prisoners in the manse, and the Russians' inexorable drive across the snowy fields towards them all. She felt as if she were tumbling through space. 'They'll have to go. We can't keep them here; it's not safe.' The words burned her tongue. How could she protect those British men and turn these German boys out into the cold? It was treachery.

Her mother sighed again. 'I know.'

'How long have they slept?'

'An hour or so.'

'Well, it's almost dark. They need to eat and leave. You're not doing them any favours by keeping them here. Weren't the SS round earlier looking for *terrorfliegers*?'

'Yes, how do you know about that?'

'They came to the manse as well. They're bound to come back to do a thorough search, and what will you say when they find two deserters on the premises?'

'At least they're not the escaped prisoners.'

'But this is just as bad. They are traitors to the Reich. You'll get yourself shot along with them.'

'You're right,' Mother said, but neither of them made a move to rouse the sleeping boy-soldiers.

'Right. I'm going upstairs to look out some of Papa's old clothes. We can swap their uniform jackets for something more civilian-looking and warmer. That will help them. But you need to wake them up, and they have to go, soon. Mother?' At last her mother nodded, and Detta went upstairs.

When she came back down with the clothes, the soldiers were already scraping up the last of the thick lentil soup, and wiping the bowls with hunks of black bread spread with goose fat. Detta took their uniform jackets from them and swapped them for jumpers and thick coats that had once belonged to her father. They smelled mostly of moth-balls, but still held the faint smoky bite of his cigars, which always made her want to cry. Her mother gave them each a 'necklace' of dried sausage to wear underneath their coat, a bottle of plum brandy for their pockets, and a handful of Reichsmark notes to help them on their way. When Mother went through to the kitchen to brew a pot of coffee to put something warm in their stomachs before they left, Detta slipped upstairs.

Her little suitcase was still packed, on her bed, ready to go. She undid the clasp and pulled out her things, put the two folded Wehrmacht jackets underneath, then put her clothes and toiletries on top and closed it again. Then she went back downstairs.

The soldier boys were in the kitchen, gulping down hot coffee. They thanked Detta and her mother again and again, and Detta felt so guilty she gave them a whole packet of cigarettes each.

Then they were gone: out of the back door, through the kitchen garden, and away down the lane, heading towards the point on the horizon where the sun had slid away, and leaving nothing behind but a curl of icy air and the faint scent of masculine sweat.

Detta washed the soup plates in cold water, listening to her mother bustling about in the games room up the corridor: folding the travel blanket; rearranging the furniture; putting the dampeners on the grate. Detta dried her greasy fingers on a tea towel, and reached for the coffee jar. As Mother said this morning, there was no point hoarding the 'brown-gold' any longer, and she'd need to stay awake tonight. From her bedroom window she had a clear view of traffic coming along the road from either direction, long before it could be heard. She was to keep watch. If she saw the SS coming, she was to give a three-ring warning telephone call to Father Richter. But they'd agreed to keep everything secret from her mother – the less she knew, the safer she was.

'Coffee?' she said now, as Mother came back into the kitchen.

'Why not? I doubt I'll be able to sleep tonight, anyway.' Her mother pulled the shutters to, pausing to look into the darkness as she did so. 'Do you think they'll be all right, those boys?'

'With your plum brandy inside them, they'll be invincible,' Detta said, wishing she believed it.

Mother smiled a sad smile and clicked the shutters closed. 'There's more lentil soup on the hob,' she said.

'I'm not hungry.'

'No. Me neither.' Her mother lit two cigarettes and passed one to Detta as they waited for the coffee to percolate.

That night Detta did not change into her nightclothes. She kissed Mother goodnight as usual at the top of the stairwell, but once inside her room she put her boots back on, pulled a chair across to her window, quietly opened the shutters, and waited. The skies were clear, and although there was no moon, the starlight reflecting on the snow meant she could see the road well enough. Distant artillery splashed angry flares across the horizon, the sound crashing just seconds after each flash. The road was empty of traffic, for now.

The SS would come back, she knew it. They had been lucky this morning. It seemed madness that whilst a desperate battle to save the Fatherland raged just kilometres away, they had time to organize a manhunt for a couple of unarmed, escaped prisoners. But, Dear God, that was the SS – they never gave up.

Detta waited, watched and smoked. But the road that tugged and stretched towards the eastern front remained empty, without even a stray cat to break the stillness. Her eyes ached with adjusting to the strobing skies and her ears buzzed with echoes of heavy gunfire. She had almost given up on her intuition, and was checking her watch to see how late it was – despite the coffee her lids had begun to feel heavy and ready for sleep – when she saw them: wavering headlights in the distance.

It might be an ambulance, of course it might, but she couldn't wait to check and take the risk. She tumbled down-stairs and into the lobby, and made a lunge for the telephone, lifted the receiver, fingers jabbing the dial. Her hand trembled as she listened, pushing the phone hard against her ear to hear: some clicks, a hiss, then three clear rings. She banged the receiver back in its cradle and went back upstairs.

She couldn't resist the impulse to watch from her window. She thought nothing of it as three vehicles pulled up in the inn car park – everyone always parked on their side because there were beech trees in front of the manse. In her mind's eye she saw the men inside the top room: one sliding into the space under the floorboards, the other crouching in the alcove behind the bookcase, and Father Richter, waiting for the knock at the door.

She'd done all she could, Detta thought, she'd bought them some time but would it be enough? She heard the cars cut their engines, saw the doors beginning to open.

She thought of the blue-eyed airman, and she held her breath.

# Chapter 16

## November 1989, East Berlin

*Miranda*

I still have the postcard in my hands as I go through to the hallway. I place it next to the old brown Bakelite phone that squats on Gwen's telephone shelf. From the kitchen there's a clatter of crockery as Gwen makes a start on supper. I pick up the receiver and dial, waiting as it rings.

'Hello, Gran?' I reach out with a fingertip and touch the torn postcard of Lossen.

'Miranda!' She asks how I am, how my head is. I tell her I'm fine, Gwen's given me aspirin and weak tea, and she begins to talk about concussion, and how important it will be for me to rest well tonight.

'Why didn't anyone ever mention Granddad had a sister in East Germany?' I interrupt. And I listen as she talks about the great shame, the stigma, of any connection with Germany in the post-war years. She says Granddad was still in the RAF when Gwen defected. She says they were both pulled in for questioning by M15 when it happened, that it put an end to Granddad's RAF career. 'And I suppose it didn't help that he was already married to a German?' I say.

'So Gwen told you about that?' Her voice is so quiet I strain to hear. 'A Nazi wife, a Commie sister – at least, that's how people viewed it, back then.' I hear her exhale – she must be smoking and in my mind's eye I can see her, perched against the telephone table, with the receiver in one hand and one of her long, pastel-coloured cigarettes in the other. Her smoke drifts past Granddad's painting on the hallway wall, the one of the POW camp at night: the spiky loop of barbed wire, the curl of the guard's smoke, bristled tops of fir trees, and a bird in flight, silhouetted against the half-moon.

I hear the doorbell jangle–clang outside Gwen's front door. 'Why didn't you ever say you were German? It's not like you did anything wrong, is it?' I say.

I sense Gwen walking behind me as my grandmother answers. 'The same reason we never spoke about his sister: the shame. It must be hard for anyone of your generation to understand how one can be ashamed, feel complicit almost, in acts of violence committed by others.'

I lift my fingertip off the postcard and touch my forehead, the tender pulpy skin above my brow. And I think that I do understand something of what it is to feel ashamed and complicit in aggression perpetuated by another.

I turn my head to see Gwen open the front door to reveal a dumpy grey-haired woman with a purple hairband. I notice the woman in the doorway smiling and gesticulating in my direction. I see pale curls wobble as Gwen shakes her head at something the woman has said.

'Gwen found an old postcard of yours,' I say. 'Of a place called Lossen – she thinks it's where you grew up, is that right? I'll bring it back with me when I come home. And maybe I could ...' An idea has begun to form in my head, about finding this village and taking some photographs for her, even before my grandmother interrupts.

'The postcard! That's where it went. I've been looking for it. But now you have it, it makes things easier, perhaps.'

'Makes what easier, Gran?'

'Could you go there for me? You see I left something behind, something very precious to me.' She tells me then about a silver locket, hidden inside a tree trunk. She says the locket contains a photograph of her own mother, secreted when she fled. She doesn't tell me why she left it behind, just that she'd like me to look, see if it's still there. 'It's all that's left,' she says. 'That, and the postcard – the only connection I have with the girl I used to be.'

I see the woman in the doorway has stopped speaking and is staring at me, head tilted, like a dog watching its supper bowl being filled, even as Gwen begins to close the door in her face.

'Yes,' I say, picking up the postcard. I hear the front door slam shut. 'I can do that.' There is a draught of lavender water and bonfire-scented air as Gwen walks behind me along the hallway.

After I've hung up I go through to the kitchen, where

Gwen is whisking batter in a bowl. She has switched on the radio on the windowsill. The newscaster talks in dry tones about the temporary changes to border controls in Berlin, and how there is no truth in the rumours that the Wall will be demolished. I tell Gwen that I just took photos of young men with sledgehammers, that the hole they made in the Wall is the one I came through today.

'Thank God Karl-Heinz isn't alive,' Gwen says. 'It would kill him, this destruction of everything he believed in.' The expression in her eyes makes me feel uncomfortable, so I look away, at the family photographs still scattered on the table.

I clear my throat. 'I owe you for the call to England,' I say, rummaging in my jeans pockets for Ostmarks.

'Don't worry about it. You're family,' Gwen says, putting down her whisk and wiping her hands on her slacks. 'And I'm sorry Frau Vetter interrupted your call. She was offering to send her husband round to help with clearing the leaves, but I know she really just wanted to find out who my visitor was. She is so nosey that woman, honestly – Karl-Heinz used to say she was probably a Stasi informer, the way she's always twitching her curtains and inviting herself in.' Gwen laughs a little. 'Poison dwarf,' he used to call her. 'And she wouldn't have found anything out about Karl-Heinz, in any case. He was utterly beyond reproach, ideologically, at least.' She sighs, looking past me to the fading light outside. Then, as if remembering I'm there, she looks across at me and smiles. 'Your grandmother asked me to look after you, so I'm making my special potato pancakes for supper.' She goes over to the table, collects the photos and taps them together into a neat pile. 'Then we can have a couple of glasses of plum brandy and set the world to rights. Although,' she gives a nod in the direction of the chuntering radio, 'it sounds as if others may have beaten us to it.'

I thank her but say I've decided to get on my way. It would be pleasant to stay and get to know Gwen, to eat pancakes, drink brandy and get some sleep. But now I know about Lossen, and the lost necklace, I want to keep moving. I put the postcard in my Filofax at the top of my rucksack, pull on my denim jacket, and sling my Leica back round my neck. When I hug Gwen goodbye, it feels like I've known her for more than the stolen hour I've passed in her home.

As Gwen waves me off from the doorway, I see the woman with the purple hairband sweeping up leaves in the garden of the house opposite. Her curtains are still open, and the yellow light causes pulsing purple shadows to fall from her as she sweeps. When she notices me she drops her broom and scurries indoors.

In the distance, I see the tram approach, and I rush to catch it. And this time it feels as if I'm running towards something, not running away.

# Chapter 17

**January 1945, Nazi Germany**

*Tom*

This time he was ready for it: the knock at the manse door. Blackness pressed in on his eyeballs and the dust crept up his nose. There was the tickle of an incipient sneeze, but he couldn't raise his hand to itch his nose, wedged as he was between solid oak and crumbling plaster in the suffocating blackness.

He'd heard the phone ring three times, dimly, as part of a dream, and woken fully to the sound of the priest's footfalls coming upstairs: it was Detta on the phone, warning them that the SS were on their way – she'd seen the vehicles from her bedroom window. The priest helped with the hurried scuffle into hiding places. Gordon was back in the space under the floorboards. Tom had squeezed into the alcove and the priest pushed the heavy bookcase in front of him with a grunt. They were more practised than last time: ready, waiting for the knock at the door.

Sounds were muffled, with the bookcase and all those leather-bound volumes in the way. There were still the guns, of course, and he'd heard vehicles drawing up and voices in the guesthouse car park as they hid, but nothing now. He strained to hear. Soon the knock would come, barking German voices, clumping boots up the stairwell. He waited, blinking in the darkness. It might be okay. The bookcase completely covered the alcove – they wouldn't suspect the hidden space in the wall. Unless they had brought dogs. Then they'd be done for – him, Gordon, and the priest, too – the Nazis had no love of the Catholic Church. Tom's thighs started to burn. He was cramped into an awkward foetal position. His breathing seemed suddenly impossibly loud, and the sneeze still threatened. Why weren't they here yet? The waiting was the worst. Dark. The black was endless here in this tiny hole. He could be falling through space, if it weren't for the pain in his limbs, and the vice-like clench of the bookcase and wall. His breath rasped, catching in his throat. He gulped down a cough, and tried to slow his breathing: in-out, in-out. Calm down. Panic won't help you, sonny Jim. But where were they? Why was there no knock at the door?

He remembered how it had been in his lonely Perspex bubble in the Beaufighter, claustrophobia in motion, hurtling through the burning night skies. They'd had a lucky escape that night, he and his skipper. Perhaps their luck would hold ... What was that, now? Not a knock, but something: a scuffle, voices from downstairs. The sounds seemed to get louder. Was that someone coming upstairs? Dear God. Stop it. Too late to pray now, you silly sod. A bang as the bedroom door was flung open. Here we go.

There was the scraping sound of wood against wood, and a sliver of light appeared beside him. 'Come out. He's told me where you're hiding.' But it wasn't the guttural shout of an SS officer, it was a woman's voice. Confusion and panic swirled in Tom's head.

He held his breath and waited for the worst.

## Detta

'*Mon Dieu!* You forced me to throw those poor soldier boys out into the cold and all the time you were hiding British *terrorfliegers* here?'

'But Mother, if we had let the deserters stay, the SS would have shot them by now,' Detta said.

'*Ah, oui, mais maintenant nous avons un problème encore plus important a régler, n'est-ce-pas?*' Mother hissed, shaking her head so that her night-time plait dangled like a noose.

'It's my fault,' Father Richter said, inserting himself between them. 'I should never have asked Detta to help me. It's me you should be angry with, Frau Bruncel.'

'You are a man of God, Father. You have no choice but to reach out to those who are in need. But my daughter should have known better, and refused to get involved.'

'But you helped those deserting soldiers, Mother. I don't see how that's any different—'

'Don't you dare take that tone with me. You are still my

daughter, and until you turn twenty-one . . .' She flung her hands up to her cheeks and exhaled through her splayed fingers. 'Oh, *mon Dieu*!'

The candle flickered, revealing lemon-white patches of flesh in the darkness: the priest's cheekbone, a taut sinew in her mother's neck, and, to one side, the angular jawline of the escapee. 'I'm so sorry,' Tom said in German. 'I should never have put any of you in this situation.'

'No, you should not!' Mother pulled her hands from her face and clamped them to her hips.

'Will you lot keep it down?' An English voice came from the bed. 'Just because the SS have requisitioned your guest-house, doesn't mean they're not still on a manhunt for us.'

'What did that man say?' her mother asked, and Detta translated for her.

'He's right,' Father Richter said. 'We should try to keep quiet, get some rest, and not overreact.'

'Not overreact? The SS come storming into my home in the middle of the night to take it over, and I come here for sanctuary, only to find that one of my oldest friends is harbouring escaped enemy prisoners, and, what's more, my own daughter has been in on the secret from the outset. The pair of you have conspired to keep it from me, and you tell me not to overreact?' She spat the words into the flickering half-dark and they all shifted uneasily.

There was a crack like lightening then, and the whole house seemed to shudder from the artillery barrage. 'I'm so sorry, Frau Bruncel,' Tom repeated as the noise died away.

'*Ach, Mensch!*' Mother reverted to German, dropped her hands from her hips, and Detta knew she was beginning to calm down.

Father Richter turned to her mother. 'Why don't you and Detta have my room, and I'll sleep downstairs in the study?' he said.

Tom offered to keep watch from the hallway window whilst they slept. The priest took a blanket from a cupboard and went downstairs. Detta followed her mother into Father Richter's spartan bedroom. They didn't undress, just took their shoes off and slid beneath the eiderdown.

Between blasts from the front line Detta listened to her mother's breathing slowly to a rhythmic assonance. She heard the scrape of Tom's chair in the hallway and the fizz of a match being struck. She waited for sleep to come to her, watching the slivery streak of candlelight under the door. There was a faint tang of fresh cigarette smoke. Tom was awake. And so was she.

Detta felt again that sensation inside. It wasn't as harsh or shocking as the first time, on the pathway in the blizzard, but it was still there, pulling her towards him. As her mother began to snore, Detta slipped out from under the covers and padded into the hallway.

He looked up as she approached. In the half-light, his eyes weren't blue, they were shadowy grey, but they still gave her that feeling, as if the air between them was brittle, and she was about to smash through.

170

'I couldn't sleep,' she said. He offered her his chair, but instead she took the wickerwork stool that had held the bathroom door ajar. The only light was from the church candle by the sink. The bathroom mirror shimmered as the door closed. She carried the stool towards him in the darkness and put it down opposite him, so they could sit on either side of the little window, looking out through the shutter slats and the bare beech branches to the Deutches Haus. He lit her a cigarette and passed it over.

'I didn't realize that was your house,' he said. 'Which is your room?'

'That one, above the front door,' she pointed with the lit tip of her cigarette. As she leant across her knee grazed his.

'So close,' he said.

'So close.' And somehow it didn't feel awkward at all, having her knee rest against his. So she stayed like that, connected to him by a little circle of warmth, as they smoked their cigarettes. 'Some SS officer is in my bed now,' she said, and shuddered at the thought. Would it be candle-wax face or bull-neck or one of the other myriads who had come swarming in from the car park, demanding food, beds, brandy, now-now-NOW! No wonder Mother had decided simply to fill up the old toboggan with provisions from the cellar and decamp to the manse. It had been futile to even attempt to dissuade her. Luckily Detta was still dressed, her suitcase packed. They were across the road within minutes, leaving the 'grey dogs' to sort themselves out. And, of course, once they arrived at the manse, the truth about the escapees had to come out.

The sky above the Deutches Haus was dark as a witch's hat, and the moon nowhere to be seen, but occasional brilliant flashes lit the main road where it stretched towards the horizon, and the air crackled and boomed. The SS had decamped their HQ to Lossen. Did that mean Schurgast had fallen? How far away were the Russians now? It didn't bear thinking of.

'What about you?' Detta said, still conscious of the warmth of Tom's leg against hers. 'Where's your home? What's it like?'

'I suppose it's a bit like this place, really. A little village with a couple of pubs, a church, a handful of shops, farmland all around. It's in Southwest England. They evacuated it for a while this time last year because the Yanks were practising for the D-Day landings on the beach nearby. Only found that out afterwards, of course. So I had an American GI sleeping in my bedroom for a while. For all I know, might have been the same one that stole my girlfriend.'

'You've got a girlfriend?' She was embarrassed by the stab of jealousy she heard in her whispered question, and flushed in the darkness.

'Not anymore. Not since the tear-stained 'Dear John' I got a while back. It was rather sweet, actually. And I can't say I blame her, given the circumstances. I was only missing in action, but they told her to assume I was dead, and it was months before word got back that I was in a prison camp out here. Well, like I said, I can't blame her, really.'

172

Detta thought, then, of Frau Moll, and the Brigadier's driver, together in the window seat. 'In times like this, only God can judge us,' she said, repeating Frau Moll's words from earlier on.

He ground out his cigarette and without the light she couldn't see his features properly. 'You're probably right.' There was a pause. The sky shivered and roared, and angry fireworks slewed above the horizon. 'And you? Do you have a boyfriend?'

She thought of Rolf, and the long-ago walks in the woods. She had still been a schoolgirl then. 'No. Nobody,' she said.

They talked more after that. The artillery fire got louder, and they had to move closer to be heard, tired heads nodding towards each other.

Outside, a full moon rose up behind the battlefield flack. Inside, Detta and Tom shared their lives with each other. Tom told her he had a sister, Gwen, who worked as an army driver, and Detta said she'd always wanted a big sister. Like Detta's own Papa, Tom's father had served in the last war, in France but Tom's father was an army padre, and hadn't fired a weapon. They discovered that they both liked hiking and nature. She liked singing. He liked painting – might have a stab at a career as an illustrator, he said, once this was all over. She told him her secret dream of becoming a writer. She'd never told anyone that before. Mother expected her to take over the running of the guesthouse, eventually. Tom told her he'd been to Germany as a child, but not here, further west, a town called Monchengladbach, which was somewhere near the Dutch border. There had been an exchange programme organized by his father's church. 'It was supposed to promote peace and understanding in the aftermath of the last great cock-up,' he said. 'And fat lot of difference it made.' He spoke in German but said 'cock-up' in English. When she said she'd never come across that phrase before, he laughed, and gave her a literal translation.

'Well, that's something else Sister Maria neglected to put on her vocabulary sheets,' she said, glad the darkness disguised her blushing cheeks.

They swapped stories of childhood. She told him about summer holidays in France, and he asked how her mother ended up marrying a German man, and coming to live here.

She explained how her mother was training to be a ballerina when the last war broke out, and had ended up as an ambulance driver instead, and that was how her parents had met, in a field hospital in 1918. The guns were loud outside and he could only hear if she kept her lips close to his ear as she spoke, so close she could smell the musky scent of him, and just as she inhaled ready to continue, there came one of those violent flashes and a booming crack. She started, and her lips brushed the stubble on his cheek, and he turned.

They kissed: soft as a pillow, smooth as cream, just a touch of lips.

Afterwards they carried on talking, telling their life stories, confiding their dreams, but each sentence was punctuated with the gentle touch of their lips and the warmth of their breath. The guns raged on, and they carried on talking and kissing, throughout it all. Her left hand curled up to the space at the nape of his neck where there was a slice of skin between his hairline and his collar. She stroked it with her forefinger. His right hand came to rest on her left thigh, thumb pressing soft pulses through the cloth of her dress.

They kissed, and told, and the tearing skies lit up like the end of days: his breath in her ear, his mouth brushing hers, and the soft urgency of their shared secrets and dreams – as if telling them would make them last.

Then, towards dawn, the guns fell finally silent. His lips were at the point where her jawline touched her earlobe. He had inhaled, and she waited to hear him whisper another confidence. But instead, he exhaled, and she felt his head loll heavy against her shoulder. Sleep had come suddenly with the quiet, creeping dawn. His head felt warm and solid against her chest. She shifted in her seat, moved her hands to better support his weight, heard his breathing slow.

It seemed to be getting light outside, but a fog was falling. She couldn't see the horizon, and the Deutches Haus looked smudged and grimy. The first of the day's military convoys slewed past. The night was almost over, and soon she'd have to let him go.

### Tom

*OhGodOhGodOhGod* – scrabbling for the rip cord and the spinning rush of space.

But then – cloud-cradled, buoyed up, somehow, the icy sucking vortex gone. Something caught him. There were hands around him, holding him. 'It's okay, you're safe,' said a voice close to his ear. It was *her*. He didn't open his eyes at first, kept them closed, smelled the scent of her, felt the warmth of her, holding him. 'You had a nightmare.'

His eyes sprang open. Fully awake: appalled at himself. 'What must you think of me? What a sad sack!' He jerked out of her grasp.

'It was just a nightmare.'

She had seen the worst of him, the scared boy screaming into the night. He put his face in his hands: the shame of it.

'Was it your plane?' she asked.

He nodded, pulled his hands away. He could barely make out her face in the dark. 'I have the same dream every night. Every fucking night since it happened. Even when we were on the march.' He couldn't see her expression, but he felt her hands reach out, pulling him back towards her. He gave in, buried his head in the space on her shoulder between her long hair and the collar of her fur coat, smelling mothballs and musk and a faint flowery scent. 'I'm sorry,' he muttered. 'You shouldn't have to see me like this.' Because men, especially airmen, are strong and cope with it all. It wasn't on. You weren't supposed to be the kind who whinged about bad dreams, because after all you were one of the lucky few, the ones who were still alive. But with this German girl, in the strange house, in the dark, the stiff upper lip somehow mattered less. He may as well tell her how he felt. 'It shouldn't have been me who escaped. There were so many others who were braver, better men.'

'But your friend, Gordon, wasn't he in the plane, too?'

'Yes, but he landed badly, smashed his head, got amnesia, couldn't remember a bloody thing, not even his rank and number.'

'You must be jealous, in a way? Did you wish you'd been able to forget, too?'

How could she know? How could she guess and how could he admit it, the combination of love and resentment he bore to his skipper. 'I sometimes wish he could remember something, so then there would be someone to share it with,' he said. He felt two spots of water on his hair, like the first fat drops that presage a summer storm. He'd upset her with his stupid sob story. What a heel. 'Don't cry,' he said. 'Crying's for girls.'

'But I am a girl.'

'So you are.'

He lifted his head and his lips found hers. They kissed as if the night would last forever. But in the lull between gunfire he heard a rooster crow, and then the bark of a dog in the street outside.

They pulled apart, and looked out through the shutter slats. The darkness was beginning to lift, leaving behind a pale veil of freezing fog. And there, coming out of the front door of the Deutches Haus Inn were dark figures, moving silhouettes, tethered to the straining shadows of huge black Alsatian dogs. They came out between the grey chunks of vehicles in the inn car park and paused, looking up and down the main road, as if making a decision.

The SS had dogs, and they were heading this way.

# Chapter 18

**November 1989, East Germany**

*Miranda*

Three elderly men sit opposite: two in fur hats, one with a bandaged hand. They hold briefcases on their knees, like stage props. They look too old to still be employed and I wonder what they do for a living – something to do with State bureaucracy, perhaps? The hatless man sinks into his double chin and stares at me, so I look away, at the window, blinking into the blackness as the train rattles on. Streetlights in the East give off different coloured light, I notice, gold, instead of silver. My face is superimposed over the flashing lights, suspended in the moving night. I look at her, the woman in the glass: Miranda Wade is a third-year photography student. She fell for a handsome journalist and ended up running off mid-term to Berlin with him, only to discover he's manipulating her to cover up his drug-running operation. Surely she's not me? My reflection looks back: the pale face with the Leica slung like an oversized necklace round my neck. No, I realize, she's not me. Not anymore.

I bought a map of East Germany at the station kiosk. I have it stretched out over my knees. I have searched, but I cannot seem to find the village of Lossen. Gran said it was between Breslau and Oppeln, and I can't find those towns on the map, either. But the light in the train is a dim sickly yellow, and the map slides around as the train sways, and I think that perhaps the place names will reveal themselves better in daylight tomorrow. I remember Gran talking about the river Oder, and that is very clear on this map, ribboning down the border between East Germany and Poland. That's why I have taken this train to Frankfurt an der Oder, the border town on the banks of the river. I will spend the night there and begin my search again in the morning.

The three men get off at the next station and the carriage is empty. My eyelids are getting heavy, gaze sleepily unfocussed. I haven't had much rest in the last twenty-four hours.

With a jerk, I am awake. The train has come to a halt. I sit up, wipe condensation from the inside of the window. The platform sign says Frankfurt an der Oder, in stark black gothic script. I am here. I push up out of my seat, pull my rucksack onto my back and pick up the map.

Doors slam, shadowy figures scurry across the platform ahead of me, but within moments the train is gone, the platform empty, and there's nobody to ask for help, nobody to ask for the way to the nearest guesthouse. The night is still and empty, the moonlight blocked by a cloud. I can't even see where the station exit is. I blow on my hands and start to walk along the platform. The platform edge slopes down onto the sidings and the half-moon makes an appearance: a shaft of silver lighting up the station. I look round for an exit sign, and that's when I see him.

The soldier is leaning up against a train in the sidings, smoking. It's the picture he makes that captures me. The moonlight highlights the curl of his smoke, and there is a loop of barbed wire at the station fencing in the foreground. He is leant at an angle against some kind of freight trailer – a huge grey silo, with a dark star painted on the side. Moonbeams catch the dull gleam of his weapon, the pale rose-gold tip of his cigarette. It is so reminiscent of my grandfather's painting, the one in Gran's hall: the colours, almost monochrome, with just a hint of lapis. As I look through the lens, a bird, disturbed from its roost, rises up towards the moon.

'Perfect,' I whisper, flicking off the lens cap and lifting the Leica to my face. I turn on the flash, not waiting to ask for permission, catching the moment before it is lost. There is a fluorescent blink as I click the shutter.

Stupid.

The soldier turns, shouts. From nowhere shadows solidify, I am grabbed from behind, Alsatian dogs snarl and bark: pink-mouthed, jagged white teeth. I feel the prod of a gun in my ribs. My arms wrenched up behind my back.

A shout and sour breath in my face: *Du Stuck Scheisse!* (You piece of shit!)

Uniformed men shoving, and patrol dogs snapping at my legs, frog-marched through a side gate and away to where a black van waits, doors howling open.

I am shoved into the bruising darkness: trapped.

# Chapter 19

**January 1945, Nazi Germany**

*Detta*

'*Ils nous tueront tous* – they will kill us all!' Mother flung out her arms, and her whisper sounded like a shout in the dead air.

Luckily the SS had started their house-to-house search at the far end of the village, which gave them some time. But if the escapees hid in their usual places then the dogs would sniff them out. The men had to leave but where could they go?

It came to Detta with sudden clarity, as Father Richter wrung his hands and the men pulled on their boots, ready to run. 'Follow me,' she said in English.

In the priest's bedroom her little suitcase lay unopened on the floor by the bed. She knelt down and struggled with the catch, then tossed her spare clothes and things on the bed. Underneath were the hidden Wehrmacht deserter's jackets. She held them out. 'Put these on.' The men began to unbutton their air force jackets. 'No, over the top. You'll need your British uniforms later.'

'Are you mad?' Her mother stood in the doorway watching. The two airmen struggled to get the German army jackets over their own.

Detta shook her head and sat on the bed next to the disgorged contents of her case. 'I'm taking them to the French barracks, but they'll need to wear these for the walk there, in case someone sees.'

'But if you're caught?' Father Richter stood behind her mother, blocking the candlelight from the doorway.

'It's foggy outside. Hardly anyone is up yet. And even if they are, people are used to me popping into the French workers' barracks with orders from the Reichsbahn. And if two injured Wehrmacht soldiers are also walking up the path towards the field hospital, so what?' She pulled on her boots.

'But, *cheri* . . .' her mother began.

'Oh Mother, what choice do we have?' Detta said, standing up. She plucked her blue scarf up from the mess of clothes on the bed covers and pulled her gloves from her coat pockets. Her mother stood aside to let her lead the airmen out of the room.

'At least let me accompany you,' Father Richter said, catching her sleeve as she reached the top of the stairs.

She ushered the men on ahead and turned to reply to him. 'No. There's no reason for you to be visiting the barracks. It would only arouse suspicion. Shouldn't you be in church this morning, anyway?' Detta pushed past and followed the men downstairs, hurrying away before she had second thoughts. She didn't want Father Richter or her mother giving her chance to pause or reconsider.

She led the men to the side door. 'You go out this way, and I'll go out the front. Cut behind the church, through the churchyard, and keep going until you reach the barracks,' she pointed up to where the track wound round through the trees. 'You'll need to re-join the track to catch up with me as I reach the entrance. But we can't be seen together. Is that clear?' She spoke in German and Tom hastily translated to English for Gordon, who nodded. 'Good. Ready?' She unlocked the door, letting them into the priest's rose garden. Gordon was still too weak to walk unaided. Tom had to shoulder his weight, and they staggered through the snow as one, just as she'd seen them that first day on the path. There was no time to kiss, or whisper goodbye. She locked the door behind them.

As she walked back through the dark corridor to the front door she sensed her mother and the priest watching from the stairwell, but they did nothing to stop her. She slid the bolt and turned the heavy key in the lock.

It was lighter now, the sun up, but hidden behind an icy blanket of fog. A line of trucks sped past on the main road: the needle-cold air suffused with petrol fumes. Detta pulled her blue scarf up over her head, slammed the manse door shut behind her, put her hands in her pockets and turned right, past the old beech tree, and along the path that wound in front of the church. The guns pounded on.

She kept thinking that at any time she'd hear the shout of the SS field police, demanding to know where she was going in such a hurry, at this time on a Sunday morning? But there was no shout, only the roar of the angry skies, and the distant barking of the search dogs. Were Tom and Gordon following?

She bent over, fiddling with the lace on her right boot, as if it had come loose and she were re-tying it. Upside down, beyond the wavering black curtain of her wool skirt, she glimpsed the men, propped against each other, staggering like drunkards between the gravestones of the foggy churchyard. They looked dishevelled, exhausted. If anyone saw, they'd think they were walking wounded, tottering towards the field hospital. They disappeared, then, out of sight behind the church.

Detta straightened up and carried on walking in the direction of the French barracks. A bird flew past, a sudden black flash against the grey-white of the morning mist, like torchlight in negative. What was it? A starling? She blinked and hurried on, head down, looking at her black boots scurrying on the snowy mud. Not much further, now, soon she'd have the men to safety.

'Good morning, Fräulein! Not at church today?' She looked up, stifling a gasp. It was the same SS officer from yesterday. He must have been walking down the track from the Schloss. She hadn't noticed his tall grey figure stalking through the shadowy trees towards her.

'Oh, you startled me! I wasn't looking. Church? No, not today, officer.'

He drew near, coming to a halt beside her. 'But it is Sunday today. I had you down as a religious girl, not so?'

'Yes, yes, I am. What I meant was I'm not going there right now, but naturally I'll be at Mass later on.'

'Naturally.' He tilted his head to one side. 'And where are you off to now? It's hardly the weather for a country stroll.'

'I'm . . .' She gestured vaguely up the hill, through the trees. 'I'm friends with Frau Moll. I often go to Mass with her and her daughters on Sundays.' As the SS officer turned to look in the direction she pointed, she glimpsed the two disguised airmen appearing from behind the church. 'How have your men found their accommodation at the Deutches Haus?' She rushed into the question, hoping to distract him.

He turned back to look at her. 'Very comfortable, thank you.' His breath billowed like smoke across her face. It smelled of brandy and cigars. 'You didn't have to leave, you know,' he said. 'Running away in the middle of the night like that, as if we were the enemy!' He chuckled a little at his own joke, showing uneven, overlapping teeth.

'Easier for your men, give you all more space, and Father Richter has a spare room for Mother and I, so really it was no bother.' Stop gabbling, she thought. Stop it. It makes you look nervous, and he'll start to suspect something. She drew breath. 'Any luck finding the escapees?' She tried to keep her voice bright.

'Not yet, but now we've got the dogs out . . .' He made an expansive gesture.

'Yes, I've heard how thorough you are with your search methods.'

He smiled, accepting the compliment. 'You should come back to the inn – and your mother, of course. It would be good for the men to have some female company.' His thin lips were grey–pink and mobile, like an earthworm. He leaned in a little closer to her, and she realized he was awaiting her response. Just then there was the thud of something falling, a muffled voice crying out, and Detta saw, with horror, just twenty metres or so behind the officer's back, that Gordon had slipped and fallen as the two airmen joined the icy path, pulling Tom down with him. The SS man turned his head to look. He tutted. 'Bloody Wehrmacht . . .' He watched as the men rolled and righted themselves in the snow. Would he choose to impress her with his chivalry, and go over to offer help to the two fallen soldiers? How could she stop him?

Detta reached over and touched his sleeve. 'Yes,' she said. She had to raise her voice a little, to counter a sudden boom of ordnance. 'Yes, of course we'll come to visit you all, Mother and I. We'll need to check up on the pig and the chickens anyway. I hope there were enough eggs for your breakfast this morning?'

He swivelled his head back and fixed her with red–rimmed eyes. 'Ah, about the chickens, Fräulein . . .'

'Yes?'

'There was an unfortunate incident. I'm afraid someone left the coop door open, and then someone else let the dogs out.' He shrugged. 'So you see . . .'

She saw, in her mind's eye: bloody feathers on the snow, and imagined the sound of the dogs' salivating jaws crunching through bones. Don't show your feelings, Detta. Just don't. There was movement on the path behind the SS man, but she wouldn't let herself look. She swallowed. 'These things happen, I quite understand. But you and your men had eggs for breakfast today, at least?'

'Yes, thank you. Eggs and rye bread. What a pity there was no good coffee in your establishment, though.'

'But who has real coffee, in these times, officer?'

'Who indeed, Fräulein? At least there is still the pig. When the manhunt is concluded we can have it butchered – the men will deserve a decent meal after all their hard work. You do have a butcher in the village?'

'Not anymore.' She thought of Herr Lipp and what happened last year. 'Unfortunately.'

'Shame. We shall just have to shoot it and do our best with your kitchen knives. Perhaps you could help us?'

'Yes, of course,' Detta said, her voice rising in desperation. How to get rid of him? She made a show of rubbing her arms. 'It's very cold, isn't it? I think I should probably—'

Just then there was the sound of shouting from halfway along the village street. 'Looks like I'm needed,' the SS man said, giving a slight bow. 'It was a pleasure to bump into you again, Fräulein, and, as I said, don't be a stranger. Consider the Deutches Haus still your home, please.'

Detta forced her lips up at the corners. 'Thank you. That's very kind of you, sir.'

He smiled again, showing his jostling teeth. 'Not at all. See you later, Fräulein.'

She waited on the track, watching him stride off, past the manse and into the village. Had he suspected her of something, or was all that just some kind of clumsy flirtation? She released a breath. At least he was gone.

But where were Tom and Gordon? The morning fog would soon begin to lift, and villagers would be making their way to church for Mass. They were running out of time. Detta looked round, but they were nowhere to be seen. She just had to hope they could see her, and that there was still time. She half ran the last fifty metres to the barracks, feet sliding on the frozen mud beneath the impacted snow.

She banged on the door. 'Open up, it's Fräulein Bruncel here!' The French would be asleep, she thought, and shouted again, pounding with her fists. But the door opened almost immediately. Henri and Jean-Paul were up and dressed, already in coats and hats.

'Fräulein!' Jean-Paul bent to kiss her gloved hand in that half-mocking way he had.

'There's no time for games. I need your help.' It all came in such a rush that her fluency suffered. She stammered and stumbled over the French words, blurting out about the British escapees and the SS manhunt.

'Wait, wait a moment. Slow down. What British prisoners? What are you talking about?'

'Shut your mouth, Jean-Paul, look, there are soldiers coming,' Henri said, slapping his friend on the shoulder.

Detta turned. Tom and Gordon appeared through the thick air, but all you could see were two men in Wehrmacht jackets. Jean-Pierre muttered an expletive and began to pull the door to. Detta put her foot in the way. 'Wait.'

'What are you doing, you silly girl? We don't want any trouble.'

'You need to let them in!'

'You're crazy.' The door banged against her foot, a hand shoved at her shoulder.

Tom and Gordon were now almost at the doorway. A kick dislodged her foot, and the door was shutting. She jammed the fingers of her left hand inside as it slammed to.

The pain was immense, despite the protection of her glove, and she cried out. At the sound, Jean-Pierre relaxed his grip on the door, and she managed to get her boot wedged back in the gap. 'Show your RAF uniforms, they don't believe me,' she called out behind her, praying there was nobody walking up the path behind them to see or hear what was going on. '*Regardez*,' she yelled, as the airmen crowded towards the sliver of open doorway to show their RAF badges hidden under the Wehrmacht jackets.

Then the barracks door was flung open, and the two British men were welcomed in with back slaps and laughter. Jean-Paul, distraught at the pain he'd just caused her, ushered Detta away to run her bruised fingers under a cold tap. Henri spirited the escapees upstairs.

Between apologizing for hurting her hand and forcing her to drink a tot of vodka to numb the pain, Jean-Paul explained that he and Henri were just on their way out to visit their Polish girlfriends up on the farmstead. He said they could leave their ID papers for Tom and Gordon. That way, if the SS searched the barracks, at least every man would have documents to show. Word was sent round, and Detta saw that the old Wehrmacht jackets were tossed on the kitchen fire.

Tom, now wearing grubby worker's overalls, came back downstairs with Henri (Gordon had been left to recover upstairs). Detta, already on her way to the door, quickly translated the plan about the ID papers. 'I should go,' she said, as soon as it was settled.

Tom took her right hand as she made to leave. 'You've just saved my life. Thank you.'

'*Nicht zu danken.*' She wrenched her hand away. Nothing to thank me for. If she said any more, she would have broken down. Better to leave now, while she still could. She pulled open the barracks door and ran out into the icy blankness, not looking back.

# Chapter 20

## November 1989, Devon

*Odette*

I touch the base of my neck, feeling the bare skin there. I notice my hands are shaking. I realize there's only one thing I can do now. I pull on my camel coat and pluck my car keys from the hook. My Fiesta, my little old faithful, waits at the kerb. People always blame cars for being unreliable, I think, shifting in behind the wheel, but to my mind it is people who are not to be relied on. I slam the car door and twist the key in the ignition.

I squint into the low autumn sunshine, negotiating the Saturday morning traffic queues on the bypass, chugging through the industrial estate, and out on to the dual carriageway. I push my foot down hard on the accelerator and change lanes to overtake a lorry on the hill. I exit the slip road and turn off onto the country lanes, flexing my fingers on the steering wheel. What is this feeling that is stuffed so far up my nostrils and down my throat that I feel as if I'm suffocating? There's a sharp pain in my forehead. It flickers on and off like a loose connection. But I have driven this way so often I do not need to concentrate. It is almost reflexive, the points where I need to indicate, turn, get into a low gear for a sharp corner. The hedge banks are high, the road a twisted shadow pulled between. As I slow into second to negotiate a blind corner at the top of a hill there is a flash of red, a sudden lurch, and a thud as two vehicles make contact.

I look up and see the startled chubby face of a woman, through the windscreen of a post office van. Her mouth gapes in a surprised 'oh'. I switch off the engine, pull on the hand-brake and turn on the hazard lights. I reach into the glove compartment and take out the photocopy of my insurance policy. I do these things slowly, deliberately, giving myself a chance to calm down. I get out of the car. The woman gets out too, wobbling under her too-tight polyester uniform. We face each other across bonnets. 'Are you okay?' she says.

'Fine, I think,' I reply, rubbing the back of my neck where it pulled with the momentum.

'Oh, God, I'm so . . .' The woman stops herself. 'But you are okay, aren't you?'

I look at the position of the vehicles. The post office van is on the wrong side of the road. 'I think we should exchange details,' I say, and pass her the sheet of paper.

'Yes of course.' She gives me a Royal Mail business card. 'It's my first day,' she says as she hands it over. 'I've not been this way before and I didn't realize how sharp the corner—'

'These lanes can take a while to get used to,' I interrupt,

glancing at the damage to my car: the wing will need beating out. I look at the van: crumpled bumper, shattered glass. I think of all the sacks of mail in the back – bills, postcards, birthday presents, catalogues and love letters.

I think of the postcard of Lossen: torn and fixed, lost for years. Miranda has it now. She has promised to go there, take photographs, find my necklace. She thinks this is a favour for her grandmother, but it is more than that, it is a chance for her to escape.

And then I remember one particular letter, sent without a stamp, forty-four years ago. How it changed my life forever. 'It was my fault. I was going too fast,' I say to the post office woman. 'You can tell your boss I've admitted liability. I'll make sure my insurance company pays.'

'Really?'

'Really,' I say. 'The Royal Mail did me a favour, once, a long time ago. I'll just think of this as payback.'

'You're sure?' A hesitant smile begins to take hold on her anxious face.

'Certain.'

'Thank you. Thank you so much!' she says. I get back in, and manoeuvre my car into a niche in the hedgerow, letting the red post office van inch past. The woman mouths a final thank you as she drives away, and I drive on.

The church is at the far end of the High Street. It is old, Norman, with a rectangular tower and castellations. A large yew tree casts long shadows across the gravestones, and the church itself is a solid silhouette against the fuzzy golden morning fields behind. I park the Fiesta by the lychgate. I follow the path around the side of the church, skirting the granite buttresses, and then strike off between the graves. Behind the church the long grass is still dew-drenched. Cold water seeps into my suede shoes as I walk towards the far corner, where a bramble-topped dry stone wall separates the graveyard from the fields beyond.

I kneel on the rectangular patch of quartz aggregate in front of the black headstone. The stones dig into my knees as I reach across and stroke the cool marble with my fingertips. 'We need to talk,' I say aloud, confident that no one but the crows are listening. 'I know I promised. No dragging up the past, no going back. But that was forty-four years ago, darling. And everything has changed, don't you see? So I have had to break that promise. Can you forgive me?'

There is no answer, just the distant cawing of crows and a rustle as the wind catches the branches overhead. But I know he's heard, and I know he understands. For forty-four years I have been a British wife, mother, widow, business owner. But I can't hide from the past anymore.

# Chapter 21

**January 1945, Nazi Germany**

*Tom*

He went upstairs after she left. Not all the Frenchmen were as friendly as the two who'd given them the ID papers; most ignored them, but they'd been given a cup of black ersatz coffee, and he'd shared out a few cigarettes in return. Gordon lay under the covers of a thin cot bed. There was one other man in the room, with a drooping moustache, who looked up from the piece of wood he was whittling as Tom walked in, and nodded in his direction, before returning to his task.

'D'you know what happened to our RAF jackets?' Tom said.

'Inside the palliasse – the SS boys are not likely to look there, not if I'm lying on top of it, asleep, anyway.'

'Let's hope it doesn't come to that. Is it sewed up?'

'Chap over there did it, fast as lightening.' Gordon had colour in his cheeks, underneath the scrubby week-long growth of beard. The rest, food and medicine had begun to revive him, despite the circumstances.

'*Merci*,' Tom said to the man with the whittling knife. It was just about all the French he remembered from school. He hoped to God the SS chaps had been as slack in French classes as he had.

'*C'est rien.*' The man parted his lips in a snaggletoothed smile.

'Smoke?' Gordon pulled out his almost empty packet of Pall Mall from under the bedclothes and offered them out. There were only three left in the packet, so Tom offered to share, but Gordon said no, he felt like celebrating with a whole one. So they all sparked up. 'Did us proud, your girl, in the end,' Gordon said, sitting up in the thin bed and sucking on his fag. 'Made it seem like a piece of cake, getting us in here.'

'Suppose she did,' Tom said, swilling smoke round his mouth and turning towards the window before exhaling. He viewed the outdoors through a triple screen: the smoke, the frosted pane and the foggy air beyond. He could still see her, just about, a distant figure with a blue scarf over her head, hurrying down the track past the church. Beyond the line of trees that bordered the main road, army trucks flew past. His girl, Gordon had said. His – had she been his? Just for those few short hours? Tom narrowed his eyes, inhaled again, watching her get smaller and smaller, getting swallowed up in the grey-whiteness. At the point where the track met the path from the church, she was joined by another figure. It was the priest, coming from the other direction, going to church to prepare for the Sunday service, Tom supposed. He watched them meet, saw their heads bend, bodies lean inwards, momentarily, then pull apart.

The priest has just whispered something to her, Tom thought. What has he said?

This time when he exhaled Tom blew the smoke sideways, and moved closer to the frosted glass, wiping a patch away with his forefinger to see more clearly.

She was just a tiny distant blur, now, approaching the beech trees that separated the manse from the road. Then, as he watched, shadows seemed to separate themselves from the tree trunks: dark silhouettes of men and dogs. The manse door opened like a mouth and gulped them all inside.

Had her mother had enough time to erase all traces of their stay: wedge the loose floorboard back in place; push the bookcase against the wall – and what about the half-used medicines and the razor in the bathroom? Had they been well hidden, too?

He'd almost finished his cigarette now, the ash was a toppling chimney in his shaking fingers.

With the artillery sounds from the frontline, and the traffic from the road, he couldn't possibly hear anything from the manse. He wouldn't hear if there were barks, screams or gunshots. His face was so close to the cool glass that he could feel the kiss of frost crystals against his cheek. There was a huge barrage, then, and the windowpane shook.

'It won't be long, now, will it?' Gordon said, in the momentary silence that followed. 'How do you say "close" in French?' Tom yanked his gaze away from the manse and looked at his friend, lying there on the bed, fag in his mouth. Gordon nodded at the Frenchman, and made a gesture with the thumb and forefinger of his right hand, putting them so close that they were almost touching, with just a tiny chink in between. 'Those Reds are this fucking close,' he said, squinting through the gap at the Frenchman.

'*Oui*,' the man replied, pausing from his whittling to look up.

Tom turned away from them and gazed back outside. The manse door was closed now. Who knew what was going on inside? But spilling up from the village street and towards the church were clusters of people in hats and coats. I should be happy, Tom thought. For two years, eleven months and two days, all I have wanted is to escape and get back to Blighty, and I'm almost there – this close – I should be over the bloody moon.

The church bell began to toll, a baleful clanging adding to the symphony of war. The church doors opened, and he watched as villagers began to roll along the main road and towards the churchyard, pulled in by the sound. A starling suddenly fluttered in the bare tree branches, at eye height to his vantage point, making a sphere of mistletoe wobble like a Christmas bauble. Christmas mistletoe– they hadn't needed that excuse last night. He remembered the touch of her lips on his and warmth rose up inside him at the thought.

Tom inhaled the last vestiges of lit tobacco and stubbed the butt out in the cracked saucer on the windowsill. He turned away from the outdoors. She was gone, and it was too late. Gordon lay in bed, blowing smoke rings at the ceiling. He caught Tom's eye as he turned and raised quizzical brows.

'Why didn't I tell her how I felt when I had the chance?' Tom said.

### Detta

Her knees ached from kneeling. Father Richter was having them pray even longer than usual: forgive those who sin against us; deliver us from evil. The scent of damp clothes mingled with incense. Detta couldn't think about God. She kept wondering what was happening in the French accommodation block.

When they'd completed their fruitless search of the manse, the SS field police had allowed them to go to the Sunday service, but had followed them on the path, stalking up past the church towards the French barracks.

Detta opened her eyes and lifted her head, unable to focus on the droning prayers. The church was fuller than she'd seen it in weeks. She looked out over the sea of bowed heads: the long-nosed pharmacist and his dumpling-faced wife; the singing teacher, who always dressed in shades of beige, and her frowning husband with his toothbrush moustache; the baker and his enormous tribe of boys, all dressed in brown, plumped like a batch of burnt rolls all along the pew beside him; the elderly couple from the corner house, who liked to leave out food for the half-starved farm cats.

And the scrawny butcher's wife, Frau Lipp, hard and sharp as a shard of glass – she had shrunk to half her size since they'd executed her husband for refusing to be conscripted. (He'd done his duty in the last war, he'd said, stony-faced, with brawny arms folded over his blood-spattered apron. He would do anything they asked, but he was too old to take up weapons and fight.) They shot him in front of her, right there in the middle of the village. Could Frau Lipp forgive, Detta wondered? And when would they be delivered from evil? When the SS were replaced by the Red Army – what kind of deliverance would that be?

Father Richter's prayers were momentarily drowned out by another ferocious volley of fire from across the Oder. The giant chandelier above the altar wobbled. Detta saw the priest mouth 'Amen', and open his eyes. He looked straight at her, over the still-bowed heads of the congregation, and made the sign of the cross.

There was a pause, a shuffle, as everyone got up off their knees and sat back in the pew, and the guns were silent, just for a few moments.

That was when she heard it: two clear shots, one after another, crack–crack, somewhere close by. Detta flinched, and her hand flew to her mouth. Two shots. A shot for each of the *terrorfliegers*.

So, that was it. He was gone. They both were. It had all been for nothing.

*

202

When they stood up to sing, she felt dizzy and had to reach out to the pew in front to steady herself. The words in the hymn book swam like minnows. Her throat was too dry to do much more than croak.

Afterwards, she waited with her mother in the churchyard for Father Richter to finish saying goodbye to the congregation: holding hands and muttering words of comfort as they filed past through the open church doorway. Despite the freezing fog, everyone seemed reluctant to go home – the unspoken thought was that this would be the last time the whole village attended church together.

The baker's boys played tag amongst the tombstones with the Moll girls, who were dressed in identical red pixie hats, looking like swirling drops of blood against the snowy ground. Detta felt sick. She turned so that the French barracks weren't even in her peripheral vision, tried to deliberately tune in on what people were saying in order not to think about what had just happened. She kept avoiding her mother's gaze; Mother must have heard those shots, too, and would know what they meant. But even an exchange of looks could be enough to give their complicity away. So instead she looked at the gossiping villagers.

There were flattened lips and head shaking, eyes rolling heavenwards as the skies reverberated.

*Those Reds can't be far away – heartless Ivans!*

*I heard those bastards even get their womenfolk to fight. Women, firing guns, commanding tanks, can you imagine?*

*It can't be true – but we'll find out soon enough because it can't be long now. I've been telling Norbert that we should leave this morning, whilst there's still time, but he won't listen.*

*I think we should wait for the evacuation order. There will be a plan, and transport laid on. Let's wait for the authorities to take charge, they'll know when it's time.*

*Well, I'm not going anywhere, I've nowhere to go, and in any case, why would I leave and let the Russians smash my windows and rob my till. Over my dead body!*

*It will be over your dead body. You heard what those refugees said.*

*Ach, that's just the big towns where that sort of thing happens. A little place like this, the front line will just pass through. We can go to the cellar for a few hours and it will all be over.*

*You're talking nonsense – they'll ransack the place and you know it. And talking of ransacking, did anyone else get a visit this morning?*

*What, from the SS?*

*No, from Saint Nicklaus – yes of course from the SS, what did you think I was talking about? They made a terrible mess in my front room. One of those dogs knocked over my Delft vase with its stupid, big tail, not that anyone thought to apologize. They didn't even close the door behind them when they left.*

*Did they catch them?*

*Who?*

*The terrorfliegers they were looking for.*

*I don't know. Who cares, anyway. I don't know why they're wasting energy on a manhunt at a time like this. You'd think they'd have better things to do, wouldn't you?*

*I suppose it's a matter of principle – remember what happened at Sagan the other year?*

*What's that?*

*Oh, you must remember – there was a mass escape from the prison camp and they shot them all, all fifty of them.*

*That's the SS for you, they never give up.*

'Detta, can I have a word?' Frau Moll was at her side. 'It's about the girls' French lessons.' French lessons, for heaven's sake. Two men had just been murdered, the front line was within walking distance of their village, and yet Frau Moll wanted to talk about French lessons. Nevertheless, Detta nodded – anything to distract her from dwelling on those two shots she'd heard. She let herself be pulled away from the cluster of gossiping villagers. The Moll girls, cheeks flushed and giggling, were still playing tag with the baker's boys, taking no notice of the shudder and roar in the skies.

'I've got us a way out,' Frau Moll leant in close to Detta to speak.

'But there'll be transport, won't there? Everyone is packed and ready, waiting for the evacuation order.' Even Mother, she thought, who claims she doesn't want to leave, but will surely change her mind now the SS are in the guesthouse.

'There won't be an evacuation order. There is no organized transport.'

'What?'

'The HQ and the field hospital are going to move today, and I expect the SS will retreat at the same time.'

'And they're all just going to leave, without lifting a finger to help the villagers?'

Frau Moll nodded. 'Don't say anything. And like Frau Lipp said just now, in all likelihood the fighting will pass through and they can sit it out in their cellars.'

'Do you really believe that?'

'No, not really. But I have a plan to get us away, at least.'

She explained that the Brigadier's driver had deliberately disabled one of the field ambulances by disconnecting the distributor. 'We wait until they've gone, then we take the ambulance – he's shown me how to reconnect it, it's quite simple really. And he's hidden some spare fuel in the old ice house. The trick will be to get out at the right time, just as the front line is passing through. Johann – Corporal Mann – says to take the side roads and head south-west. I've got a map. He says the Red Army will keep going north, on to Brieg and then Breslau, because they need to capture the major towns before they can go onto Berlin. So we'll go sideways, south-west, slip down towards France, and disappear.'

'We?'

'You speak French, and your mother is French. And I think there'll be enough space for Father Richter, too.'

'Father Richter doesn't speak French.'

'No, but he's a Catholic priest. Think about it: an ambulance with a priest and a handful of French-speaking women and girls – it's our best chance of getting out.'

'And what about your husband? Once this is all over then the British will release him, and then—'

'They'll put him on trial, and he'll be executed for what he's done.'

'You can't possibly know that.'

'Can't I? Listen, Detta, once we leave, there's no going back. Whatever these people say, our old lives are ending, one way or another. Tell your mother and Father Richter, and come and visit me at home, so we can discuss the details in private.'

Detta nodded. 'Thank you. I will.'

As they turned to join the main group, Detta saw old Herr Schneider, the railway guard, coming down the path from beyond the French barracks. Herr Schneider had an air rifle over one shoulder and carried something in his left hand. He grinned at her, and held it up: two birds, black and lifeless as a pair of gloves. 'Starlings,' he called out. 'All I could get, but it'll do for the pot.'

Two shots, she'd heard: crack-crack, clear as day – two dead starlings, that was all.

'Did you see whether the SS got the escaped prisoners?' she yelled back. 'They were about to search the French barracks when we went into church.' She walked a few paces towards him, winding through the toppling tombstones.

'Nothing doing. Angry as hell they were. That's it, those escapees are free, probably across the other side of the Oder already, if they've got any sense. And d'you know what, I say good luck to 'em, those cliff-pissing Britishers. It's every man for himself now, and if they can escape, I say so what. Good luck to them.' He was yelling to be heard over the sounds of the guns, and everyone could hear his treacherous words, but nobody seemed to care. He waved his dead starlings as a goodbye, and went on his way.

Father Richter was closing the church door. The villagers had started to walk home. She would need to join Mother, go back to the manse, help cook lunch, and tell them of Frau Moll's escape plan. But before she went back to join them, she turned so she could look up along the path through the trees and see the barracks.

Was he still there, and was he still alive? She had to find a way to get back and see him, just to be sure.

## Tom

'I heard shots. I thought you were dead,' she said, hurling herself into his arms.

'I've fallen in love with you,' he whispered into her hair as they embraced. And it was as if they'd made some kind of contract, there, standing in the doorway of the barracks in the freezing fog. When they kissed this time it wasn't the tender brushing of lips it had been last night; now it was deep and urgent, like slaking a thirst. She pulled away at last, and he opened his eyes. Darkness was falling, as if someone were shading pencil through the air, turning everything grey and featureless.

'I came to tell you that we're going to leave, soon,' she said. 'My friend has a plan to get us away in an old army ambulance.'

'You've got transport. That's good news. If you're in an ambulance then you've a much better chance . . .' He stopped himself from spelling it out. 'You'll be safer there than on foot with the other refugees.'

She nodded. 'I know.' She pulled a postcard from her pocket. It was a picture of the village guesthouse – her home. 'Keep this, so you'll remember me, whatever happens,' she said.

She pulled away, turning to leave. 'No, wait!' He tore the postcard in half, took a pencil from his pocket and wrote his parents' address on the reverse. 'We can find each other again. After this,' he said. 'After this is over. I'll come and get you. We'll find each other, somehow, somewhere.'

She glanced down at the address. 'You want me to write to you in England?' she said, looking up again, into his eyes.

'No.' He opened his arms and drew her into him one last time. 'I want you to join me in England and be my wife.'

They couldn't kiss forever. She tore herself away, with exquisite slowness. Then she was gone, swallowed up by the icy fog. He stayed in the doorway, looking out into the freezing blankness, even though he could no longer see her. He tried to imagine her in a white wedding dress in a shaft of stained-glass sunlight, aunts in best hats and confetti in pockets. Gordon would be beside him in a morning suit, with a rose in his buttonhole and a gold ring in a velveteen box. He tried to imagine it, but the image wouldn't stick. It was stupid to try.

He sighed, and realized he could hear his own breath. The artillery had gone quiet. The front line was momentarily silenced – odd.

It was just as he turned the handle to go back into the barracks that he heard it: the clatter-rumble of tanks coming along the main road, followed almost simultaneously by the yell of a low-flying plane, and the stuttering rattle of straffing machine-gun fire coming right through the centre of the village.

# Chapter 22

**November 1989, Devon**

*Odette*

In all likelihood it is nothing, the dizziness I feel as I stand up from the grave. One leg has pins and needles so bad I can barely walk. Perhaps I'm in some kind of mild shock from bumping the car. Still, I decide not to drive until I've taken in some fluid. The village shop doubles as a post office and should be open by now. As I turn away from the grave a starling flies past, over the headstone and on into the golden sunshine beyond.

Still unsteady, I pause to rest at the lychgate. In the distance, beyond the muddle of village rooftops, I can just make out the silver-blue shimmer where the fields end and the cliffs smash into the sea. Grey clouds have begun to mass over the southern horizon. An autumn gale is on its way. I go down the steps and cross the street to the shop, tucked like an afterthought on the corner by the pub.

The doorbell jangles as I push it open. It hasn't changed

that much over the years, I notice: fewer vegetables, more greetings cards, but still the same scent of brown paper and gossip. I shiver, even though it's warmer here than outside. I feel a pain in my head, again, only this time it's like a spark shooting from my neck to my forehead. I scan the cluttered shelves for painkillers.

There is a woman posting a parcel at the counter: short and plump, with a brown woollen hat pulled down over her perm. She gives me a sideways glance as she bustles out, and I know she recognizes me, as I do her. It is Anna Riddaway. Her uncle was killed in the North Africa campaign, and two of her cousins in the Plymouth Blitz. I know all about her – everyone knows everything, round here, it's not a place for incomers or secrets.

We'd had to come and live here, with Tom's parents, after the wedding. There hadn't been anywhere else. Now, as I smell the peppery scent of Anna passing me by, I remember how everyone in the village managed to be icy-polite with me when I was with my husband, or his family, but assaulted me with aggressive silence whenever I was out alone. Tom's parents and Gwen agreed to perpetuate the half-lie: that I was a German-speaking French girl from Alsace. But the villagers all guessed the truth. It was in the way their eyes veered away from mine, and muttered conversations came to an abrupt halt whenever I approached. It was a relief to move away to RAF quarters and, later, to our own home in Exeter, above the typing school we set up together.

The doorbell jangles again as Anna Riddaway leaves. The

whey-faced post mistress, who I don't recognize from my earlier life here, asks pointedly if she can help me. I push a packet of paracetamol and a plastic bottle of cola across the counter to her. She has just told me a price when I suddenly remember, and grab a tube of Rolos from the shelf. There is a faint click of her tongue against the roof of her mouth and she revises the figure. I give her a five pound note. She asks if I haven't any change, and tuts again when I apologize, saying I only have a note.

Outside, the skies have darkened, early morning sun now shrouded and dull. The wind whips grit against my cheeks as I cross the road. I take a detour on my way back to the car to find the village telephone box. It smells of stale urine and cigarette smoke, but the windows are intact, and at least it offers some shelter from the south-wester blowing in.

Some things don't change, I think, looking out through the smudged panes at the village street. I unscrew the cola bottle and push the chalky tablets from their silver blisters. The paracetamol is pebbles in my throat, the cola fizzy-sweet. I see Anna Riddaway, again, walking a small beige dog on a lead, shoulders hunched against the windy morning. I knock on the telephone box window as she passes, and she turns to look. Her face is very close to mine, through the glass: wide nose, small eyes, curranty in their basketwork of worry lines. I smile, even though the sparking pain between my neck and forehead has returned, even though smiling is the last thing I feel like doing. I smile so hard I feel my jaw will crack from the effort. And for a fleeting moment, Anna Riddaway cannot help herself. She lifts the corners of her mouth and smiles back, fraternizing with the enemy. Then she frowns, and is gone, tugging her dog away towards the park.

Things don't change unless you make them, I think, taking another swig of the sickly cola. I put it down on top of the telephone directory, reach into my pocket for loose change, pick up the phone, and dial.

It goes to answerphone, as usual. Helen is out, or call-screening. 'It's your mother,' I say. 'I've taken your advice and given Miranda a distraction, so Quill can't find her. But I've been thinking, things need to change. It's not right that you two aren't speaking. I can't bear it anymore, Helen. I just can't. So I'm going to fix things. I'm going to visit Jono.'

I hang up and walk out of the phone box into the windy day. I have helped Miranda get away from that awful man, I've got back in touch with Gwen, and I've even got Anna Riddaway to acknowledge me. I drain the last of the cola and put the bottle in the rubbish bin by the bench. I push through the rushing air to where my car is parked by the church wall. I look down at the crumpled metal on the wing. Ignoring the spasming twinge between my neck and forehead I get back into my damaged car and drive, turning left out of the village, towards Plymouth.

Cars can be mended, rifts can be healed, and families can be fixed too, can't they?

# Chapter 23

*Detta*

Detta checked her watch in the flickering candlelight. How long since she'd seen Tom, seen him for the last time? At some point she'd have to stop counting the minutes and give him up for good.

Wait, Frau Moll had said. Wait until the front passes through. For hours they'd sat in Father Richter's windowless study, under the stairs, listening to the interminable rumble-clatter of the German tanks heading towards Breslau, and the roar as Russian planes flew along the lines, gunning them down, even as they retreated. The sound of strafing was like an avalanche of stones on the manse roof.

Now there came an answering boom of anti-aircraft fire from the street outside, and the candle flames flickered. Father Richter clasped his hands tighter in prayer. Mother worried the rosary. Detta paced. Were they just to stay here like sitting ducks? To leave for the Schloss now would be madness, but being stuck here in the airless study brought its own insanity.

'I'm going to the bathroom,' Detta said, next time there was a pause in the relay of airborne machine-gunners.

'Are you sure?' Her mother looked up from the rosary.

'Better to go while it's quiet, no?'

Mother shrugged, face white and hopeless, and Detta left, picking up one of the candles from the desk. She closed the door behind her and turned right towards the stairs. The moving candlelight pooled and threw shadows as she went.

It got louder, colder and brighter as she climbed the stairs. When she reached the top step she realized why: there hadn't been time to shutter the upstairs windows before it started, and the one above the front door, where she'd sat with Tom that night – was it only last night? – had blown in. Shards of glass spangled the floorboards, reflecting the exploding sky. The smashed window let in the noise, and the bitter chill. Through the missing window she could also see the branches of the old beech tree, crackling with orange flame. The air tasted burnt.

Detta knew she ought to be quick, to take advantage of the lull in the fighting, but she couldn't help but inch towards the broken window, take a look out beyond the burning tree. She flattened herself against the side of the wall so as not to be seen.

Flames crawled over the Muller's rooftop, and the bakery was gone, nothing but rubble. The straggling line of tanks clattered up the street, with some men trudging alongside in weary escape. Detta edged closer to the window, shoes crunching on broken glass and splintered wood. She couldn't help but look, to her right, up the track. The French barracks were still standing, thank God. Surely they would have gone down to the cellar to shelter, wouldn't they? And soon he'd be free. As soon as this line of Panzers was replaced by T–34s. How soon would that be, she wondered? How many hours did she have left?

She felt in her pocket for the torn postcard. Maybe one day, somehow, they'd find a way to be reunited. But for now the angry night held him tight in its fist. She pulled her gaze away, biting her lip, telling herself she had to forget him, that the only thing she could afford to focus on right now was getting through this night alive.

But, just as she turned away, the sky tore apart with white fury and there was a deafening yell.

## Tom

A high-pitched scream tore through the dark sludge of his dreams and the ground juddered in response.

*Katyushas, non?*

*Oui, oui, ils ont pres d'ici.*

Banshee wails came again and again, followed by shuddering crashes. What was a Katyusha's range? How close was the Red Army now?

When the Russian planes started strafing the village they'd decamped into the barracks cellar, hauling palliases and blankets down the outside steps in the pauses between attacks. They spent the night shoved up against each other in the clammy darkness, passing round roll-ups, the tobacco cut with foul-smelling dried herbs to make it last. A bottle of vodka went round, too: just a few acid-sweet gulps each, but enough to take the edge off their fear and let them drift into semi-consciousness. The air smelled of smoke and stale piss, and was chill as a crypt, even with them all holed up down there.

There was a grille in the cellar wall, just at head height. Tom stood up and looked out. It was lit up like daylight out there. He checked his watch. He thought she'd made it back to the manse before the Russian planes began their shoot up. She was probably still alive. Probably. And if she were, was she awake in the manse, hearing the howling Red Army rockets, just like him? He wished he could hold her, and tell her it would all be all right, just as she'd held him when he'd had his nightmare last night – was it only last night?

Turning away from the rectangle of incandescent explosions, the cellar felt darker than ever, a blackness that pushed right in on his eyeballs as he blindly picked his way over the bodies of the other men and found his way to the cellar steps.

'Where the hell d'you think you're going?' He could barely hear Gordon's voice over the din.

'Nowhere. I'll be back soon.' The metal rail was cold under his palm. His boots scraped against the damp concrete stairs.

The stairwell came up beside the barracks' back door. It was louder out here – deafening. The streaming flares assaulted the eastern skies. He ran the few steps to the back door, pushed through. In the strobing brightness he saw a cup fall and break on the floor, the sound of it smashing masked by the tearing explosions outside. He ran through the kitchen and up the barracks stairs, back to the room they'd been in earlier, smoking Gordon's last cigarettes and watching the man whittling his stick. The windowpane had blown in: saw-edged shards glinted and shivered.

Coming up the street, just approaching the manse, was a single German Panzer tank. As he watched, one of the tanks paused, the gun turret swivelled, and fired a salvo before roaring off. It was almost parallel with the barracks when a single Katyusha rocket screeched over. Tom lost his footing as the whole place shook. Outside, a reverberating blast turned the tank into a huge orb of orange flame. Smoke belched through the broken window and the air was momentarily hot and burnt-tasting. 'Poor bastard,' Tom muttered, unable to hear his own voice over the ringing in his ears.

After that, the Katyushas paused their incessant screaming. He looked out through the empty window, past the quivering silhouettes of trees. The church had a chunk missing from the far end, like a bite from a sandwich. But the manse looked intact, thank God. He drew breath. The full moon dangled like a dog tag, but the eastern skies were turning paler, a line of rose-gold threading the edge of the snowy plains. It would be daybreak soon.

But then the silence was broken by a metallic clatter. Coming up the road from the east were two snaking columns of tanks. It was too far away to see clearly from here, but he knew that each one would be emblazoned with a Soviet star: the Russians at last.

The Red Army rumbled closer. He was as good as free, but when he thought of her, the thought of freedom felt like a betrayal.

He stood and watched as tanks, foot soldiers and trucks bulging with troops began thundering into the village, in a never-ending stream. Distant gunfire from the west rumbled, barely audible above the din of clanking tanks, roaring engines and jubilant Russian voices. Then, in the murky pre-dawn, shadows began to break free from the convoy and swarm into the remnants of the village houses. He heard shots and laughter carried on the icy air.

He imagined her there, waiting in the darkness, rigid with fear and numb with cold. He imagined the heavy thuds on the front door, the throaty Soviet shouts, and the hail of bullets splintering the oak door.

The world was still twilit and vague. He leant further out through the necklace of glass shards. The trees obscured his view but he thought he could make out figures at the front door already. But, coming out through the back, the way he and Gordon had escaped earlier, were three distinct shadows. They scurried through the graveyard. He could just about make out her scarf, trailing like a pennant, as she ran. They disappeared up through the trees. He exhaled. Of course. She'd said they'd go to the Schloss, join her friend with the ambulance, take their chances as the front passed through. Good luck and God speed, he thought.

# Chapter 24

**November 1989, Devon**

*Odette*

I gulp down the sense of panic I always feel in this place, with its slippery lino floors and institutional smell – the dreary dislocation of it all is so reminiscent of my own incarceration, all those years ago ...

I stop at the nurse's station on the way in and ask how Jono is getting on. I knock on the glass window, and the young nurse with the black-framed glasses looks up from the filing cabinet, smiles, and gestures for me to come in. The door to the medicine store is open, and I glimpse his colleague reaching to get something from the top shelf. The air is fuggy with old smoke, and there's a metal ashtray stuffed with butts next to the spider plant on the windowsill. The nurse says Jono's responding well to the new drugs. In good weeks he's been doing crosswords, he says, closing the filing cabinet. Not doing, creating, his older colleague calls out from the store room. She comes to stand in the doorway, hands on ample hips. Your son-in-law creates cryptic crosswords for one of the papers, she says. The *Sunday Correspondent*, that new one, calls himself Phaedrus, she adds.

'That's good, isn't it?' I say, looking from one to the other. The male nurse pushes his glasses up to the bridge of his nose and nods. The woman says that Jono is a clever man. She says it in an accusing way, chin thrusting, as if I underestimate my son-in-law's intellect. 'And has he had any problems with the paranoia or hearing voices recently?' I ask. The male nurse says no, he's been stable for a while now. 'I heard something on the radio about care in the community, halfway houses, that sort of thing . . .' My voice dithers – I realize now I'm here that I'm not quite sure what I'm asking for. I have a vague idea that if Jono is out of the mental institution then this will be a beginning of getting Helen and Miranda to speak to each other again, of reuniting their torn family.

But that painful pulse between my neck and forehead comes again, and it's hard to think or articulate clearly.

The female nurse says there's been a lot of nonsense written in the press about care in the community, and the man says it's something I'd have to take up with Jono himself, before making an approach to his consultant, and I thank them both and leave. It's a start, I think, beginning the long walk through the common room, up the stairs and along the corridor. At least I've flagged it up.

\*

'Hello Jono,' I say, walking across the ward towards the man sat on the neatly made bed. He looks up, and there's a flicker of recognition but he doesn't respond. In front of him, on a tray, is a half-finished jigsaw puzzle. There are three other beds in the room, but they are empty – their occupants must be downstairs watching TV.

Outside the window I see the leafless oaks tremble and jerk in the incoming gale, but inside is warm as a summer's day. 'How are you?' I say, now I'm closer. He doesn't answer, but looks at me, green eyes, receding ash-coloured curls, cheeks pale beneath a blue-ish haze of stubble. I sit down on the brown blanket beside him, careful not to disturb the jigsaw. Now I'm close I can see that it is a map of the world, with dozens of tiny pieces to slot into place. Africa, Asia and the Americas are mostly complete, but Europe is a jagged hole in the centre. I pick up a piece of jigsaw: plain blue, with four lugs. 'Can I help?'

'Why not?'

Someone turns a radio on in the next room, and chart hits are a tinny mosquito whine through the thin hospital wall. Some girl pop star singing about being lucky in love. 'Your nurse says you've been doing well recently,' I say, turning the jigsaw piece in my fingers. He nods. I see how his fingers quiver as he slots in a sliver of the Adriatic coastline.

I think about what the nurse said about him starting to create crosswords and selling them to the newspapers. Jono always was a clever man: clever, sensitive, and

223

good-looking, too, in his slender, boyish way. No wonder Helen fell for him. He led her astray at university, I suppose, but after her father died it was hardly surprising she went off the rails a bit. And Jono was a good dad to Miranda, for a while, before his mental health problems became fully apparent. If he's getting better now then maybe he could provide a steadying influence, a 'positive male role model', something to make her realize that there are good men around, that she deserves better than the one she ended up with in Berlin.

'The nurses say you're doing really well,' I repeat. 'I was wondering if we could start thinking of you moving out of here? If we talk to your consultant. What do you think?'

'Is she coming?' he says.

'Who?' I ask even though I know.

'Miranda.'

'No. She's in Berlin, taking photos.'

'But who's picking her up from school?'

'Nobody. She's grown up now, Jono.'

'Of course. I forgot.' He picks up a piece of Italy. The shake is more pronounced now. It is an effort for him to fit the piece into its place, but I resist the urge to help. 'I'd like to see more of her. But not her mother. Helen is still trying to poison me, you know.' He says it in such a dull voice, that I almost find myself nodding, as if he's just mentioned the weather, or something that's happened in an episode of *Eastenders*.

'She's never tried to poison you, Jono, you know it was just the—'

'I had a message last night.' He interrupts in that same flat, matter-of-fact voice. 'At the end of the six o'clock news. It was Michael Burke – of course he had to speak in code, but I understood. She's after me again.'

'No. No she's not, Jono.' The uncomfortable pump from neck to temple comes again, and I feel prickles of sweat on my hairline.

He sighs, pushing in pieces of the Alps, then glances up at me. 'I'm not stupid, Odette.' He grins, then, unexpected, small, white teeth, like milk teeth. And my heart pulls, because even after all these years, he's still the sweet young man my daughter fell in love with, and he's still Miranda's father. 'The sound's come back,' he says. 'It's my mind singing to me. I wish you could hear it, such a happy sound – a male voice choir, humming. Like a brain full of Welsh bees. You'd like it, because you like music, don't you?'

'Yes.' I nod. I feel like crying. It was stupid of me to think Jono was well enough to get out of this place, that having a functioning father figure again could somehow help my granddaughter.

He starts a tuneless whistle, that cuts across the muffled radio from the next room. I pick up my piece of blue jigsaw and slot it into the English Channel. Jono makes a start on Poland. I remember the packet of Rolos I have in my bag and give them to him, and he says thank you, and puts them under his pillow. Eventually the male nurse pops his head round the door and says it's time for me to leave. I kiss Jono on the cheek; he smells of soap powder and toothpaste, like a Monday morning schoolboy. He breaks off his whistle to say goodbye. The jigsaw is almost finished, just Germany left to complete.

In the corridor the nurse asks if everything is okay. He is measuring coloured pills into plastic pots on the trolley. I tell him that Jono is talking about brain noises, and messages through the TV again. He pulls out a clip-board, makes a note, and says he'll talk to the consultant about it. He thanks me for mentioning it and we smile and say goodbye.

I resist the urge to run as I get to the communal area, all those saggy-saliva mouths and dead-eyed stares swivelling as I pass through. The television is a loud, waspish buzz, the atmosphere thick and sweaty.

The plump nurse lets me out of the main door, and I lean a hand on the stonework at the top of the steps, paus-ing to draw in cool, fresh air. The pain pulses again and again, neck to forehead, like electric jolts. I didn't sleep well last night, worrying about Miranda, and there was the collision earlier on. It's just a mixture of exhaustion and mild whiplash, I think. What I need now is to go home and lie down in the cool darkness of my bedroom, and sleep.

I look up to my left. I can see Jono at the window, watch-ing, and I try to raise my arm to wave goodbye, but my hand is leaden-heavy. I cannot lift it.

## The Escape

In the car park my white Fiesta is just a few paces away, but it seems to recede as I look. There is a sudden inverse pressure, air being sucked out. I see a black halo round everything, and hear a high-pitched ringing in my ears. Then my leg gives, and I crumple to the ground.

# Chapter 25

**January 1945, Nazi Germany**

*Tom*

Where was the gushing relief at his imminent liberation? There was nothing but the sour sting of grief in his throat at the thought of losing her, of what would happen to her. He watched from the window, waiting. The litmus dawn spread pink into navy overhead, and silhouettes came slowly into focus with the daybreak: the bottle-brush trees, the torn edge of the church with its onion-shaped spire. She would be up there somewhere, beyond the church, through the trees: Detta, her mother, the priest and the others, packing themselves into the ambulance, ready for their flight. Then she'd be gone, for ever. He thrust a hand into his pocket and felt the edge of the ripped postcard. He felt like that: torn apart. What were the chances they'd manage to find each other again? If only she weren't German. If only he could take her with him, keep her safe. He stared out at the black outline of the church, clenching his jaw.

Distant ordnance still boomed, and from the road came shouting and the sounds of military traffic. He looked, but could see no sign of an ambulance careering past. And what would he do if he saw it – wave like an impotent idiot? He turned away from the window and went back down to the cellar.

In the stinking darkness he felt more trapped than he'd ever felt as a PoW. 'I retrieved this whilst you were out on your little stroll.' Gordon handed him back his RAF jacket, ripped from its hiding place in one of the palliases. There was a swish of cloth as Tom slipped it on, in readiness for meeting the Russians. The guttering candlelight glanced off the gilded edges of the insignia. He touched the uniform badge, above his heart. *Per Ardua Ad Astra* – through adversity to the stars, whatever the hell that meant.

'Thought we'd lost you for a moment there, old man,' Gordon said. 'Gone AWOL on me.'

'What?'

'Thought you'd gone to make an honest woman of her.'

'What are you talking about?'

'The girl, the priest, the church – all you were lacking was the best man, and given the circumstances I would have understood if you'd gone and done it without me.'

The realization struck Tom with sudden force. 'You're right. Christ, I'm an idiot!' And, grabbing his coat, he pelted up the cellar steps.

There was a priest, a church, and the woman he loved. He thought he'd have to wait until the war was over, wait for her letter, then come out to Europe to find her and bring her home. But no, he could marry her now, take her with him, keep her safe. If it wasn't too late already?

## Detta

'At last!' Frau Moll called from the cab, as the engine finally stuttered to life. Detta heard the Moll girls clapping from inside the ambulance. Through the passenger window she saw Father Richter make the sign of the cross and roll his eyes heavenwards. She, Mother and Father Richter had just made it out of the manse before the Red Army arrived. When they got to the Schloss Frau Moll was ready to go, but the vehicle wouldn't start.

Luckily Mother had some knowledge from her time as a driver in the last war. Now, she straightened up from under the hood, wiping her hands on her coat. 'Come on, then,' she said, and Detta slammed the bonnet shut. But as she did, the engine died again. Frau Moll turned the ignition. The engine choked. 'Stop, stop!' Mother gestured at Frau Moll through the windscreen. 'If you keep doing that, it'll flood. We'll have to wait a couple of minutes.'

'We don't have a couple of minutes!'

'I'm telling you, if you keep trying to start it like that, it will just make it worse, and then we really will end up stuck here.'

'But the Reds could be on their way.'

'They won't be. Not yet.'

'How can you know that?'

230

'The infantry will pass through the village like a plague, but they won't trouble themselves with walking through the woods and up the hill, they'll be keen to keep going on to Breslau while the weather holds.'

'And what makes you an expert in military strategy? I've got my daughters to think about!'

'Ladies,' Father Richter's low tones interjected. 'Can I ask for calm?'

'No, Father, you cannot!'

Detta turned away from the quarrel. Beyond the Schloss, beyond the treeline, beyond the Oder river, the sun was already rising: red–gold and angry, shooting out livid orange skeins of high cloud above the Eastern skies. The stars were fading. Soon it would be daylight.

Last night she'd kissed Tom – kissed him properly – for the first time. Would it be the last?

He'd told her he loved her, and she hadn't responded. Why hadn't she told him she loved him, too? Now it was too late.

She span her body away from the sunrise to look down through the trees towards the French barracks. It had survived the Katyusha barrage. He was safe, just there, down the snowy hill, not more than a few hundred steps away, through the silver birch and firs.

'Are we going now, Maman?' one of the Moll girls called from the back of the ambulance.

'Soon, darling. As soon as we can get this thing going again,' Frau Moll called back.

\*

231

Detta felt oddly detached, as if she were viewing them all from up in a mistletoe ball, looking down at the van with the red cross on the side, the black-robed priest in the passenger seat, the panic-faced women, shouting through the glass windscreen at each other, and the girl with the blue scarf, a splash of sky against the snow. They all looked very small, far below.

Any moment now the ambulance would cough back to life, the girl with the blue scarf would get inside with the others, and they'd be gone, driving along the estate road, turning past the barracks, and away.

She could hear Mother and Frau Moll yelling at each other, the judder-rumble of tanks through the village, and the twitter of birdsong from high up in the trees but it was all muffled, as if heard through glass, as if her whole little world were captured inside a snowglobe, and she was outside, looking in, ready to shake it up.

Then with a rush, she was back inside herself, the cold biting her forehead, and the Moll girls calling from the ambulance: come inside with us, Fräulein Detta, it's time to go! She took a step towards the vehicle, ready to get inside with the little girls. She would be in the back with them for the journey, so she wouldn't see the barracks as they passed by. She wouldn't see if Tom were standing at a window to wave goodbye, and they wouldn't stop, so she couldn't tell him – why hadn't she told him when she had the chance? – that she loved him.

There was a feeling, then, like the panic-tug she'd felt that last morning in work at the Reichsbahn office, when she saw the Russian bombers fly overhead. She'd listened to the pull in her gut that morning, and it had taken her running to safety to catch the last train across the Oder. What was it telling her to do now?

*Come on Detta, get in!* The call came from the back of the van.

There it was again, that inner clench, like homesickness. But not for a place, she realized, for a person. For Tom. 'I'm going,' Detta said, turning on her heel.

'You're what?' Her mother looked up from under the hood, frowning.

'By the time you've got the engine going, and driven all the way round by the estate road, I'll be ready,' she said. 'I'll meet you outside the barracks in five minutes.'

'You can't, it's not safe!'

But Detta was already gone. She heard her mother's voice dwindle as she ran, feet slipping through the crusted snow. 'Just five minutes,' she called out, holding her splayed fingers in the air as she ran. 'I'll see you outside the barracks in five minutes.'

Five minutes: enough time to tell Tom she loved him, to kiss him, just one last time. Five minutes was no time at all: they'd still be able to get away safely, wouldn't they?

## Tom

The air was sharp as a razor's edge. The night was beginning to lift, stars fading into blue. He hurried up the slippery path between the trees. He could just make out a large building

233

with a curved portico and steps. That must be the Schloss, mustn't it? He needed to reach her before they set off. He broke into a run, feet sinking through the ice and into the powder snow. It was as effortful as running through sand dunes. What could he say? Don't go – come with me to England. It was stupid, audacious, reckless. It could never work. She'd say no. He had to try. Afterwards – if there were an afterwards – he could tell himself that at least he damn well gave it his best shot. That was all.

Lost in a swirl of thoughts, pushing through the drifts, chest heaving, he looked up to check the way. And there, through the trees, someone was running down the hill towards him. Someone in a fur coat, with a blue scarf flapping free from her pale face: it was her.

She was there.

'I was coming to find you.'

'I couldn't leave without saying goodbye.'

'I love you.'

'I love you, too.'

'How long have we got?'

'No time – they're just starting the ambulance now.' Her skin was cold as porcelain, as his lips touched hers. She spoke through kisses. 'I ran. They tried to stop me, but I told them to pick me up at the barracks. We've got as long as it takes them to drive round along the estate road, that's all.' She took his hand, tugged him back in the direction he'd come from. 'I can't make them wait any longer, it's not safe. We have to go now.'

'Marry me.'

'I wish I could.'

'The church is right there. There's a priest driving down the road and there are two witnesses with him.' The words spilled without thought, but they made sense, complete and utter sense. If they were married she could stay with him; he could take her back home to safety. 'It will only take a couple of minutes to do. Come back to England with me, as my wife.' He could see it now. There were to be no best suits or confetti, not even a ring, just a few snatched moments in a war-ravaged church.

'You're mad.'

'And you call all this sanity? It's a chance, don't you see? It's the only chance we've got.'

They paused, as he gestured round at the shattered village below them, the line of tanks rumbling on through.

He saw her lips part, ready to respond.

## Detta

She was here, between the Schloss and the manse, just as she had been when she'd seen him stagger through the blizzard supporting his colleague. It was the same, but utterly different, here on the path with the man she should have known she was in love with from the outset. He had asked her – impossibly, wonderfully – to marry him. His blue eyes searched her face.

And she was about to say yes, surrender to his barrage of kisses, when she noticed something: a black dash scudding in her peripheral vision. A bird? There was a sound, too, a whining drone that tore through the air.

'Drop,' he yelled, but she was down before the words left his lips, snow shoved up her nostrils, grit on her cheek. The plane screamed through, spraying bullets that whizzed like angry hornets. She could feel his body next to hers as the sound veered away. She half-sat up to watch where it went. The dirty snow stung as she wiped it from her eyes.

The plane hadn't been aiming for them. It flew along the length of the village street, and down the tank columns, picking off the foot-soldiers and infantry-stuffed trucks. Machine-gun fire crackled like burning twigs. She looked back at him. He lay quite still. His eyes were closed.

'Tom?'

'Your lot picked their moment to do a counter-attack,' he said, getting up in one swift movement, reaching down a hand to help her. They heard returning fire from the Russian troops, saw the German plane bank and turn, a black bow in the Prussian blue sky. 'Buggers are coming back for another go. Better make a run for it.'

They sprinted downhill towards the barracks: slipping, ricocheting from tree to tree, tumbling down the concrete cellar steps, and falling inside.

Her breath burned in her throat, heartbeat a speeding train. The faces of the Frenchmen were pale blobs in the gloom. There were shouts and the sound of metal clanging from the main road as anti-aircraft guns were positioned.

The plane's bullets sounded like sudden hail, a summer storm passing overhead.

'You okay?'

She nodded, unable to speak.

'Detta, answer me. Are you all right?'

'Yes,' she said, realizing that he couldn't see her nod, waiting for her eyes to adjust to the dark.

'Busy out?' Gordon shouted from somewhere across the cellar.

'Nazi counter-attack. But just one plane, by the looks of it.'

They picked over supine bodies, some snoring, oblivious to the battle going on outside, and found their way to Gordon, who shifted up to give them space next to him on the straw-filled mattress. Her eyes adjusted to the darkness.

Gordon had the remnants of a candle burning next to him on the concrete floor, and was shading in a Union Jack on a large piece of cardboard. 'Let them get on with it all out there for a bit longer. Gives me more time to finish this,' he said. 'Which should have been your job, seeing as you're the artist.'

'Thought I'd let you have a turn, for a change,' Tom replied.

Detta thought of Mother and the others. Had they managed to start the ambulance? Had they taken cover when the plane flew over or driven away? Tom put an arm round her and she let her head rest on his shoulder, blocking one ear, so the stammer of the guns wasn't as loud, and that side of her face felt warm and safe.

Eventually the sounds died down. She thought that surely Mother and the others must be coming now, and made a move to get up and go to find them. She was just turning to say a final, awful goodbye to Tom – it must surely be too late for the reckless wedding plan? – but just as she stood, there was banging on the cellar door, and the shout of a Russian voice.

'Quick, Detta!' Tom grabbed her and bundled her into the triangular hole under the stairwell. The men had been using one side of it as a temporary toilet. She huddled in the opposite corner, gagging at the smell. Tom and Gordon shoved the mattress in front, and Gordon leant his back against her – in the darkness it would have looked as if he were just sitting up against the wall. Someone blew out the candle, and she couldn't see anything except the faint grey-pink smudge of Gordon's neck. There was the stench of old urine, and the loud Russian voice echoing inside the dank cellar walls as the door opened above her head.

He spoke first in Russian, but then in heavily accented German as his footsteps descended the steps: '*Fransosich?*'

'*Oui, oui,*' the Frenchmen chorused. His footfalls continued. She counted eight, nine . . . He was almost at the bottom.

'And British,' Gordon called out.

'British? How many?'

'Two. RAF,' Tom chipped in.

Detta heard a shuffle as Tom got up, meeting the Russian on the lowest step. 'Ah, RAF.'

'Yes, I'm Warrant Officer Jenkins and over there is Flight Sergeant Harper, my skipper.'

'Warrant Officer?'

'Yes, it's like a Sergeant Major rank in the army.'

'Ah, ma-jori! Ma-jori Jenkins.' They must be shaking hands, she thought. 'Come.'

Two sets of footsteps began tramping up the steps, above her hiding place. 'He thinks I'm in charge, thinks I'm a major. I've got to go,' Tom's voice called down.

'Let's say it's a field promotion, acting rank only,' Gordon said. 'Enjoy your new position. But don't be too long, eh?'

'No, I'll be back soon, I promise.' Tom raised his voice as he replied, for her benefit, Detta was certain. Then there were more footsteps and the sound of the cellar door opening and slamming shut. He was gone.

She nudged at Gordon's back. 'Let me out.'

'It's not safe. What if more Russians come and see you? You need to stay where you are, I'm afraid.' He shunted back against her. She shoved him, then, hard as she could. He grunted, more in surprise than pain, as she pushed past him and stood up. The darkness span, but she ignored her dizziness and reached out, stumbling over bodies on the floor. 'Wait!' Gordon yelled, but she was too fast for him.

She reached the concrete stairs and began to climb. She had to get out, had to find her mother and the others. But just as she reached the top step the cellar door slammed open again.

It was too late to run back and hide.

# Chapter 26

## November, 1989, East Germany

*Miranda*

*'Aufstehen Sie, sofort!'* Get up immediately!

I open my eyes, squint to focus: peeling paint, high-up frosted window, tiny sink and unlidded toilet, a rough grey blanket edge, the whole room no bigger than a double bed. Room? No, cell. I remember now. I am in a cell at the Stasi HQ in Frankfurt an der Oder.

*'Schnell!'* The guard bangs on the other side of the door. I see his dark eye and the greyish-pink square of his razored cheek through the peephole in the airlock-thick metal door. I stand, rubbing my eyes, mouth dry, head swimming. The door opens and a hand reaches in and grabs my upper arm. I'm drunk with exhaustion and dread.

Our shoes make plasticky noises on the lino, and the air smells of old men. I'm not sure how many times I have walked this walk already – four, five times, or more? They don't let me sleep in between questioning. Each time my eyes close, the guard bangs the door. If I don't respond he enters, shakes me awake. They took my watch off me when I arrived, along with my other things. I can't tell how long I've been here, or even if this is the same guard.

The walls are painted three-quarters up with gun-metal grey, only the tops of the doors and the ceiling are creamy-white, like a head on a pint of beer. Doors are shut, close-lidded, unseeing, on either side, except for one, further along to my right. As we pass, I glimpse a man feeding the contents of an open filing cabinet into a buzzing paper shredder. A telephone rings but nobody answers it. The guard sees me looking.

'Eyes to the floor. Walk on.' He tightens his grip on my arm as we pass the open doorway. Should I feel violated by his bruising fingers? The truth is, I'm grateful. I'm now so weak with hunger and lack of sleep that I need his support. We reach the door halfway down the corridor, on the left, with the red light above it, which flickers to life at his knock.

'Enter,' says a voice.

'Address him as Captain,' says the guard, opening the door, releasing his grip, and hustling me ahead of him inside the room. A seated man fiddles with something in his desk drawer and clicks it shut at my approach. He doesn't get up.

'Hands under your thighs, palms down.' The seated man – Captain – gestures to the empty chair in front of the desk. I sit as I have been told.

He is clean shaven, greying hair shorn to disguise the bald patch, with not one single distinguishing feature in his stony

241

face. He could be any middle-aged, middle manager anywhere: a bureaucrat in a suit, a college lecturer in jeans and
a jumper, a dentist in a white coat. But he is none of these
things. He has the shiny epaulettes and grey wool jacket of
a Stasi officer.

He thinks – they think – that I am some kind of spy. I
had a camera, a map, and I was caught taking photographs,
at night, of a Russian armaments train. I have no ID. In
the confusion of capture, instead of sticking to speaking
English, and pretending not to understand, I responded in
German – the good German taught me by my grandmother,
with an East German accent. I can see how it looks, and I
have nothing to prove them wrong. I tell them to contact the
British Embassy in East Berlin, where my emergency travel
documents are being processed. But the Embassy is closed
for the weekend. And anyway, they say, they don't believe
me. So the questioning continues:

'What have you to tell us, Fräulein?'

'I have done nothing, Captain.'

'You think we imprison people on a whim?'

'No, but—'

And so it goes. The same as the last four – five, or more? –
occasions: what was I doing taking photographs of a Russian
train? Who am I working for? Who do I report to?

I say I am just a photography student, getting photos for
my portfolio. I didn't realize what I was doing. I talk about
the moonlight, the smoke, the barbed wire and the bird . . .

'Nonsense.' He says British students don't speak German

this well, don't have East German accents, don't take study trips mid-term.

I tell him I lost my passport.

'Then how did you come through to the East without ID?'

'I walked through a gap in the Wall,' I say. A flicker passes his face as I say this and he takes a drag of the cigarette that lies half-burnt in the metal ashtray.

'Ridiculous,' he says. 'The part of the Wall that was reported as damaged has been replaced and is occupied by border guards.' He exhales. Smoke hangs in the air between us. I say I lost my passport in West Berlin, then walked through a vandalized piece of the Wall and reported my missing passport in East Berlin.

'But why? Even if it's true that you're a student with a lost passport, why would you run to the East, and come here? There are more holes in your story than a sieve, Fräulein.' The almost-finished cigarette smoulders on in the ashtray.

I tell him that I've come to try to find my grandmother's old house, it's in a village called Lossen, somewhere near Breslau. Does he know it? He smirks. 'Breslau does not exist,' he says. It is in Poland and is called something else now. And how could I hope to get to Poland without a passport?

He seems to get angry, then stubs out the remains of his cigarette and half rises from his chair. I am a stupid little girl. Do I want to start World War Three?

'Do you realize how delicate the situation is at present?'

'Yes,' I say. 'No.'

I confuse myself. 'No, I don't want to start World War

Three. Yes. I realize how delicate the situation is.' But do I? What is going on outside this office, out in the real world, in real time? I think of the man pushing paperwork into the shredder, and the unanswered phone, ringing off the hook.

I ask about my camera. He says it is impounded as evidence. No, of course I cannot have it back.

He sits back in his chair and sighs. 'You will tell the truth in the end, Fräulein. Everyone always gives way eventually. Are you worried about betraying your superiors, perhaps? But could betrayal mean freedom? Think about that, Fräulein.' He tells the guard to take me away and I am marched back to my cell.

And so I continue to be shunted, starving, thirsty, sleepless, between my cell and his office. How long between each interrogation? An hour, two? I don't know. There are no clocks. All the curtains are closed, there's no daylight. I lose all track of time. My head is thick as lard. I am so cold and angry. It is pointless telling the truth because nobody believes it. Why can't I sleep?

Back again: hours, days, later, I can't tell. The same stupid question:

*What have you to tell us?*

Nothing. Let me sleep.

*What have you to tell us?*

The Wall is coming down.

*What have you to tell us?*

Why don't you believe me?

*What have you to tell us?*

I hate what I have become.

*What have you to tell us?*

I feel alone in crowds.

*What have you to tell us?*

My boyfriend hurt me.

*What have you to tell us?*

My father was a junkie. It turned him insane.

An angry confessional, a shivering delirium. I shout my answers. The tape is running. The man making notes on a pad. I don't care. I don't even know where I am anymore.

*What have you to tell us?*

He had a bad trip, and I found him. I found him. I called the ambulance. And you know what my mother said? He'll be fine. He'll be home before you know it. Daddy will be fine: the biggest fucking lie of the many lies she's told. He wasn't fine. He never came back.

*What have you to tell us?*

My boyfriend is a drug dealer. He's not my boyfriend anymore.

*What have you to tell us?*

He says he's just selling a lifestyle choice. My father made a lifestyle choice and look what happened to him. Look what happened to him! Are you writing this down? Are you? Because somebody should. Nobody else gives a fuck.

*What have you to tell us?*

It's all set up, you know. The journalism is just a front. I am part of his cover. So that's the truth, okay? I'm here as cover for my drug-dealing boyfriend so he can turn the whole of the GDR into cocaine guzzling monkeys the moment the Wall comes down. Okay? That what you want to hear?

I am still shouting when the telephone on the desk rings. I yell – what, I barely know – ranting like a lunatic. I see the Stasi officer mouth a response into the receiver, hang up the telephone, frown at me.

I am screaming, rising to my feet, pointing at the bruise on my temple, calling out how ironic it is that 'You Stasi idiots actually treat me better than the man who said he loved me!'

I see the captain lift a hand and bang it down, flat on the desk. The telephone jingle-jolts. I shut up then. 'The guilty ones merely cry and repeat their stock phrases,' he says. 'Only the innocent get angry. And we have just received corroboration of your ridiculous story.' He smiles then, looking like someone's kind uncle. 'For you, it's over. You are free to go, Fräulein.'

# Chapter 27

**January 1945, Liberated Germany**

*Tom*

Sunlight exploded onto his face as he emerged from the darkness of the cellar. To his right, behind the lines of trees, the military traffic growled along the main street. Above the remains of the village wispy trails of black smoke curled up into the empty blue sky. The cold air bit his bare cheeks and his feet slithered on the icy path as he walked alongside the Russian major, past the church, with the chunk taken out of the transept.

'Field HQ,' the major said, gesturing at the manse.

'Your HQ?' How soon everything had changed. Only yesterday he'd been hiding from the Nazis there, now it was a Russian headquarters.

'For today, only. Tomorrow, maybe Breslau.' Tom glanced sideways and caught the major's smile. The Red Army were proud of the rate of their advance into Nazi Germany. There was no stopping them now.

'And Berlin?' Tom said. 'How soon until you take Berlin?'

'Soon.' The major's smile slipped, and a look of determination froze his angular features. 'Very soon.'

As they approached the manse, Tom noticed the old beech tree in front of it was blackened, cauterized, still smouldering. His nostrils filled with the acrid smell of it. The major ushered him ahead, and they went inside.

Already the place was irrevocably changed: windows blown in, shattered glass on the lino, the faint stench of excrement. A single brown leather boot lay discarded at the foot of the stairwell, halfway up a few items of male underwear hung draped from the bannisters in a dreary striptease. Pictures had been ripped from the wall and smashed. The vase of dried roses in the hallway was gone.

Perhaps the Russian major saw the shock on Tom's face. In any case, he seemed to feel the need to explain. 'The men, they have nothing. The soldiers' pay is not good. When we win, they take.' He shrugged, as if forgiving naughty children who'd had their hands in the biscuit tin.

'They are allowed to take everything?' Tom said.

'They are poor. They have nothing, so they take.' The major made grabbing motions with his hands, and shrugged again.

Tom thought of Detta then. These conquering Red Army infantiers were free to take with impunity. And would the 'taking' include the taking of women, the fleeting thrill of violent pleasure? Of course it would.

He told himself to calm down. Detta was hidden in the cellar with Gordon. She'd be fine, wouldn't she?

## Detta

He held her hand as he said it, and lifted it to his lips, not in the flirtatious way he usually did, but with sad tenderness: *'Je suis désolé.'*

'I don't believe it. They're coming for me. They'll be here any moment. You must be mistaken, Jean-Paul.'

'No, no, we saw them. It was definitely them, wasn't it, Henri?' His friend nodded. Two skinny women stood behind them in the doorway, wide-eyed and shivering. Jean-Paul explained that he and Henri had taken advantage in the lull in the fighting as the front line passed through the village to make a dash back from the farmstead with their Polish girlfriends. Like Detta, they'd had to dive for cover when the German plane flew over, spraying bullets. They were coming across the football field. He said the ambulance was in the back lane, at the junction with the main road, beside the old stable block, its engine running. A priest and a woman in a green coat got out. 'It looked as if they were about to run across the road to the barracks when the plane came. They dropped to the ground. But afterwards, they didn't get up. We passed close by the bodies. It was definitely them.'

'Yes it was. I'm sorry,' Henri said.

'But it can't be true.'

'We both saw. I'm so sorry.' Jean-Paul let go of her hand. The two women shuffled silently down the steps beside her and on down into the darkness, and the men followed on behind.

'Detta, please come back,' Gordon called from the cellar below. But the door was still ajar. Detta stepped out into the cold and slammed it shut behind her. The sun was fully up and her eyes squinted in the sudden glare. She turned right, almost blinded by the flash of sunlight on snow, keeping her right hand on the cellar wall to guide her: round the corner, behind the line of trees, parallel to the main road. She paused in the bright, brittle air, taking it in. As her eyes adjusted, she saw. The village, as she knew it, was gone. Houses and shops bore the scars of last night, their walls pock-marked and crumbling, windows and doors blown in. Some, like the bakery, were just reduced to rubble. Others, like the Muller Farm, had collapsed, rooftops smouldering. Through the treeline, along the main road, she saw two columns of tanks with red stars painted on their sides, ragged-looking infantry soldiers jogging alongside. Choking exhaust fumes rose to meet the icy-clear skies.

She heard the cellar door bang open, and Gordon's voice calling her, but she ignored him and carried on walking the line between the side of the barrack block and the beech trees.

Jean-Paul said the ambulance had stopped up the street, beyond the barracks. Perhaps it was still there? But the road was filled with the clatter and stink of the military traffic and it was impossible to see clearly past the stable block to the junction with the estate road.

She paused, scanning along the moving mass of men and machines, looking for a glimpse of a red cross on the side of a vehicle, or the dark green of her mother's coat. One of the soldiers spotted her, and ran over, yelling something incomprehensible. His grimy face was flushed, sweat beaded his black brows. Detta shrugged and shook her head to show she didn't understand what he was asking. But he yelled again, jabbing a finger at his left forearm, as if wanting to know the time. Detta pushed back her coat sleeve to reveal her wrist watch. The glass glinted as she angled the face towards him so he could read it. But he just grabbed her wrist, put a finger under the watch's gold band and ripped it off, laughing as he stuffed it in his pocket and ran back to join his comrades.

Stunned, Detta just stood still, seeing him go. The watch had been a gift from her mother following her first communion. At the thought she jolted back into herself: Mother. She had to find out if what Jean-Paul said was true.

She turned left and along the tree-lined verge until she reached the old stable block. She was just lifting her leg to step over what she assumed was a fallen tree branch, when she looked down, and saw a face.

She leant over. There, looking up from the mud beside a storm ditch, was the face of a boy. He had wide grey eyes, staring up at the sky with a surprised expression. He had a tip-tilted nose, and on his cheeks, the livid pink speckle of adolescent acne. From the waist down, his body no longer existed, mangled into mush beneath tank tracks. His Wehrmacht helmet had slipped to one side a little. Out of respect, Detta bent down to straighten it up. As she touched it, it slid off, rolling away to reveal a red-grey slimy mass.

The boy's face was intact, but the rest of his skull had been blown clean away.

She withdrew her trembling fingers, straightened up, gulping down choking bile. Then she stepped over the corpse, as if it really had been nothing more than a fallen branch in her way. To allow the Red Army infantiers to see her weeping over the body of a Wehrmacht soldier would have been inviting a bullet.

She staggered a few steps forward and leant against the edge of the mounting block next to the old stables, telling herself to breathe and calm down. If the Frenchmen were right, then she'd be able to see the bodies soon. Perhaps they were mistaken, and it wasn't Mother and Father Richter at all. Or if it were, they might still be alive, able to be saved. The tanks still rumbled relentlessly onwards. As she paused, she noticed a Russian soldier, urinating against one of the trees a few paces along. She turned away, but not before he'd seen her looking at him.

She pushed her sleeves up, showing her empty wrists, proving she had nothing for him. He left his fly undone and swaggered over to where she stood, saying something in Russian. He was short and stocky, with ammunition draped over his shoulders and a bayonet slung at his waist. She made a move to cross the road but he yelled '*Stoy!*' and lifted his weapon. As he came closer she could see that his uniform was bedraggled and filthy, one flap missing from his fur cap. He said something else in Russian and made a gesture with the gun, shoving his face in close. He had high cheekbones and sinkhole eyes. His breath reeked of alcohol. She didn't need to understand Russian to know that he wanted her to go into the stables with him.

'*Nyet*,' she said. No. Just about the only Russian word she knew. But he took no notice and prodded her in the ribs with the gun. She winced and repeated '*Nyet*,' casting her eyes round for someone to help her. But there was just the endless thunder of the passing tanks, the swirl of choking exhaust fumes, the onward thrust towards the next battle. Nobody took any notice of the local girl saying 'no' as the drunken soldier lifted his gun.

'*Je suis française!*' she yelled in desperation, shaking her head. If he thought she was French he might not attack her. It was the Germans they hated, wasn't it? '*Je suis—*'

The gun hit her hard and swift in the solar plexus. She fell back, winded, landing awkwardly against the mounting block, legs splayed, unable to breathe, unable to move.

The soldier had just dropped his gun on the ground and was reaching towards her when one of the tanks veered up onto the verge beside them, glancing off a tree trunk. The turret hatch flew open and the commander's head appeared. The soldier paused, turned to look. The commander took off the helmet and goggles and a shock of fair hair tumbled out from underneath. There was the sound of a woman shouting in Russian.

She roared at the soldier, pointed at the discarded weapon and his undone fly, gestured up the Breslau road. He didn't move, at first, until the tank turret swivelled round, until the gun barrel pointed directly at his head. The commander barked and gesticulated some more until the soldier did up his fly and picked up his weapon.

Before he left, he spat in the snow, a thick green–grey clot, right at Detta's feet. Then he went, away up the road with the others, lost in the machinery of war.

The commander put her helmet and goggles back on, nodded at Detta, withdrew into the T-34, slammed the turret shut, and swivelled back onto the road to join the rest of the column.

'. . . *française*,' Detta said, having breath now to finish her sentence. She stood up, pushed her skirt back down.

*'Je suis française,'* she repeated, pulling her German ID documents from her pockets and tearing them into tiny pieces. She let the torn strips flutter down into the place where the Russian soldier had spat, stamping them underfoot, so they mixed in with the dirty slush and his phlegm.

All that was left in her pocket now was a torn postcard, with an address in England written in pencil. She folded her arms to stop herself from shaking, her mind empty of all thought. *'Je suis française.'* She repeated it to herself under her breath, as she carried on walking, past the stable block, to the junction where the estate road joined the main road to Breslau. *'Je m'appelle Odette, et je suis française.'*

### Tom

'So, what do you need from me?' Tom said.

'First, we drink.' The major indicated the open door of the priest's old study. The books were still there, although they'd

254

been pulled off the shelves and were strewn on the floor. The picture of the Virgin Mary had been wrenched from the wall and lay near the desk, glass smashed, a footprint across her impassive face. 'Here, to your freedom!' Tom realized the major was handing him a hip flask. He took a swig. Fire ran down his throat and ignited his insides. It was the strongest vodka he'd ever had. He made a face. The major laughed, took the flask from him and gulped down some himself, smacking his lips and wiping his moustache on his sleeve. Then he raised the flask in the air. 'To Stalin!' he said, taking another gulp and passing the flask back to Tom.

'Stalin!' Tom echoed, and took another swig.

After that, the major had him fill in a form with his name, rank and number, and Gordon's too.

'Two British prisoners only?' he said, checking the details.

'Two,' Tom nodded, thinking of Detta. If only there had been time to marry her, and claim her as British. If only there were a way to keep her safe. 'We can go home – to England – now?'

'Yes, yes. Allies go home. Today. Transport is coming.'

'Can I go back now? My colleague will be wondering where I am.' (What about Detta, how the hell was he going to keep her safe if he was being sent home?)

'Yes, yes, ma-jor-i. I come with you. I need – how you say – head count. How many French workers.'

'You're repatriating the forced workers, too?'

'Repeat please.'

'The French workers – you are sending them home?'

255

'Yes, yes, they go in truck with you.'

So he and Gordon were to be sent east on transport with the French. Tom's mind began to work.

They left the manse and went out into the aching-bright sunshine together, back up the path past the wounded church, towards the French barracks. As they got closer he could see that Gordon stood in the cellar doorway, his cardboard Union Jack dangling from one hand, the other shading his brow as he looked out across the ruined village.

He seemed to be looking for something. As if something – or someone – was lost.

# Chapter 28

**November 1989, Frankfurt an der Oder, East Germany**

*Miranda*

Somewhere a bell chimes. I adjust the rucksack on my back. It is lighter than it was. The Stasi have kept my Leica and film as 'evidence'. I would be angrier if I had the energy but I'm just relieved the ordeal is over. At least they left the Rolleiflex, perhaps thinking that it is just a bit of antique junk. I can feel the bulge of the old camera prodding the base of my spine through the fabric. I take a breath, the air a cold catch in my throat.

I'm free to go, they said, shoving me out of the metal doors. But free to go where? I look at my surroundings. Beyond the scrubby park and the wide street a hypodermic church spire pricks the dark underbelly of the clouds. It's twilight already. Streetlights droop like snowdrops.

I try to force my wrung-out brain to make a plan, but it is all I can do to make my legs move forward along a path between trees like upturned witches' brooms. A woman in orange trousers and a black fur coat sits on one of the park benches smoking a cigarette. As I get closer I see her coiffed poodle sniffing at a metal litter bin and cocking his leg.

I ask the woman if there are any hotels or guesthouses nearby, thinking only of the need for food and sleep. She gestures with her cigarette: the Stadt Hotel is just down Karl-Marx Strasse, she says, past the Oderturm, see it? She points at a rectangular tower, head and shoulders above the other city blocks. It's on the far side of Brunnenplatz, past the fountains, you can't miss it, she says. I thank her and walk on, remembering the last time I stayed in a hotel.

Not long after we met, Quill took me for a weekend at the Salcombe Hotel, on the South Devon coast. He had part ownership of a yacht with a friend of his, who was due to be bringing it into port after a transatlantic trip (now I realize how naive I was, not to have made the link between Quill's five-star lifestyle and the fact his yacht regularly criss-crossed the Atlantic between South America and Europe). That weekend we had candle-lit suppers, long afternoons in bed, stroking skin and hair, dozing when we felt like it, waking up with kisses, murmuring endearments, making impractical plans about our future. I even remember discussing what we'd call our children.

My throat tightens but I hold back the tears. What's the point?

I've reached the edge of the park now, and turn right along Karl-Marx Strasse. A tram skids to a halt beside me. The automatic doors disgorge a squat man with a brown belted PVC jacket, carrying an empty string bag. The doors snap shut and the tram careers away, clanging along rails embedded in the cobbles. As the man brushes past me, I see his pale, sagged cheeks and the bruised shadows beneath his eyes. My face probably looks like that too: ground down and exhausted. I walk on towards the junction. On the opposite side of the street, a pale blue chimney pokes up from behind featureless grey buildings. Smoke plumes upwards, and I'm reminded of Gran's slender pastel-coloured cocktail cigarettes.

At the junction with Logenstrasse a white-gloved traffic cop twirls his baton like a conductor, the orchestra his traffic: the stuttering two-stroke Trabants, bass notes of Wartburgs, roaring motorbikes, rattle of trams, screech of brakes. I think of Berlin, the gridlocked lines of cars either side of the newly opened checkpoints. You'd have thought all the vehicles in East Germany were being sucked West through the plughole of the Berlin Wall. But there seem to be plenty left here in Frankfurt an der Oder. It feels like a rush hour. My sleep-deprived mind grasps for handholds of information. If it is rush hour, then it must be a weekday. So I must have lost a whole weekend, maybe more, locked up in the Stasi HQ. When he released me the captain said that somebody had corroborated my story, which was why I was free to leave. So somebody knows I am here. Who?

I blink gritty eyelids and glance up at the looming Oderturm as I continue my forced march, feeling the hot rush of carbon monoxide on my legs as I cross the junction. Office blocks have given way to shops on this side of the street. In one window tall stacks of canned vegetables look like 1920s' Manhatten skyscrapers. A butcher, sleeves rolled up, sweeps the day's detritus onto the kerb: beige wood shavings with spots of reddish-brown dried blood. I hear him breathing heavily, pausing to lean on his broom handle to watch me pass. Other shops have brown frontages, already shuttered up for the night. The street looks like a sepia photograph. I'm reminded suddenly of why I'm here: the postcard, the necklace, my mission for my grandmother. I can still do all of that tomorrow, after I've slept. I'm too exhausted to make plans right now.

A sudden wind, a storm's messenger, whips litter from the street. Panicked pigeons whirl upwards, a page of newsprint clings briefly to my legs then flutters away. Cigarette butts and sweet wrappings are mini whirlwinds in the gutter. The sky darkens, and icy water slews down, soaking me in an instant. I am half blinded as the torrent beats against my face. My clothes glue to my body, and I start to shiver, slowing my walk to a stagger. Cars with dipped headlights patrol past like sharks circling a sinking craft.

At last I sense an open space to my right, beyond a line of railings. This must be Brunnenplatz. I wipe droplets from my eyes and look across an acre of concrete. Across the square, a red-brick church's war-ravaged facade is like the face of a badly burnt veteran. In front, a line of fountains spew a wave of redundant water onto the shiny cement. And there, beside the pointless water feature, is a huge modern block. Emblazoned in stark black lettering above the entrance: Hotel Stadt Frankfurt.

I have just begun to walk towards it when I hear a voice calling my name, a voice I recognize.

# Chapter 29

**January 1945, Liberated Germany**

*Detta*

The sunset was a glimpse of heaven: crimson spilled into azure, the snowy fields rose and amethyst. But the foreground was hell: the shattered, spiky outlines of broken buildings – doors gaping, windows blasted. The ground underfoot was a burgundy sludge, half-frozen mud and blood mingling on the verge. Bodies had been shunted away to make way for the continual stream of vehicles and horse wagons spilling military supplies. Better to look up at the aching beauty of the skies.

The truck idled, puffing out black fumes. Detta waited with Tom and Gordon as the Frenchmen got on. They'd tried to usher her ahead, as one of the few women in the group. How odd it seemed, the veneer of manners, of civility, when all around was this inhumanity: the tangle of brown–grey carcasses that still littered the storm drains, mud, blood and torn uniforms mangled into a frozen mess.

It was impossible to tell which uniform it was, whose side each discarded corpse belonged to, and yet, amongst all this, they clung to their manners, like a life raft from a sunken ship. She'd declined their offer, preferring to stay with Tom.

'I don't see why we're still waiting,' Gordon said. 'If we hang about too long we'll get left here, and then we'll really be scuppered.' He inched towards the tailgate.

'You do what you want, pal, but I'm not leaving without something official. The major promised us a document to ensure safe passage.'

'But I don't see what difference—'

'We've got no idea what lies ahead. There's a thousand miles between us and the Black Sea. We can't risk leaving without it.'

Detta felt Tom's arm tighten round her shoulder as he spoke. It was for her benefit, this waiting for the document that the Russian major had promised, she knew. Tom and Gordon had their RAF uniforms to keep them safe: Russian allies. But she was just a girl, speaking French with a German accent. She needed something official to secure her safe passage.

The last Frenchman was clambering up the tailgate and into the back of the truck. The street, still thronged with military traffic – the tanks had all passed through, but now it was supply vehicles stuffed with ammunition, and horse-drawn carts piled high with food and blankets, bulging out from the seams of ripped tarpaulin. The truck jerked forward, the driver impatient to make a start before nightfall.

Gordon began to haul himself in, muttering that they should get going, not take any chances.

Detta could still hear the booming guns, but now they came from the opposite direction, not from Oppeln, but from Breslau. In just one day, everything had been reversed.

The truck driver leant out of the cab window and shouted something in Russian. The engine revved. Frenchmen began to pull up the tailgate drawbridge-like behind Gordon, but he tried to stop them. An angry struggle had just begun when the tall Russian major appeared, his uniform incongruously immaculate, his boots polished to a high shine that reflected the dying daylight. As he approached, Tom's arm gripped her tighter still.

'Ah, what have we here?' the Russian spoke in German.

'*Je suis française,*' Detta answered in French. '*Je m'appelle Odette Bruncelle.*'

'*Enchante, mademoiselle,*' he said, giving a brief bow and a flashing smile before pulling a piece of paper from his breast pocket. He opened it up to show Tom. It had Russian writing and was covered with the stamps of Soviet officialdom. Tom reached out with his free hand to take it. The officer let go of the document, but kept his feline eyes fixed on Detta, and continued to smile his porcelain smile.

'*Spasibo,*' Tom said.

'You are welcome,' the Russian replied in English.

'For God's sake, get in,' Gordon's voice interrupted, shoving the tailgate back down and holding out a hand. But just as their fingers connected, Detta pulled away.

She ran the few paces back along the road to the old beech tree in front of the manse. The whole world throbbed and she laid out a hand to steady herself. The bark was rough through her gloved fingertips, the trunk still warm from where it had been fire-blasted the night before. She looked through the empty, blackened branches, up the street, eyes searching between the rolling wheels, the tramping feet.

There: the glimpse of dark green cloth against the churned-up grey sludge, and the black one beside it: the hump of two bodies in the ditch beside the junction. They were still where she'd seen them earlier, half-crushed by tank tracks. She hadn't gone right up close: she couldn't trust herself not to break down, howl out her grief in her mother tongue, give herself away.

Father Richter and Mother, both lost, just like the Frenchmen said.

Detta clung to the tree, telling herself that her mother was much more than that discarded mass of flesh and cloth, left to rot in the wayside ditch. She told herself that Mother's soul would be somewhere else, no longer contained within her broken body. Perhaps she'd be with Papa, at peace. And Lossen, the village she'd known all her life, the village from the picture postcard, no longer inhabited these shattered, burnt ruins. Even were she to stay, there was nothing left for her here: no mother, no home, nothing. That's what she told herself, but she still felt like a coward and a traitor, for what she was about to do. With shaking hands she reached up and undid the chain at her neck: it had an inscription in German, identified her as German. She had to let it go.

Inside the hole in the trunk was a mixture of old charcoal and leaf mold, warm as proving dough from the fire that had ripped through the tree the night before. She dug her fingertips down, deeper, deeper, leaving the necklace there, hidden.

'Detta!' She heard Tom calling her. She let go of the tree trunk and stumbled back to the shouting voices and the waiting truck.

She scrambled up, Tom behind her, and the tailgate clunked shut. The truck revved, jerked forward, and they were gone, barrelling along, swerving and veering to avoid the endless line of Red Army traffic coming the other way. The Oppeln road cut a line between the quartered evening sky: virgin-blue on one side, blood-red on the other, the sun a burning sphere, sinking down beyond the devastated landscape. Behind them she could still just make out the Deutches Haus – ripped open, roof stoved in. *'Auf wiedersehen,'* she whispered into the icy wind – see you again. But even as she voiced it, she knew it to be a lie.

Home had gone, along with the girl she used to be, and there would be no going back.

## Tom

Was it euphoria he felt or self-loathing? Feelings ping-ponged in his chest as they drove ever further away from Nazi Germany. Distant guns volleyed like arguing deities. It was almost dark when they turned off the main road. The rutted wagon track ran alongside a wood: spiky outlines of pine trees jabbed into a dark sky prickled with stars. He hadn't heard her cry, not once, but as the truck turned, her hair brushed against his cheek, icicle-stiff with frozen tears.

The truck jolted on, and Gordon reached out and pointed out bustling figures, two with the probing antennae of machine-guns, soon swallowed up by the forest. Within moments there was the rat-a-tat of gunfire from the trees: Russian soldiers saving themselves the trouble of accommodating German POWs, as the push into Hitler's Reich continued.

The freezing air sliced through them, and he rubbed at Detta's back through the thick fur of her coat, to try to keep her warm, but still she shivered so much that her whole body spasmed. She hadn't spoken anything since she reappeared at the barracks this morning, except the repeated sentences: 'Je suis française. Je m'appelle Odette Bruncelle.' It was the Frenchmen who'd told him about her mother. When he'd spoken to her about it, she'd blinked and looked away.

It's my fault, he thought. They could all have got away together safely in the ambulance if she hadn't come to see me.

The truck came to a skidding stop on the riverbank. They all stumbled forward with the momentum, but they were packed so tightly into the truck bed that nobody fell. Tom knew that at any moment they'd have to get out. They'd have to slither and stagger across the icy expanse of river, and he'd have to help Detta and Gordon. Could he do that with both of them? He prepared himself mentally for the cold and the effort.

As they regained their balance Tom saw that the driver had got out of the cab and ambled over to where the stubbled white snow met the tarnished vista of the frozen Oder. He took something from his pocket, the size of an apple, fumbled with it briefly, then hurled it out onto the ice. There was a pause, then the burst of light and sound as the grenade exploded. The driver turned, shouting something in Russian, and gesticulating. He got back in the cab, the engine growled and the truck slid down towards the river. Surely they'd stop at the edge? No, the wheels kept turning. The ice was thick but thick enough to hold the weight of a truck-load of people?

Tom held Detta close as they eased onto the ice. The driver was careful in his recklessness, the wheels took them slower than walking pace, gently spreading the burden of the weight. Some of the Frenchmen were praying, softly, under their breaths.

They must have been halfway across, right out in the centre of the flow when it came, as much a reverberation as a noise: a chilling crack that started beneath them and spread fast and wide across the ice. 'Fuck,' said Gordon. Tom held his breath. The truck snailed forwards. The frozen river creaked and shifted like ship's timbers, but it held. At last they scraped their way up the far bank. Tom exhaled.

Voices broke out. Relieved laughter rippled through. The driver shouted something in Russian from the cab window as they sped up and careered across the snowy ground. A Frenchman nudged him, said something he didn't

understand. Tom looked at Gordon, who shrugged. The
Frenchman repeated the sentence, slowly and loudly for his
benefit, but it still made no sense. He felt Detta move her
shoulders, releasing his grasp – he hadn't realized quite how
tightly he'd held her on the river crossing. 'The driver says
he's going to take us all the way to Oppeln tonight, to the
refugee processing centre,' she said, in English.

'Oppeln?'

'Yes, it's a big town near here. I work there . . .' He heard
the catch in her voice as she self-corrected. 'I mean, I used
to,' she said. 'I used to know someone who worked there.
But I don't know her anymore.'

# Chapter 30

## November 1989, Frankfurt an der Oder, East Germany

### Miranda

'My sleepless beauty!' I hear the distant voice shout. I look round, but at first I can't see anyone, just the high buildings on three sides. 'Miranda, it's me!' I see him, then, sprinting round the corner: long strides, black hair blown back off his face, looking like a hero should look: strong, fit, determined and handsome. I put out a hand and touch the metal rail that runs between the square and the pavement, wet-slick and freezing. Quill is almost upon me: mouth parted, panting, white teeth. 'The Stasi bastards said they were letting you out of the main entrance, not the back door. I've had to run to catch you.' He is here. I am in his arms. He is warm and strong as a fairy-tale prince. 'It's okay. It's over now.' His voice in my ear, his lips on my cheek. 'Dieter told me about their interrogation methods. You must be all-in, my poor baby. I've booked us a hotel room. You can sleep as long as you want.'

'Dieter?'

'You didn't realize he was one of them? Old Dieter's been a Stasi informant for years. News about you got passed along the lines – some old biddy in Grunau said she'd seen you with a neighbour. We would have found you earlier if there hadn't been all the other palaver going on with the Wall. I wish I'd got to you sooner. I'm so sorry.' He brushes my hair away from the bruise on my temple. 'I'm sorry about everything. But I'm here to take care of you now.'

He is my buttress. Without him I don't think I can stand. I sink into him, feel the rub of his stubble against my face. The raindrops are suddenly warm: rain? No, tears – Quill's tears coursing from his eyes and running down my own cheek. 'I'm sorry,' he mutters. 'I'm so sorry. I love you so much. It will never happen again, I promise.' His words stream with his tears as he holds me fast. 'I love you,' he repeats, lifting me like a child into his arms. My head is against his jacket, and I close my eyes and let him carry me away.

What was it that Stasi officer said just before he released me? *The guilty ones merely cry and repeat their stock phrases.*

In the hotel lobby I struggle from his arms. He kisses the top of my head as I break free. 'I need to phone home,' I say, pointing at the telephone on the reception desk.

'Of course. You'll need to let your mum know you're okay. Charge it to room 179. I'll see you in the restaurant, yeah?' He blows a kiss in my direction as he turns away. If he'd ever listened to me when I talked about my family,

271

my life, he'd know that the last person I'm going to call is my mother.

The receptionist is sullen-beautiful: puce lipstick and harsh blusher like a slap around the cheeks. She looks me up and own. I must look a fright: dirty hair, clothes plastered wetly, and the glazed stare of the sleep-deprived. She must wonder what I'm doing with the handsome foreigner from room 179. I would wonder it myself, if I had the ability to think straight.

I tell her I need to make an international call. She shrugs assent, lifts the cream telephone receiver, jabs a shiny red nail on one of the buttons, and pushes it across the fake marble Formica towards me. I dial the number and wait while it rings on and on, willing Gran to pick up. When a man's voice answers I think I must have misdialed.

But just before I hang up: 'Is that Miranda?' the voice says.

'Yes – who's this?'

'It's Keith. I'm a friend of your mum's.'

'What are you doing at Gran's flat?'

'Sorry, Helen asked me to pick up some of her mother's things to take to the hospital.'

'The what?'

There is hissing on the line and I have to press the receiver hard against my ear to hear him properly.

'I'm so sorry, Miranda.'

'Sorry?'

In the pause before he replies I see a swarm of uni-formed figures push in through the glass hotel doors. The uniforms are different colours: grey, green, brown, and an indeterminate shade somewhere between all three. They have peaked caps with gold braid and shiny epaulettes. I see the receptionist simper and tuck a strand of yellow hair behind her ear as they approach the desk. I shift to the side to make space for them. They smell of damp wool and stale smoke.

'I know she wanted to tell you herself, but she said, if you called, to tell you there's no need to rush back. Your mum knows how important this trip of yours is to you, and she didn't want you to cut it short for no good reason.'

'For no good reason?'

'Yes, um,' he clears his throat and continues. 'I'm so sorry about your grandmother, Miranda. Your mum did say you two are very close.'

It is even harder to hear with a muddled conversation in German and Russian going on between the receptionist and the military men beside me.

'What?'

There is a click and the hissing on the line suddenly clears. 'Your grandmother's had a stroke. She's in hospital. I'm so sorry that you have to hear it like this.'

'That's okay,' I say. The effort of controlling my emotion makes my voice sound forced, robotic. 'Thank you for passing on the news, Keith.' I listen to this unknown man's breathing at the other end of the line for a second, then he repeats how very sorry he is, and how I should try not to worry, and I hang up.

Gran has always been there for me. When things went wrong with Dad, with Mum, with Quill, she's always there to help. Or was. Now she is ill, she's the one who needs me, and I can't get home to see her.

Quill waves and gets up as I thread my clumsy way through the restaurant to our table. He holds out my chair and tucks me in. Even though it is far warmer in here than outside, I'm still shivering. He takes off his leather jacket and drapes it round my shoulders. 'Don't worry, baby. I'm here to look after you, now,' he says, sitting down opposite and fixing me with his green eyes.

I realize I am, in fact, ravenous, as I wolf down consommé soup and a crumbling bread roll. Then the white-aproned waiter brings pork chops in some kind of blackcurrant sauce, with fried potatoes and cabbage. The cruet set in the centre of the table is brushed steel, and so is the vase for the pink plastic rose, the ashtray and the napkin holders. They look like spare parts for armaments, I think: tanks, guns or some other sleek killing machine. Quill orders champagne and I drink it like lemonade. The restaurant begins to tilt and right itself, as if we're at sea.

I speak as little as possible, skirting around the danger zone. But a nod or grunt here and there seems to satisfy him. He talks for both of us, just as he has ordered for both of us, lights cigarettes for both of us. I realize I haven't smoked a single cigarette since I came through to the East. I only seem to need to smoke when I'm near him, I think as I inhale. The nicotine gives me a head rush.

## The Escape

Afterwards I'm grateful for his supporting arm, guiding me across the restaurant and into the lobby. He collects the key on its oversized plastic fob and asks if I'm ready for bed. I smile, thinking of the blessed numbness of sleep. 'Yes,' I say. He takes my hand and leads me towards the lift.

# Chapter 31

**January 1945, Liberated Germany**

*Detta*

The door banged open and one of the Frenchmen walked out. She smiled at him, but he wouldn't meet her eye and walked past.

Detta quickly folded the Russian document and passed it to Tom, who stood behind her in the queue. He gave her a questioning look, but she frowned, shook her head and turned away. It occurred to her that if one of the men from the cellar had tipped off the Russians that there was a German girl with the English prisoners (perhaps in the hope that this information would give him some kind of preferential treatment), the document, with all its Soviet stamps, would be no use at all. Worse – it could serve as evidence of espionage.

No, she'd have to get through this on her own.

A woman's face appeared in the doorway, cold smile cutting her doughy cheeks. She nodded at Detta. The queue shuffled, bunching up behind her as Detta followed the woman through the doorway. Inside the room the air was a fraction warmer than the rest of the factory, although there was still the same gritty feeling of cement dust up her nostrils and on her tongue as elsewhere.

The woman motioned for her to sit on the metal-framed chair in front of the wide wooden desk. Behind the desk were two leather armchairs. The grinning woman sat down in the one on the left. In the other, a Russian officer, with an aristocratic nose and white hair, sat with legs crossed, heron-like, smoking a cigarette in a long, ivory holder. He looked at Detta through the haze of blue smoke but said nothing. Between the seated Russians, in front of a huge plate-glass window, stood a middle-aged man in a crumpled German Wehrmacht uniform. He wrung his hands and gulped as if he had a fishbone stuck in his throat.

She sat on the hard chair and placed her hands in her lap. She curled her fingers, balling her fists – if she fiddled, she'd look as nervous as the German soldier. Weak daylight filtered through the window onto her face. The Russians and the German were in shadow. The Russian man cleared his throat.

'*Je suis française,*' she said, before he could speak. It had become almost reflexive now. I'm French: if she said it enough times she would start to believe it herself, she supposed. '*Je m'appelle Odette Bruncelle,*' she said, and waited. The man and the woman exchanged glances. The German prisoner then asked her if she spoke any German at all, as he did not speak French. She told him that she did, and he translated to the Russians, who exchanged a few words. The woman maintained her inane grin, whilst the officer's face was set like concrete.

Eventually the officer began to interrogate her through the prisoner, while the woman scribbled notes in a file. Every question was posed in Russian and translated into German.

'Where are you from?'

'Alsace-Lorraine in France.'

'What are you doing in Germany?'

'I'm a forced worker.'

'Why are you a forced worker?'

'Because the authorities told me to report to the Labour office and they sent me to Germany. I had no say in the matter.'

'Which authorities?'

'The Nazi occupation ones, of course.'

'When were you sent here?'

'In October 1943.'

'Where were you working in Germany?'

'In a factory in Gorlitz in Silesia.'

'What were you making?'

'I don't know, we made metal parts, but none of us knew what they were for; the Germans didn't tell us anything.'

There was a break, then, while the Russians conferred. The soldier gave her a hasty, guilty apology, saying he was sorry, but he was only the interpreter. She nodded, looking up past his bobbing head and through the office window.

The old cement factory, which the Russians were using as a refugee processing centre, was on the outskirts of Oppeln. Through the first-floor vantage point she could see across the railway tracks and into the town – what was left of it: a jumble of crumbled masonry. She could even make out the remnants of the Reichsbahn building, looking as if it had been given a cuff to the side of the head by a giant hand. The fire escape had lifted from the walls of the upper storey and hung free as unpicked stitches.

The questions started again:

'Where were you born?'

'Colmar, Alsace-Lorraine.'

'When?'

'25th September 1925.'

'What's your home address?'

'17, Rue des Jardins, Colmar.'

'How old are you?'

'Nineteen.'

'Why do you speak such good German?'

'Everyone in Alsace speaks German as well as French. As I'm sure you know, Alsace has been both German and French over the years, so the people speak both languages, just as the border peoples do in Russia, like the Ukrainians.'

The man tipped the ash from his cigarette into the metal ashtray on the desk, and leant across to make a comment to the woman. She nodded, and made a note on her papers.

'Why is it that you came here with some English prisoners?'

'When I heard that our glorious Russian allies were not far away, I decided to go on the run in the hope of being freed. I walked east at night and hid during the day. When I reached Lossen I heard French voices and managed to hide with them in their barracks. There were Englishmen there, too, but I don't know them. Your soldiers liberated us and brought us all here.'

Detta waited for the German man to translate this into Russian. He gesticulated as he spoke, as if unwinding an invisible spool of thread. When he finished there was silence for a moment. The woman, still grinning, tilted her head at the officer. He stubbed the remains of his cigarette in the ashtray and shrugged.

Outside, she leant on the corridor wall, shut her eyes and exhaled. Tom was in after her – she didn't dare make eye contact. When she heard the door slam shut, she opened her eyes again. It was only then she noticed that her hands were still balled into fists, slick with sweat. Gordon was staring at her from the head of the queue. 'Okay?' he mouthed. She nodded, released her fingers and wiped the clammy dampness on her coat. But when she looked down she realized that what she'd thought was sweat, was thick-red blood. She'd dug her nails so deep into her palms during the interrogation that she'd made herself bleed. She rubbed her hands together, so the vestiges of blood became sticky. '*Pas de problème*,' she said, catching Gordon's eye. '*Parceque je suis française.*'

## Tom

'Don't look,' he said, but it was already too late. She'd seen the baby's arm, rising out of the snowdrift, a silvery glint as the sunlight caught the frosted flesh. It was only then that he realized that all the lumps in the snow they'd been trudging wearily past, these last few days, weren't drifts, but bodies. Had she known it all along? He couldn't tell. She hadn't spoken to him since the processing centre. They trudged along at the back of the line. The fields were flat and featureless white. A few snowflakes drifted, seemingly from nowhere, as the sky was endless blue – their world an empty snowglobe.

They'd left Oppeln, escorted by an old Soviet guard, gap-toothed and grumpy, gesticulating with his rifle to their billets in devastated villages en route. They were headed to Krakow, where they'd been told they could catch a train to Port Odessa in Romania, but there was no transport in Poland, just shanks pony. The villagers, what was left of them, the very old and the very young mostly, shared what they could: potato soup, herb tea, the occasional hand-rolled cigarette. They had almost nothing; devastated by the Red Army as they swarmed through. But it was easier than the forced march from the POW camp. Gordon could walk unaided now – he was up ahead with the French, having swapped his RAF cap for Jean-Paul's beret – and there wasn't the constant fear of jittery German trigger fingers.

Detta turned her head away as he spoke, even though

they'd both seen that little frozen arm, etched in silver in the morning sunshine. Her hair flipped as her head spun away from the image that couldn't be unseen, and that's when he noticed.

'Where's your scarf?'

'I left it with the woman in last night's billet.' She answered him; it was more than she'd spoken in days.

Last night's billet: six of them sat round a kitchen table, heads on their arms, dozing through the freezing night. Breakfast had been half a wrinkled apple and a cup of black tea, scrutinized by the stares of a handful of snot-nosed children. He didn't remember the woman very well. She was old, had kept herself huddled in the corners of the room.

'The grandmother?' he said.

'She wasn't their grandmother. She was their mother. She rubbed charcoal on her face to make her look older because of what the Russians did.' Detta paused then, pulled in a breath before continuing. 'Many times, they did it. In front of her children, too. She lost her husband to the war. She's terrified that the Russians might have given her syphilis, or some other disease, and there'll be nobody to care for her children. She told me this morning, while I was helping with the dishes. I just thought, it's good quality, that scarf – mohair and angora – she might be able to barter it for food.' Detta paused, and turned to look at him. 'Hearing her story just made me realize,' she continued, 'how deplorable my own self-pity has been.'

'Not at all.' He reached out to touch her. For didn't she

have every right to despair: a mother dead, a home destroyed, identity bartered for freedom.

'But I'm one of the lucky ones. I've got you, haven't I?' she said, looking deep into his eyes.

'Always,' he pulled her towards him. 'You will always have me. I promise.'

# Chapter 32

**November 1989, Frankfurt an der Oder, East Germany**

*Miranda*

I stand next to the window in the dingy hotel room. With one hand I touch the subsiding bruise on my temple. There is not much left to show for Quill's outburst of violence in Berlin. 'I love you so much,' he says, reaching out to me. But when I open my mouth to respond, nothing comes out. 'I feel so empty when you're not there,' he says, filling my silence.

Outside the rain falls, making glistening halos round the streetlights. I watch the top of an umbrella float like a black lily down the sluice of pavement below, and hear the muffled sound of the evening traffic, like a river running off the edge.

'You mean the world to me. You know how good we are together. Don't let that go, Miranda. We're special, you and me. The journalism, that's what's really important, you know that, don't you? The other stuff, the stuff you heard me talking about on the phone – it's just business, an income stream. It doesn't mean anything. It just lets me focus on what's really important, without having to worry about money. We can have a good life and still do the things we're passionate about, Miranda. With the money I make I can set you up with your own studio, buy you all the equipment you need, and it frees me up to write about the things I really care about. My business interests needn't change anything between us.'

I run my other hand along the windowsill. Dusty – my fingers are caked with the sloughed-off skin cells of the others who'd been in this yellow-wallpapered hotel room. Who? Businessmen? Stasi operatives? Mistresses, informers, prostitutes?

'I'm sorry,' he says. 'I'm so sorry about what I did. I was angry, but I promise you – I promise you – that nothing like that will ever happen again. Think about how happy we make each other, how good we are together, Miranda. Our love makes unhappiness seem to have lost our address. Miranda?'

I struggle to comprehend his higgledy-piggledy words. Perhaps the last couple of days of only hearing and speaking German have switched off my facility for understanding English. Or perhaps what he says makes no sense.

I see his hand appear next to mine on the sill. He lays down two passports, their dark blue covers the same colour as the encroaching night outside. I reach out and take them. The one on top is his. I open it. Quill DeVere: dark brows, strong jaw, flash of teeth, in the black-and-white rectangle. The other one is mine. Miranda Wade: cropped silver hair, owlish eyes with long lashes. I find my voice at last: 'You told me you burnt it,' I say.

'Yes, but of course I didn't. I just hid it. What do you take me for? I'm not some kind of monster. And I needed it for the Stasi, to prove you were who you said.'

'I smelled burning. I saw ash in the sink.'

'I burnt the toast, that was all. I was amazed you fell for it to be honest.'

'You lied to me.'

'For your own good, Miranda. For us. To keep you close.' He is standing behind me. If I turn, I will have to face him. I feel him take something else from his jeans. He places it on the windowsill in front of me, next to the passports. 'Look,' he says. 'We did it.' It is a piece of newsprint: the front page of the *Sunday Correspondent*. There is my photo, the one I took of the border guard breaking down at the sight of the lifted barrier. My name is written in tiny type at the side of the shot. My name: Miranda Wade – not Reuters, or Associated Press, but my own name. On the front page of a national paper. My photograph has captured the moment when the world woke up to history. 'Freedom?' says the headline in bold black type.

'My piece is on page three,' he says. 'They led with your picture. And quite right, too. It's amazing. You're such a talented girl. And together, we're a formidable team, you and me.' I feel his breath on my neck. 'You mustn't leave me again,' he whispers, his lips against my flesh. I feel something tug and give inside. A sudden exhalation escapes my lips, as if I've been holding my breath.

'I've been meaning to do this for a while, but now seems

like the right time,' he says, and turns me round, so I can no longer look at the photo. He tugs at the gold signet ring on the baby finger of his left hand and holds it out to me. 'I want you to have it.' He puts it in my palm.

I pick it up and hold it between finger and thumb. There is some kind of heraldic bird etched deeply into the gold oval: beak open, screaming. Quill urges me to try it on, but it doesn't quite fit any of the fingers on my right hand – either too big or too small for all of them.

'Try the other hand,' he says. I do, and it fits the ring finger on my left hand. 'Leave it there. It looks good, don't you think?'

'Yes. But on this finger it makes me look like I'm engaged?' I cannot stop my voice rising to a question mark at the end of the sentence.

'It does look that way, doesn't it?' he says. One of his hands snakes up underneath my jumper. The other hand reaches in front, catches my jaw, and I find I have no choice but to look into his eyes. They are very dark, in the light of the dim hotel bulbs. He ducks his head slightly and a lock of black hair twitches above his brow. 'I'll always be here for you. I promise. Don't you love me, Miranda?' His lips stay parted as he leaves the question hanging, and I glimpse his white teeth, his wet tongue.

I glance beyond him. Above the double bed is a huge black and white photograph of Marlene Dietrich, looking down on us with a mocking smile. I have that reassuring feeling of wanting to escape. 'Yes,' I say, letting myself sway into him.

Then his lips find mine, his hands tug my clothes, and we stumble backwards, together, falling onto the musty-smelling bedsheets, limbs tangling, hands grabbing. His skin is warm against mine and he smells of almonds and smoke and I am wet-tight ready for him as he pins my arms down and plunges into me. 'Yes,' I say, feeling the exquisite push of him. 'Yes. Yes.' And the strange little room shears and falls away. The rush of it: colours flash, a buzzing in my head, then blackness. I hear my scream as if it is someone else – disembodied, apart.

And when I open my eyes he is on top of me, sweat glue-ing our bodies together. He is so heavy. I struggle to breathe with the weight of him on my chest. *La petite mort* – that's what the French call it: the little death.

# Chapter 33

**March 1945, Romania**

*Tom*

'It's not always the best policy.' Tom felt a hand on his back.

'Beg pardon?'

'Honesty, old man. Not always the best policy.' Major Croft held a clipboard in one hand. A piece of string attached a pen to the bulldog clip at the top of the clipboard. The paperwork fluttered and flipped in the wind. He had been going down the line, ticking off all the allied prisoners and forced workers on his list: the line of ticks looked like the seagulls that whirled on the thermals above the docks. But there was one missing. Where a gull should be, there was instead a worm – a question mark next to Detta's name.

'But I told you, and so did Flight Sergeant Harper, she saved our lives. You have that in writing in our repatriation statements, don't you?'

'Yes, of course, but—'

'But she's German?'

'It does put me in rather an awkward position with London.'

'An awkward position?'

'Yes. Rather.'

Major Croft was a reservist. Too old for combat, he'd spent the war desk-bound, somewhere in London. This jolly to the Black Sea to log the homecoming prisoners under the reciprocal Yalta agreement would be the closest he'd ever get to the action, Tom surmised.

'I just thought, better to come clean now. I had to claim she was French to get her away. But we wouldn't want anyone from our side to think we were being underhand about it. It was a matter of survival, don't you see?'

The major's hand was still between his shoulder blades in what was probably intended as some kind of paternal gesture. Tom shook it off. An awkward position? Try being shot out of the sky and having to survive on your wits for the next three years, that's ruddy awkward, sunshine.

The wind had whipped the grey clouds into peaks, mirroring the tumultuous sea. He could taste brine on his tongue. 'Would it be "awkward" for London if I refused to get on the ship without her, and telegrammed the British Press to explain why?' Tom said, looking out to where the *Highland Princess* strained her bulk against the anchor lines, like a horse at the reins – as if she, too, couldn't wait to be rid of this Godforsaken port. A line of Russian POWs were filing off the ship, like a trickle of oil, spilling down the gangplank and onto the docks.

'Don't quite catch your drift.' The major's greying moustache was lifted by the gale as he spoke.

'I'm not leaving without her.'

The major sighed. 'Why the hell did you have to tell me she was an enemy alien?'

'The war will be over soon, maybe even by the time we make it back to England. What difference does it really make?'

The major didn't answer; he looked out to where Detta sat, on the sheltered seat he'd encouraged her to sit on, behind the pile of pallets. What had seemed like chivalry, was in fact cowardice, Tom realized – the old buffer had wanted her out of the way whilst he broke the news to Tom that she wouldn't be joining them on the long voyage home. Sensing their gaze, she turned and waved, smiling, unaware that her freedom was in the balance.

Behind her, the sea and sky were the same grey-green as the Wehrmacht uniforms she'd found for them to escape in, all those weeks ago in Lossen. 'Look, she helped us escape from the SS. She saved our lives. I'm not leaving her,' Tom said.

'I'm afraid my hands are tied. I can't have a German on board without explicit authority from London.'

'You're not seriously planning on leaving her here with the Ivans? You know what they'll do to her, don't you?'

'As I said, my hands are tied.'

'Do you have any children, Major?'

'Yes, two daughters, Dinah and Eve.'

'How old?'

'Sixteen and eighteen. Dinah's just joined the Wrens.

Funny to think she was only twelve in September '39, still a child, really, and now she's off doing her bit for King and country like the rest of us. Time flies, eh?'

'Would you leave your eldest daughter alone here with the Russian soldiers?'

'Well, of course not, but – look here, you're putting me in an impossible situation.'

The last of the Russian POWs were filing off the *Highland Princess* now, and the queue of allied escapees and forced workers bunched forward in anticipation of boarding. Tom glanced at Detta again. He couldn't – wouldn't – leave her here.

He grabbed the major's pen and scrawled a tick over the question mark next to Detta's name.

'What the hell are you playing at?' Major Croft snatched the clipboard away, and in doing so the ink blotted the line of type. 'The record is spoiled now, you chump.'

'Yes it is. It's impossible to be clear on this passenger's details, isn't it? Perhaps you could have London wire the ship when she docks at Port Said to request clarification?'

The pen swung like a pendulum below the crumpled sheets of paper. 'Oh, I see what you mean.' The major stopped the swinging pen with a thumb and forefinger. 'Dashed windy, pen seems to have slipped.' He ran a line through the remainder of the record, obliterating Detta's nationality.

The barriers were lifted, then, and the queue began to surge forward. Detta got up from her seat and came over to join him.

'Thank you, sir,' Tom said, shaking his free hand.

'Not at all.' Major Croft cleared his throat and turned to Detta. 'Bon voyage, dear,' he said. Just then there was an enormous honk from the red funnel. Major Croft stepped sideways, away from the queue, and Tom and Detta were caught up in the human swell. 'Bon voyage to the pair of you!' the major called out, and was lost from view as they rose like a tide with the others towards the waiting ship.

## April 1945, The Irish Sea

*Detta*

'There it is!' He pointed East and she looked. It didn't seem much, that doodle on the horizon, a shade darker than the cloud-laden skies and churning sea. A honk reverberated from the ship's red funnel, and white froth laced their stern. Seagulls mewled and swung overhead. Tom grinned, dropped his pointing arm, draped it round her shoulders and gave her a squeeze. Detta leant into him, hoping that by sheer proximity some of his homecoming joy would rub off on her. 'Bloody good to be back,' he murmured, kissing her temple, where the wind whisked her hair from her forehead.

Home. Was it her home?

Until now she'd managed to put the future from her mind, drifting in the day-to-day routine of life on board. At Port Said there had been oranges – oranges! She had forgotten what they even tasted like. Their waistlines thickened and their cheeks tanned as they chugged across the Mediterranean. The French had all jumped ship at Naples. Detta wondered if they'd got back home with their girlfriends by now. Tom had joked that they should make the most of the trip, saying it would be the only time he'd be able to take her on a sunshine cruise on his RAF salary. It was almost like a honeymoon, the lazy, drowsy days. Almost – there was precious little privacy on a troop ship, of course. She'd had to share a cabin with a Polish girl called Wanda, and Tom was down below with the men. Even so, they had managed a few snatched moments of intimacy, and he'd promised to marry her the second they disembarked.

The port – Liverpool, it was called – was closer now. She could distinguish the outlines of buildings and ships in the dock. 'We'll be off this tub by nightfall,' Tom said, and started to talk about which hotel they could stay at, and how they could get a special licence for the wedding so they wouldn't have to wait. 'I want to have a ring on your finger before I take you down to Devon to meet the family,' he said.

As he spoke she was wondering distractedly whether there might be somewhere to get her hair done. It felt like a luxury, even to think about it, but she indulged herself in girlish thoughts, just for a moment. She glanced up at the ship's red funnel and thought of lipstick. Could you get hold of cosmetics in Britain, after all these years of war? It would be wonderful to have lipstick to wear on her wedding day, she thought, half-listening to Tom and watching Liverpool get larger as the ship steamed into port. When a figure came up behind them, she assumed it must be Gordon, coming to join them as the ship finally docked.

'Warrant Officer Jenkins?' It was a voice she didn't recognize. They both spun round. It was a naval officer: white jacket with braid, florid face beneath his cap.

'Yes, sir.'

'And Miss Odette Bruncel?'

'Yes,' she said.

'If you wouldn't mind coming with me, please.' An order phrased as a question: they had no choice but to follow him inside.

The saloon was empty, save for the table at the far end by the bulkhead doors, where two other uniformed men sat. They looked up as Tom and Detta came over, but did not stand to greet them.

'Don't worry, darling. I'm sure it's just a formality,' Tom said. But a shiver ran right through Detta as she was told to stay where she was, and Tom was called up to the table alone. He was not invited to sit, but stood 'at ease' as they spoke to him. She strained, but was too far away to hear what was being said. All she could hear were the sounds of the ship coming into port: the honk from the funnel and the answering toot-toot of one of the port's tug boats; the clang and thunk of metal chains being lowered, and, faintly, the strains of a military band striking up, tinny as a scratched gramophone record.

When they led Tom out she felt the thud as the bow made

contact with the docks. His eyes slipped sideways to meet hers, and she had the urge to reach out and touch him as he passed, but he was too far away, and then he was gone, together with the first officer, the saloon door slamming behind them.

'Miss Bruncel?' The officer on the right looked up, and she knew she should approach. Her legs felt weak, as if she'd got up for the first time after a long illness. She forced herself forward. Close up she could see the man was quite old: what was left of his hair ran in grey furry strips above his large ears. The other man had dark brown hair oiled flat across his forehead, and didn't look up, just continued to write something in red ink on his papers. It was the same red as the ship's funnel, she noticed, that curling ribbon of text, the same colour as the lipstick she'd hoped to find for her wedding day. She couldn't read the words he wrote: upside down in that funny foreign language.

'Miss Odette Bruncel?' the older man repeated. She nodded. 'From Lossen, in Germany?' She nodded again. 'Date of birth 25th of September 1925?' Another nod. 'As an enemy alien, you will be taken to a reception centre for questioning as soon as the ship docks. Do you understand?'

'Yes,' she said. 'I understand.'

She'd said she understood, but she hadn't, not really. She hadn't known that she'd be handcuffed immediately, without even the chance to say goodbye to Tom or collect her things from her cabin.

# The Escape

There were flags and bunting swagging the docks, people waving handkerchiefs and cheering, and the band played 'Rose Marie I love you' as she was shunted down the gangplank. The waiting crowd's happiness swelled like an overblown balloon, fit to burst. Detta's eyes flicked round, looking for a glimpse of Tom, but he was nowhere, nowhere at all. Just as her head was pushed down, ducking her into the back of the waiting black car, she saw a blonde woman break free from behind the barrier and rush up to one of the disembarking prisoners, kissing him, long and hard, like she'd never let him go. Then the door was slammed shut.

The wipers pulled grey raindrops across the oblong windscreen, but the rear of the van was blacked out, so she couldn't see the docks, the ship or the endless grey seas, or whether Tom had seen her being taken away at all.

# Chapter 34

**November, 1989, East Germany**

*Miranda*

I freeze. Is he waking up? He grunts and flings an arm out into the empty space on my side of the bed. I hold my breath, thinking of what to say if he opens his eyes: *I can't sleep, I need some air, I was just going to get a glass of water . . .* He starts to snore, and I release a breath. But I daren't risk putting the bedside light on. I walk across the room, feel for the rough cloth of the curtains and reach behind. Yes, there on the windowsill: two passports. I put them both in my rucksack and head towards the door.

He stops snoring as I turn the handle.

I turn to look back at him, ready again with excuses. He is all blurred shadows in the darkness, his hair a black scrawl on the pillow. His bare shoulders are free of the bed covers, one strong arm spread wide. I see his broad chest rise and fall in the slow rhythm of sleep. Even from here I smell the faint bitter-almond smell of his aftershave.

His eyes stay shut.

If he were to open his eyes now, smile that smile of his, invite me back to bed, would I curl up into his arms and give in?

I turn the door handle, but his eyes stay closed. I open the door slowly, just wide enough.

I try to stay calm, but find myself running down the stairwell. The nighttime receptionist barely looks up from her novel, and I speed across the orange lino, through the glass doors and out into the cold, wet, pre-dawn.

The streets are almost empty. Some of the streetlights aren't working, and the town has a groggy, half-asleep feel. I run towards the high-up security lights by the bridge, fixing on one like the North Star. A delivery truck lumbers past in the opposite direction, splashing oily droplets on my jeans. There is the smell of exhaust fumes. Icy rain sheds tears on my cheeks and my rucksack bangs between my shoulder blades as I run on, through the dark streets.

My breath comes in painful bursts. But I hear no following footfalls, and when I check over my shoulder, there is no dark figure catching me up. It is just me, the cold rain, and the grey post-war blocks interspersed with the crumbling brickwork of the old town, as I approach the River Oder.

I slow to a jog, reaching the corner of Karl-Marx Strasse and Rosa-Luxemburg-Strasse. The road is floodlit here. Security lights run between a barbed-wire-topped chainmail fence. A dog barks, somewhere down towards the river. The blue bridge arcs over the dark water, up ahead, beyond the border checkpoint. I am almost there. A single white car rushes away from the checkpoint, headlights on full beam, making me squint, veering past in a Doppler zoom of noise.

I get closer to the bridge. There is a central cabin with the shadowy figures of border guards inside. Roads run either side of the cabin, towards Poland, and in the other direction, back into East Germany. Grey-painted metal struts hold up the clear plastic roof. The air is dry underneath, echoing with the dull drum of raindrops. I wipe the wetness from my face with the sleeve of my denim jacket, pull off my rucksack and take out my passport as I walk the last few steps towards the cabin. The border control guards come out to meet me.

There are two of them: a chubby man in browny-beige uniform with a beret pulled almost down to the bridge of his nose, and a dark-haired woman in a bottle-green jacket and trousers with a gold star on her peaked cap.

The man reaches out and I hand over my passport. He furrows his brow as he takes it and blows a harrumph through his thick moustache. Then he shrugs and mutters something in the woman's ear, passing the passport to her. She peers down her pointy nose and flicks through the pages. She looks at my passport photo, then to my face, and back again. She nods at the man and motions for me to follow her inside the cabin. The man stays outside.

Inside the cabin smells of stale cigarette smoke, body odour and some kind of cheap, fruity perfume. 'You don't have a visa for Poland,' she says in English. 'Why do you want to visit?'

'My grandmother came from Poland. I want to see the place she came from, that's all.'

'And where is that?'

'It used to be called Lossen, when it was part of Germany. It's between Breslau and Oppeln. I'm actually not sure what those places are called now.'

'You don't have a visa, and you don't know where you're going, and you turn up at the checkpoint at five in the morning?'

'Please don't send me back.'

'They always say that. But then 'they' are usually East Germans, trying to get through Poland to the West. You're British, though. Nobody could stop you going home – why come this way?'

'It's like I said. My grandmother was from Poland. Look—' I take out my Filofax and rifle through the pages to find the old postcard. 'This is where she grew up.'

The woman nods. 'So why not just fly in from London to Poland? There are flights every day from Heathrow to Warsaw.'

'I was in Berlin, and—'

'You can fly from Berlin, too. Why come this way?'

'If I go back . . .' I falter. How can I explain? 'I've come so far. I need to keep going. Please.'

The woman glances at her East German colleague's back through the glass. 'I can only authorize a day visa, under the circumstances.' She reaches for the rubber stamp and the ink pad on the desk.

The rain is easing slightly as I walk out into the centre of the bridge, under the metal arch, where East Germany meets Poland. The security lights on either bank glitter and reflect in the slow-moving expanse of water. I still hold my passport in one hand, but I pause to put it in the rucksack, and take out Quill's instead. I open it and look at his photograph: his charming smile, dark brows – that knowing look. Then I lean out over the metal rail, holding it for a second above the broad river, before letting it drop down into the inky water below. It barely makes a splash, his face gone in an instant.

There's a glimmer of silver on the horizon, beyond the town of Slubice on the opposite bank. Dawn is coming. I walk on eastwards, towards the light.

# Chapter 35

**April 1945, England**

*Tom*

'When can I see her?' Tom said, as soon as he was allowed to sit.

The man on the other side of the desk lowered his heavy-lidded eyes and sucked in a breath. 'Fräulein Odette Bruncel has been taken to a reception centre, where she will undergo debriefing.' He emphasized the word 'Fräulein', as if speaking in italics, drawing out the word with his public-school vowels.

'Where? And how long for?'

'I'm afraid the location of reception centres are confidential – for security purposes, you understand?' The man raised his tired gaze and waited for Tom's nod of acknowledgement before continuing. 'And she will be held for as long as it takes the centre to sort out the sheep from the goats, as it were.' He opened a file on the desk in front of him. 'Now, old chap, run me through your story again.'

'It's not a story. It's the truth.'

'Yes, well, run me through your version of the truth again, if you would.'

So Tom retold how it all happened: escaping from the forced march with Gordon; finding sanctuary with the priest in Lossen; Detta coming with food and medicine, hiding them from the SS manhunt, and helping them get to the French barracks.

'And she was his housekeeper?' The man dangled a black fountain pen between thumb and forefinger.

'No, she was a bi-lingual secretary with the railway. Part of her job was translation for the French forced workers.'

'That's odd. Your skipper said she was the priest's housekeeper.'

'Well, he was mistaken. He – he didn't get to know her as well as I did.'

'I'm sure he didn't.'

Tom felt anger rising hot in his chest at the inference. But losing his rag would do no good. He took a deep breath of the musty air and gazed out of the window, where the grey rain lashed in an impenetrable torrent, blocking whatever view there might have been.

'Why do you suppose she told him she was a housekeeper, but confided in you that she was a secretary?'

'Why? I don't know why. It's just a misunderstanding. Flight Sergeant Harper must've got the wrong end of the stick.' He met the man's impassive gaze. 'She's not a liar, if that's what you're getting at.'

'I'm not getting at anything, old chap.' The man's suit made a swishing sound against the leather seat as he shifted in his chair. 'What we're doing is trying to establish the facts. Which are somewhat in doubt. Was she a house-keeper or a secretary, for example. Anyway.' He paused and gestured with the pen. 'Let's move on, shall we? Is it true that she brought the SS directly to your hiding place, with the priest?'

'Yes, she did. But she had no choice. She was protecting us.'

'Protecting you?'

'She knew the SS would search the manse in any case, and she thought that by showing willing, by pre-empting them, she could bluff them into thinking she was a loyal citizen, and then they wouldn't bother undertaking a full search. Which is exactly what happened.'

'Indeed.' The man turned over a sheet of paper and looked down at the typed document. Something was underlined in red. 'It says here that she gave you some Wehrmacht jack-ets to wear?'

'Yes, when we escaped to the French barracks, to disguise us when we walked up the public road.'

'How do you suppose she came by those jackets?'

'She told me some deserting soldiers left them behind.'

'How convenient.'

'What are you saying?'

'Oh, I'm not saying anything, merely clarifying a few points from your earlier deposition. There are some incon-sistencies between your account and your pilot's, you see.

We just need to clear a few things up, old chap.' He made a note in green ink on the sheet in front of him and turned to the next page.

Tom realized that his hands had bunched into fists. He opened them slowly and clasped them together on his lap instead. Aggression would get him nowhere – months in POW camps had taught him that.

'So, there's something here about how Fräulein Bruncel had the opportunity to escape the approaching Red Army in an ambulance, together with her mother and some family friends. However, she chose to join you in the barracks with the French workers and their Polish girlfriends.'

'Yes.'

'Why do you suppose she did that? Why did she not leave when she had the chance?'

'She came to see me.'

'Yes, but why?'

'She came to tell me she loved me.'

'She hadn't told you before?'

'No.'

'And how long had you two known each other, at this point?'

'I don't know. Two, maybe three days.'

'Two or three days.' There was a pause. 'After two or three days she was already so in love that she would risk everything to be with you?'

'Of course she was. So was I. I would have done the same in her shoes. It was—' Tom shook his head. How could he explain the intense emotions of those times to this lizard of a man?

'Warrant Officer Jenkins, you were a prisoner of war for rather a long time, weren't you?'

'Two years, eleven months and one day.'

'And, I suppose, you were utterly starved of female companionship throughout your incarceration?'

'You could put it like that.'

'I do put it like that. I put it that seeing a pretty young girl like Fräulein Bruncel may well have had quite an impact on a man in your situation. A pretty young girl who, moreover, spoke English and seemed to want to help you, to find you attractive, even.'

'Detta is a very special woman.'

'I can see how you'd think that.'

'With all due respect, you're twisting my words. It wasn't like that at all. She wasn't after anything. We fell in love. I love her. You must understand that?'

'Love can mean different things to different people.'

'She's not some kind of honey-trap. She's not a German spy, if that's what you think?'

'I'm not paid to think.' The man put down the pen, folded his arms and sat back in his chair. 'I'm only paid to ask questions. And the question I keep returning to with this little scenario is why? Why would Fräulein Bruncel throw her whole life away for a man she'd only just met? We cannot rule out espionage. But this may also just be a case of sheer survival. Perhaps she thought the odds were more in her favour with an allied airman than on the run in a stolen ambulance? Perhaps, hearing what the Ivans were doing to German girls, she knew which side her bread was buttered? And one can hardly blame her for that. In any case—'

'I'm going to marry her,' Tom said, unable to hold his rage any longer. 'I don't care what you bastards think. We love each other and we're going to be together.' His clenched hands jerked apart as he spoke.

'I don't doubt the intensity of your feelings, but you may start to see things differently once you've had your leave and returned to the RAF. In the meantime, we'll talk to Fräulein Bruncel and come to our own conclusions.'

Tom jolted out of his seat. 'But I need to see her. When can I see her?'

The man remained seated, unfolded his arms and made a vague gesture at the papers on the desk in front of him. 'The process needs to run its course. Thank you for your time, Warrant Officer. You may go.'

'I'm not going without answers.'

'Then you will be here a very long time. There is such a thing as national security, you know, and bringing an enemy alien into the country in wartime is a very serious matter. I'm sure you understand.'

'I ...' He wanted to argue, but what was there to say in retort to that? He closed his mouth and gave the smallest of nods. An image of Detta as they marched her off the ship came into his head. She'd looked round for him, but she hadn't seen him, hadn't heard him yelling his love from the upper deck.

Where had they taken her? And how the hell was he ever going to find her?

## Detta

They could barely fit into the cubicle together, she and the bony, uniformed woman, who refused to make eye contact. Detta's bladder felt as if it would burst.

'Well, get on with it, then,' the woman said, looking up at the bare electric bulb that swung above them. 'What's wrong? Too shy to drop your knickers? You weren't so shy when you dropped them for your RAF fella were you? But that was different, I s'pose. He was your meal ticket, wasn't he?' For the first time since the journey began, back in Liverpool, the woman looked directly at her. There was hatred in her deep-set eyes.

There was no point responding to the insults, Detta thought, turning away to look at the handcuffs that dangled from the woman's hand. But surely she wasn't expected to – to perform – in front of this stranger? 'Are you staying in here?' Detta said, face hot with embarrassment.

'Can't leave you in here alone. Who knows what you'd get up to,' came the reply. Detta pulled down her knickers and sat on the cold toilet seat. She stared at her shoes, the funny cork-soled things that Tom managed to find for her when he was off the boat in Naples (she hadn't been allowed off herself, of course – nobody would risk letting an 'enemy alien' out of sight). At first she thought she couldn't, not here, in this tiny box, with this horrible woman watching. But she was desperate, and it came, at last. She'd been holding it in for so long, that it stung, and she bit her lip with the sudden pain. It made a gushing sound as it hit the bowl. A faint smell rose. There was nothing she could do. The woman tutted. 'Do all German girls piss like horses, or is it just you?' she said. Detta did not answer. She reached for the toilet roll. It was shiny and hard. When she pulled her knickers back up, her gusset still felt damp. She reached for the chain and flushed.

The woman clicked the handcuffs back on her before unlocking the cubicle door. 'But my hands,' Detta said. 'I need to wash my hands.'

'I think pissy fingers are the least of your worries, duckie.' The woman jerked her back towards the waiting van. The driver was leaning up against it, having a smoke. 'And do get a move on, we'll be late getting to London as it is, without having to stop for your so-called comfort break.' Detta saw the driver frown at the last remark. 'Oh, give over, Alf,' the woman said, opening the van door next to him. 'It's not like I told her the centre's address. Does it really matter?' She shoved Detta into the gloomy interior. 'No, don't answer that. Just do your job and drive.' The woman threw herself inside and slammed the door after them.

London, then, Detta thought, as the driver got in and turned on the engine. They are taking me to a reception centre in London. She slid to one side as the van swerved away from the kerb.

Later – much later – the woman fell asleep, head bumping against the blacked-out window, lips mumbling something incomprehensible and barely audible above the engine's growl. Although the side windows were blackened, she could see out through the front windscreen to where bridges and houses, hedges and ditches tumbled past as they sped on into the twilight. There were no road signs on the main roads, but Detta could guess when they'd arrived in London: curling through a maze of streets, van wheels jolting over potholes. There were rows of large houses, and sudden gaps of flattened rubble. They turned into a small side street, slowing down as they passed a sign next to a pillar box: Nightingale Lane, it said in thick black letters against a white background. The car ground to a halt in front of large metal gates. The woman suddenly sat up straight, eyes wide open. 'Not asleep, just resting my eyes,' she said, her voice slurred as a drunk. The driver left the engine running and went out to a side entrance. When he got back in the van, the gates had already begun to swing open to reveal a huge old house, with two gables like arrows, pointing up at the London sky. The car slid inside, wheels crunching on gravel. The driver killed the engine, and got out to open the door next to her, as if he were a chauffeur, not a gaoler.

The woman shunted her up the steps. The double wooden doors opened inside to a yellow-beige hallway that smelled of boiled vegetables and disinfectant, where another woman was waiting. This one wasn't wearing a military uniform, but instead had on a dark-grey dress with a white pinafore apron over the top, and steel-grey hair rolled away from a crumpled face.

311

Detta's handcuffs were taken off and the military woman left. The door thudded shut behind her, and the new woman – her wardress, Detta supposed – locked it immediately from a set of keys she wore on a chain round her waist. She was ushered upstairs and along a featureless corridor to a door at the far end.

'You'll be sleeping in here with the others. The bathroom's just across the way. Quick now, it's past lights out.'

'And tomorrow?'

'You'll be interviewed.'

'By whom?'

'Well, Miss, I'm not at liberty to say.' The crumple-faced woman wore an expression of habitual worry.

'And then will I be free to go?'

'The process can take time.'

'But I will leave here?'

'Oh yes, this is a repatriation centre, Miss. You will be moved on from here, no question.'

Detta hesitated. On the boat they'd said she'd be taken to a 'reception centre', but this woman had said 'repatriation centre'. The British had so many words that meant the same thing. Perhaps 'reception' and 'repatriation' were just different versions of the same word. It probably wasn't anything to worry about, was it?

'Good.' Detta allowed herself a half-smile. So this incarceration was merely temporary. Once they'd heard her story – and Tom's corroboration – they'd let her go, wouldn't they?

# Chapter 36

## November, 1989, Poland

*Miranda*

The adrenaline is starting to wear off, leaving me stale and exhausted.

I take another sip of the gritty coffee and glance round the roadside cafe. A dejected-looking red-headed waitress wipes the countertop. Apart from me, the only other customer is a fat man, tucking into scrambled eggs. He sits beneath an improbable print of a little girl holding a sunflower. The sunflower is the same colour as the daubs of scrambled egg smeared on his plate. Outside, the rain is easing, bleeding away with the night outside. Beams of early sunlight flash rainbows through the spray from the speeding wheels of passing trucks. I check the clock above the till: Mum will probably be up by now. I go over to the payphone by the door.

The receiver presses against my hoop earring. I prod the metal buttons with a forefinger. 'Hello? Yes I'll accept

313

reverse charges.' The voice at the other end is muzzy and high pitched.

'Mum?'

'Oh, it's you, Miranda. I thought it was the hospital.'

'How is Gran? I spoke to Keith, but he didn't tell me how it happened.'

'She was visiting your father and collapsed in the car park. She was lucky she was there, not at home, because someone found her and called an ambulance. They took her to Derriford because it was closer.'

'Is it serious?'

'It's a stroke, Miranda. Of course it's serious.'

'I mean, will she be okay? What's the prognosis?'

'Too soon to say. She's not fully conscious yet, very confused. So they're keeping her in to assess the extent of the, well, the damage, I suppose. But the important thing is that she's going to pull through, so there's no need for you to rush back.'

'Mum, I—'

'Look, I've got to go, darling. I was just on my way out, and it's a hell of a drive to Plymouth from here. You're alright, aren't you?'

'Yes. I'm fine.'

'You know your gran was trying to sort something out for your father, when it happened. It made me think. It's good to talk to you again, Miranda, even though it's under such difficult circumstances. Love you.' There is a click and a hiss as she hangs up, grabbing the last word, as usual.

I cling on to the receiver for a moment, then I go back to my table.

I take the torn postcard from my rucksack and put it down on the cream Formica. I look at the postcard: the inn, the cars, and the trees. It seems more important than ever to get there now. But where is Lossen? All I know is that it lies somewhere between Oppeln and Breslau, but they'd have different names now, since becoming part of Poland.

The waitress has disappeared into the kitchen. The fat man dabs clots of scrambled egg from his moustache and lights a cigarette. I get up and cross the empty cafe towards him. I put the postcard down near his plate. 'Lossen?' I point at it, and he squints down, eyes almost lost in the fleshy foothills of his face. His pungent cigarette smoke catches in my nostrils. 'Near Breslau?' I say. He grunts, pulls a map from his coat pocket and spreads it out on the counter. 'Breslau,' he says, shaking his head and pointing a pudgy finger at a town on the map. The letters spell Wroclaw, but he says 'Rots-lav! Rots-Lav!' jabbing a pudgy index finger at the map.

'Oh.' I smile and nod. So Breslau is now Wroclaw. 'Are you going there? Are you going to Wroclaw?' He smiles and shakes his head, and I don't need to understand Polish to know that it means 'sorry, but no'. I smile my thanks and go to stand near the till.

There is a draught of chill air as the cafe door opens and closes. I see a couple with matching long grey coats come in. They sit at a table nearby. She's quite young – mousey hair in a neat bob. He has fair hair, thinning at the temples, although he can't be more than thirty. His coat is undone and I see a sky-blue scarf at his neck and some kind of uniform underneath: white shirt, tie, navy trousers and jacket. I wonder what they are doing here?

I can't help hearing their conversation as they wait for the waitress to reappear – they speak German, and my ears are still attuned. I find out that they are pilots for Lufthansa. Their plane is in Wroclaw, but it's been grounded overnight for repairs. The woman decided to take the opportunity to visit a cousin in Slubice, and the man has just driven over to pick her up so she'll be back at the airport in time.

They are at ease with each other, but not intimate. I think they must be colleagues, not a couple. The man seems to sense my eavesdropping and looks my way. I feel as if I've seen him before. It is like bumping into an old classmate at a crowded station – familiar and unfamiliar at the same time. But he can't possibly be anyone I know, can he?

The waitress reappears and I point at the till to show I am ready to pay for my coffee. When I hold out a handful of Ostmarks, she frowns and shakes her head. We exchange sign language: open palms and shrugs and pointing at empty coffee cups. Not knowing how else to pay for my breakfast, I pull Quill's signet ring from my left hand and hold it out. The waitress looks confused. 'Take it,' I say. 'For my coffees.' I put it into her palm and close her hands over it. She opens her fist and looks down at the ring, then she shrugs, smiles, and our exchange is complete. She puts the ring on her own finger and begins to come out from behind the counter to see to the waiting couple.

I have to be quick. Before the waitress gets to them, and before I lose my nerve, I take the two steps to their table: '*Entschuldigen Sie, bitte.* I need to get to my grandmother's house. Can I get a lift to Wroclaw with you?'

# Chapter 37

**May 1945, England**

*Detta*

'That will be all, then. You're free to go.' The man with the sagging eyelids tapped the papers into a pile and clicked the lid back on his fountain pen.

'I can leave?' Hope lifted her voice. Was it finally over, this never-ending queue of days?

Every day here had been the same, since the night they'd brought her from Liverpool. Every day tepid and unremarkable as the food, and the weather, in this place. Every day there had been breakfast of toast and margarine, an obligatory walk (three times round the perimeter fence), then to the kitchen to help to prepare the midday meal, and floor polishing or laundry duty in the afternoon. Except four times – five if you included this one – she'd been sent up to the top floor interview room straight after breakfast for questioning. There had been three men in different coloured military uniforms, the French intelligence officer and now this man, in his baggy brown suit. Surely she'd done enough, at last, to be released?

'You are letting me go?' she said, to be certain she'd heard correctly.

The man looked up, catching her tone. 'You can leave, yes.'

'So, am I to leave this place today?' She clung to the hope. She shifted in her seat, and the sealed letter she'd written to Tom made a faint crumpling sound in her pocket – she wrote every day, although she still hadn't heard back from him.

'Oh dear me, no, Fräulein. That was just a figure of speech. You need to remain within the boundaries of the centre, of course.'

'And what about my fiancé, Warrant Officer Tom Jenkins from the RAF. Hasn't he been in touch?' She thought about all those letters. They must have questioned him, too, she supposed. Why hadn't he written back?

'Fiancé?' The man looked pointedly at the empty ring finger on her left hand. 'No, I'm afraid not.' He looked up again. 'So, as I said. The interview is concluded. You may leave.'

'But, can I ask, how long will I have to stay here?'

He cleared his throat, rifled through the papers in the folder in front of him. 'Let me see.' He frowned, then got up and went over to the filing cabinet next to the window. He opened the top drawer, and his fingers picked through the files.

Detta looked down at the open folder on the desk. There was the man's scrawled notes from the interview they'd just had, black ink still wet on the paper. But, poking out from underneath was something else, another sheet of paper, handwriting she recognized. Detta let her fingers steal across the desk towards the open file, pushed the top sheet sideways to get a better look at what was underneath.

'Someone must have mislaid your registration document, or filed it incorrectly ... maybe it's been put in the wrong place ...' The man was still searching the filing cabinet.

Detta looked down at the open file again. No, she wasn't wrong. There, under the top sheet, was her own handwriting: the last letter she'd written to Tom. She nudged it with the tip of her finger, and under that, the one she'd written the day before. She looked at the wedge of paperwork on the desk. Had they stolen all her letters? Had he even received one of her daily letters to him? The wardress collected the post every day after breakfast, claiming she would stamp each one and put it in the box to catch the first post. But she'd lied. They'd all lied. Her letters were here. Tom would never have heard from her, never even known where she was, all these long weeks.

'Ah, yes, here it is.'

Detta withdrew her hand quickly as if she'd touched a hot iron. The man came and sat back down. His reptilian lids blinked slowly before he continued. 'You're quite correct, Fräulein. You've been here almost a month now, and you've been seen by each of the agencies, so, yes, it probably is time to move you on. I'll have a word, and we'll see how soon we can get things in motion for you.' He smiled, revealing uneven, yellow teeth.

'Moving on? Where will I be moved to?'

He tapped the sheets of paper together again and closed the cardboard folder. 'Back home, I shouldn't wonder.'

'Home?'

'Yes, that's right, Fräulein.' He spoke very slowly, like a teacher to the dunce of the class. 'Back home to Germany.'

Detta closed the door slowly behind her on her way out, and managed to make it across the corridor to the windowsill next to the fire door. She leant against it, finding it hard to breathe, as if there were a heavy weight on her chest. She rested her cheek against the cool pane, the rumble of a nearby train station faintly audible.

They were sending her back to Germany.

What about Tom? What about their life together, the one they'd planned? Her thoughts tumbled in chaos as she looked out over the morning street. Had nobody read any of her statements? Hadn't they corroborated her story with Tom? Did nobody believe her?

She remembered how the woman in the car had spoken to her, on the journey down from Liverpool, with derision and fear. She recalled a phrase she'd heard the wardress use in conversation with the cook: 'All fur coat and no knickers,' wrinkling her nose in outrage. She thought about the way the man had looked down at her missing engagement ring just now. No, nobody believed her. They thought her a fantasist, an opportunist, a whore. She was the enemy. They hated her and they wanted her gone.

She looked out of the sash window, waiting for her breath to slow, her thoughts to still. The black-painted fire escape zigzagged down the brickwork. Oak trees, lush with new spring leaves, spilled over the barbed wire that spooled the top of the high fence. Beyond that was what she supposed was a typical suburban British street: red-brick houses with shiny brass doorknobs, hopscotch paving slabs, and the post-box just below. As she watched she saw the familiar figure of a little girl skipping towards the gates, ahead of a woman pushing a pram. She'd seen them before at this time of day, when she'd been up here for interviews. The girl had a navy blue coat with a fur collar, and a shock of blonde curls. She looked, Detta thought, with a tug of grief, just like one of Frau Moll's daughters.

It came to her almost as a reflex, bypassing conscious thought. She pushed the release bar on the fire escape and was outside, feet sliding a little on the metal step. The building hugged the perimeter on this side. She could see right down onto the red circle of the postbox, the dandelion-headed girl. She took the letter she'd written for Tom out of her pocket and hurled it, hard as she could. The faint spring breeze lifted it, so it whirled over the barbed wire, falling like a giant snowflake, just at the girl's feet. Detta held her breath.

The girl stopped skipping, picked up the white envelope, waved it at the woman with the pram, who nodded at her. As Detta watched, the girl posted it through the mouth of the postbox.

'Fräulein! What are you doing out there?' A voice from inside.

She span round. 'I'm so sorry, I felt faint, I needed some air,' she said, hearing his approaching footsteps.

'If you are feeling faint, then I suggest you go to your room and lie down, instead of standing out here in the cold.' He was there in the doorway, nudging her inside, pulling the fire door to.

Detta's letter to Tom was in the post. It had no stamp, but it was the best she could do, to trust her future to the British postal system, and hope.

## Tom

'Perhaps it's for the best, T,' Gwen said, flicking ash into the kitchen sink. Since when had his little sister started smoking? So much had changed in his absence, Tom thought.

'How so?' He couldn't keep the irritation from his voice.

'Well, I probably shouldn't be telling you this, but Colonel Carruth says they'll just repatriate her, in the end, once they've established she's not a spy.'

'Well of course she's not a spy!'

'But how do they know that?'

'Because I've signed a statement saying exactly how she saved my life, and so has Flight Sergeant Harper. And what the hell makes your Colonel Carruth an expert in all this, anyway?'

'I don't know. Old school chum in the Home Office or something. Anyway, maybe you should be prepared to let this one go . . .'

'If they've sent her back, then I'll just have to go out to Germany and find her, marry her, and bring her back as my wife,' he said.

'Oh, Tom.'

'What?'

'You know what it would be like, if you did do that. She'd barely be able to show her face in the village. So many people lost everything in the Plymouth Blitz.'

'Which had nothing to do with her. She was still a schoolgirl in 1941, for Christ's sake.'

'But people won't see it like that, will they? Not round here, at least. Nobody will be able to get beyond the fact . . .' she trailed off, taking another drag of her cigarette, her eyes like marbles, glassy and hard.

'The fact that she's German?' he said. She wouldn't meet his gaze, looked out of the window at the bluebells by the hedge, ran a hand through her blonde curls. 'What about you, Gwennie? What do you think? I mean really. Do you think I'm on a hiding to nothing?'

A wood pigeon began its uncertain coo-coo from the monkey puzzle tree, in the pause before she answered. 'It's not about what I think. It's about you, and your happiness. You've been miserable since you got home, and we all think it might be better if you just, well, you know, move on. After all, your leave's up next week, isn't it?'

'What, I should just go back to work and forget about her?'

'Well, the authorities clearly aren't going to tell you anything. You've had no joy from any of the letters to the

Home Office, have you?' Gwen sighed, a pained look on her pretty face. 'And, T, how well did you know the girl? I mean, really?'

'She saved my life, you know.'

'Sorry, I know. It's just we've all been so worried about you, these past few weeks.' She stubbed out the cigarette and threw it into the dustbin under the sink. As she straightened up, the church bells started ringing. 'Well I suppose we'd better get a move on. Don't want to get Pa late starting the sermon and upsetting old Mrs Riddaway again. Last week she claimed her stew was burnt because the service went fifteen minutes over time, the old battle-axe.' She plucked her handbag off the back of a chair.

He forgave her. He would always forgive Gwennie, his curly-haired little sister. She meant well. He could imagine Ma and Pa with their anxious expressions exhorting her to talk some sense into him – *You try, Gwendolyn dear, he listens to you*. Tom sighed and picked up his cap from the kitchen table.

'Oh blast, I've got nothing for the collection,' Gwen said, shaking out her purse. All that fell out was an old bus ticket, a tightly rolled-up pair of nylons, and a gold lipstick case. 'I used up the last of my change on the excess postage on that letter of yours yesterday; you'll have to sub me. Or, better still, pay me back what you owe, you rotter.'

'What letter?'

'The one that came whilst you were out collecting your new uniform yesterday. I told Ma to pass it onto you.'

'She didn't.'

'Her mind is all over the place these days, poor thing, it's her "time of life",' Gwen said the last phrase under her breath, as if it were some kind of secret. 'They're probably in the Davenport. Everything seems to get shoved there.'

He followed her out of the kitchen and into the hallway. It was dark and cool, with the tiles underfoot, and the morning sunshine streaming in through the stained glass panel above the front door. She lifted the rosewood lid of the old desk, next to the umbrella stand. 'Here. Thruppence you owe me, T, and don't say you can't afford it because I know what a warrant officer earns these days, and that's without the three years back pay you have owing.'

She held out the envelope. It was dirty, crumpled, and his name and address was written in curly black ink letters on the front. But there was no stamp. Postage due – 3d was scrawled in red ink across the front. He tore it open:

*Home Office Repatriation Centre, Nightingale Lane, London.*
*3rd May 1945*

*Dearest Tom,*

*I've lost count of the number of letters I've written, but I still haven't heard back from you.*

*Tom, if you've had second thoughts about us, I'll understand. I'm sure that coming home has put things in a new perspective, and if you feel differently about me, then that's just how it is. But if this letter reaches you and you do still feel the same way as you did in Germany, in Russia, on the ship*

*and in Liverpool, then know that I feel that way too, and I
always will.*

*If you still love me, please come and find me.*

*Yours forever, Detta x*

He passed the letter to Gwen, watched her face as her fur-
rowed brow smoothed as she read. Tom's mind worked.
They were keeping her prisoner. He had to get her out,
because if Gwen's colonel was right, she could be sent back
to Germany any day. He needed to get to London, but trains
were a nightmare on Sundays, and anyway, how the hell
was he even going to get to Totnes station at this time on a
Sunday morning?

Gwen handed back the letter. She didn't say anything
immediately but instead reached back into the davenport. She
held out a key fob. 'It's got a full tank and the spare coupons
are in the glove compartment,' she said.

'But what about your colonel?'

'I'll think of something. The old boy's taken a bit of a
shine to me, so I doubt he'll have me court-martialled just
for lending out his staff car on a mercy mission.'

'Gwen, I can't drop you in it.'

'Oh, for God's sake take the damn thing before I change
my mind!'

# Chapter 38

**November 1989, Poland**

*Miranda*

'I'll just drop Silke off at the airport and you can give me directions.' At the sound of his voice I'm awake. I open my eyes and things swim into focus, but still make no sense. I am on the back seat of a car. I push myself to sit up. Through the windscreen I see a wide road with coloured cars strung like beads, and in the distance the scribble of a cityscape horizon. I remember then how I hitched a lift with the Lufthansa pilots to Wroclaw from the roadside cafe. I must have fallen asleep almost as soon as the journey began, lulled by the warmth and the gentle throb of the car engine. I blink into full consciousness.

'You wanted to be dropped off near Wroclaw?' The woman in the passenger seat turns, her tip-tilted nose in profile against the gunmetal skies beyond the glass. 'I've got to be at the airport for flight checks but Michael should have time to take you to your grandmother's.'

# The Escape

The road snakes on between featureless fields, but the buildings on the horizon are looming larger. A few minutes later the car pulls into a space in front of the cargo bay of a small airport. The woman – Silke – gets out of the passenger seat, smiles at me through the car window and waves. 'Good luck with your search,' she mouths through the glass, and walks off in the direction of the hangar.

Michael invites me into the front. I feel the blast of cold air as I get out, and then I'm back inside in the warmth again, slamming the passenger door. I thank him for taking the trouble to help me. 'Not at all. Just tell me where we need to go,' he says, pulling out into the road.

'The thing is, I'm not sure. It's a little village called Lossen, somewhere between Breslau and Oppeln. You can just drop me off somewhere in Wroclaw if you want. I can find a taxi or something, I'm sure.'

'I don't mind driving to the village. There's plenty of time.'

'Okay. If you're sure you don't mind?'

'I'm sure. Look for signs to Opole – that's what Oppeln's called, these days.'

We drive on in silence for a while. The Silesian skies above us are thick grey-purple, the vast fields stubbled brown and beige. A line of roadside trees seem to topple towards us as the car rushes forward. I point out the Opole road and we head south. He gestures at the tape deck on the dash: 'You can put something on, if you want?'

I rifle through the cassettes in the space below the stereo: Suzanne Vega; The Smiths; U2. Quill's MG only had a radio.

Quill – by now he will have realized I've gone, along with his passport. A cocktail of guilt and relief makes my stomach churn. 'You okay with Suzanne Vega?' I say.

'I was hoping you'd choose that one.' He turns to me and smiles, then fixes his gaze back on the road. Suzanne's voice comes through the stereo. 'So, I have to ask, how did you end up in a roadside cafe near Slubice, hitching a lift to your grandmother's home village?' he says.

'I'm sure you don't want to listen to me rattling on all day. Anyway, there's not much to tell.'

'Please, tell it anyway. There's time, and it's good for me to practice my English.'

So I do. From the moment I decided to come to Berlin, photographing the night the Wall was breached, Quill making me believe he'd burnt my passport, the realization that the journalism was just a cover for setting up a cocaine-smuggling network. I even tell him about Quill headbutting me, feeling oddly ashamed, as if I somehow invited his violence.

Tears come, unbidden, but I wipe them away and carry on talking. It's cathartic, letting it all out. And it doesn't matter – I'm hardly likely to see this stranger again, am I? So I tell Michael about slipping through the hole in the Berlin Wall, about finding Aunt Gwen, the torn postcard, Gran sending me off to find her hidden locket, and being picked up by the Stasi for questioning. I tell him about Quill's 'rescue', hearing about my grandmother's stroke, my pre-dawn escape to Poland, dropping Quill's passport in the Oder and using his signet ring to pay for my breakfast at the cafe. 'And that's when I asked you for the lift,' I say, wiping my wet face with my palms.

'Not much to tell?' Michael says. He turns to look at me again, one eyebrow raised. His eyes crinkle kindly at the corners. They are the same shade of blue as his scarf, I notice. I smile through my tears, then look away, out to where the clouds bruise the winter horizon, piling up over the Opole road. Although it's the middle of the day, the light has become thick and low. He flicks on the headlights.

'I feel guilty,' I say. 'I shouldn't have thrown his passport in the Oder, or given away his ring.'

He laughs as I say that. 'But not guilty about telling tales to the Stasi about his drug-running operation?'

'What?'

'You said you ended up shouting out everything in your interrogation.'

'I did. But Quill said he had the Stasi on side, so they won't do anything, will they?'

'I'm not sure. It's one thing for a local informant to accept a bribe and turn a blind eye. It's another for an officer to ignore a taped statement given during interrogation. In any case, things will be different for the Stasi now – with what's happening. Information like this could just get handed on to Interpol.'

'You think?'

Michael shrugs. 'It's all going to change, now the Wall's coming down.' He indicates off the road towards a huddle of concrete buildings: a shop, petrol station and diner. 'But you mustn't feel bad about it,' he says, pulling into a parking space. 'He deserves it, and more, from what you've just told me.' He turns the key and the engine is quiet, and there is just Suzanne Vega's voice, still singing about changing her destiny.

'Why have we stopped?' I say.

'Why do you think?'

'I don't know.'

'We need to buy a map or ask where Lossen is, if we're ever going to find your grandmother's house.'

'Of course.' I click the stop button on the tape deck and reach for the door handle.

For a moment I'd forgotten what I was doing here, lost in conversation with the blue-eyed pilot.

# Chapter 39

**May 1945, England**

*Tom*

He dropped his head in his hands in defeat. All morning he'd been shifted from pillar to post in the Home Office. Nobody seemed to have heard of Odette Bruncel, or to care. *We are not at liberty to disclose the details of confidential files,* they told him. And the expressions on their faces added: *why would you want anything to do with that filthy Nazi spy?*

He looked up through the window beside him to see a droning swarm pass overhead from right to left behind the dirty glass, like migrating birds, heading eastwards, along the Thames and over to Germany. And then they were gone. The skies outside were back to the usual cloudy blue, and the sound was just a distant vibration in the glass. That's what they'd do if he didn't find her in time, he supposed: put her on a troop plane back to Germany. Or a ship, more likely. After all she'd been through. It didn't bear thinking about.

Feet pattered along the endless Home Office corridors, typewriters chattered, filing cabinet drawers swooshed open and clunked closed. A patch of spilled tea lay unnoticed on the beige linoleum. The woman at the desk nearest him finished licking a manila envelope and let it fall onto the stack in front of her. Tom felt a pull in his chest and his throat constricted. Breathe, he told himself. Just breathe. The hand on the big clock by the door jerked forward. 'I'm going for lunch,' said the envelope-licker to her typing colleague. 'You want me to pick something up for you?'

'You're alright, I'll be off myself in a sec.' One of the metal hammers stuck out on her typewriter. The typist tutted and pushed it back into its position in the ranks. 'I've got the afternoon off for a dental appointment. But I've got to finish this one. It's urgent.'

'They always say that. I say nothing's as urgent as my shopping. If I don't have something to put in the oven for tea then my Harry will have my guts for garters.' The other woman made a face, and left, plucking her handbag and coat from the stand on her way out.

Tom's final hope was a man called Witherington, who was in charge of the 'Aliens Department'. He was told he might be able to get hold of Witherington at lunchtime. He'll swing through the typing pool to pick up his bowler and umbrella from his office. You might catch him then, a spotty young clerk told him, not sounding optimistic. So Tom waited, on the hard chair by the edge of the typing pool, in the gap between the window and Witherington's office, where a small mirror hung on the wall next to a fire warden's tin hat.

He sighed, looking round. Where was the fellow? Most of the typists and clerks had already gone. The chatter of typewriters was almost silent, except for the one in front of him, an older woman with grey streaks at her temples – more conscientious than most, it seemed. Then she, too, finished. Pulled out the cream sheet of paper, placed it in a manila file, and got up. She walked right past him to Witherington's office, went in, and came out without it. Was she his secretary?

She paused in front of the mirror and pulled a lipstick from her pocket, dabbing the remains of an orangey colour on her lips. She must have sensed him looking at her. 'Not hungry?' she said. 'The canteen's pretty good, considering. It's in the basement.'

'I'm waiting for Mr Witherington. I was told I might be able to catch him.'

'Well, I don't know who told you that, I'm sure, but you'll be lucky if you find him here. He's in conference and they've had sandwiches sent in. Sometimes they go on all afternoon. You'd be better off having a bite to eat, or even leaving it until tomorrow, I would. He's usually in a foul temper by the end of the day.'

'But I can't. I can't afford to wait around. What if they send her back, after all she's been through?' All the woman did was shoot him a sympathetic look, but he found himself blurting it all out: the escape with Harper, how Detta hid them from the SS and came back with them on the boat to Liverpool. 'So you see, that's why I'm prepared to wait for Witherington, as long as it takes, even if I end up sleeping here.'

When he finished, she said nothing, but continued to look at him, squinting her eyes a little. 'I'm sorry,' he said. 'Rambling on like that, and you about to get off on your lunch break. Don't let me keep you.'

'That's where I know you from,' she said, still looking at him in that strange way.

'What?'

'You're one of Gordon's crew: the one who made it back with him – the one who saved his life.' Her face brightened as she spoke. 'You were at the wedding, weren't you? In January '42?'

'I'm not sure I follow you.'

'Gordon Harper, married my niece Dorothy. We all got roaring drunk in the mess and someone played the bagpipes. I seem to remember you doing a foxtrot with Aunty Maud.'

'Good Lord. Did I?' January 1942: it would have been just before the sortie when they took the hit. It felt like pre-history.

'You're Tom Jenkins, aren't you?' She'd moved to stand in front of him, her face breaking into a grin. 'My family owes you so much, for bringing Dorothy's husband home. I can't thank you enough.' Tom stood up to shake her hand, which seemed to be the right thing to do, but she grabbed him and hugged him close. 'We're all so very grateful,' she said.

'Nothing to thank me for,' Tom said, his voice muffled by her hair. 'He would have done the same.'

The woman let him go, wiping a tear from her cheek and sniffing loudly. 'Silly me. But let me buy you lunch. It's the least I can do. It was so wonderful for Dorothy to get her husband home safe. So many weren't so lucky.'

'That's very kind, but I'd rather wait for Witherington,' Tom said.

'Is it about the girl? Gordon said there was a priest and a girl who helped you hide, and the girl came with you.'

'Yes,' Tom said. 'Her name is Odette Bruncel. She's my fiancée. But they've got her locked up in Nightingale Lane somewhere and nobody will even let me see her. So I was hoping that your Mr Witherington—'

'Oh, you'll get no joy from him,' the woman interrupted. 'Even if she's cleared of espionage links, he'll have her deported. He's awfully strict.'

Tom frowned. 'There must be something I can do?'

The woman sighed and continued. 'No, he'll have her sent back. They're not re-interning them now, just sending them to parts of Europe that have already been liberated and letting them make their own way home. That is, unless she has a permit to stay for the purpose of marriage to a British citizen. Does she have one of those?'

'I don't think she has anything. That's why I'm here. So do you think Witherington will be able to help with the permit?'

'No. He'll chuck you out with a flea in your ear.' Her eyes met his. 'If he gets to hear about it, that is.'

She went back round to her desk, pulled a form from a drawer, and wound it into the machine. 'I need her full name and date of birth, and yours, and your home address. He gave them to her, watching her type the details in the form.

'And this means she's free?' he said, as she pulled the paper from the machine and held it out to him.

'It means you can get her out of that repatriation centre and get a ring on her finger. But as for getting a naturalization certificate and so forth, you'd have to ask Mrs Clarkson about that, and she's not due back for another half an hour. If you want to wait?'

'No, I've done enough waiting to last me a lifetime. Thank you. Thank you so much.'

She smiled as he took the permit. 'Nothing to thank me for. Good luck.'

## Detta

'Anything for me?'

The wardress shook her head and walked past, distributing the second post: doling out envelopes and packages to the rest of the dormitory. Many of the other women got mail every day; they'd been in internment centres for most of the war, but pre-war friends kept in touch, sending sweets and toiletries. The other women talked openly about how, even if they were repatriated, they'd find a way back to Britain. For them, it was home, despite it all.

But there was never any post for Detta. The authorities had been taking the letters she wrote, reading them and filing them. None of her letters had been sent, none of them had reached Tom. Unless? She thought of the unstamped envelope fluttering down like a giant snowflake in front of the postbox last week, and the little girl popping it in the slot.

No. She would have heard by now. It was a foolish hope. Either that letter never made it to Tom or, worse, he received it and chose not to respond.

She looked out through the sash window beside her bed. The skies were duck-egg blue, and the trees vibrant green with new leaves. The flowering cherry shed pink petals like confetti on the empty lawn. Spring was here already, and still no word from Tom. She could just see over the fence and into Nightingale Lane, where a khaki green military vehicle was pulling up at the kerb, beside the postbox.

The wardress stopped on her way back. 'Have you packed your things ready?'

'Yes.' Detta indicated to the small string bag packed with her few possessions, which lay on top of the grey blanket, next to her fur coat. 'Do you know what time the transport is coming?'

'I can't rightly say, Miss. This afternoon is all I was told.' She shrugged and walked out, closing the door behind her with a click.

Detta smoothed a hand over the white pillowcase: damp, always, from the silent tears she shed every night after lights out. The second post had been her last chance. But now that, too, was gone.

There was a tiny choking mewl from the cot between her own bed and the next. Detta turned her face away from the window to see Gabi – the baby's Italian mother – groan and roll over under the sheets.

Detta took out the remains of a precious tin of Vaseline from her pocket. She pushed off the lid and took out a dab, smearing it on her lips, first, for the shine, and then over her eyebrows, to tidy them. She pinched her cheeks to redden them: preparing a face to meet the future. As she took out the broken comb to run it through her hair, she heard the reception centre doorbell buzz. She thought of the army car she'd seen drawing up outside. It must be the transport to take her away, back to Germany – what was left of it – back to the mud and blood and chaos.

The baby began to howl in earnest, and Gabi sat up, bleary-eyed, and began to unbutton her blouse. Detta shot her a sympathetic glance. Gabi had been a friend, of sorts, these last few depressing weeks.

Detta stood up and put her hand in her pocket, feeling for the torn postcard she'd kept with her all these months. Did Tom still have the other half, or had he thrown it away weeks ago? It didn't matter, now. Tom didn't want her. England didn't want her. So be it.

She took out the scrap of card, and walked over to where the metal waste-paper bin was, by the dormitory door. She glanced down at the picture of the Deutches Haus Inn that she held between her fingertips: that had been home. She turned it over. On the other side was Tom's address: that could have been home. But neither existed for her, anymore. Marriage to Tom, a new life in England, all that had been a dream, and now it was time to wake up.

# Chapter 40

**November 1989, Poland**

*Miranda*

It isn't even there. I hold up the torn postcard with the yellowed strip of peeling Sellotape holding the two halves together. Looking at arm's length, I can see exactly where it should have been. But my grandmother's childhood home no longer exists. Gone is the half-timbered brick and the thick oak door. Gone, too, are the trees and hedge on one side. Instead there is a dusty patch of bare muddy gravel, rutted with tyre tracks, an unofficial widening of the main road where it swoops round the corner. There are houses further back: boxy grey things that look more like bunkers than homes, blankly utilitarian, like the rest of the village.

My neck aches from falling asleep on the back seat earlier. I stand, looking at the place where it should have been, where a family lived and a history began, and now there is nothing but an empty lot.

A lorry thunders past behind me, and the postcard wobbles

in my hand. 'There's nothing left,' I say, turning my head to Michael. I feel as puffed-up and angry as the thick clouds that tower above us.

'Does it matter?' he says.

'But I've dragged you all this way, and it's not even here.'

'What were you expecting? What wasn't blown up by the Red Army was probably flattened by Communism.' He sounds matter-of-fact. 'We might as well look around, as we're here. I don't know about you, but I could do with a coffee and something to eat before we head off. And you might feel differently about the place if you've seen more of it,' he says, touching me lightly on the sleeve and pointing over the road behind us. 'Look, the church is still standing – that would have been the church your grandmother went to, wouldn't it?'

I turn to look. I hadn't noticed it when we pulled up: a large white church, outlined in thick terracotta paint, with an onion shaped spire. 'Yes,' I say, my mood lifting a fraction.

Three cars pass in quick succession and then we walk through a veil of exhaust fumes to the other side, where there is a pebble-dashed house, with a garden that attaches to the churchyard. There is a single beech tree in front of the manse. I falter, and a shiver runs through me. 'You okay?' Michael says, slipping a hand under my elbow. 'You look pale.'

I have a swimming feeling, as if I've got up too quickly, and the whole world throbs. 'Just a little light-headed,' I say, reaching out to steady myself on the tree trunk. The bark is rough beneath my fingertips.

'Maybe your blood sugar is low – you didn't have much breakfast, did you?' he says. I shake my head. 'Let's find somewhere where we can get you a drink, at least. And you're shivering. Here – take this.' He unwinds the sky-blue scarf from his own neck and wraps it round mine.

He is right. I am cold. The temperature, already chill, seems to have plummeted further. I pull the scarf up so it covers my head. 'Thank you,' I say.

'That might be a hotel,' he says, pointing up behind the manse, beyond the churchyard, to where a large Schloss is glimpsed through the winter-bare trees. 'Why don't you have a look round here, and I'll go on ahead and see if we can get something to eat and drink up there?'

'Okay,' I say. I hear his footfalls crunch away up the path.

I hold up the postcard again. I was too close, I realize. The photograph would have been taken from here, across the road. And the leaves in the foreground may well have been the branches of this tree. I put the postcard in my jeans pocket and run my hands over the trunk.

The tree has been fire damaged. It looks as if it was hit by lightning once, long ago, half of it withered and blackened. There is a hole the size of a head, at shoulder height. Inside it new growth sprouts, like arms, reaching up, pushing through the blackened space. There is a mixture of old charcoal and leaf mold at the base of the hole: dark brown and moist. I dig my fingertips down, through the clamminess of it, feeling, deeper, deeper, down through past years of blown leaves and detritus. But I can't find anything. Maybe someone else has been treasure hunting since 1945. Maybe it's the wrong tree. Maybe the necklace was never there.

As I rub the muck from my hands, I look up through the empty tree branches at the upstairs window of the manse, and for a moment I think I see the pale outlines of two faces behind the glass. There's an odd smell in the air: not the fading scent of exhaust but stronger – acrid smoke – something burnt. I wrinkle my nose, and blink, and when I open my eyes again the faces have gone. I must have imagined them.

I decide to have one last look, just to be certain, and plunge my hands back inside the trunk, scrabbling down as far as I can. There's something stringy, like a root, in the way, catching the edge of my baby fingernail. I pull to get rid of it, this sinewy thread. As I tug it out, there is a tiny sparkle, as the light catches something hidden. Underneath the grime is metal, tarnished dark grey and cold. And on the end of it a blackened lozenge. A chain and locket. I smile, and put it safely in my jeans pocket, next to the torn postcard. I have two things to take back to my grandmother. And a hundred questions to ask about the story that lies behind them.

I hear a rustling sound and look up into the bare branches. Two black birds with silver speckles on their wings – starlings – flutter away over the rooftop, as if disturbed by something.

I pull my grandfather's Rolleiflex from my rucksack, hugging it into the space below my heart. I take photographs: the tree, the manse, the church, the churchyard, the empty space where the guesthouse used to be. I'm planning to put together an album of photographs to take to Gran in hospital.

The storm clouds are piling up, skies darkening overhead, and I decide to go and find Michael. An icy blast of wind tugs the scarf, and I wind it closer round my face, pushing my chin into my chest. I begin to walk along the path that winds in front of the church. There is frost on the ground: fallen leaves bronze-silver and slippery on the surface of the beige mud. A few ragged old rose bushes trespass spindly branches over the manse fence into the graveyard. One still holds half a yellow rose, quivering in the chill air.

The track continues, past a flat piece of earth that is covered in a rectangle of concrete, with jagged spikes of rusted metal poking up above ground, and a dark hole with crumbling steps disappearing downwards – there would have been a large building there once, but all that is left is the cellar. As I pass I have another moment like the one just now: a swooning feeling and the scent of burning. Perhaps Michael is right and it's just low blood pressure causing these odd sensations.

The track narrows to a path and rises through some trees. There are firs like green bottlebrushes, and bare silver birches with blots of pale green mistletoe clotted on high branches. I can see the Schloss through the trees. I look up at the sky: the dense clouds make twilight of the daytime. The air feels charged. There is a rumble, like distant ordnance. I carry on walking, uphill, across the frosted ground.

I see him then, between the trees, coming down from the Schloss, striding in his long, grey coat, with his fair hair dull

The Escape

gold in this strange light. As we get closer to each other I notice the chink of blue, as his eyes meet mine. There is an uncomfortable sensation inside me, like numb-cold fingers thrust in front of an open fire.

And that's when it happens: the sky is rent with electric yellow, and there is a blinding flash, followed a split-second later by a tearing roar, as the dark clouds rip apart above our heads. White snowflakes spew down. The storm has broken.

I raise the Rolleiflex to the space below my heart. 'Snow!' Michael holds out his arms, lifts his head, then opens his mouth wide. I see him through the lens, caught in a moment of childish excitement. He snaps his mouth shut, looks across, and grins. 'My first snowflake of winter!'

He looks straight through the viewfinder, right at me, as if the camera isn't there at all, catching my gaze and holding it fast. From this distance his eyes are like twin blue sparks seen through the snow-veil between us.

That's when I know. It's only when I see him through glass that I realize: Michael is the man from the kerbside in Berlin, the one who called for me to phone for an ambulance, the one who used his long coat to cover the overdosed junkie, who waited on the kerb for the medics, the night the Wall was breached. It's *him*.

I click the shutter. I capture the moment.

And it's perfect.

# Chapter 41

**May 1945, England**

*Tom*

As he reached for the buzzer his fingertips grazed the barbed wire that looped round the high gateposts. He pushed and waited, looking round. The skies above Nightingale Lane were the faded blue of baby clothes on a back garden washing line. Baby clothes on a line – he had a sudden image of the future, walking home from an ordinary job, down an ordinary street, perhaps with a paper tucked under his arm, and seeing Detta in a flower-freckled garden, hanging washing, with a pram parked under a cherry tree. He smiled at the mundanity of his vision, realizing it was everything he wanted now. The street of his dreams might be just like this one in Wandsworth: oak trees sighing with crowds of new leaves; distant traffic clattering and grumbling – an ordinary suburban street on an ordinary Spring day. Just like this, but different, with a wife and baby to come home to.

Tom looked up at the ivy-fringed windows of Oak Lodge. Somewhere up there an extraordinary woman – his future – was waiting for him. But the gate remained clamped shut between the barbed-wire ringlets. He pressed the buzzer again. He wasn't leaving until he got her out of this place. With its high walls and Victorian red brick, it looked just like the school it had no doubt been before the war – a good school in a decent part of London. But Tom knew from the barbed wire and the blankness of the shut gate what it really was these days: a prison camp. And there was no way he was letting her languish in there one second longer. He pounded the gate with his fists. If he shouldered it hard enough he could probably break it open, he thought. He would, if it came to it – break in, pluck her up, and carry her away, like a prince from a fairy tale.

'Yes?' A bored voice came at last through the intercom system. 'Who is it?'

Tom leant close to the punched holes in the metal plate. 'Warrant Officer Tom Jenkins, here to collect my fiancée, Odette Bruncel.'

'Have you got the relevant documentation?'

'Yes,' Tom said. 'Let me in.'

A sigh came like a hiss through the grille. 'I'm sorry, sir, but Mr White's gone home already, and I can't authorize anything without his signature. You'll have to come back tomorrow.' The line went dead. Tom hit the buzzer again. 'I said, come back in the morning,' the voice repeated. The line went dead again. Tom felt the fingers of his right hand bunching into a fist. Little Hitlers, the lot of them. He flexed his fingers and let out a breath, rolling his eyes upwards. Was she up there, somewhere? He scanned through the branches, hoping to see a face at a window, but there was nothing.

Above the oak trees a hazy cloud of starlings doodled and dodged, plummeting and whirling in formation, air dancing, just for the joy of it. The murmuration suddenly banked, swilling right across his line of vision, as if a distant squadron of planes were flying past. And he was taken right back to that day at the camp, watching the Russian bombers, the twist in his solar plexus at the thought of freedom.

He turned back and pressed the buzzer again, hard, for a very long time.

'Yes, what is it?'

'I'm here to collect Odette Bruncel. I'm her fiancée, and I've got her release permit with me.'

'Well nobody's told me anything about a release permit. Somebody should have telephoned.'

'It's here. Come and take a look.'

'It's not my job to come out and have conversations with visitors, sir.'

'I'm not a visitor. I'm a liberator. Odette Bruncel is free to leave, and I shall push this buzzer all ruddy night if I have to.'

'Now, be reasonable—'

'Reasonable? That girl is free to come with me. You are holding her against her will. And if this gate stays shut then not only will I carry on buzzing this stupid thing, I'll bloody well sue for false imprisonment.'

'There's no need to take that tone.'

'For God's sake, will you just open the damned gate?' The catch was suddenly released, and he stumbled inside.

A paved path led up to a short flight of steps. Dormer windows were a frown above the front door's petulant mouth. He bounded up the steps, hearing the gate clank shut behind him. The front door opened on a chain to reveal a rodent-like face: prominent teeth and an upturned nose.

'I can't let you in until I have had sight of the official documentation,' she said. Tom pulled the permit from his pocket and thrust it into the gap. A small hand plucked it from him.

He touched the wings on his uniform badge, like a charm, leant forward, and called out into the dark hallway behind the half-open door: 'I'm here, Detta. I got your letter and I'm here to take you home.'

## Detta

Just as Detta was about to drop the useless remains of the postcard in the bin, the door banged open. It was the wardress, panting a little from the stairs. 'Get your things, Miss, you're going home.'

'Home?' Detta said. So it was true. They were sending her back to Germany today. She slipped the postcard back in her pocket as she went back over to her bed. She picked up the string bag and her fur coat. What would they do? Put her on a plane to Berlin? Who would pilot the plane, she wondered, perhaps a colleague of Tom's? Perhaps if she could get word to him . . . ?

No. Don't be stupid. It's too late for that.

'Hurry up, Miss.'

The baby had stopped crying, now nuzzling at Gabi's swollen breast. Detta could hear voices from downstairs: a man and a woman. She quenched her hope immediately. Of course there would be a man's voice, some lance corporal, tasked with bundling the 'enemy alien' away in the army car. She stepped across the floorboards and leant over to kiss Gabi on the cheek and the baby on its peachy head. 'Goodbye,' she said.

Gabi looked up with round, weary eyes. They would have embraced but with the bag, the fur coat, and the suckling baby, it was impossible. 'Good luck,' Gabi said, almost managing a tired smile.

'Come on,' the wardress said. 'He's waiting for you.' Detta turned and walked through the open doorway and into the dark corridor, her feet sliding a little, as they always did, in these cork-soled shoes, on the polished lino. The string bag bumped against her leg, and the fur coat slithered in her other arm. Thoughts whirled as she walked. She was stupid to think she'd fly to Germany. Someone like her would hardly be worth the expense. No, they'd send rejected refugees like her by boat: in her mind's eye she saw those famous white cliffs dwindling to a small snapping white bite on the horizon behind her, as some old troop ship chugged across the Channel, eastwards, carrying her back, all the way back to where she'd come from.

Detta could hear the wardress's footfalls following, just out of step with her own as she made her way towards the stairs. Would she just get dumped at the port, or would she have a choice of where to go, a one-way train ticket to somewhere? If so, where? To Hannover, to try to find out if Aunt Hedwig had made it through alive? Or to Alsace, to try to track down Frau Moll and the girls, if they'd survived?

She was at the stairwell, and put out a hand to grasp the bannister, mind still full of plans for the future that was being thrust upon her. She barely heard the voice calling: 'Detta!' She blinked, paused, staring down the stairs into the dark hallway, hearing a voice she thought she recognized. But it couldn't possibly be ...

'Well, what are you waiting for?' The wardress prodded her from behind, and the silly summer shoes slipped on the polished lino, and suddenly she was falling, falling down and down-down-down into a spinning rush, and dark blackness.

But then a panic gasp awake, and there were arms around her, holding her. 'Got you. It's okay, darling. You just blacked out for a second there.' Strong arms holding her close, the scent and warmth of him. The feel of his uniform badge against her cheek. Yes, it was him. It was *him*.

She looked up and his face swam into focus: the fair hair brushed away from his wide brow, the eyes such a dark blue in this light, they were almost lapis. 'Tom?' But it was too late. Too late. 'They're sending me back,' she said, remembering what the wardress said, the khaki army vehicle waiting outside.

353

'No. No, you're not going anywhere without me – we're getting married tomorrow. That is, if you'll still be mine?' A look of anxiety passed over his features.

His face blurred out of focus again as she leant up towards him. 'Always,' she said. 'I promise.' She closed her eyes as her lips met his, soft and safe – home.

# Chapter 42

**November 1989, Plymouth**

*Odette*

Who is this old woman with the droopy eyelid? I hold the mirror in my good hand and look carefully but I do not know the woman who returns my gaze.

I know one fact about myself. My name is Mrs Odette Jenkins. It is written on my forms, and the nurses call me Mrs Jenkins when they come to take blood or help me to the bathroom. They have capable hands and tired eyes. One of them reminds me of my mother: worry lines, bony fingers, a smell of perfume, cigarettes and hard work.

The face in the mirror doesn't look like the remembered face of my mother, but it doesn't look like me, either. I am away and somewhere else, even though the forms say I am Odette Jenkins.

You were lucky, Mrs Jenkins, the nurses say, drawing the curtains round my bed, bringing food, or taking it away, inserting cannulas or dishing out medicines. Lucky your son-in-law saw you collapse, lucky there were trained nurses nearby, lucky there happened to be an ambulance in the area. Time is brain, Mrs Jenkins, and you were lucky to have survived your stroke.

Lucky? I am reminded of a girl pop star singing about being lucky in love, and a man with sad, green eyes and a receding hairline. But I don't know who he is, either.

I have come to terms with the now. At first it was all a muddle of faces and sensations and noises that were so loud I felt sick. But now there is the regular gravy-drenched food in its plastic tray, the swish of the pale orange curtains, and the bleep of the machine, and the three old ladies in the other beds on the ward. This is my now: I know I have had a stroke and I am recovering in hospital. What I do not know is who I am.

Through the window opposite my hospital bed I can see the sky. Throughout the day it changes colour: rose quartz, opal, topaz, and finally lapis blue. Now I close my eyes and wonder what colour it will be when I open them again, but when I do, instead of the sky, I see a face zooming in close up, a swinging brown-haired ponytail, someone speaking in a fuzzy voice, asking me my name.

I can't answer that one, even though I know. I know I am supposed to be Mrs Odette Jenkins. But I'm not. It might have been Mrs Jenkins in the mirror, which has slid out of my grasp and onto the bedsheets, but I'm not her. I have tried to explain this to the nurses, but nobody understands.

Palsy, it's called, the droopy eye, says the doctor in the

white coat. My hand and leg are heavy on that side, and they tingle. The doctor smiles and says it's nothing that physio can't help with. She says I'll need rehab, but the prognosis is very good.

Prognosis? I repeat the word and hear myself slurring like a drunk.

Yes, the outlook, the cheery ponytailed doctor says. We're expecting a full recovery, given time, Odette. And you're lucky you've got family locally who can help support you in the meantime.

*Lucky* – that word again. Family? I remember my mother: her face and embrace and the smell of her. But I do not know where the memory is from. Do I have other family? A husband? Children? I must have, I suppose. I just wish I knew.

The doctor wears a white coat and calls me Odette. The nurses wear blue tunics and call me Mrs Jenkins. There was another woman who came before. She didn't have a white coat or a blue uniform. She had chestnut-coloured spiky hair and smelled of hairspray and perfume. I saw her hand resting on my bad one, but I couldn't feel it because of the pins-and-needles. I closed my eyes for a moment, and when I opened them the sky had changed colour again, and the woman was gone. Maybe it was she who left this mirror, and the brush and lipstick, which I can't use, because my bad hand won't let me.

The doctor has gone, now, and I look in the mirror again. The women in the other beds are old: grey hair and walnut faces. This face in the mirror is old, but not as old as the

357

other women. Or, if she is, she is a little better maintained. At that thought, the reflection smiles a lopsided smile. The hair around the heart-shaped face is white, the eyes dark brown, the features tidy. It is a face that would once have broken hearts, I think.

Were you a heartbreaker, Odette Jenkins?

For a brief moment, then, I smell pipe smoke and feel inexplicably sad. But the moment passes, like a wave breaking on the shore.

Outside the window I see a seagull rise on a thermal, and disappear into a sapphire sky. I close my eyes, wondering what colour it will be when I open them again.

A touch on my shoulder. 'Mrs Jenkins. Someone to see you.' Hands help me to a sitting position. 'I'm afraid she's a little confused,' the voice says, as I begin to open my eyes.

There is a face: silver-blonde hair with dark roots beginning to show, a worried expression, a china-blue scarf. 'Gran,' she says, and suddenly there are arms round me. I think for a moment this person must have confused me with one of the old women in the other beds. Surely I am not anyone's grandmother? The voice just now said I was confused, but it is not confusion I feel, it is dislocation. There is an elderly woman in a hospital bed called Odette Jenkins, and she is embracing her tearful granddaughter. And I know I am this woman, but I am not her. I try to answer but my voice is stuck, so I let myself be held.

She is crying, I realize, this girl: tears warm and wet, dripping on my floral nightie. I have no words, but I rock her, this woman-child in my arms, and it feels right. It is a comfort for us both somehow. 'Ssh,' I say to the crying woman in my arms. I pat her denim jacket with my tingle-numb hand. 'Ssh. It's okay, dear.'

Eventually she stops crying and pulls free, looks at me through wide, watery eyes. She takes a tissue from the box on the locker and blows her nose. 'I got it, Gran,' she says.

'What?'

'This.' She reaches into her jacket pocket and pulls out a tarnished silver necklace with an oval-shaped locket. And there is a fizzing feeling in my head as she does so, like water on sherbet.

I bring my good hand up to touch the patch of bare skin at the open neckline of my nightie. '*Mein Halskette?*' The words spill without prior thought.

'Yes, your necklace. At least, I hope so.' She passes it to me. I fumble with it. Good hand, bad hand, struggling. I know I need to see inside the little blackened silver lozenge. 'Here, let me help.' She undoes it and places it open on my palm.

It opens like a book. On the right-hand side is an old, mottled photograph of a woman holding a baby. I know the woman's face. It is my mother. The baby must be me. On the left there is an inscription. *Für Liebling Detta an ihrem 18. Geburtstag. Solange du lebst, wirst du mein Baby sein.*

'For my darling Detta on her 18th birthday. As long as you live, you will always be my baby girl.'

As this young woman reads the words, my memories come, like a domino track in reverse, all suddenly standing up in line again. I see myself as a character in a story: a frightened secretary in an office, a girl with a blue scarf over her head, going out into the snowy woods, a stolen kiss with an escaping airman, mud, blood and my mother's forbidden corpse, the interrogations, frozen fields, the steamship with the red funnel, the man with the kind blue eyes and the strong arms. I remember it all now.

'I am Detta Bruncel from Lossen.'

# Chapter 43

**May 1945, Exeter**

*Detta*

She heard distant bells chime the half-hour. They walked arm-in-arm under the colonnades. To her left was a row of shuttered shops; to her right a small road, bounded on the other side by a parapet, and beyond that a vast expanse of grass, big as a meadow, in the centre of which was the cathedral. She had the sudden urge to break loose, slipped her arm from his and dashed across the empty road, through a gap in the wall and onto the grass. For so many months she'd been trapped: in the train from Krakow to Odessa, in the boat from Odessa to Liverpool, then in the repatriation centre in London. When was the last time she'd been able to run like this?

She flung her arms wide and span in a circle, till the stars rushed sideways and her heart pounded. She stumbled, laughing, and he was there, holding her, breaking her fall. She swayed giddily into his embrace, happy to be caught.

'My runaway bride,' he said.

'It's just so good to be free.'

'Christ, yes.' They embraced. Hugging hard, clinging tight, both lost in their own unspoken memories. At last they pulled apart. A warm spring breeze whipped a strand of hair across her face, and he pushed it away. 'You look done-in, darling. Shall we just go straight to bed when we get to the hotel?'

She answered with a question: 'Must I sign in as Mrs Jenkins, even though we won't be married until tomorrow?'

'I think that would be best,' he said. 'Save awkward questions.'

'Isn't it bad luck to see your bride on the eve of her wedding?' She faltered a little, and he sensed her meaning.

'There is a sofa in the honeymoon suite,' he said. 'I'm sure one of us can manage a night on that, if that's what's bothering you?'

She would never have the kind of wedding she'd dreamt of. She'd never be married by Father Richter, in the Lossen church, with her mother to watch and the Moll girls as bridesmaids. All of that was gone, that other Detta, that other life. But to be a true wife, to withhold herself until after marriage, that was one convention she could keep. 'You're sure you don't mind? I know it seems silly. It's just one night, I know. But I was brought up to think that a girl should wait, and I—'

'I don't mind at all.' He kissed her cheek. 'One more night won't kill me, Mrs-almost-Jenkins.' The pale facade of the hotel looked down on them as they walked back across the road. There were columns and curlicues of wrought ironwork at the entrance. 'I say, it's a bit posher than some of the places we've stayed in,' he said, pushing open the double doors.

'Yes,' she said. And she knew that he, too, was recalling some of the awful billets during the freezing walk to Krakow: the itch of lice, the stench of unwashed bodies, and the constant gnaw of hunger. She reached for his hand and he squeezed it tight as they walked inside together.

The concierge looked up from the reception desk as they walked into the lobby. 'Good evening, sir, madam,' he said, nodding at them in turn, his smooth white hair shining like a pearl in the glow from the standard lamp by the desk. From a door to her right, Detta could hear voices, the chink of glasses and muted chatter. 'Lounge Bar' said a brass plaque on the door. She thought for a moment of the public bar in the Deutches Haus, before the war: the radio on, the half-cut banter of the locals, her mother smiling and refilling steins of beer. So long ago. A loud cheer broke her reverie – someone's birthday, perhaps? The man lifted his eyebrows and continued: 'Do you have a room booked with us tonight?'

'Yes,' Tom said. 'The honeymoon suite.'

The concierge smiled. 'Warrant Officer and Mrs Jenkins?' Tom nodded. The sounds were getting louder from the bar, as if a party were in full swing. Odd, for a Monday night, Detta thought. There were scuffle-thumps in between the cheering, as if furniture were being cleared aside. 'If you'd both like to sign here, please?' The concierge held out a pen, and gestured to a large ledger on the desk in front of him. Just then the telephone rang. 'If you'll excuse me for one moment.' Tom signed his name as the concierge took the call. He held out the pen for Detta. She hesitated. Mrs Jenkins – but she wasn't Mrs Jenkins, not yet. 'It's for you, sir,' the concierge said. He held out the black telephone receiver towards Tom, then walked a few discreet paces away, to give him some privacy.

Tom took the call. 'Hello?' Detta watched Tom's face, as he spoke. His expression changed, as he listened. He passed the receiver to the other ear, motioned for her to pass the pen so he could scribble something down on the blotter as the person on the other end carried on at length. 'I see,' he said, nodding. 'Yes I can quite see that. Of course I under-stand.' The pen slipped from his hand, landing with a soft thump, spilling black ink over the notes he'd just written. He turned slowly back to face her, still holding the receiver in his other hand. 'Darling,' he said, and something in his tone made her stiffen with tension. 'I'm afraid we can't get married tomorrow.'

She looked at Tom, telephone receiver dangling, issuing a faint tinnitus buzz – whoever was at the other end had already hung up. It's because I'm German, she thought. Someone in the RAF, or the clergy, or maybe even a close family member has just told him it's impossible, irresponsible and morally wrong. You can't marry her, she's the enemy, Detta imagined a disembodied voice hissing down the line. Tom wouldn't marry her, and she'd be sent back.

'We can't get married?' she said.

# The Escape

## *Tom*

He saw her face crumple in panic. 'Don't look like that, Detta.' He hung the receiver back in the cradle. 'It's a dreadful shame we shan't get married tomorrow, but it solves the dilemma as to who sleeps on the sofa.' He smiled at her but her expression didn't change. The volume of cheering and laughter had increased in the bar. Someone had turned off the radio and started thumping out tunes on a piano. 'We'll have to get married this evening, darling. That was the vicar on the phone. He's busy all day tomorrow, because—'

But he didn't finish the sentence because at that moment the door of the lounge bar burst open, and a line of revellers spilled out, hooting and whooping, kicking their legs out in a conga line, stumbling and shouting as they snaked round the lobby. The concierge appeared, frowning, from behind the desk. 'Gentlemen, ladies, please,' he began.

'Don't be like that, you silly sod!' yelled a puce-faced man waving a cigar. 'Haven't you heard the news?'

'The news, sir?'

'The war is over!'

The concierge looked as if he'd just been slapped: 'The war is over?'

'Just came through on the BBC!' The conga line passed between them: roaring, exultant faces, and the concierge was grabbed in with happy hands, disappearing with them back through the door, into the bar.

The lobby was empty. 'Took the words right out of my mouth,' Tom said, stepping forward and crushing her so tight in his arms that a gasp of breath escaped. 'The war is over. It's VE Day tomorrow and our vicar has special thanksgiving services to do all day, but he says if we meet him in St Stephen's Church in five minutes, he'll marry us tonight. You don't mind, do you, rushing it like this?' He released her then, looking into her eyes.

She shook her head, laughing now. 'Of course I don't mind!'

They ran out of the hotel, hand in hand, and he led her down a side alley and up a deserted street, their feet tapping on the empty pavements, to where a brick church stood, on the right-hand side. They stopped, breathless, leaning against the heavy wooden door. A skinny sickle moon was rising above the blitz-broken horizon, picking out the edges of rooftops and rubble in the darkness. As they waited, sounds of music and laughter drifted towards them through the night. Amber lights began to appear in city buildings, like doll's eyes blinking open, as people ripped blackouts and threw open windows, waking up to peacetime.

You're going to be safe now, he told her. You'll be my wife. You'll be British. I want you to forget Germany, think about the future we'll have together here instead. There will be no more Fräulein Bruncel, you'll be Mrs Jenkins from now on. Do you think you can do that?

She held his hand tight, and promised to leave her past behind, for both their sakes.

The vicar arrived, a friend of his father's: a man so tall and thin he looked as if he would topple over in a sudden gust of wind. With him was a dumpy woman in a green turban and camel coat and a short, thin hunchbacked woman dressed entirely in black, who he introduced as his housekeeper and her mother – their only witnesses. Unfortunately there was still no electricity in the church, he said, unlocking the door. He lit the huge candles on the altar, and asked if they minded him not changing into his vestments. Tom apologized to them both for getting them out at this hour, but they both said 'not at all', and that wasn't it such wonderful news about the war being over. The housekeeper produced a brass curtain ring from her coat pocket and said to Tom that she guessed he'd need it, and he laughed, agreed, and apologized to Detta for not having had a chance to get her a real one.

Detta said nothing except 'I do' as the metal ring was slid onto her finger: a dim gleam in the guttering candlelight. Tom looked down at her face – his wife's face. Her eyes were melting pools, looking back at him.

And for a moment he was back there again, on the path between the church and the Schloss, in the bitter cold, catching the dark-eyed gaze of the girl in the blue scarf. Catching it and keeping it, forever.

## Detta

The windowpane quivered as a formation of aircraft swooped overhead. The hotel windows were very old, the glass uneven – it was like looking underwater at a shoal of passing fish. They flew quite low, but Detta could barely hear them above the sounds of celebration drifting up from the cathedral green: gramophone records played through loud-speakers, and the happy shouts of the crowds. She glanced round the room: wooden floors, woollen tufted rugs, gilt-framed pictures of hunting scenes. In the corner there was a china basin where taps occasionally belched drips. The air smelled of lavender floor polish, cool where it touched her bare shoulders and chest, rising out from the rumpled bedsheets.

Tomorrow, when the shops would re-open, they were going to a jewellers to buy a gold wedding ring. Tom had been very definite about it. I am not taking you to the Rectory without a proper ring on your finger. You have no idea how small-minded some of father's parishioners can be, he said. If anyone gets wind of the fact all you've got on your finger is a bit of brass, it'll be round the village in no time. Detta thought back to her home in Silesia. She had every idea how small-minded villagers could be. At least here in England the gossip would be just that: gossip. Not a prelude to a visit by uniformed men and a one-way trip in the back of a black truck. She blinked away the memories. She shouldn't think such things. If only Tom would wake up. She could forget when he was awake, talking to her, kissing her. She thought again of last night. Ah, that was a better memory to dwell on.

She looked down at him. Her husband. His tousled hair was a sandy smudge on the white pillow. One arm shielded his face: smooth skin and a bulge of muscle. As she watched, she saw him convulse. He made a gagging sound and sat up, eyes wide and unseeing, fingers scrabbling at something invisible against his naked chest – a ripcord that wasn't there. *G-God!* His stuttered cry.

She leant over and wrapped herself round him. She drew his head onto her shoulder, held him close until his panicked trembling stilled. He was warm and soft and smelled of musky smoke. She stroked his hair. 'It's okay. You're awake.' She kissed the top of his head, held him closer. A starling landed on the window ledge for a moment, and she saw the glistening sheen of the bird's feathers as it took off into the morning sunshine. 'It's okay,' she repeated. 'We're home.'

# Chapter 44

## October 1990, Germany

*Miranda*

'Have you seen this?' Keith says, waving a newspaper in front of my face.

'Not here, Keith!' Mum's hand swats it away, but not before I've seen the headline: *Sunday paper's drug bust*, it says. 'Sorry, love. This isn't really the place. We can show her when we meet up tomorrow,' Mum says. Keith folds the paper and puts it in his pocket, but I glimpse the grainy grey photograph poking out of the mustard corduroy: Quill's swarthy features snapped through the back of a police car. I blink and take a breath.

'So, did you enjoy the preview?' I say, gesturing at the vast white room, walls studded with spot-lit photographs in matching brushed-steel frames. The gallery is filled with a cocktail of suited city-types and tangle-haired artists. Mum wears an orange dress, and looks happier than I've seen her in years. Keith has on a smarter version of his usual leather-elbowed jacket.

'Wonderful!' Mum says. 'I'm so proud – I just wish your father and grandmother were well enough to have been here to see it too.' Over her shoulder I see Keith rubbing his nose and looking uncomfortable. I smile at him and mouth 'thank you' – I know he's had to bankroll their trip to Berlin to see this – and he flushes beneath his ginger beard.

Mum releases me. We laugh awkwardly to cover up our emotion, and she asks me more questions about the exhibition. 'Through the eyes of others' is curated to show the history of foreign photographers' impressions of divided Germany, from the end of Second World War to the end of the Cold War. There are only two of my photographs: the ones I took at Jakobstrasse last November, of the boys playing football by the 'Go West' poster, and the young men starting to knock down the Wall – urchins and oiks turned black-and-white heroes through the Rolleiflex lens. Only two, but my first professional show – a beginning, at least. I tell Mum and Keith about my plans to document other borderlands, places where there are literal or metaphorical walls: divided cities from Johannesburg to Jerusalem. Mum nods, tilting her head to one side, asking questions, and actually listening to the answers.

The gallery begins to empty behind us: waitresses clearing lipstick-smeared wine glasses and ashtrays. Gwen joins us, looking like she's just walked out of one of the photographs herself, with her black trousers and white twinset. She takes my hands, tells me how proud my grandfather would be, especially as I used his camera to take the shots.

I am getting used to it, this idea of family. For so long it felt like Gran was the only one. But now Mum and I are speaking again, Keith's been good for her, Dad is out of hospital, and there's Great-Aunt Gwen, too. A kind of invisible safety net, that I didn't realize I had.

Keith looks at his watch and says they should really get going. We arrange to meet for lunch at the Paris Bar the following day. Mum insists I make a note of it in my diary. I grab my rucksack from one of the hooks by the door, and pull out my Filofax. When I open it, a photo falls out: a black and white shot of the off-duty pilot on the snowy path, arms outstretched, like an angel. 'That's a nice one,' Gwen says, picking it up. Her blue eyes dance as she passes it back to me. I write down details of our lunch date, we hug our goodbyes, and then they're gone. I turn to look out of the uncurtained windows. Stars speckle the clear night skies.

There's a tap on my shoulder. I turn. The gallery is empty now. The owner, in a black silk dress and leather choker, asks me what my plans are. 'I'm meeting Dieter and some other friends down near the Reichstag, if you'd like to join us?' she says, a smile splitting her glacé cherry lips.

I hesitate. 'It's a kind offer, Petra, but—'

'Or you can watch from here, if you want?' I nod and she hands me the gallery keys. 'Lock up afterwards and post them through my letterbox on your way home.'

'Thank you. I will. Enjoy the rest of the night.'

'Oh, I intend to,' she says, laughing as she plucks her blue fur coat from the hook. 'I've waited a lifetime for it.' The door bangs shut as she leaves, and I'm alone.

I pick up my denim jacket and the sky-coloured wool scarf, put them on, and head in the opposite direction. There is a fire door at the far end of the gallery. I glance at the frames as I pass, rewinding German history until I'm back in 1945 with the first photograph: the Berlin streets a mess of rubble, Russian tanks in front of the Brandenburg Gate, onlookers with hard, dark-eyed stares.

I push the cool metal of the fire door and then I'm out into the night. The fire escape ricochets down the grey brickwork to the dark alley below, but from up here there's a good view between the rooftops to the Reichstag building. The fire door comes to a soft close behind me. I reach out to grip the handrail, feeling the rough, rusted metal beneath the shiny paint.

It is almost midnight.

I taste the tang of city air, hearing the honk and growl of cars and buses below, and the distant murmur of the vast, massing crowd. The Reichstag is floodlit, the stone-work looking pink-yellow in the bright lights, like cliffs above the rising tide of people. I hear the sound of a door opening and closing, somewhere at street level. I catch my breath. With my free hand I touch the soft wool of the scarf round my neck.

I look across to the Reichstag, and see the wind whip the German flag, tiny as a page of discarded newsprint, from this distance. A bell begins to chime, and the crowd roars as the flag is hoisted up the flagpole: black, yellow and red streaming out above the people – one flag, one nation, one people. It is midnight and Germany is reunited, at last. The cheering continues, and the tolling of the bell, drowning out the voices of politicians and their speeches. Then the national anthem begins: *Deutschland Uber Alles*.

As I watch, I see sudden bright sparks in the sky, and hear a distant crackle, like gunfire. Then a neon chrysanthemum blossoms, and spears of incandescence shoot upwards. A firework display, of course, something else to remember the 3rd October for.

As the anthem comes to its rousing close, I hear the fire door open behind me. A moment later I feel his arms round my waist and his face in my hair. He says sorry for leaving me alone like this. The flight was delayed, and getting to the centre of town was a nightmare, crowds clogging the roads. I lean back into him, say it doesn't matter. Mum, Gwen and Keith were here for the preview, and the exhibition will be on for weeks. 'I just feel so incredibly lucky to be here,' I say, feeling the warmth of him encircling me as we watch the remains of the fireworks and the fluttering flag of a united Germany.

'Me too, *schatzi*,' he says, kissing the nape of my neck. 'Me too.'

Afterwards, when the last firework has fizzled away, he pulls free from the embrace. 'Where are you going?' I say.

'I'm going to take you home – unless you'd rather be down there with the revellers?'

'No, I always feel so alone in crowds.'

'I know you do, so let's just go back to our place, have our own private celebration of unity.' He reaches for my hand. The diamond on my ring finger sparkles as it catches the light from the gallery behind us. 'Yes?'

'Yes, Michael,' I say. 'That sounds perfect. Let's go home.'

# Chapter 45

**October 1990, Exeter**

*Odette*

At the sound, my fingers still. I was about to type the letter 's'. The type hammer has stopped halfway to the paper. My ring finger quivers above the key, the gold wedding band catching the lamplight. The carriage clock has just chimed quarter to. Fifteen minutes to go. I let out a breath, flex my fingers above the keyboard, push the release, lift the lever and turn the platen knob. I pull out the sheet of paper, and place it in the yellow file marked 'memoirs'.

The letter 's' still hovers indecisively above the keyboard, so I push it down into position and get up to turn on the television, where the sandy-moustachioed news anchor announces that they are going live to Berlin for the reunification celebrations. I take the champagne from the ice bucket and pop the cork.

He should be home by now, I think, checking the champagne glasses for dust. On the TV screen the Reichstag is floodlit, and the red, yellow and black German flag billows out above the jostling crowds. He said he'd be back in time for this. Where is he?

I go to the window, lift the heavy chintz curtain and look out into the darkness. I see the door of the Clarence Hotel opening: an oblong of yellow light. There is a conjoined silhouette, two figures together in the hotel doorway. At first I think it can't be him, because he'd be alone, but the two shadows begin to walk across the cathedral green towards my flat, and I hear through the glass the muffled sound of his voice, and a woman's laughter, lifting up towards the dark autumn skies. I let the curtain fall.

Symbiotic is the word, I think. Jono helps me with the practical things: shopping, cooking, putting out the bins – things that were once easy, but I still struggle with, despite almost a year of physiotherapy. I help him with routine, reminding him to take his pills, eat regularly. Over the past few months my flat has been busy with visits from social workers, community nurses, family, supporting us both in our new lives. At the start we tiptoed round each other, relying on polite notes and rotas. But these last few weeks we have relaxed. I shout at him for leaving his sweaty football socks on the bathroom floor, not putting the toilet seat down. He nags me to give up smoking and write my memoirs. And now he has a part-time job as a bar man at the Clarence Hotel. And, it seems, a new girlfriend.

On the television the crowds are cheering as the German national anthem strikes up: *Deutchsland Uber Alles*. Who would have thought such a display of German nationalism would be tolerated on the BBC, let alone celebrated? Forty-five years ago is another life, another world, I think, as I scribble a note to Jono to help himself to the champagne, and prop it up next to the glasses.

I leave the television on, hear the pop and spit of fireworks above Berlin as I go to the bathroom. I slather cream on my face and wipe it off with cotton wool. The mirrored medicine cabinet doors bisect my reflection. I am Odette Jenkins. I am Detta Bruncel. I am British. I am German.

I am.

I hear the front door being pushed open, two sets of footsteps in the hallway. Good for him, I think, brushing my teeth. I hope she is understanding, and kind. Whoever she is, this new girlfriend, I hope that one day when people ask how they got together he says, I looked into her eyes, and I just knew.

As I leave the bathroom and cross the hallway to my bedroom I hear the chink of glasses from the living room, the sound of laughter. I pause to unhook the painting of the prison camp watchtower from its place on the hallway wall, and take it with me into the bedroom. It doesn't feel right there anymore, and in any case, I need to make space: it won't be long before there's Miranda's wedding photos to hang.

I prop Tom's painting up on my bedside table and change into my night things, taking off the silver locket and hanging it on my dressing table mirror.

Through the walls I can just about make out the muted

voices from the other room. They have turned off the television, put on the radio: voices, music, the sound of a man and
a woman beginning to share their lives, fall in love, perhaps.

As I push back the bed covers I smell tobacco smoke, feel
the familiar current of emotion running through me. I turn
to switch off the bedside light. I lie between the cool sheets
and put a hand out to stroke the empty pillow. 'It's okay,
darling,' I say. 'We're home.' I smile and close my eyes.

The torn-apart feeling has gone.

# Author's note

Although *The Escape* is a work of fiction, I must credit Michael Hingston's book *Into Enemy Arms* (Grub Street, 2006), for providing the stepping-off point; I am indebted to Hingston for recounting the remarkable story of his aunt's flight from Germany in 1945. Another work of non-fiction that helped inspire the 1945 timeline of my novel is John Nichol and Tony Rennel's *The Last Escape* (Penguin, 2003), which details the forced march that British POWs had to make ahead of the incoming allied forces at the end of World War Two. And anyone who has read Ian Walker's fascinating *Zoo Station, adventures in East and West Berlin* (Secker & Warburg, 1987) will find echoes of his observations of Cold War Berlin in *The Escape*'s 1989 timeline.

If you're interested in discovering more of the books and films that helped create *The Escape*, take a look at the 'extra material' page of my website: clareharvey.net

# Acknowledgements

I am very grateful to my editor Jo Dickinson and my agent Teresa Chris for support, encouragement and patience (and a couple of rather tasty lunches) during the writing process.

Thank you to my children for having to suffer a research trip to Berlin that was thinly disguised as a family holiday, to my husband for all his help on my freezing cold weekend of 'optical research' in Poland in February, and to my mum and sister Tessa for looking after kids & dog whilst we were away.

And thanks, too, to anyone who has had to read any of my unedited shizl or put up with me banging on about plot wrinkles, etc. whilst *The Escape* was still a work-in-progress. You know who you are, and you are all fab.

Thank you xxx

P.S. I nearly forgot – thank you to the 'real' Miranda Wade (she knows why).

# Clare Harvey
# The Night Raid

World-renowned war artist **Dame Laura Knight** is
commissioned to paint propaganda portraits of factory girls
and is sent to the ordnance factories in her hometown of Nottingham.
At first, she relishes the opportunity for a nostalgia trip, but when
she starts work on a portrait of two particular women, **Violet Smith**,
and her co-worker **Zelah Fitzlord**, memories begin to resurface
that she has spent half a lifetime trying to forget.

Violet is an industrial conscript, and her wages help
support a sprawling family back home in Kent. But working in
munitions also meant freedom from a small-town mentality, and the
disappointment of a first love turned sour. For Zelah, too, working in
the gun factory meant escape after her dreams of the future
were dashed in the carnage of the Plymouth Blitz.

But, just like Laura, Violet and Zelah have something hidden:
mistakes that they have tried to leave behind.

Will the night shift keep these women's secrets, or will the past
explode into the present and change all of their lives forever?

**AVAILABLE NOW IN PAPERBACK,**
**EBOOK AND AUDIOBOOK**

**SIMON &**
**SCHUSTER**

# Clare Harvey

# The English Agent

*How far will two women go to survive WWII?*

Having suffered a traumatic experience in the Blitz,
**Edie** feels utterly disillusioned with life in wartime London.
The chance to work with the Secret Operations Executive (SOE)
helping the resistance in Paris offers a fresh start. Codenamed
'Yvette', she's parachuted into France and met by the two
other members of her SOE cell. Who can she trust?

Back in London, **Vera** desperately needs to be made a
UK citizen to erase the secrets of her past. Working at the foreign
office in charge of agents presents an opportunity for blackmail.
But when she loses contact with one agent in the field,
codenamed Yvette, her loyalties are torn.

**AVAILABLE NOW IN PAPERBACK,
EBOOK AND AUDIOBOOK**

**SIMON &
SCHUSTER**

# Clare Harvey
# The Gunner Girl

**Bea** has grown up part of a large, boisterous Kent family.
But she hasn't heard from her soldier sweetheart in months and her
mother is controlling her life. She needs to take charge of her future.

**Edie** inhabits a world of wealth and privilege, but knows only
too well that money can't buy happiness. She wants to be like
Winston Churchill's daughter, Mary, to make a difference.

**Joan** can't remember anything of her past or her family,
and her home has been bombed in the Blitz.
Desperate, she needs a refuge.

Each one is a Gunner Girl: three very different women,
one remarkable wartime friendship of shared hopes,
lost loves and terrible danger . . .

**AVAILABLE NOW IN PAPERBACK,
EBOOK AND AUDIOBOOK**

**SIMON &
SCHUSTER**